SCRAP

Also by Calla Henkel

Other People's Clothes

SCRAP

A NOVEL

Calla Henkel

THE OVERLOOK PRESS, NEW YORK

This edition first published in hardcover in 2024 by
The Overlook Press, an imprint of ABRAMS

Abrams books are available at special discounts when purchased in quantity
for premiums and promotions as well as fundraising or educational use.
Special editions can also be created to specification. For details,
contact specialsales@abramsbooks.com or the address above.

First published in Great Britain in 2024 by Sceptre

Library of Congress Control Number: 2024935817

Printed and bound in the United States
1 3 5 7 9 10 8 6 4 2

ISBN: 978-1-4197-7522-2
eISBN: 979-8-88707-334-7

ABRAMS The Art of Books
195 Broadway, New York, NY 10007
abramsbooks.com

For K.R.

It is to have a compulsive, repetitive, and nostalgic desire for the archive, an irrepressible desire to return to the origin, a homesickness, a nostalgia for the return to the most archaic place of absolute commencement.

Jacques Derrida

X

There was something about the unspooling of a sociopath over computer speakers that enabled me to fall into my deepest state of concentration while binding books. Someone is always guilty—this is the intrinsic propulsion of true crime, and after countless hours I was an expert on cell phone towers, cadaver dogs, rogue psychics, genealogists, fibers, and credit card trails. I could recognize a psychopath from speech patterns and I was deeply familiar with the sparked flint of a serial killer's eye. Now that I look back, it was almost as if I'd been preparing for Naomi's murder, lifting the metaphorical weights, readying myself to unwind my red ball of yarn and trace her life on my wall.

1

It was early June and I was in jeans and my only button up—my ambitions for the evening were simple and mildly selfish. I wanted to flash my engagement ring and tell my old friends about my house and barn-converted-studio in the mountains and hint at our baby plans. I needed them to know I was all right. I was better. I gulped a glass of white wine and observed the rehearsed lines slide from acquaintances' lips, "I love the show." "Congrats." "Memphis, you're a genius." I found the art world so surreally suffocating, so filled with performative affirmations—I couldn't believe I'd lasted seven years in New York City.

I pulled my phone out and sent Jessica a text. *Miss you.* It was her last night teaching a four-week workshop on silver enameling in Oregon. I assumed she was hosting an open house with her students, eating Sam's Club cracker sticks, drinking light beer.

I forced my teeth into a smile while watching Memphis talk to a guy in the standard dockworker-artist costume, Carhartt and a small knit hat, standing in front of one of her massive cubist palm frond paintings. It was easy enough to push away the ancient simmer of jealousy when staring at Memphis, because the truth was, I was grateful. She was one of the only ones who'd kept in touch after the incident. And she, despite being in head-to-toe Gucci, was still the same girl who had drunkenly peed in my laundry hamper freshman year. When Memphis Emerald had invited me to this opening, she meant it; she didn't think I was crazy.

The gallery's intern flipped the lights off and began corralling the hundred or so people to the street. I was looking forward to the dinner at Franco's. It was Memphis's favorite from college, with brick walls and pasta hand rolled by a small man on display in the kitchen and always some beautiful aloof model girl hostessing who'd look through me like a bus window.

The chosen forty invited to dinner rolled into a fleet of Ubers. Memphis was whisked into the first black car—I found myself a few cars later, wedged between two strongly perfumed women in stiff designer jackets. A blonde and a redhead, Naomi and Natalia. I was looking for my phone when they had said their names so didn't know which was which. The Ns. Late forties, or maybe early fifties, clearly extremely rich, the kind of women who burned two-hundred-dollar-candles and had fifth houses. I kept my eyes glued out the window in hopes of avoiding conversation. After getting stuck at a light, our Uber took a wrong turn and we ended up arriving at Franco's after everyone else had already been seated.

The hostess, tall and ethereal as ever, with widely set eyes and a large gap between her teeth, waved us in. I saw Memphis and to my relief, an empty seat next to her. I turned to say goodbye to the Ns, then just as I began to walk away, the gallerist, Sylvia Burton, with her Anna Wintour bob cut, sat down in the chair next to Memphis. I froze.

"We must be over there," the red-haired N said, firmly pulling my sleeve toward the far corner of the restaurant where the last three empty seats gaped. The dinner was seated.

I smiled to cover my frustration and followed. Of course, I would spend tonight with these banal peacocks. We approached the table, all politely bobbing our heads. I found my name on a tiny folded rectangle written in some intern's overzealous cursive and we sat.

"So, you're an artist?" the red-haired N asked me over the roar of the adjacent table.

I nodded, not wanting to explain myself.

"That's lovely."

The air settled heavily around our shoulders; the evening would be long. I ripped a piece of bread and chewed. The Ns had begun talking to each other at a gallop, using names and places that sounded like code—Whitney's COO is from Delta; Well Abe's bringing Marc to Alec's.

I pulled out my phone and texted Jessica, *stuck with two obscenely rich women, save me.*

A few minutes later, the blonde N's phone began releasing a meat-grinder of vibrations and beeps. She picked up, after a pause, she released a "Fu-ck," the screen's glow strobing under her chin, "Uh-huh, yeah, got it." She looked up at the red-haired N and made an apologetic grimace. After she hung up, she turned to both of us, "I am so sorry to do this, but there is an emergency—I have to go."

The tenor of her voice indicated she was about to slice a tumor from a child's frontal lobe, but from her outfit, I knew that was not true.

"No problem, and good luck," the red-haired N replied.

The blonde left, her Chanel boots clucking across the tiled floor.

"She's in PR," the remaining N said with a wry smile.

A void opened up between us. "That's a good book," she said pointing to the *Sharp Objects* by Gillian Flynn sticking out of my tote bag that was slung off my chair. I had bought the book at the Strand while killing time before the show. It was a gift for Jessica, who loved thrillers and, stretched on the futon in sweatpants, her nose glued to her phone, had proclaimed wanting to read it.

I nodded, "I'm sorry, what was your name again?"

"I'm Gillian Flynn," she replied with a cutting smirk, nodding to the book.

It took me a second. It was a joke. I released a forced chord of laughter.

"I'm Naomi, and you are Esther Ray, correct?"

I nodded, but didn't remember giving my last name and I knew she couldn't see my place card from her vantage. An uncomfortable pause settled between us. I picked at the tablecloth. Then a guy wearing a ratty Grateful Dead T-shirt appeared over Naomi's shoulder and my heart leapt: he was a blessed dinner crasher, he would join us—he would do the talking. He would tell us about guitar pedals and egg carton sound insulation.

"Is it free?" he asked, pointing to the chair.

We nodded. The guy breathed a heavy thanks, then lifted the chair over his head and walked away. I was stuck.

"Are you enjoying it?" Naomi asked, again nodding to *Sharp Objects*.

"It's for my fiancée, she likes trash."

"Well, it's hardly trash. *Gone Girl* is my absolute all-time favorite. I love a frenetic plot. You know, it's embarrassing, but I even love Dan Brown. I'll read anything he writes. Or Stephen King, or David Baldacci, oh god, or Donna Leon, which are all set in Venice. But you have to read *Gone Girl*."

"I prefer true crime . . ." I said flatly. I believed fiction was for idiots. How could you connect if the violence wasn't real? How could you care if the need for justice wasn't truthful?

Naomi said nothing, looking oddly disappointed as if my disinterest in *Gone Girl* had rendered me unworthy of further conversation.

"So, what do you do?" I asked trying to fill the void.

"I run WAC, a water-management nonprofit, in places of extreme poverty—Madagascar, Nepal—all over."

I knew that meant *housewife*. I shifted my weight, noticing the shimmering gold-flecked thread of her MoMA Design Store–inspired sari wrap.

6

"And how do you know the artist—Memphis?" Naomi asked.

"We went to school together."

"Ah, and what sort of art do you make?"

"Well not art, I make—craft."

Naomi cocked her head, "What's the difference?"

"One is about process and use, and the other is about market and value." I paused looking around the room, "And ego. Craft has no ego, anyone can learn it, anyone can master it. Art relies on the isolation of genius. Whereas craft is—moral."

Naomi extended her lower lip, "So you think this is all bullshit?"

I nodded to indicate yes.

"Me too," she clucked, laughed, then hushed her voice, "I'm only here because Sylvia Burton, the gallerist, is on my board." She took a sip from her wineglass, "I mean, I do like the paintings."

"As do I," I said, relaxing into my wooden chair, remembering one of the lines I'd seen people repeat earlier, "Memphis is a genius."

Naomi flagged the waiter down and ordered a new bottle of wine. I watched as she spoke, her lips were sealed in a subtle natural color and she seemed more earthy and less glamorous now that Natalia had left. "Beauty by proxy" was a concept my mother had introduced me to. My mom Caroline was an angel faced Betty Draper type, ever aware of the favors she performed for the world, scooping her good looks like ice cream just by showing up. I touched the lump of fat under my chin. Whenever I thought about my mom, I grasped that un-work-out-able piece of flab. We looked nothing alike.

I took a sip of water and stared at Naomi. She was a small woman with high shimmering cheekbones and small burrowing eyes, like marbles pressed into bread dough. She had a sort of prophetic new age look, part Florence and the Machine, part aspirational Jane Goodall. She was wearing a huge hunk of rose quartz caged in silver around her neck, and a dozen or so bangles that moved up and down her wrist as she drank.

"So, where do you practice your craft?" she asked after setting down her glass of the new piss-hued natural wine.

"Hammersmith, in the Blue Ridge Mountains—I bought a house and studio with my fiancée."

"Near Asheville?" She asked exuberantly.

"Yes, about an hour away," I was surprised she knew, but Asheville was a hot spot for well-heeled hippie retirees. I fidgeted with the folded piece of cardstock bearing my name.

"I go to Asheville frequently. I love that it's vibrant, yet still remote. My astrologer actually told me that I should be there. I've been really interested in astromapping, have you ever tried it?"

I shook my head.

"Well, with their advice, I decided to base my latest project out of Asheville."

"For the water management stuff?" I asked.

"No, well—actually, hydroponics are involved," she said with a wink I couldn't compute. Maybe a weed joke?

"But no, it's not WAC," she followed up flatly, then leaned as if she were telling me a secret, "It's a *very* special project."

The way she said "special" sounded perverse; too round and warm. The other tables had quieted, gnocchi in mouths. I snuck glances at Naomi as she arranged her napkin on her lap. Despite smelling faintly like patchouli, she was extremely neat, as if every red hair on her body was accounted for. There were probably multiple people in this city who would notice if she lost a strand. Her stylist. Her dermatologist. Maybe a husband. What would we talk about for the next hour?

Naomi looked at her thin gold watch, I assumed thinking the same thing.

"Do you have kids?" I asked, inadvertently placing my hand on my empty uterus, my mind reeling backward to the image of my kitchen calendar, garnished in Jessica's handwriting with the words: *fertility clinic 12:30.*

"I do—Tabitha, she's nineteen."

"Nice," I said, unsure how to follow up.

"So, what crafts do you make?"

"Mostly bookmaking."

Naomi smiled, then sat up, "Yes, tell me about your books."

"Well, I make the paper—then I sew the signatures together, and make the covers with linen stretched on board. Each one is unique. For me, I like that I make these empty vessels which get to be filled, they create space. You know? Rather than add to chaos. I used to be a photorealist painter, so it's nice to facilitate emptiness, if that makes any sense."

"That's excellent," Naomi replied. Her demeanor shifted, now intently engaged, she leaned in as if she had a list of questions ready. What was the size of my studio? The average number of pages? The weight of the paper I used? Was I ecologically conscious in my work? Did I have storage? Was it secure? What sort of scale of projects was I used to working? Did I do custom jobs? Finally, Naomi dipped her head over the table, her longest beaded necklace nearly grazing the cocoa-dusted tiramisu, "I have a proposal."

I looked at her and smiled, unsure of how to shape my face. She brought her right hand up and rested it on top of mine, her black-brown eyes opening up like mushrooms. "I actually really believe in fate. I think people are put in each other's lives for a reason. When Natalia left earlier, I considered following her. I mean, what was the point of me sitting here tonight?" She paused, "Can I be fully open with you?"

I nodded, wishing I could leave.

"Here is the thing. I am an emotional hoarder," she said as if introducing herself at AA.

9

Nothing compares to the vortex of wasted time that is the periphery of the art world, husbands of dealers, daughters of collectors, estate lawyers, and fellow board members like Naomi—I had no choice but to let her blather. She continued, "My husband is an extreme minimalist in almost all aspects of his life. Our house has black wooden floors, white walls, no art, no photos, no nothing. And for the most part, I love it. It's not like we're Amish, but we keep things 'clean.' He sees it as an aesthetic oasis but we joke it borders on fascism. Anyway, for as long as my daughter has been alive, I have been, well—I have actually never told anyone this."

She took a sip of wine, gathering abstract courage.

"I rent a storage unit in my building—I save everything."

"Mmhmm," I added blandly.

"Schoolwork, notes, photos, letters, sometimes I even print emails and texts. I always put them into a plastic bin which I keep in my office. My husband thinks it's just one plastic bin, but the reality is—every time it's full I bring it to my storage unit, then replace it with a matching bin and start again. I have—oh, two hundred. I think? God bless the Container Store."

I nodded, unsure why she was telling me.

"I have always wanted to transform these bins, well, this archive, into scrapbooks. And I want them to be a surprise gift for my husband's sixtieth birthday. Do you think you would be interested in a scrapbooking job like that?"

I bit the inside of my lip, then tried to politely find words, "Oh—interesting—hmmm—sadly, that's really not what I do. I mean, I appreciate the thought, but I am—more of an artisan." The word *artisan* reminded me of the cheese counter at Whole Foods, but it seemed like it might hammer the point.

Naomi looked shocked.

"I could have all the boxes shipped to you, and then you could take your time, in your own studio."

I inhaled, "I'm sorry. I just don't really scrapbook."

"Money is no object."

I laughed at her trite, maraschino cherry of a statement, of course money was no object, but then I saw it—vibrating in her eyes: a look of desperation that scared me. I sat up. "It's just not what I do," I said firmly. Maybe when I had told her I'd studied "crafts," she had imagined glitter and glue sticks, not the historical tradition of making fine, useful objects by hand. I felt insulted. I took pride in needing nothing. I didn't want to meet Memphis's gallerist, or get on the good sides of collectors. I could see artists for what they were, court jesters employed to liven-up the real estate above sofas. I didn't want to be a clown-servant for the criminally wealthy. I made books that anyone could afford. Naomi released my hand as if she could hear my thoughts. She then dipped into her pocket and retrieved a white rectangle. "Please keep this conversation to yourself—and if you change your mind, call me." I stood awkwardly as she got up to leave and watched her small form vanish out of the restaurant.

I pulled out my phone and wrote Jessica again, *Bb you'll never believe what one of the rich ladies just proposed.* I took a deep suck of air, then scanned the room, a seat near Memphis had opened up. I relocated.

"So, Es, who'd you get stuck with?" Memphis asked, pouring champagne into my wineglass.

"Naomi," I paused, then fished out her card, "Duncan."

"Oh fuck—right, she's worth a bazillion dollars, you know she actually—"

Whatever Memphis was about to say was cut off by Mitch, one of our fellow ex-classmates, arriving to the table with a skull shaped bottle of vodka.

An hour later a big group of us trudged to Sly Fox, a basement level dive bar attached to the Ukrainian National Home on Second Avenue. Memphis ordered three pitchers of beer.

11

"Esther, it's good to see you," Slade, a sculptor who I knew made his living applying Venetian plaster walls in penthouses, said as he filled my glass.

"It's nice to be back," I replied.

"And you're not goth anymore?" he laughed.

"I donated my Slipknot shirts to needy teens," I said gamely.

Slade smiled, someone put on George Michael.

"So, how've you been since—" Slade stopped himself.

My stomach spiked, I could see him thinking about the incident at Michael Valentine's studio, but Slade seamlessly pivoted and asked to see pictures of my house. And *oohed* and *ahhed* at the barn. And in turn, he showed me photos of his newest sculptures, surrealist bodies cast in concrete, I reciprocated the *oohs* and *ahhs*. When he got up to order another round, I wrote Jessica.

You ready to fly home?

I'm so happy I get to see you in less than 24 hours.

Someone just spilled a beer on me.

"I can't believe you use a flip phone and live in a cabin," Memphis laughed, pointing to the brick I was texting on, "you're a real live hermit."

I shrugged and slipped the phone into my pocket.

"I want to make a toast," Memphis held her glass to the low-slung lamp.

The table quieted.

"To an anonymous man," she bowed her head, then lifted her eyes, "I showed up to town ten years ago and some off-his-tits-on-coke banker at the Bowery Hotel told me that my name Katie Jones sucked. He said if I wanted to be a successful artist, I should change it to a city and a precious stone because rich people love only two things—real estate and rocks. And I, being a shameless runt, took his advice and I guess it worked, so cheers to him."

The table laughed. Even I thought it was funny, but I caught a wrinkle of pain in Slade's face—he was still in it.

Still trying to get shows. Still trying to be the most interesting man in the room. I wanted to shake him. To tell him the Venetian plaster walls were more interesting than any abstract twist of art he could shit out. Why couldn't he see that use was valuable?

The next morning, I woke up on Memphis's uncomfortable designer couch. I knew she had a coffee "date" with a reporter from the *New York Times* and was long gone. We'd drunkenly said our goodbyes the night before in the kitchen. The evening had ended in tears. Just as we'd been leaving the bar, loitering on the gum-pocked sidewalk, Mitch had shown Memphis a photo of Ivanka Trump hamming for the camera in front of one of Memphis's old paintings which, apparently, now hung in her Palm Beach living room. Memphis, drunk and emotionally wasted from the day, felt humiliated. But that was part of the game—there was no controlling where your work ended up once it hit the waterslide of liquid capital. Tear gas producers. Developers who bulldozed affordable housing. The spoiled grandchildren of Nazi auto-parts manufacturers. Racists. Or all of the above.

I was groggy. On the train to the airport, I took my phone out, still no word back from Jessica. She'd had an early flight so maybe she was already napping at home. I closed my eyes and imagined her curled up in bed, a pillow wedged between her legs to keep her knees from touching. I tried calling anyway. No answer.

I arrived in Asheville feeling strangely rested. I paid the Elvis-looking attendant at the park-n-fly lot, then cruised off in my banged up red truck. The radio was blasting twangy country, and I felt a sense of calm which I would never have predicted upon returning from New York—and I had Jessica to thank. When she'd found the invite card in the trash with Memphis's deranged handwriting months ago, she had taped it to the fridge with a Post-it that said, *Go*. She had been insistent, telling me it was *time to face the past*—she'd even booked my ticket.

Forty minutes later I turned onto the dirt road that led to our house just past the Christmas tree farm. There it was at the end of the steep climb. It always took my breath away, our beautiful seventies bungalow with slanted windows and rough pine beams. The house's previous owner, Ed, was a woodworker, so everything gleamed with love and ample varnish. I hadn't been afforded the boldness to imagine a life like this. I had been raised in a shitty duplex in Dayton, Ohio, by my alcoholic beauty of a mother and my barely-there father. Home was never somewhere I wanted to be. I had spent many early teenage nights walking around, staring into the pudgy brick houses of the nicer neighborhoods, astral-projecting into the glowing living rooms until I could feel their throw blankets scratching my own shoulders. I never thought I'd end up somewhere like this.

The Hammersmith Craft School hosted twelve resident artists every winter. I was in the paper studio, Jessica lower metals. I saw her first at orientation; she was wearing a daisy printed sundress over long-johns and I was in my usual jeans and a T-shirt. We were the only lesbians on the mountain and our romance was immediate, intense, and all-consuming. Jessica was my opposite, loud and funny—her jewelry, flashy and wildly popular on Etsy and Pinterest, while my books had garnered a quiet following of grandmothers and poets. But we became inseparable and when winter thawed, we wanted to beat back spring's snowdrops and daffodils, in hopes of never being evicted from our sanctuary. And then one Sunday while I was working a shift at the school's coffee shop, I watched as Moyra, the town's real estate agent, pinned up the bungalow's "For Sale" ad. $110,000, five acres. Mountaintop. After she left, I ripped the ad down and drooled, and only a few hours later, on the porch of Jessica's studio, we decided.

I parked the truck and opened the door, relishing the familiar crunch of gravel, it was my cowbell—my happy supper's-ready sound. I dropped my duffel in the mudroom and noticed instantly it was too clean. Whenever Jessica came home from a trip it looked as if her bag had detonated with a house-size impact radius. Her purse wasn't scattered across the bench. There were no smears of peanut butter on the table, no dirty laundry streaking the floor. I walked to our lofted bedroom. Her collection of shoes which usually graced the entrance was gone. So was our quilted bedspread. Had we been robbed? I looked to my right; the pounds of Jessica's silver jewelry that lived on the oak vanity had vanished. I tore open the cabinet drawers, my things were there but hers weren't. No underwear. No sundresses. No sweatpants. It had to be robbery.

A spike of heat ran across my spine, and I stumbled to the kitchen to check on the only material objects that mattered to me: four Polaroids duct taped to the inside of the junk drawer. I thrust my hand in and dramatically felt the square edges. They were still there. I sighed, not even Jessica knew they lived silently in the darkness of that drawer. Then I saw it. A note in the ceramic fruit bowl, printed out on a piece of Jessica's sky-blue jewelry stationery.

Esther,

I feel like a coward for doing it this way but I've decided to stay in Oregon. I have been under so much pressure. The house. The engagement. All the talk of having a baby. Work. Everything. I wasn't paying attention to me. I have been so unhappy and out of touch and it took leaving for me to truly understand.

I hope you had a healing trip to New York. I'm really proud of you for going back—I suppose I'm realizing how much your issues have taken from me. And I really wanted to help you take that next step in your journey, but now I have to face mine. I am going away for a month and a half to a retreat at an ashram in the mountains. I've paid my next two loan payments, but after that—I want to sell. I spoke with our realtor, and she said it should be easy enough. The deed is on the fridge.

I had Melanie come pack up most of my things and leave you this letter. I have a few boxes I'll pick up at a later date. My phone is off. I'm open to talking when I emerge. And I truly hope you can focus on moving forward. I love you.

X Jess

I called her. No answer. Just endless rings, not even a kick to voicemail. I hung up. Tried again. The rings pulled me under, I couldn't breathe. I sat down in the nauseating emptiness of the kitchen, and eyed the deed to the house which was stuck to the fridge with a teapot shaped magnet. Its saggy yellow form taunting me like a losing lottery ticket. Where was she? Cross-legged on some hilltop? I played through the past weeks, rewinding our conversations which I now realized had been sparse—always initiated by me. How long had she known? When had she talked to our real estate agent? Had she canceled the appointment at the fertility clinic? And when had she arranged for her idiot studio assistant Melanie to pack up her stuff? I released a string of trombone sobs.

My thoughts swirled like an oil spill. All of the fantasies we had constructed; *our life*, unlashing in bright toxic waves. We'd had plans. She had made promises. She'd grabbed my hand at dinner when I'd been quavering on the subject of parenthood—global warming, microplastics, Russia—and she'd looked me dead in the eyes and said, "But baby, let's give

16

our life some meaning." Had that not happened? *Our life*. I thought to her arms outstretched in bed. To her jagged mornings. Her grumpiness before coffee. Her elastic use of the word *fuck*. The grocery bags she stored under the sink, and the way she sighed after sending emails. She, and all her habits, had been mine. How could they be out there, orbiting loose in the universe?

Then I saw something dark stirring at the corner of my eye. A snake was on the floor of the bedroom weaving its way under the dresser. I let out a high-pitched scream and ran into the kitchen. I was world-shatteringly terrified of snakes. Jessica had always calmly removed them from the porch, or the dryer, or barn floor with a broom, laughing at my Jell–O-cowering. I put on loud music and debated calling Chester, the eternally cheerful potter who lived a mile and a half away. Maybe he would come over and wrangle the snake. But I didn't want to see him. In fact, I wanted to kill Chester. I wanted to kill everyone. Without Jessica, I wanted humanity and time and reason to cease.

On the porch, I shakily drank down a nearly spoiled bottle of Trader Joe's wine, my knees tucked to my chin, still ravaged by the waves of *our life*. What was I supposed to do? I let out a wail. Then another. Big Mediterranean heaves of grief. I called Jessica forty-three times. The rings were water torture. Finally, it dawned on me to call her sister, Alisha.

"I know, I know," she answered already annoyed. Someone was shrieking in the background, I assumed she was at work at the methadone clinic in Chicago.

"What do you mean? *You know*," I gargled.

"I mean, I know Jessica left you. And I know she didn't like do it face to face, but like . . ."

"How could she—leave me?" I burst.

"This isn't my place."

"Alisha, please."

Silence, then finally, "Look, she felt bad about it. She was really torn up. I don't know."

"Tell me why."

"I can't."

"Please," I cried.

"She just, I guess she just felt like you were too . . ." she paused.

"What?"

Alisha clicked her tongue, hesitating.

"Just say it," I pleaded.

"Fine. *Intense*, or something."

"Intense?"

"Look, do yourself a favor. Just like, play it cool all right? Maybe she'll meditate it away. Just like, don't chase her. Don't like do anything extreme. I'm at work all right. I gotta go."

"Alisha wait, where is she?"

"Oh, hell no, Esther."

She hung up.

Without any other way to release my rage I threw the now almost empty bottle of wine against the side of the house. It cracked and thudded, leaving a smear of ruddy sediment on the side wall. It felt right that our home should bleed. *Intense*. I debated calling Alisha back but she was my only line to Jessica, I didn't want to sever it. Not yet. I was now drunkish and my jaw was sore from rage-clenching. I gathered my courage to peek back in the bedroom.

There was a braided leather belt laying right where I'd seen the reptile. I took a breath. There was no snake. I still slept on the couch, wrapped in a twist of sheets and beach towels, waking periodically only to be consumed into quicksand that she was no longer here.

The next morning the house felt craterous and bombed out; when I wasn't crying, I listened to true crime podcasts. I revisited the classics like the Gilgo Beach murders and Ted Bundy.

Taking solace in the extraterrestrial world of sociopathic behavior, convincing myself that Jessica was no different from them—I was after all a woman she had abandoned in the mountains. She had a sparkle in her eye—maybe I just hadn't realized it was murderous. Around six at night, I gathered the strength to make a bag of microwave popcorn. I ate it in large mouth-splintering handfuls. I debated killing myself. I debated buying a gun at Walmart and driving to Oregon. Revenge was an easy well for me to dip into.

A few miserable hours later, I pulled on my boots and walked up to the Hammersmith School dining hall to steal Wi-Fi. Slumped against the dumpster in the parking lot, I looked up every ashram within three hundred miles of Portland and narrowed it down to four. I stalked Jessica's Instagram and noticed she'd stopped posting two weeks ago. That was unlike her. She always shared updates from the studio to *stay close* to her customers. She had to be hiding something. I searched for recent tags of the school where she was teaching and found several accounts from students. There she was. Grinning in three group photos—always seated next to a black-haired girl with shimmery almond eyes and red lips. The beautiful girl was tagged; greenchristina1. I clicked on her. Sure enough, two photos down her grid was Jessica, alone at night, sitting on a picnic bench in her short yellow sundress, eyes smiling. I wanted to digitally terrorize this woman, but then I heard Alisha's voice in my head; I needed to be cool.

I had been replaced. And I would probably be replaced again and again, because Jessica would fuck more girls. They would pile up. Each one better at something I had failed at, each one an improvement upon me. I zoomed in on greenchristina1. She looked radiant and forgiving. She probably loved going to dinner with big groups of friends and never complained about income tax. On the walk back I decided that if a car came, I would throw myself in front of it.

No car came. The next morning, still in pajamas, I put on my boots and headed down to the studio with a hammer. Flipping on the barn's power, the Bluetooth connected to my previous evening's Bundy podcast, instantly filling the hallowed space with a description of all of the items found in Bundy's car: torn strips of sheeting, a flashlight, handcuffs, a crowbar, green plastic garbage bags, an ice pick. I looked around the studio, most of Jessica's tools were gone, but the anvil was still there. I slid off the engagement ring she'd made me and gently set it down, then lifted the hammer, bashing until it became a formless strip of silver. When I finally stopped, I heard wheels turning in gravel and my heart fluttered out of my mouth like a butterfly on amphetamines. It would be her. She had made a mistake. I would forgive her. We would draw a bath. She would make me a new ring. I turned on my heels and threw open the door.

I caught the car just as it was turning at the bottom drive of the neighboring Nelson cabin, a beat-up Jeep Cherokee with a burgundy leather La-Z-Boy strapped to the top. No one was supposed to live there. I'd spoken to George at the post office about the cabin and he'd said the last Nelson had died six years ago. I always cut across the property to get down to the river and Jessica and I had even joked about buying it. The cabin was ancient, one of the old Appalachian relics, one room with a sagging roof and chinked logs that were sinking into the earth. Was someone living there now? Of course, I was losing everything I loved, even my privacy.

I returned to my room and curled into a ball, from my bed I could still see the hill of Christmas trees out the window, the winding stone path, my shambolic garden. I didn't want to sell and give up on the only life I had ever loved. And a part of me knew as long as I had the house there was a chance Jessica would come home. But there was no way I could afford the mortgage on my own. Everything felt like it was compressing in around me. Then I remembered the white rectangle sitting in my coat pocket—Naomi Duncan.

The next morning, I googled her. There she was, her red hair glistening at a luncheon table packed with petunias. Posed in a camel dress on a veranda. Standing on a red carpet next to a man that looked like a bizarre cross between Nathan Lane and Benicio Del Toro, who I assumed was her husband. I scrolled through more photos, at fundraisers and ribbon cuttings, then read her Wikipedia. She was born in Connecticut, the heir to a condiment fortune. Married to Bryce Duncan, the CEO of Red Rock Capital. She liked to garden. She had nearly qualified as an Olympic skier, but dropped out after her father's death to manage the family company. I zoomed in on pictures of her at the premier of *Wicked*, posing with her family. Tabitha Duncan, her only daughter, was tall with waist-length brown hair and an angry stare. I pulled out my phone and dialed.

2

I watched as the unmarked moving truck moaned up the dirt
road. For the past week my pride had been living in my
stomach like an accidentally swallowed wad of gum. I could
feel my back tensing as the vehicle moved closer. The air thin-
ning. I was yet again the jester, catering to the sympathies of
the upper class. I had sworn after spending all those hours
painting women in Michael Valentine's studio in New York I
would never be indentured to them again. But I reminded
myself that I had negotiated enough to cover my mortgage
payments for the next two years. It was worth it.

Once parked, the short stocky driver stepped out with a
clipboard and a sullen expression. "You Gillian Flynn?" He
asked, in a throaty New York accent.

I nearly laughed, then caught myself and descended the
wooden staircase, my boots clipping the boards. Naomi had
explained on the phone that she would organize the delivery
under a pseudonym to protect the surprise, because *Bryce
always figures everything out!*

"I'll need about thirty minutes to unload, but first I need you
to sign," the driver said, extending a thin tablet. I scrolled
through the digital pages, quickly realizing it was not a simple
receipt-of-delivery form I was signing off on—it included a five-
page NDA that Naomi had failed to mention on our phone call.
And this had my real name, this was not veiled under the wink-
wink of birthday secrecy, this was legally binding. I looked at
the delivery man, raised my eyebrows, he shrugged.

I felt a cold spread across my shoulders. I had signed an NDA after the incident in Michael's studio. I knew the repercussions—how you lost your right to talk but not think. It was purgatory. No matter what, all of your endless hours of replaying would be stuck inside of you like an unbalanced burning ecosystem. I looked out at the barn, trying to weigh my options, then felt a rip cord of disbelief—Naomi believed her daughter's class photos warranted an NDA. She must be a military-grade helicopter parent. I pressed the stylus to the glass.

"So, where do you want 'em?" the driver asked.

I pushed open the studio door and pointed to the long empty stretch of wall on Jessica's side of the barn. The driver assessed the uneven gravel then started unloading by hand. I joined despite his protests. The boxes were all white plastic, medium-size, maybe fifteen gallons, with tapered bottoms, some heavier than others. We lined them up, stacking as high as we could, a little over two hundred in all. The driver disappeared into his truck and came back out with a metal box of tools.

"I'm supposed to secure the building."

"What?"

"I've been instructed to make sure that the doors and windows all have secure locking mechanisms."

"It has a wooden barn latch," I protested, "this seems excessive."

Again, he shrugged.

As he set about installing a series of shiny bright latches and bolts on the sliding door and window, it dawned on me that this was not a normal truck driver. Finally, when he finished, he gave me a set of new keys, and pulled out his clipboard again, "Last signature."

I twirled the beveled stylus, and he handed over another envelope and gave me an awkward military salute; I waited till the truck disappeared to open it. Inside I found another smaller white envelope, holding the first payment of thirty thousand dollars. On the phone I had given Naomi a number I thought was impossibly high, explaining it sounded like a full year of work I'd have to condense into six months, and she had doubled it without pause. I squeezed the inch-thick stack as hard as I could and let myself bask in a flare of relief.

Dearest,

I hope you are well. And if you are reading this then you have received the materials for our project. I am extremely excited to begin—but there are a few things you must understand. What you are producing must remain private, hence the added security. I find it ideal that you will process the boxes in the seclusion of the Blue Ridge Mountains. I do hope the NDA wasn't too much of a shock, but it really is standard fare. And I am afraid I have to be strict—under no circumstances should these books or the contents of the boxes be shared with anyone. Even if Mother Teresa should rise from the dead and rap on your studio door, kindly turn her away. And please stay sensitive to the time frame, it is imperative the books be ready by January 30th. I will arrange a visit as we near the end of the project to check on the final product.

Now that the housekeeping is out of the way, you are about to intimately get to know us. It is all there in the boxes. Tabitha, Bryce, and myself. Every piece of paper that passed through our hands for a little over two decades. Tabitha would be completely embarrassed if she knew I was doing this—but that's the beauty of this being a surprise. I want an honest portrait of our family—so we will begin in 1998, the year Tabitha was born.

As we discussed, I would like at minimum two books per year, Spring–Summer and Fall–Winter. I want schoolwork, as well as photographs, emails, and more colloquial notes included. I have not looked through the boxes after placing them in storage, so I'm sure there will be some surprises. I often wrote notes on photos, and any document with a light blue Post-it—please always include. I must admit, I am slightly Type A, so precise chronology is paramount, as is captioning. There are quite a few photographs which I had printed over the years, so I've made a small key/dossier of important people so you can keep track of who is who. As well, there is a list of where we go on vacation and important dates such as birthdays and anniversaries.

I would like you to include as much of the material as possible. <u>Under no circumstances should you throw anything away.</u> I will arrange for a pickup of any leftover material after completion.

If you have any questions whatsoever, please do not hesitate to reach out. And for all our communication, I have included a cell phone from which I have programmed a number you can call me on, I know, I know, it's all very 007, but really, Bryce figures everything out!

And thank you so much, it really is fate!

Warmly,
N.

I pulled out the phone, it was a slim Samsung, nicer than mine, and even had a camera. I opened the contact list, there was one number saved under "N." This paired with the NDA seemed over the top, but the stack of cash was reassuring enough to silence my concerns. I took the money and put it in the freezer, then retrieved a jar of pickles from the fridge. I ate on the porch and eyed the barn. How was I supposed to start? Just pick a bin? Despite being *Type A*, Naomi hadn't dated or numbered the boxes.

I'd told her I wanted to assess the material, then send her a sample book. I calculated. Two books for each year since Tabitha was born was forty minimum. That alone would be weeks of work of stitching, folding, gluing, and binding. I ate three more pickles, took a shower, then wasted thirty minutes trying to find a podcast in my downloads—I settled on one about two young girls who were dismembered in a Waffle House parking lot in the mid-nineties.

With the grisly demise of the girls blasting over the speakers, I lifted the white extruded plastic lid of the bin nearest me. The box was a chaotic salad of colored paper. The first thing I pulled was a stapled piece of schoolwork from Tabitha's second grade geography class. Her name was dumbly printed in blue ink at the top of a grid of maps: America, Europe, Australia, all colored in with pencil. Was this important? How was I supposed to know? There was a date on the back that said March 2, 2007.

I inhaled and listened as the podcast explained why one of the girls had not been reported missing for five days—something about her parents' impending divorce. I sighed, and decided I would make piles, first by year, then I'd separate each of those by month. I took a sharpie and a Post-it stack, and marked 1998, 1999, 2000, and so forth—spreading them down the wall of the room up to 2018.

I returned to the bin and continued, pulling out a pack of sheet music from what appeared to be Tabitha's violin class. In the upper corner a teacher had written: *Tabitha this is the second bow you have broken this month. Nothing positive comes from you taking out your aggression on your instrument. Instead of becoming angry, I would like you to change your mindset—and think about these obstacles as challenges to overcome. Please make sure you take your violin on vacation this Christmas,* followed by a frowny face. My interest was piqued, but then I remembered Tabitha was just another materially unconscious trust fund kid, who would never understand the actual cost of replacing a violin bow. And was this note really important? Naomi had said she wanted an honest portrait. I decided to wait to make value judgments. The majority of that first box turned out to be from 2012. Not everything had dates, so I began an "unknown" pile.

I took a break; the podcast was *liberally* using foghorns to amplify the drama of the search for the dismembered girls. I looked back to the boxes and tried to imagine Naomi emptying Tabitha's backpack before they flew off for some vacation. If the husband hated this sort of detritus, why would he want this shrine-of-shit for his birthday? I grabbed the dossier Naomi had prepared and flipped through, which included a dozen or so pages of tiny headshots identifying family, teachers, friends, neighbors, and colleagues. I skipped to the list of vacations.

*Christmas: The Little Nell in Aspen, with our entire extended family, Bryce's sister, Danielle Brudall, and her husband, Peter Brudall (vice president of UBS bank), with their three boys, Mike, Bradley, and Tobias.

*Spring Break: The Ranch at Rock Creek in Montana. (Bryce likes to fly-fish and usually brings Conor Copeland, an old friend and current NYC police commissioner.)

*Summers: The Hamptons at our home on 271 Gin Lane, our neighbors are Robert and Chrissy Ash (Chrissy is a divorce lawyer to the stars, and Robert is an exec at NBC) and their two kids, Eleanor and Ernest.

*Pam Gorson was our primary nanny, who accompanied us on all trips.

*Elena Tester was our secondary nanny, who filled in on Pam's off days.

The noted occupations of her acquaintances seemed crass—I snarled as I put the dossier down and returned to the bin. After dozens of multiplication worksheets, I stumbled on my first stack of photos, still in their paper sleeve from Duane Reade. The images were glossy, all taken on a bright day. Three kids running around a topaz pool, a squirt gun floating in a sunken hot tub. A woman in a white dress with black hair in the foreground. This had to be the Hamptons. Maybe that was Chrissy Ash, divorce lawyer to the stars. The grass looked like it had been cut with scissors, the house was light blue with perfectly weathered shingles and happy round shrubs. The next photo, four kids lined up on stools in a gleaming white kitchen, with a fleet of stainless steel fridges behind them. I felt the old flush of real estate envy.

I took a break; it was already dusk. I walked the trail to Hammersmith. Once in range of the dining hall, without thinking, I pulled out my iPad and googled the Duncans' Hamptons address on Zillow: $17.6 million. I entered a scrollhole, hitting red dots, sifting through photos of houses with ocean views, gargantuan fabric curtains, and children's beds that looked like sailboats.

I returned to the barn and became robotic. I stopped looking at the contents of the photographs and focused on sorting everything by date, but I couldn't help it; I liked the secondary nanny, Elena Tester. I always paused on the photos with her in them, my gaydar gently peaking. She was young. Early twenties, with eyeliner that was a little too heavy and lipstick a few shades too dark. And in a photo of her lifting Tabitha off a swing I had spied what looked like a solid block of tattoos on her torso. Maybe she was a dyke.

I filtered through more schoolwork. State capitals. Presidents. Tabitha's failed French quizzes and endless columns of numbers with Red Rock Capital's logo printed at the bottom, all with pale blue Post-its, marking them as important. My attentions weaved between the podcast's dismembered girls and the sorting of paper, but I was good at this type of boring. Ever since I had stopped painting and begun bookmaking, I had given in to mindless focus. A care for precision but not emotion. It was never all of me.

I unearthed another forty-two-page bank statement from 2011, and I took a breath and looked around the room. What was all this shit? Why the financial stuff and receipts? The photos I understood, even the homework, but the invoices and spreadsheets made no sense. Should I really include all forty-two pages? I felt the gnawing need to ask. I dug out the Samsung from under a pile of papers and punched the only number in the phone.

It rang and rang. No answer. Ten minutes later, the foreign buzz made me jump.

"Hello?"

"Hello dear," Naomi said over the sound of a passing ambulance.

"Hi Naomi, I'm just starting to sort—" I fell silent as my eyes tracked the piles of paper on my concrete floor. "What do you want with like, with the invoices and bank statements? And receipts? Do you really want to include these?"

Naomi cut me off, "Esther, I don't envy you. Did you read my note?"

"I did—"

"Well, there isn't much else I can tell you. Whatever I saved has value. It all has its place in the tapestry—just trust the process. And don't throw anything out."

Another ambulance charged by in the background, she paused, then returned, "You know, I've been thinking a lot about legacy," she paused, "and reincarnation."

"Oh—"

"I've given you the thread, just weave it together. I can't tell you what it will look like. And darling, it's fate remember?"

"Right, fate. Bye."

Fate was easy for rich people to get behind because it meant they were supposed to have what they had. I sat down on my wooden stool. The tapestry metaphors had done nothing to clarify the mess in front of me. Why was she thinking about legacy? I knew rich people thought more about dying than normal people. They had wills and assets, endowments and lawyers and beneficiaries, but it still seemed bizarre, she was only in her midfifties and I honestly couldn't even begin to unpack the whole reincarnation thing. I sighed and returned to sorting, slipping deeper into the current of the Duncans.

In the next box I found another note from Tabitha's teacher, informing her parents that she had hit one of her fellow students in the face with her metal pencil case. I felt a shudder, imagining the oblong imprint on the cheek of a classmate. Hungrily, I looked at the surrounding papers hoping for more details, but there was nothing. I found photos from Tabitha's fifth-grade dance, she was posing alone in front of a beach themed backdrop, her eyes wild, her forehead greasy and reflecting the flash of the camera. Even with all the world's wealth at your disposal, being a preteen was painful to look at. In the next box I found my answer: dozens of reports from Tabitha's child psychologist, Ben Kenworth. One citing the pencil case incident—among others—described Tabitha as moody and volatile. I checked the date, she would have been thirteen; who wasn't moody and volatile at thirteen? And why would anyone want these sorts of reports pasted into a scrapbook?

I moved on. More vacation photos. Bryce rarely looked at the camera while Naomi was ever aware. Always poised, sunglasses perfectly tipped. Tabitha had braces in some. There were pictures of them on a private jet. Bryce waving the camera off while talking into his phone. And Naomi hadn't been lying about their house in Manhattan; it was nearly empty, except for a few pieces of woven leather furniture. All wood, glass, and several bonsai trees on marble plinths overlooking Central Park. Not a stitch of carpet. No art. Not even a book.

I closed my eyes, tuning my attention back to the podcast. The narrator was waxing about every amateur detective's new favorite tool—genealogy. 23andMe and a swath of other similar companies had webbed together the data of millions willing to shell out money to spit in a tube. What had driven all of those people to slobber on demand? A desire to know their great-grandfather was Irish, or find out they were one five-hundredth Neanderthal. To me it was such mundane information—so wholly irrelevant to the reality of being. But a few years ago, a victim of an abduction had the idea to use it to track down her relatives and so was the beginning of forensic genealogy, which worked inversely as well, tracing the DNA of killers to their relatives: Big Spit data had become the microwave for cold cases.

It was nearly eight at night. I had only gotten through nine boxes in six hours. Walking up the stone steps back to the house, I was crushed by the warm quiet of the mountain. I was careful to almost never be in silence. Even when Jessica was only away temporarily, teaching, or out at the grocery store, I was terrified of the night's blankness. I missed her banging around the kitchen, squawking on the phone. Making a mess. I stood frozen on the path, listening to the hollow slips of sound—animals, wind, then nothing. I looked down the driveway, willing her car. I knew there had always been an imbalance, she made too many plans. I made none. She always wanted to adopt a dog. Or sign up for a CSA farm delivery. Drive to Montauk, go to Bali for the summer, enroll in law school.

I had arrived at Hammersmith after attending a string of craft schools. Haystack. Arrowmont. Anderson Ranch. Shakerag. I took classes in pottery, basket weaving, natural dyes, and bookmaking, doing work-study when I could, but it was still shockingly expensive. Mostly the classes were filled with retired people who had always longed to use their hands; ex-accountants, stay-at-home moms with grown sons, schoolteachers, professors, and court clerks. The classes were fervid, the odd assemblages of students developing bizarre closeness through long hours ignoring reality in the studio. There was always an angry man. A lonely widow. A twentysomething avoiding college. I ended up spending most of my settlement money unlearning everything I had absorbed in New York. I had a teacher at Arrowmont who explained that whatever we touched, touched us. And I knew I had touched evil in Michael's studio: a dark current of greed and immense ego. In those craft workshops I chipped away at the layers of anger and rage that had sealed my short painting career in the Big Apple.

I went out onto the porch with a glass of red wine. The night air felt good. I stared at the barn. I'd met a guy in my ceramics class at Haystack, named Dave, who had worked his whole life at a nuclear storage site in Aiken, South Carolina. Dave's job was to monitor the turquoise wells of water that cooled the spent radioactive fuel rods. "Just like Homer Simpson," he joked. I had enjoyed hearing about his work. The yellow hazmat suits. The pulsating toxicity at the bottom of the pool. From the porch, my barn filled with Naomi Duncan's plastic boxes felt similar. I wanted to seal them off—to keep their poison from seeping into my life. I could already feel the pull. My desire to slip into obsession. And I knew proximity to wealth had the power to dement. Soon enough I'd find myself absentmindedly comparing stainless steel fridge prices online. I promised myself that tomorrow I wouldn't go on Zillow. I would focus on the podcast, wear a hazmat suit—like Dave.

3

The next morning, as usual, I went for a walk, cutting over the Nelson property. Upon crossing, I could see the Jeep Cherokee was parked in the drive, the La-Z-Boy no longer strapped on top. I dipped out of sight and followed the murky river, which had been polluted by a coal plant a hundred miles up. Back at home I ate breakfast and felt disgustingly alone. I debated walking to the school and downloading Tinder. There weren't any lesbians on my mountain but Asheville was crawling with dykes. The unofficial slogan of the city, coined during a '90s Indigo Girls concert, was *ten thousand lesbians can't be wrong*. And they of course all brewed kombucha, ate off handmade ceramics, believed in astrology, and "liked to hike." I could tolerate most of it, but astrology was too close to fate—I hated the idea that everything was traceable, already drawn in chunky permanent marker in the cosmos. And anyway—there was no way to ascertain my rising sign: I had no idea what time I was born and my mother was dead. Two facts that had iced several first dates.

Despite my hopes that Jessica would breeze through the door, I was still filtering through the house, opening drawers, speculating on what was or wasn't still there. Taking stock. For the most part, all the good stuff was gone. The Le Creuset Dutch oven, the quilt, the Ayurvedic face oil, copper-bottomed pans, the shibori place mats, and her ceramics. I was left with the crap: a headlamp, broken sunglasses, bathtub-swollen mystery novels, flip-flops, a half-used bottle of lavender Dr.

Bronner's. Each object was like a small land mine, simultaneously affirming her once presence and now absence. I picked up the cylinder of organic lavender soap and tossed it in a high arc across the bathroom. It landed with a satisfying *clunk* in the trash. The sound made me crumple. A hollow familiar drum. The weeks after my mother died, whenever my father was home, he'd aimlessly roam the house throwing her things into the kitchen's metal trash can. Her curling iron, *thump*. A hairbrush. Old yearbooks, *thump*. She had been completely erased in under four months. I had saved nothing, paralyzed by my father's methodical gruffness.

But I wasn't as cold as him. I stalked the house picking up Jessica's flotsam, dumping it into one of Naomi's now empty bins, neatly, albeit passive aggressively, labeling it—*j's junk*. I fought the itch to take everything to the backyard and load it up in the firepit. I wanted to watch it burn. To have flames dement her objects, to turn them into an equalizing ash—but I was still hoping she'd come back. I carried the box to the barn and loaded it on top of the pile of Jessica's other left-behind cardboard boxes which I stacked, like a totem pole, on top of my sturdy metal filing cabinet which held my passport and various important papers. Before turning back to the house, I stared at the bin of j's junk. I was hit with the sensation that maybe I could reconstruct her from the contents, my Frankenstein bride made of half-used nail polish bottles, flip-flops, and nutritional yeast.

In the kitchen I poured another cup of coffee, then picked out a new podcast, a cold case from seventeen years ago about a missing Canadian woman. Ethically speaking, coldcases were the only form of podcast that were acceptable. They sautéed long dormant hopes of families looking for closure. I walked to the studio and the podcast popped on in through speakers. In the first five minutes it is so obvious the boyfriend killed the missing girl it's excruciating, but there is no body.

No murder weapon. No hard evidence. Yet on the day of her disappearance one of the boyfriend's hockey bags goes missing. A hole was punched in her bathroom door. A neighbor later saw him carrying bulky trash bags. He had her car keys. He lies to the cops. And he tries to kill himself. According to the boyfriend's side-piece-fuck-buddy, she even saw bite marks and scratches on his back. Yet somehow this man is free. I was so enraged I mindlessly tore through eight of Naomi's boxes by two p.m.

For lunch I ate two string-cheese sticks. I needed to go grocery shopping, but the idea of buying things just for myself was too devastating. I knew I would still pick up what she liked because I wanted her to recognize the fridge. I wanted to smell chickpeas bubbling on the stove. And I wanted Jessica to be happy when she came through the door. I ignored my hunger and went back to hunting for dates on various pieces of paper—my brain spinning on the missing Canadian girl.

I quit at nine p.m. but I'd made a sizable dent in the boxes. At this point, I thought a nice, recycled eggshell medium weight paper would be ideal for the books. Something to make all the printer paper pop. I also needed to figure out the best method to adhere the scraps. Which raised the questions of how archival these books actually needed to be. Who would truly care to see Tabitha's failed French quiz in a hundred years? And how should I deal with things that were double-sided which I couldn't just glue down? I debated photo corners but they were finicky. I ended up eating a jar of olives over the sink while scrolling through a series of tabs I'd preopened en masse on soccer-mom-scrapbooking websites, picking up tips on acid-free photo glue.

The blogs were full of sad women taking selfies in underlit lady-caves. Visual clutter seemed paramount. Lots of gold and silver pens. Paper antiqued with tea. Name tags cut from burlap and accented with twine. Laminated wedding invitations.

Stickers. Stamps. Tissue flowers. In my spiral, I had googled scrapbooking origins. It appeared to have begun in the 1800s, mostly people gluing family photos, obituaries, and birth announcements into bibles—and sometimes locks of hair, I'm sure to the delight of all the amateur genealogist and forensic freaks. But essentially it was an architecture for displaying familial narrative, 23andme before 23andme. It pained me to imagine filling the Duncans' life-garbage into my books, I never wanted to see how people used the things I made. But my desire for emptiness hadn't always been there, at least not in art school.

I had showed up stupid. Everyone shows up to college stupid but I looked like an angry Monica Lewinsky, as Memphis had so kindly pointed out on our first weekend drinking at La Caverna. I was out but not even generally OK with queerness, or myself, or my height or intensity or the way my voice sounded in a classroom. I was painfully aware of the cut of my shoulders, every black hair on my body, and my Hot Topic hangover wardrobe. My face was always painted an off-white and my neck draped with layers of silver chains. I was not cool. I hung out mostly with the foreign students, and the kids who'd graduated from the pipe schools, which were military-style arts high schools that ignored academics but drilled students in form and technique and were then "piped in" to New York universities. All the pipe kids had a shared and disparaged polish, and most of them, like me, loved photorealism.

I could draw a coffee cup so three-dimensionally sound that one would impulsively reach for it. I could perfectly capture the shimmer of condensation on a chopped strawberry. The fog in the corner of an eyeball. A tangle of matted hair. The trick was never looking away. Staring so deeply into the form that it became the only thing I understood. The coffee cup replaced me. The strawberry became me. I started with colored pencil, but Mrs. Galloway, my very encouraging high school art teacher, bought me oils—so I began. I could take whatever I wanted and replicate it. I was a bank robber. Everything and everyone was a puzzle that I could solve. Whatever I loved I could own. I could consume. But I knew being dexterous with a paintbrush was not enough. Not in art school. Not in New York. You had to have a concept. A meaning. A story. A philosophical intention to bolster your movements on canvas. I tried to read the classics and keep up. Adorno. Clement Greenberg. Baudrillard. Derrida. But the truth was, I only liked the process, the consumption of form.

The following morning, I was groggy. The Jeep Cherokee–driving asshole, who'd moved into the Nelson cabin, had been using a chainsaw from four a.m., cutting in angry whining strokes, till sunup. I imagined a meth head slurping Mountain Dew. A redneck railroading fentanyl. A Juggalo free-basing Faygo. Who else was up at four a.m. with a chainsaw? If I hadn't loathed confrontation I would have marched down in my pajamas, but instead, pouty and depressed, I'd turned up my rainforest sound machine and tried to go back to bed. Standing at my sink, I drank a shaky cup of coffee, then walked down the curving gravel road to the Hammersmith craft store and put in an order for recycled eggshell paper.

Slumped near the dumpsters, I hungrily checked my email. Living without the internet felt good when I'd cohabitated with Jessica. She'd had an iPhone. If we needed to see a picture of Kristen Stewart's new girlfriend, she had it up in seconds. Now I was untethered. I had no new emails. I was so lonely I read my spam. HOT GIRLS NOW 18. PENIS ENLARGEMENT FOR YOU ESTHER 6969. K.E.T.O.S.L.I.M. The bizarre strings of letters and numbers that constructed the email subjects felt like tiny alien strippers twisting and shouting for my attention.

Their unorthodox prose were somehow soothing and I was grateful for their concern. Maybe I did want a bigger penis? Maybe I did want hot girls now. But all I wanted was Jessica. *Jessica, Jessica, Jessica.* I couldn't stop saying her name. I ached to alter the fabric of time. To reach out and touch her pregnant belly. To rest my head on her silky thighs.

I hadn't always wanted a family and I was too butch to imagine my own uterus being used as it was intended, but Jessica had planted the seed. She'd started bringing it up right around the time we'd moved in, and this child entered my daydreams like a sparkling jet of hope in a world so dark I could barely read the news. I began putting my hand on Jessica's stomach whenever I could, letting myself imagine a line of stockings on the mantel and visits to the local library. And when she made the appointment at the fertility clinic, we started talking seriously about sperm donors. So, we made a list of male friends alongside their pros and cons in a notebook we kept in the kitchen for grocery lists.

Greg = nice sense of humor, chews with his mouth open,
   weirdly competitive.
Nathan = good looking, tall, questionable soul.
Ben = hot, very bad at math, Republican siblings.

Once I was back in the barn, I cleared off my worktable, and began cutting the backing board with a blade. There was plenty to do before the paper arrived. I stretched an indigo piece of linen for the cover while listening to an interview, set to plonky dulcimer strumming, of a man who firsthand saw his sister get beat up by her husband but he never said anything to the police about the incident after she went missing.

I had become successfully numb to the content of the Duncan boxes. The yearly piles were now massive—a slush of inanities, I was like a mail sorter at the post office; on the brink of mental breakdown yet no less efficient. In the more recent boxes, I'd found even more bank statements and receipts. It seemed bizarre, like some form of emotional accounting. I tried to imagine Naomi's mental state when she'd slip yet another piece of paper into the box's plastic mouth. Maybe she was drunk or rolling on Ambien or maybe she just thought of it as a recycling bin. After two more zoned out days of sorting, the eggshell paper arrived and I began putting together the signatures, pressing my bone folder along the creases, and punching holes for the needle with my bulbous wood-handled awl. It felt good to return to this work, my hands darting furiously.

When I was finished, the example book looked clean, simple, and I thought beautiful. I wrapped the rectangle in tissue paper and slipped it into one of Jessica's leftover jewelry delivery sleeves, then wrote out the P.O. box Naomi had instructed. In the echo of completion, I felt confused about the path forward; Naomi had told me to make a tapestry. If the boxes had been all family photos maybe I would have understood, but this was such a bizarre mix of shit. Mostly refuse and some, like the notes from Tabitha's psychologist, were disturbing. What sort of story would I be telling? Soon I would have to start making narrative choices beyond chronology, and that would have to come from understanding.

It was almost the Fourth of July. Ingles, the only grocery store in town, was decorated with plastic American flags and the windows were sprayed with red, white, and blue stripes. I had been living on a steady diet of microwave Amy's burritos, rotating between black bean and Indian, inhaling them while sorting papers. Standing in the aisles, overwhelmed by a complete lack of inspiration, I bought fifteen more burritos. Eating was no longer a cause for celebration. Jessica had smuggled so much joy into the ritual of setting our table: linen

41

napkins, beeswax candles, and the flaky French salt. Now I thought of my stomach as a gas tank. Something that simply needed filling.

Later that evening, I went to start my bath, and turned the tap. Nothing.

"Motherfucker."

I knew immediately. I put my clothes back on, grabbed a flashlight, and headed down to the hill. Just beyond my property line, I lifted the large gray piece of plywood that covered the spring box, praying the snakes were elsewhere—preparing for their holiday weekend. There was no water. It was empty. I sighed; it was shared with the Nelson cabin. Jessica would have breezily talked to the neighbor, maybe brought an offering, some flowers, a zucchini, or a head of lettuce from the garden. I sucked in a hiccup of air and turned to continue down the hill. I had no choice. It was dusk. A desert orange was emanating from the thin rectangular windows of the cabin. I would have to knock. I would have to speak to this idiot. Around fifty feet away, I debated turning back. Then the door swung open with a harrowing creak. A short man with a white mustache and a blue polo shirt appeared. He was older than I was expecting, his face deeply creased, his forearms tan. He lifted his right hand, and I realized he was holding a small silver gun.

"Who's there?" he yelled, with a lumbering Southern accent. "This here is private property."

"It's me, Esther. I'm your neighbor. The spring box is drained."

The man huffed, then let his shoulders drop.

"Are you running any continuous water?" I asked, trying my best to sound calm.

"What?"

"Like a leaking faucet or loose toilet handle."

"No," he said, soft but incredulous.

There was a strange pause, both of us just staring. Something inside of me hardened. Who pulls a gun on a neighbor? Who cuts logs at four a.m.? Who says *no* like that?

"I've seen you walk on my property."

"What?" I asked.

"Don't, it's private."

I couldn't believe him. I knew those who lived alone in the mountains were a weird breed. I had not chosen this life. I had wanted a cottage-core lesbian fantasy, and it had been ripped from me, unceremoniously via a note in a fruit bowl. I had not intended to become a Ted Kaczynski festering in my cabin, but this man clearly did. A streak of fear ran through me, followed by anger. I knew better than to lash out with the gun in his pocket. I knew it could be tense between "locals" and the craft people, and I had heard about mountain teenagers torching clay studios citing "devil worship." Then I saw it, a hose in the corner of the yard gurgling a steady stream. I stomped over and turned off the golden spigot attached to the side of his shed.

"Have a nice night," I sneered, then trudged home and turned my music up loud enough that he could surely hear it. I tried to ignore the vibrations of the interaction in my veins. It felt like a curdling of the mountain, everything spoiling at once.

A part of me wished the book I'd made for Naomi had gotten lost in the mail. The whole project felt overwhelming and despite my best efforts to keep my distance from the material, the Duncans were consuming my thoughts. I'd even spent a full evening googling the family's hedge fund, Red Rock Capital, which they'd started at the end of the nineties using Naomi's father's money, betting big on e-commerce and winning.

I was alerted that the package I'd sent to Naomi had been delivered to her P.O. box. But there was nothing, no phone

43

call. No chipper voice note from Naomi, *Go ahead dear! I love it!* It was a long weekend, and I knew there was a good chance the Duncans were already barbecuing a rack of ribs by the pool in the Hamptons. From photos of Fourth of Julys past, I knew they draped red, white, and blue streamers on the terrace and ordered an oversize cake from Carissa's bakery. While my burrito was spinning in the microwave, I tried to imagine what it would be like if I were part of their family. Maybe I could be an aunt, or an older sister. Somebody who would join for these exorbitant vacations and drink from six-hundred-dollar bottles of wine. The high-pitched beeping signaling the finish line of my burrito's circuitous journey ended my fantasy.

I purposefully cut across the Nelson property on my evening walk to Hammersmith. Fuck him. The school was buzzing with new happy students. I felt a kick to my spleen remembering the cloud of possibility I had arrived on. All those potential new friends. *Jessica.* I sat on the steps stealing Wi-Fi and stared into my iPad, willing myself to get lost in my old role of highly effectual studio assistant—overbuying glue sticks, plastic sleeves, and Post-its. I ordered Derrida's *Archive Fever* and a coffee table book about the history of scrapbooking. I impulsively bought Kurt Cobain's journals, rationalizing something about "the importance of looking at alternative formats." Amazon then suggested Frida Kahlo's diaries, Peter Beard's, then Anne Frank's and then Zelda Fitzgerald, and I just sat there in the dark pressing *Buy. Buy. Buy.* I had forgotten about the rush of knowing that everything could be expensed. It was research. I would be reimbursed. Normally, for my own purchases, when I watched my debit card slice through a plastic card reader I felt as if a piece of my own body was being chopped off.

Four days later and still no word from Naomi. I was annoyed. I drove down to the post office to pick up one of my packages. The old-timey glass-fronted mailboxes with their brass combination locks conjured a long-gone mining boom–era town, but now the mildewing two-room building was held together by a mix of duct tape and aluminum patches. George, who was nearly blind, and had worked there for the past forty-odd years, popped into the wood framed vestibule.

"Oh, hey there, is that you, Esther? I got something for ya," he said in his thick drawl.

"Thanks," I paused to seem casual, "and George, I was wondering—do you know who's in the Nelson cabin?"

"Oh, well—I'll be damned. There was a Nelson left after all. I thought when Shelt died that was it, but Patrick is apparently Shelt's nephew on his sister's side." George leaned his head over the wooden divider, a flutter of dandruff following, "Nice fellow, but he gets a lot of mail from the correctional institute."

"Oh," I said lightly, not wanting to tip my hand to our current neighborly dispute, but the news affirmed my belief—correctional institute—Mountain Dew Kaczynski. I nodded politely to George, thanked him for the package, and turned to leave.

"Oh, and sweetheart, I'm sorry Jessica broke it off."

I swiveled, stunned. My eyes were barely able to meet his, "How did you—"

"She asked to get her mail permanently forwarded."

I felt my cheeks flush. George, with his possum gray hair, took an almost imperceptible step backward, as if to say—*I can't tell you where, don't even ask.* So, I didn't.

I stopped at the school before going home, and googled *Patrick Nelson* on my iPad. Nothing. Had he been in prison? I tried again. *Patrick Nelson Inmate North Carolina.* All that popped up was an insurance agency in Greenville, I gave up. Maybe he was into those prison pen-pal websites juggling the attention of dozens of lonely jailbirds. I shuddered and pulled out the coffee table book I'd ordered from its cardboard sleeve.

The book was overdesigned and weirdly shaped. What was I looking for? Large glossy photographs stared back at me, Victorian ladies on bicycles, old candy wrappers glued next to sheet music. Dance cards. Five girls sitting on a log. A man in an air force uniform. It all seemed so stylized. So neatly vintage. What could I even make with Naomi's mess? A how-to guide of criminal wealth and child rearing on the Upper East Side? A who's who of the Hamptons elite? Near the end in big letters was an Ezra Pound quote that fit my feelings on the subject: *We do not know the past in the chronological sequence. It may be convenient to lay it all out anesthetized on the table with dates pasted on here and there, but what we know we know by ripples and spirals eddying out from us and from our time.*

To keep working I needed to know if Naomi had approved of the test book I'd sent. I wallowed for two more days then broke down and drove to Hammersmith and googled the WAC offices. I called, rationalizing that maybe she had misplaced her burner. I knew insecurity was a side effect of my having slipped back into the role of the highly effectual studio assistant. I needed to please. Head pats. Treats.

"Naomi Duncan's office, Fern Sawyer speaking," a harried voice finally answered.

"Oh, hi—I'm looking for Naomi."

"And may I ask who's calling?"

"Esther Ray."

There was a pause, the phone clicked over.

"Why are you calling me here?" Naomi's voice was frosty.

"I wanted to know if you liked the book."

"I was very specific about our communication, Esther."

I gulped a wad of hot discomfort, "I'm sorry, I just didn't hear from you . . ."

"It's a very hectic period. I did receive the book. It's perfect, and I apologize for not reaching out sooner."

46

I felt a swell of pride, "That's great to hear, and I solved the issue I mentioned in the note, I'm going to use adhesive plastic sheets for the double-sided pieces of paper."

"All right, just make sure not to throw anything away." She turned hard again, and she lowered her voice, "And never call WAC again."

"Why?" I asked without thinking.

Naomi paused, then her tone shifted into a forced lightness, "For the birthday surprise."

"Oh, right," I said, returning her false levity.

I drove back to my house feeling like a child who'd done something wrong, replaying the conflicting tones of Naomi's voice. Midway up my road I hit the brakes, my whole body jerking forward, then back. Screwed to a large tree, on the entrance of the drive to the Nelson cabin, were three new signs, painted in red on brown wood—NO TRESPASSING, PRIVATE PROPERTY, KEEP OUT. I flung open my door and hopped onto the back of my bumper and ripped down the signs. Flinging them one by one, off the side of the road.

4

It is a feeling that always arrives on a flashing highway of speed and cinematic emotion; I am on horseback, dressed in leather at full gallop. I am a cop in a bad movie. I am a vindictive mobster with nothing to lose. I am in pursuit of justice.

The first time I felt it was when my mother died. A soft warm day, June 21, 2002. My dad was off somewhere in Nebraska selling tractor combine components and I was in my room, sketching in my spiral notebook while Jerry Springer expounded who on his small stage was parentally bound to a drooling toddler. My own mother had spent the better part of the morning in the mirror trying on dresses she'd bought at Kohl's, scrutinizing a mound of colorful fabrics with tags still attached. She was deeply vain, and with her long wavy blonde hair, olive skin, and surreal robin's-egg-blue eyes, she had reason. Men stared in the grocery store, doors were held, bank teller windows magically popped open. She was very aware of her power and ritually rubbed herself with creams and oils, her sheets always stained with residue. She even refused to use her forehead, reacting without physical emotion, turning her neck in slow motion, to stave off wrinkles.

When she married my father at twenty, she'd thought he was rich. But Greg Ray, the young salesman, had lied, or really, just not told her the whole truth. My dad burnt through the small inheritance he'd received from his Aunt Mildred while wooing my mother on trips to Chicago, buying her dresses from Saks and a fat diamond engagement ring, pantomiming a life he could never sustain. My mother was already pregnant with me when she'd found out there was next to nothing in their bank account, and she was too proud for divorce, so she made do, punishing him by drinking and applying for credit cards, spending money he didn't have.

That soft June night, my mother was heading to Madeline Lancaster's. Madeline was her childhood best friend, a gin drunk who owned seven Appaloosa horses and relied on the charade of the party to keep knocking down ice studded beverages because she didn't like to drink alone. She hosted a weekly ladies' night which started around four p.m. My mother rarely missed one. Madeline's husband Wayne owned a string of Ford dealerships. They lived in a sprawling suburban compound, boasting an indoor pool with a waterslide and a fully built-out bar framed by tiki torches. My mother was envious and I knew it made her physically ill to go into Madeline's closet, or see her candy-apple-red KitchenAid mixer or the rows of MAC lipsticks that lined her vanity like erotic ammunition. Madeline loved to give tours, and my mother had a habit of bitterly mumbling, *Someday I swear, I'll just burn her house down.*

Madeline may have been materially wealthy for Ohio, but she was short with a perpetually squinched face. "No amount of MAC is going to save her," my mother had remarked tartly one day while I peed in the Eiffel Tower–wallpapered bathroom at Madeline's. They were always trying to one-up each other, and my mom took extra care to get dressed up for ladies' nights. When I close my eyes I can see it, the fog of the oversize windows, the stench of chlorine and mentholated cigarettes, Neil Diamond or the Beach Boys whining from the speakers. The chorus of vapidity. Music mixing with women talking about laser hair removal, the purr of a blender lashing pineapple, rum, and ice into submission. Madeline didn't have kids. Wayne didn't want them, and she didn't mind, she liked that she could do whatever, whenever she pleased.

When I was younger, I loved swimming in the pool and the goofy demeanor of the women, with their glazed eyes and loud laughs. Most of the time the crowd thinned by dark, the women had their husbands to pacify and kids to put to bed. But because my dad was on the road my mother also did as she pleased, and she usually spent the night in one of Madeline's spare bedrooms. I would sleep over too until around age twelve. I stopped going. I hated it. From the second she opened the door, Madeline plied my mother with liquor. She preferred my mother drunk. "She's just more fun hammered," she'd told me once with coral lips as she added Malibu to the blender. I didn't know what *hammered* meant. But if my mom wanted to leave, Madeline would pop a bottle of champagne, which no matter how far gone, she could never turn down. I despised how my mother moved with added weight when drunk. Spit roping from her mouth, lipstick smudged. Words slurred. Everything that embarrassed me magnified.

That last night, before leaving for Madeline's, my mom had turned to me in the doorframe of the duplex and tilted her head to ask how she looked. I thought the raspberry dress seemed cheap, but I bit my lip.

"You look gorgeous."

She beamed.

"I'll be home tomorrow around noon, there's lasagna in the fridge."

I nodded, not even looking up from Jerry Springer.

If there was lasagna in the fridge, why did her car end up wrapped around a median a little after midnight? Why had she tried to drive home? What happened? I felt a need bright blooming inside of me, expanding in spirals of neon cursive tubing—Justice.

How many drinks had Madeline given her? The timeline of that evening became my obsession. After the funeral, I called Madeline daily. At first, she answered, dropping into low

51

syrupy tones, probably drunk, and crying along with me, telling old stories about my mom—but I only wanted to know about that night.

"Honey, it was like any of those evenings. We had some drinks, then we went to bed—I didn't even know she'd left."

I'd call again the next day and ask her the same question—waiting for a deviation in her story, for some sort of clue.

"What happened? What did you talk about?"

"Oh, I don't know, baby, I told you, that new George Clooney movie with the aliens."

After a few weeks she became annoyed, "Honey, you have to stop calling. I've told you everything. You know, I lost a friend too."

I tracked down the numbers of the other women who were there that night. Justine, Karen, Melissa-Lee, Eleanor, Susan. Everyone had left before my mom, they all said the evening had seemed normal, bordering on boring. Justine had shown photos from her vacation to the Wisconsin Dells. Karen had brought a pound cake. I returned to calling Madeline, sometimes late at night, hoping the fog of sleep would bring new utterances—a confession.

Had they fought? Did she force my mom into the car? Madeline changed her number.

Once I got my driver's license, I'd show up at her house, ring the doorbell, and wait on her sloped lawn. After a few weeks she installed a camera on her porch. And four months later she took out a restraining order. I tried another route: hiring a lawyer. Under the Dram Shop Act of 1862, whoever sells alcohol can be held liable for injuries of, and perpetrated by, their customers. In a small, carpeted office in a strip mall that smelled like rubber, I tried to argue that because Madeline had a full professionally stocked bar built into her house replete with tiki torches, the law should apply. A tall, gaunt-faced man explained that the Dram Shop Act only pertained to licensed alcohol vendors. There was no case against Madeline.

"You can't blame Madeline for this," my dad grimaced after I'd returned from my third strip-mall lawyer, "Caroline drove drunk, that's her cross to bear."

That was the other thing. There is only so much sympathy for a drunk driver. She could have killed a school bus of Christian children. She could have hit a jogger. She could have rear-ended a pregnant woman or flipped a car of mock-trial champion teenagers. Killing herself and only herself was a good outcome—no one says this, but they think it.

My dad was home even less. He had never been overly affectionate, always quiet in his care, but he had worshipped Caroline. He was now brittle and angered easily. And I could no longer predict his temper. We rarely spoke, brushing silently side by side in the kitchen. Whatever warmth that had simmered inside of him was frozen.

I began laying out the spreads of the first book. Tabitha Duncan's early days were documented in extreme detail. The year 1998 pile was on the north wall, and amongst hospital papers, prints of her tiny feet on card stock, and wet nurse referrals, were dozens of Duane Reade photo envelopes. I opened the first stack. Naomi looked young, her cheeks flushed, propped up on pillows in the white hospital bed. Later Bryce and Naomi took a photograph in a mirrored elevator with the pram covered in white cloth, the flash fracturing the upper quadrant of the image—but you can just make out the small silver camera Naomi is holding. I wondered what Bryce had imagined happened to all of these photographs? There must be some part of him that knew she'd held on to everything?

As soon as I'd started to glue down each page, it became impossible to keep my distance. Each image. Each receipt and squiggly pencil drawing. Everything staring back at me with impossible singularity. Tabitha was a fat baby with a round head and a puff of brown hair, born at New York-Presbyterian on November 9, at 7:10 a.m. A Scorpio. On my lunch break at Hammersmith, I opened Jessica's favorite astrology site and plugged in Tabitha's time of birth; her ascendent sign was also Scorpio. She was the Slytherin of the astrological world. Scorpios are notoriously dark, jealous creatures. At one point, I'd tried to fuse Jessica's love of astrology with my own penchant for true crime and we spent a night on the couch deep-diving into the astrological signs of serial killers—surprisingly Scorpio came in second, only behind the gentle, fearful, overly trusting Pisces. But Charles Manson was a Scorpio, so was the Golden State Killer, and one of my favorite lesser-knowns, Nannie Doss, who had been given the brilliant moniker "self-made widow."

When I returned, I pried open more Duane Reade envelopes. There was a lightness between Bryce and Naomi during this period, a joy sliceable like cake. At least two hundred baby cards were saved in a ziplock bag—from friends and family, some tasteful on monogrammed stationary, and some garish with cartoon storks and diaper jokes, and even several from fashion houses like Givenchy and Yves Saint Laurent. It was almost all sweet. Grandparents *ooing* and *gooing* in photographs. Happy brunches, christenings, and sandy vacations in St. Barts. The procession of time in the Duncan household felt like a ten-thousand-person stampede of nannies, assistants, drivers, aunts, and cousins circulating around this singular child. After seven hours of gluing and sorting I was completely drained.

I spent the evening in my kitchen, away from the photos and piles of papers, stitching together blank scrapbook signatures while listening to a podcast about a girl who vanished from a hippie hotbed in Colorado that sounded oddly similar to

Hammersmith. Despite living where I lived, burning palo santo and using bamboo toilet paper, hippies still made me uneasy. I knew the sunshine of the self-described healers and free spirits was often laced with shipwrecked libertarianism—every man for himself. The Colorado girl disappeared after a drum circle, which the podcast took aural advantage of, thumping away, as the hippies explain in different tonalities that no one in the area likes talking to law enforcement, people do a lot of drugs, and everyone is only known to each other via nickname— Barboy, Wind Grip, Big Cat.

This is perhaps the essential perversion of true crime, and what I like best—it is just a guy in a Uniqlo vest with a condenser microphone and oversize headphones. An amateur journalist, a weekend psychologist or retired grocer with a love of LexisNexis. Podcasters are not cops. They sit on front porches of accused killers and wait outside of McDonald's bathrooms, mics on, without having to file paperwork or get approval from *above*. They are emailed in the middle of the night in all caps by the family members of victims who think the police aren't doing enough. They are drunk dialed by suspects and follow clues which seemed too ludicrous to be written down in official notebooks. Despite the obvious fetish for forensics, there is a low-key cop-hating culture baked into true crime; because it's always either the pigs' laziness or racism or obsession with the wrong suspect or unwillingness to see sex workers as people, or just their old-fashioned botching of things.

I felt restless and wanted to get out of the house. I walked down the trail to Hammersmith with Jessica's headlamp strapped over my ponytail. Once in the school's parking lot, I checked my emails as if I were gulping for water. I had received a mass invite to a batik workshop in Idaho. An announcement for a gallery in Brooklyn. But again, nothing really for me. I was just another alphabetical chain clasped with an @ sign in a splash of self-promotion. I refreshed my inbox. Nothing. I could hear voices coming from the large porch on the opposite side of the cafeteria. People were probably drinking. Eating leftover chips and M&Ms from the Friday night welcome mixer. I could walk around, say hi. Maybe it was Carston or Lily, people I knew, but they would ask about Jessica.

Instead, I began looking at pictures of Naomi on Google. I clicked through a series of images of her standing in front of completed water projects in sandy parched-looking areas of the world. I was impressed. WAC had financed and managed the digging of eleven hundred wells, "all created in close collaboration with the surrounding communities in an effort to build sustainable long-term water systems." I decided a life dedicated to bringing water to the needy was not the worst for a woman living on Central Park—at least she wasn't hosting thoroughbred dog shows, or buying stainless-steel balloon art. I wondered if Tabitha had Facebook. I typed her name into the blue search bar. Private.

The top result on Google was a link to Instagram. I almost dropped my iPad. Her circular profile photo stared back, smiling in a sunflower field wearing a seafoam-green tube top, her midriff bare, with a tiny pair of sunglasses balanced on top of her head that made her look like a nineties supermodel. She had 2.6 million followers. I scrolled down, past images of her on a private jet with two blondes holding champagne glasses, all boasting pastel claws. A slideshow of four photos posing in front of a glowing Manhattan skyline, Tabitha's skull haloed in multicolored berets. Photographs of frozen yogurt. A latte resting on a slab of marble next to a small beige Birkin bag. Tabitha, lathered in oil, splayed in a bikini on a shockingly white boat. Somehow, I had never imagined Tabitha grown up—she had been relegated to the sinewy-facelessness of all children. I gawked at her tan body and green-eyed mean stare. She was a celebrity. It seemed absurd, but of course, America loved the performance of generational wealth. I walked back home as Tabitha's contemporary body rang like an impossible alarm.

The next morning, I tried my best to push the sultry after-image of present-day Tabitha from my mind and began gluing in photos from her first day of kindergarten. She was grinning, exposing two rows of excited teeth. In the next picture, Bryce and Naomi were crouched down, joining Tabitha at her miniature height, on the front steps of school. Bryce was wearing a suit, Naomi a starched button up. The photos were followed by a bundle of welcome literature on light orange paper, then a tuition packet. Yearly $49,700, not including field trip costs. How could kindergarten cost so much? In the stack I found a letter, folded in thirds, from her teacher with the school's crest proudly centered.

Mrs. + Mr. Duncan,

Firstly, I want to extend a warm welcome to your family! We love having Tabitha in our classroom and are overjoyed with her warmth and energy; it's been a great first month of school. I am, however, writing because we have had several incidents in which Tabitha has lashed out physically. She seems to have an extremely short fuse and we would like to open a discussion with you about adding behavioral therapy into her morning sessions. This is quite normal, as entering school is a major life transition! We think a little extra help will get her where she needs to be. If you are available to come in at the beginning of the school week, Monday or Tuesday, it would be great to discuss in person.

Thank you, and look forward to a fabulous school year,

Mrs. Ronaldo

My mind wandered back to her Instagram, to the curated tones of Tabitha's pastel grid and the obvious flaunting of affluence; her penchant for violence seemed even stranger in the suds of muted beige and pink. There was a bang on the barn door. It was aggressive. I froze and debated not opening, I assumed it was the neighbor. There was another series of knocks, this time faster, then a male voice calling my name.

"Esther Ray, you there?"

I slowly rolled open the door, and there stood two cops.

"Good afternoon Ms. Ray."

My eyes moved to their useless torsos harnessed with violent tools.

"Ma'am your neighbor, Patrick Nelson, has filed a complaint."

"Wha—at?" I stuttered.

"He's alledgin' that you tore down his NO TRESPASSING sign."

"I did not."

"Well, that would be a destruction of private property."

"Well, I'm tell'n you I didn't," I said with the venom of a preschooler. They let me off with a warning. I returned to gluing but felt like I was going to explode—the need for revenge itching at each of my cells.

Even in the dewy brightness of the following morning I could still sense the stale, stupid breath of the officers in the barn. My hatred of police blossomed in high school, after my mother's death. I had spiraled. I refused to shower or do homework. Instead of going to class I hung out in the art room in the back of the building, reapplying black lipstick and brooding, refusing to even paint. My art teacher, Mrs. Galloway, who wore clogs and had frizzy red hair, turned a blind eye to my truancy, patiently listening to my endless tirades against the police, my obsessions with Madeline, and justice. She'd bring in extra canvases, oils, acrylics, and even her own battered books on Van Gogh and Klimt, trying to soften me. Nothing worked. Then one November afternoon, Mrs. Galloway handed me a how-to book on forensic artistry. Initially I thought it was an attempt to bridge my interests in justice and art, but now I know it was a ploy to reinstill my faith in the system.

I had initially wanted to throw the hardbound tome back in her face: no rendering, no matter how lifelike, would bring my mother back. But I grumbled a thank you, and a few bored weekends later, I found the book in my bag. And after reading it cover to cover and completing the book's test-your-skill section on composite drawing, I realized I was good. I could translate the descriptions of the middle-aged-would-be-rapist to page effortlessly. My photorealism had purpose. Value. But most of all I loved working on the age progressions—adding give and looseness to once taut forehead muscles, mapping the drape of skin across eyelids and estimating the sag of cheeks— always keeping in mind the book's adage that "everything softens, but the eyes never change."

Unbeknownst to me, Mrs. Galloway came from an old Ohio cop family, and she'd tucked my drawings in a manila envelope and brought them to dinner at her brother's house. I assume she waited for the beers to temper the room before pressing my charcoal pages onto the table, because three weeks later I got a phone call in which a gruff man named Hank Horner explained he was "impressed, and would I have any interest in giving them a hand at the station?"

I arrived early to the precinct on that frigid Friday in freshly laundered black pants and a new-to-me velvet blazer from Goodwill. The secretary ushered me into a windowless room with a faux wood table, and I sat until Hank Horner, Mrs. Galloway's uncle, a fat man with bizarrely bushy eyebrows, detailed the task at hand. Missing children. I would produce age progressions for kids who had evaporated over ten years ago.

"Normally we work with the same in-house artists, but we haven't had any luck."

I was nodding along, serving up my best performance of serious adult.

"Where will the images go?" I finally asked.

"Phone poles, bulletin boards in post offices, *Dateline*. Wherever."

Hank haphazardly pulled out three photographs from a white envelope. The first was a blond, barely teenage boy on a silver-blue mountain bike, he moved the rectangular image closer. Staring into the hazel eyes of the boy, I could tell he looked like a class clown, destined for trouble; a baseball through a window, busted with a homemade bong, maybe a suspension for a super-glue prank gone awry, but not a missing child.

"Dylan Henderson, he was last seen in a Dave's Markets parking lot ten years ago, he'd be twenty-three today."

I nodded.

The next was a small girl with black hair in pigtails, who was last seen in the backyard of her family's house wearing a pink jacket and gold boots. Did her older sister turn away for a second? Or was she left alone for hours? I knew I wasn't supposed to ask. Gazing at the picture, I wanted to hold her, to tell her it would be ok. She would be thirty-five. The next image Hank pulled was a teenage-ish girl. I recognized her angst, her heavy black eyeliner and hoodie, she looked like me. Maria Delgado was last seen leaving her friend's house in Marietta.

"She would be twenty-one."

I exploded with purpose. I would find them.

"You can take the pictures with you," Hank said with a sweeping gesture of his hand. He turned before leaving, "And I can't promise we'll use whatever you draw. It has to run through our network, and then the families have to approve."

I spent the next days sitting at my desk adding weight and years to those three faces. Imagining a decade of jaw-chomps and surprised eyebrows, did they work long hours in an overlit lumber warehouse? Were they big laughers? Smokers? Or did they wake up at five a.m. for a swim at the Y? I tried to predict the drag of time, the faint droop of a thirty-year-old cheek. And I began to see them everywhere. Maria's soft nose. Dylan's thin lips. I took out yearbooks in the school library and studied the faces of my classmates with similar features, tracing their progression from grade school to high school. Georgie Werther, who graduated the year before, had the same jaw as Dylan. I stared at each of Georgie's Lifetouch photos, mimicking the pockmarks from acne and the curve of his teenage neck. I found the round face shape of Maria Delgado in Elisabeth Carlton who had been in my honors chemistry class. Elisabeth had gotten fat two summers ago. Would Maria be fat? Was she even alive?

I turned in my drawings nine days later—it took eleven weeks for the approval to come back from the police station board, and then another week to hear from the families. Once Hank told me they had been sent out, I drove to every post office within fifty miles and checked telephone poles and the corkboards in the entrances of grocery stores and gas stations. I saw my drawing only four times. Four measly black and white pieces of paper stapled next to advertisements for used boats and piano lessons.

"Why aren't there more posters up?" I asked Hank after I finally got paged through to his desk.

"We just send them out, if a location puts them up, they put them up. It's protocol."

"So, then what is the point?" I asked angrily. "What is the fucking chance someone is going to recognize them from four posters?"

"It's just the way it is."

"This is insane. How can you—"

He was annoyed. I kept hammering him with questions.

"Look, no one expects to find them," he said, finally cutting me off.

"Then why did I make the drawings?"

He paused, inhaled a spike of air, "Sarah is my niece. It was a favor—she begged."

It took me a second to understand who Sarah was—then I remembered her first name—Mrs. Galloway. *Sarah.* I slammed the phone down and drove to OfficeMax and printed three hundred posters myself, stapling them to trees and taping them to bus shelters and securing them under windshield wipers up and down Stewart Street. None of the kids were ever found, but this is when I learned the police don't care. Do you know how many rapes end up with a conviction? Five out of one thousand. There are currently two hundred and fifty thousand unsolved murder cases in America. And if you get killed by a police officer, you know how likely the officer will be held accountable? One in two thousand. Police are the dystopic hangover of slave patrols—only around to protect the property of the rich. And police follow protocol, and protocol is the bare fucking minimum.

5

I had given in. I was again sitting in my truck outside the Hammersmith cafeteria's loading dock, scrolling through Tabitha's Instagram. I had become obsessed with the impossible slickness of her digital image. My attraction to things that were beautiful often made me curl with embarrassment, but I was an artist. I couldn't help it. I stared at Tabitha's dimpled smile by the pool of the Hamptons house, her hair bouncing in styled tendrils for sponsored content for Pantene; she was an absolute filter for the moment and made me feel completely collagen-less. She was fluent in the details—the glasses by the water's edge all filled with slushy piña colada in just the right shade of pastel yellow, the layers of spider-silk-thin gold necklaces, her face just ridiculous enough to seem self-aware.

It all reminded me of Jessica's uncanny ability to style her jewelry for Instagram: the linen tablecloths, soy-wax candles, and a half-unwrapped clementine that casually framed the jewel-adorned hands. What were they even really selling? Shampoo? Gold ore? Themselves? It had always shocked me. How Jessica could lower herself—back bending onto the dining room table of strangers, letting people take slices from her body like pie, cherry guts oozing. She loved to overshare, posting pictures of me without permission, constant studio selfies and "process shots." She wanted everyone to know exactly who she was. At first, I thought her honesty was an act of radical transparency, then later I saw it as a sort of craft-world naivete, but eventually, I understood—she knew exactly what she was doing and her cult-of-personality packaging, which hinged on a solar system of polite millennial fantasy, felt as putrid as the hypercapitalist art world. Why couldn't something just be beautiful, without having to gyrate on a platform?

Back in the barn I let myself be consumed by scrapbooking. But it was too late. *Jessica. Jessica. Jessica.* Her name shook through my thoughts like a ferret in a cage. I tried to concentrate. Tabitha was now seven and Bryce's sixtieth birthday was in a little under four months, and at this rate I would have to complete two books per week. I worked through the afternoon without stopping for lunch.

I had attempted to be as accurate as possible while sorting, but every now and then things were out of order. Usually, Naomi added the packs of photos a month or so after they were taken, but sometimes a Duane Reade envelope would show up years after the fact in a different box entirely and I'd have to run it back to its proper pile. This kept happening with pictures of Naomi pregnant with Tabitha which were constantly popping up years later. Naomi, with her slicked-back hair and red lipstick, had a Carolyn Bessette-Kennedy thing going on then—an early 2000s Calvin-Klein-cum-Armani-Exchange coolness that seemed entirely antithetical to the woman with bangles and rose quartz necklaces that I'd met at Memphis's gallery dinner. I flipped through the latest stack. She was standing on the side of a playground, her giant bump peeking out of a billowy white button up, her lips painted chemically bright red. But in the next image she was holding Tabitha's hand. Still pregnant.

There was a second child. I felt like I'd been smacked. How had I missed this? What happened to the baby? Miscarriage? Tragedy? I sat down holding the photo when my boot kicked something soft. My whole body lurched. I jumped up. This was not an apparition or a leather braided belt. This was a thick brown snake coiled around the wooden leg of the stool. Jessica had instructed me that black snakes were like squirrels, funny rodents with long tails, but brown snakes with triangular skulls were venomous. I had studied them voraciously online and I was certain this serpent was a copperhead, ubiquitous to western North Carolina. I felt my organs rattle with operatic sound, a freight train of octaves barreling through my throat. I climbed up on the workbench. The snake's muscly body leered, extended in my direction. But there was no exiting the barn without going past it. I was stuck in a bizarre standoff; all I could do was scream.

I closed my eyes. Then minutes, or maybe seconds later, I heard the door slide open, and a deafening crack. I opened my eyes clocking a trail of blood, then hiccupped, lost in my own hysteria, gulping for air. When I finally quieted, I saw Patrick Nelson was standing in the entrance, staring at his hand. I instantly wondered if he'd been bit—but his posture was too strange, he seemed lost in a deep welling sadness, then I realized he was holding a gun. I looked down at the writhing snake and felt suddenly sick. The room got dark.

"Are you ok?" he asked a second, or maybe third time.

I still had no words, eyes pressed shut.

"Would you like some soup?" he asked, softly, as I came spinning back to earth.

"What?" I finally croaked.

"I'm making tortilla soup. It's on the stove at my house."

I nodded shakily and climbed down from the workbench, too stunned to know how else to respond and desperate to get out of the barn, away from the dying snake. Neither of us spoke as we walked down the gravel road, the crunching of our feet at synced tempos.

I could still taste the metallic bile of my fear in the back of my throat as Patrick pushed open the squeaking door. The cabin smelled of garlic, vegetables, and decaying wood. I looked around, it was indeed an Appalachian time capsule, with a potbellied stove and daguerreotypes of old mountain men leaning against the stone mantel—but a new fridge, small flatscreen TV, and a strip of blue-ish LED lights grounded us in this century. Patrick busied himself with whatever was boiling in the large pot and I sat down in a spindly chair at the round oak table. A minute or so later he brought over two white bowls of bubbling liquid.

"I'm Patrick," he said, as he sat down awkwardly.

"Oh—I'm Esther."

We both silently marinated in the strangeness of our introduction.

"Do you live here alone?" I asked finally, trying to make conversation.

"Yes," he said softly.

Of course he lived alone.

We ate in silence. I hadn't realized how hungry I was. The soup was surprisingly spicy; I finished quickly. Patrick looked pleased at my appetite and offered seconds. I nodded and snuck glances while he added shredded Sargento cheddar to the bowl; he was maybe sixty, with a perpetual hunch and dark eyes that seemed like two flashlights that had been turned off.

"So, you're afraid of snakes?" he asked dryly, placing the refilled bowl in front of me.

I took a sharp inhale at the reminder of the slithering form on my studio floor and nodded. "How did you know to—come?" I asked, pointing toward the barn with my spoon.

Patrick looked out the window, "Your scream. I thought someone was trying to kill you."

I nodded, assuming he probably also listened to too much true crime.

He looked down at his hands and said nothing.

"Thank you."

"I shouldn't have shot it."

"You have good aim."

"I used to hunt." Another pause. "I'm sorry we got off on the wrong foot," he said, fidgeting with the corner of his sweater. "I just really prefer privacy. I have trouble with—people," he added, "I just want to be alone. I shouldn't have called the cops."

"I get it if you want privacy, I usually do too," I added.

"Well, if you wanna cut across the property, you can."

I smiled, "I'll keep out of your hair."

We went back to silently eating until Patrick stood and cleared the table.

"I should get going," I said with unnecessary urgency.

He made a small sound of agreement.

Rather than face the snake's carcass, I avoided the barn for almost a week. The mystery of the second Duncan child pressed, but I twitched with fear when I looked at the wooden building—the snake was still too fresh and reanimation seemed possible, or maybe it took longer for a serpent's soul to twist its way to hell. Either way I wasn't taking chances. I decided to throw myself into running errands.

One can live out here in the mountains and be a spinner of yarn, or clay, or plyer of any raw material and see oneself as spiritually tuned to the planet—but you'll still find yourself at Walmart. In the autumnal light, the parking lot burst with its usual bizarre mix of Phish bumper stickers, Rebel Flags, Trump fucks, and my-other-car-is-a-broom-ers. I wandered to the outermost aisle to get Gorilla Glue, then loaded up on groceries and a pack of Miller High Life for Patrick: a thank you for his efforts in slaying the snake.

On my way back home, I couldn't help it: I pulled off at the Hammersmith parking lot and googled Tabitha again. I sifted through her normie makeup content; how-tos, and videos posted under variations of "people keep asking for my skincare routine." Then a few clicks deep, I stumbled upon a viral clip in which she was dressed in a tiny butterfly-shaped dress in her kitchen, making fun of her Jamaican housekeeper's accent. I felt my insides turn. The comments revealed the internet had demanded her cancelation, but a week later she'd posted a blubbering apology video, and somehow, thanks to the paltry tide of digital memory, she had redeemed herself. Tabitha was not a good person. I didn't need more proof, but here it was.

I left Patrick's beer on the top of his driveway. Once home, I gathered my confidence and entered the barn with a large bamboo stick and jerkily removed the horrifying carcass which was far heavier than it should have been, flinging it as far as I could into the thicket behind my house. I burnt some of Jessica's sage to remove the smell and returned to tracing the timeline. It was clear that Naomi had become pregnant in the winter of 2006, sometime around Christmas. I imagined her and Bryce fucking on crisp white hotel sheets, snow drifting out the window, a DO NOT DISTURB sign hanging idly on the golden doorknob. There were plenty of photos of Naomi with a big bump at Tabitha's school, and later in the back of a limo with Bryce's parents, sitting on a bench outside Rockefeller Center. She was still dressing sharply for work at Red Rock Capital in tailored suits, carrying a stiff Saint Laurent Sac de Jour bag.

In 2007, just before the birth of this second child, I found the usual paperwork from doctors' appointments, ultrasound images, and a second ziplock bag full of cards of congratulations. Then the customary Duane Reade packet of photos, including an image of a very tired-looking Naomi sitting in a gray hospital bed surrounded by flowers and balloons looking down at a pink squealing baby. A copy of a birth certificate for

Marcella-Marie Alistair Duncan. There were around four months of the usual baby photos, and then the pile got dramatically thinner. I found a cartoon drawing of a cat on a Dean & DeLuca bag, then an NDA signed by Elena Tester, the dykey-looking secondary nanny, and a subsequent receipt of payment for $25,000.

The next piece of paper was a clipping from the *New York Times* in which the Duncans announced a massive donation to the American SIDS Institute, and briefly discussed losing their second child Marcella-Marie to the condition which affects 2,300 babies a year. Why pay off the nanny if she died of sudden infant death syndrome? And as if an answer, I found on thin cream paper a stapled series of notes from a brand-new child-behavior specialist recommending several types of therapy programs for Tabitha at a center in Connecticut for problematic preteens. I could feel the neon highway open back up; I was, again, dressed in head-to-toe leather, full gallop on a moonless night. I was deep in the jungle in a Hawaiian shirt, a machine gun draped across my chest. I was in a catsuit wielding a samurai sword. I was Hamlet, clutching my dagger. Tabitha and her "unbridled violence" must have done something.

I knew that I listened to my bloody podcasts, in part, to keep my own homicidal thoughts at bay, but all those hours of being ear-fucked by amateur detectives had taught me how to *really look*. And in sifting through the Duncans' raw material, I had seen fossil fragments, those shimmering pieces of some secret, bleached and bedazzled; covered up. But this was the big one, the skeleton. And it was on display, like a dinosaur at the natural history museum. I felt a strange sense of purpose settle over me. Whatever happened to Marcella-Marie was at the heart of why Naomi had hired me to make these books.

I cracked my neck, then tore through the remaining piles. There was a loud gap. Nothing had been saved for two years. Why had Naomi ceased saving things? I needed to get on the internet. I drove back down to the Hammersmith School and parked behind the cafeteria. Terrence, the weekend cook, waved from the loading dock, I raised a singular finger from the steering wheel, signaling both *hello* and my desire for no further discussion. I took out my iPad and put in *Marcella-Marie Duncan*. Nothing. My brain whirred. Then I tried the nanny's name—*Elena Tester*. A resounding emptiness filled the truck. The nanny returned no links, no Facebook. No abandoned Suicide Girls account or garish MySpace.

I returned to the barn and surveyed the landscape of paper—whatever sentimentality Naomi was trying to preserve now felt dark. I began looking for any sign of Marcella-Marie. Maybe a miniature tombstone or a dried wreath of rosebuds. There was just an echoing blank until June, two summers later. Beginning with a mountain of Duane Reade envelopes filled with glossy rectangles, the shift in the family was clear. Naomi's entire look changed, the tight black suits were replaced with flowy linen dresses and jewel-toned shawls. She'd founded WAC exactly two years and three months after the SIDS donation, and at the opening of the offices she wore a Mexican style embroidered dress, her neck layered in glass beads. I stared at photographs from the WAC ribbon cutting, noticing how Naomi's body was always angled away from Bryce, the distance between them new and palpable.

I woke up with the nagging feeling I had to find the goth nanny. Partially because I had a crush on her and partially because I knew she was the one person who would have the details of what had happened with Marcella-Marie. After all, she had been paid off—I had proof. She must know something. I once again found myself loitering outside of

Hammersmith. I punched Elena Tester into Google but again the blank reappeared. How had she simply vanished? My information was thin, all I had was a name and a time period in which she had resided in New York City. What did people in podcasts do? They hired private detectives.

I googled *P.I. North Carolina*. I was stunned to discover the sheer volume of active investigators in Western North Carolina. What were they all doing? After a little reading, I discovered that most of them were following unfaithful spouses and exposing fake workers' comp claims, and most of them were men. I didn't want to deal with a man. There was one page for a Brenda Millwater. I liked the looks of her. She had a Dog-the-Bounty-Hunter thing; one of those women who worshipped dick while looking like a sunburnt bull dyke. I sent her an email. *How much to find someone?* It seemed relatively hopeless. Maybe Elena Tester was dead. How else could someone my age exist without a digital footprint?

Back home, I took a nap and woke in a brief bubble of happiness. I'd forgotten Jessica had left me. And then, a collapse. Like a shipwreck in fast forward, I was back at the bottom of the ocean, a deep-sea creature slithering through the wreckage of a once bright life. I guzzled coffee, then drove to Hammersmith to check my mail. There was no news from the Dog-the-Bounty-Hunter PI. I let my head rest against the side window of the truck. I debated going home and getting my burner phone and trying to formulate a cohesive question to Naomi about Marcella-Marie; but after the coldness of our last phone call, my *Dateline* instincts told me not to—I needed to sort this out on my own, I had to be smart.

I drove down to the post office to pick up six boxes of adhesive plastic sleeves.

"Esther, dear, nice to see you," George said as he popped up from the back room, "I have a couple letters and packages for you."

"Oh great, here, let me grab them." It was painful and cartoonish to watch his loose-skinned arms lift the heavy boxes to the counter.

"I feel rain com'n," he said, pointing to the window, trying to distract me from his huffing.

"Cats and dogs," I chimed.

George laughed, and I loaded the packages into the bed of my truck. On my way back up the mountain, I pulled over in the back parking lot of Hammersmith and checked my email again. Still nothing from the PI. I opened Instagram. She was trapped, buzzing in my mind, like a mosquito. *Tabitha.* In her latest photos she was promoting a tour for her new signature gold palate, her manicured hands draped across her face, one shimmering eye peeking out at the camera. The next image was of her wearing a cowboy hat, under the caption: Nashville see you TOMORROW for the launch of #GoldenGodsPalette I'll see you in Atlanta THURSDAY! I double-checked. It had been posted yesterday which meant Tabitha was near me. Only five hours away. It felt like a sign. This was my answer.

I pulled out of the lot, and headed west in the direction of I-40. I felt a magnetic force moving me. I'd driven to Nashville the year before for a class on natural dyeing taught by a plump woman with a light voice and vicious eye for detail. My insides swayed at the thought of that class—I had been so patient while simmering dried avocado pits on the big white stove, waiting for the water to turn pink. The teacher had talked endlessly about wholeness. How everything was infinitely connected to what we were making—from the soil that grew the avocados, the wooden spoon which turned the water, and origin of the pot's metal. She explained that our own emotions could alter the color of the dye and had us chant before beginning class—I'd had to work hard for that calm. And I knew I was slipping. I hadn't even watered my garden in a week. All of my thoughts were wrapped up in the Duncans. I turned up the radio to drown out my skidding brain.

It was three p.m. by the time I rolled into the town. I had stolen Wi-Fi from a Starbucks, and discovered that Uncommon James, the shop hosting Tabitha, was located in the Gulch neighborhood. I parked a block away and put on a baseball cap then walked toward the line of girls all dressed in soft-toned tops and either yoga pants or too tight denim. The queue wrapped the outside of the concrete building. I took my place behind an athletic brunette and her pouty daughter. The mom looked at me and smiled. I nodded and pretended to check my phone.

"Kristin is here till three so don't worry," the mom said overly nicely.

"Who?" I asked.

She looked momentarily stunned.

"Kristin Cavallari."

I didn't know how to respond.

"She runs the store."

"Oh . . ." I replied.

My lack of understanding seemed to shock this woman.

"She's a reality celebrity."

"I'm just here to—" I couldn't think of why I was there. "Buy a gold—palette."

The woman nodded, content with my answer. In my torn-up pants, hiking boots, and oversize white T-shirt I did not look like someone who wanted a palette or would wait to meet a reality celebrity. The line wasn't moving. I began sweating and suddenly felt hungry and needed to pee. I debated leaving. Then we crept forward and I saw her, and all my bodily needs evaporated.

Tall and radiant, Tabitha's brown hair was fluffed in waves. She was wearing a short gold leather skirt, a fitted cream top that revealed her shoulders, and that stupid cowgirl hat I'd seen in her earlier post. I felt my heart stutter. She was standing in front of a sequined backdrop, taking photos with girls who looked like cheap photocopies of herself, posing, with her pink tongue sticking out as if they were all best friends at a backyard bachelorette party. I wanted to call out Tabitha's name. I had seen the photos of the day she was born. I had poured over her teenage handwriting. I knew that she liked rye bagels with strawberry cream cheese. She'd had her first kiss with Hunter Wisedale at French camp. And she had a shimmering violent streak. Would I confront her? I didn't have any proof she had done anything to Marcella-Marie, just a gnawing hunch. The line grew closer. A blonde woman sitting at a makeup-stacked table informed me if I wanted a photo, I had to spend at least seventy dollars on cosmetics and pay for a makeover.

"What?"

"Everyone who is being photographed with Tabitha and Kristin have had their makeup done by one of our artists. It only takes about fifteen minutes."

"Oh."

I picked out the advertised gold palette, and a dark red lipstick in a shiny tube, neither of which I would ever wear.

"Looks like you're still nine dollars under," the blonde said without looking up.

"Ok, I'll have a blush too then."

"The blush is great."

I felt for my wallet. I had two hundred dollars of Naomi's money which I had planned to spend at the Hammersmith school store on four more reams of paper. I wondered if Tabitha, who was standing mere feet away, would notice, and intrinsically know that I was holding her mother's crisp bills.

I pressed the twenties into the blonde's palm, and was then handed off to a redhead in skinny jeans, with massive breasts choked in a black baby T-shirt that read #GoldenGod.

"So, my name is Desirée, and I'll be doing your glow-up."

I feigned a smile and followed as she motioned toward a director style chair in front of a mirror.

"So, how do you usually do your makeup?"

"I don't."

I'm a long-haired-butch-ish ex-goth, I wanted to say. *And I was just dumped. And I have a raging feeling that Tabitha murdered her sister.* After all, isn't this what women did after breakups? They sat in chemically saturated air with black capes tied around their necks and spilled their secrets to women like Desirée. She removed my hat, setting it on the vanity in front of me, and I felt suddenly exposed.

"I really love a blank slate," she said mindlessly, as she sponged cold goo onto my forehead.

A few seconds later I was completely washed out in foundation, then Desirée set about mapping the bridges of my face in a dark oily brown streak. I looked cubist.

"Don't freak, it's just contouring," she laughed. Desirée smudged the edges down with a pink teardrop sponge and gradually I started to look sharper—as if Vaseline had been rubbed off a lens.

"Now we'll add the #GoldenGod shimmer and you're done."

I nodded. Desirée's hands smelled faintly of chicken salad; it felt good to be touched again. I didn't like how I looked in the mirror but I didn't want her to stop. I wondered what she could do to me if I sat for an hour. How many versions of my face she could produce from her magic sponge? My mind traveled back to the forensic artistry book from high school, and my sketches of those three missing kids. Sometimes I googled their names but nothing new ever showed up. Maybe they had just been repainted by someone like Desirée, their faces restructured by foundation and brow pencil and maybe they were out there—all glown up. Desirée made a popping sound with her pink lips signaling she was finished. I stood and forced a smile, then she led me to the waiting station just beyond the backdrop, handing me off to a short girl with a pixie cut. I put my hat back on.

"Do you want me to use your own phone?" the girl asked.

"What?"

"So, you have the photos—on your phone?"

"I don't have a camera on my . . ."

"Oh ok, well I can use the store's, and then we can email the pictures to you. If you want her to sign your name on the promo bag, you can fill this out and just be sure to add your email."

"Great," I mumbled, as I took the pen and slip of paper. I'd been lulled into submission by Desirée's cold fingers, but standing in line to meet Tabitha my heart began raging. I took my place behind three teenage girls, all with the same makeup as mine. Eventually, the acne-encrusted sprite in front of me smiled in position on Tabitha's right side, a flash of tongue and light, then she scurried off. It was my turn.

Tabitha let her green eyes dart to mine and dipped her cowboy hat with the rehearsed coyness of a showgirl, "Hi there."

I felt flayed with embarrassment for being so moved by the symmetry of her face. But I also knew she was cruel and capable of casual racism and possibly murder. Yet she had Naomi's cheekbones and was tall and her skin was perfect. Bryce, her father, was Brazilian. So was Gisele Bündchen. So was Adriana Lima. All the impossibly hot Victoria's Secret models I'd ogled in my mom's flimsy pink catalogues.

"And who should I make this out to?" Tabitha asked, taking the folded slip of paper from my hand. She read the name I'd written: Marcella-Marie. My eyes greedily watched the bitchy-cheer-captain-demeanor evaporate. A flash of terror cut across her face, then she was momentarily frozen, her lips caught in an open ring. It was enough proof for me. Tabitha shook herself back to reality, straightened her spine, and wrote, *For Marcella-Marie xx Tab*, on the side of my white shopping bag.

"Ok, and look here," the short girl with the camera chirped, cutting the tension.

Tabitha returned to her role, sticking her tongue out for our two-second bachelorette party. I could feel the heat radiating off her exposed tan shoulders and I wanted to move closer, to dangle one of the millions of scraps of information I knew about her life and ask her about her sister. But just as I opened my mouth, Tabitha turned her gaze to the girl who had been behind me, beginning her act all over again, "Oh, hi there!"

I walked away from the store quickly, my entire body ringing, replaying Tabitha's flash of terror when she'd read the name Marcella-Marie. There was now no question in my mind: she had done something.

When I finally opened my truck door, I was hit with the return of my dire need to piss, and squatted behind my wheel hub, feeling drunk and delirious like I was outside some packed bar in New York. Once I'd drip-dried and was seated behind the steering wheel, I peered into my paper bag at the plastic shells of makeup I'd just purchased and opened the palette as if the answer to what I was supposed to do next was laying in the tightly packed shimmering cubes of powder. What would a true crime podcaster do? Maybe I should go back. Confront Tabitha with a hidden USB microphone. Maybe she would admit to it. Then what?

I jerkily decided to leave and pulled into traffic, then gunned it to the McDonald's near the freeway. I needed to eat, to try and calm myself—figure out what to do next. In the parking lot I shoved hot mounds of french fries into my painted lips, while absentmindedly leafing through the mail I'd picked up earlier. A gas bill, some Greenpeace spam, and a letter from the correctional institute addressed to Patrick Nelson from *Jupiter A. Nelson.* I took out my iPad and logged in to the barely functional McDonald's Wi-Fi. The top five hits were nearly identical: Jupiter A. Nelson was named as the school shooter at New Lake High School, in Applemont, Virginia, March 3, 1998. Three dead, two injured. Each article was accompanied by the same photo of a sad teenager wearing an oversize blue polo shirt with a string of puka shells barely visible, his hands cuffed behind his back.

George, at the post office, in his ancient, near-blind state had done this before, but usually it was postcards for some student at Hammersmith, or a Lands' End catalog meant for Chester down the road. I knew I shouldn't read the letter. It wasn't for me. It was Patrick's and he had told me he just wanted privacy—but I couldn't help myself. I tore it open. The writing was jerky, in blue pen on yellow legal-pad paper. *I hear your point dad, but I still think that the transporter consumes the whole body. I mean, if you're going to turn "matter" into "energy," then you would have to kill the original. You know? So realistically they're all just copies of themselves . . .* Anyway the last episode we saw was *Requiem for Methusela.* It took me a second to understand what the fuck he was talking about: *Star Trek.* The following paragraphs continued on and on discussing the minutiae of galactic universes. I got a smear of ketchup on the second page, and haplessly tried to wipe it off. I kept reading. More blabbering about spaceships. I wanted to hear shower horror stories, and descriptions of shanks made from Altoid boxes, and plots for more scholastic murders, but it was all so mundane; dinner was potatoes, peas, and grape juice, the next evening a burger that "wasn't so bad."

I thrust the truck in motion, my mind alternating between the radiating heat off of Tabitha's shoulder and the fact that Patrick's son had brought a semiautomatic rifle to school in a gym bag and killed a teacher and two students. I began talking out loud while I drove as if I were playing both roles on one of those podcasts where husky-voiced platonic girlfriends compare murders, talking pornographically about genetic material under fingernails and the Venn diagrams of ex-boyfriend-husband violence, all while rapid firing self-deprecating jokes.

"But how is it possible?" I asked myself.

"They are both child murderers?" I responded.

"But only one is in prison?"

"What were the fucking odds?"

A few hours, which felt like minutes, later, I pulled into my driveway with the thrust of Vin Diesel and threw open my door. Then I noticed—there was someone standing right next to me in the shadows. My heart stopped. The form stepped forward. It was Patrick, wearing sweats and holding a barely functional flashlight.

"Sorry to startle but I was waiting for you, because George at the post—"

Then he saw it. The truck's overhead light perfectly illuminated the six pages of yellow legal-pad paper with the scratchy blue writing in a mess of McDonald's wrappers. Patrick eyes bounced in recognition, he leered, moving his head back initially confused, then reached around me and grabbed the sheets off the seat.

"Why would—" he stopped himself, his voice cracking, then turned and stormed off, disappearing into the driveway's silent darkness.

"It was a mistake—" I called, then stopped. I caught my reflection in the truck's window; my makeup was smeared across my cheeks. I looked insane.

6

"To quote my dear friend M.C. Richards: 'centering has nothing to do with center as a place. It has to do with bringing the totality of the clay into an unwobbling pivot, the equilibrium distributed throughout in an even grain,'" Andra shouted to the class as we all watched her wrinkled hands warble through a cone of wet spinning clay.

It was nearly November. Three months after I'd seen my smeared makeup in the reflection of the truck. I knew I had moved off course, my equilibrium lost. I had wobbled. I should have never driven to Nashville or opened Patrick's mail—it was the kind of behavior that had gotten me in trouble before. My compulsive side. My Nancy-Drew-cum-Nev-Schulman side. But in Andra's night class, under the fluorescent lights of the clay-spattered studio, I felt back where I belonged. I still listened to true crime, lulling myself on the banality of stranger's pain, and I still spent my days in the barn gluing the Duncans' ephemera onto eggshell paper, but I was resolute in keeping my distance, like Dave and his spent nuclear fuel rods.

I now saw the scrapbooks mostly in colors, as if they were a Gee's Bend quilt, ecstatic and imperfect. I let the tones of the papers guide my hand. Gluing yellow receipts together. A page of concentric metro tickets. An undulating pattern of Columbia Grammar School fall announcements. A procession of photographs, birthdays blending with vacations. I kept the dates straight, but I was no longer absorbing the details; what they ate at dinner or who was sitting next to whom. I was not going to obsess. Whatever happened to Marcella-Marie was not my problem, and for all I knew, she probably did die of SIDS. I stayed off of Tabitha's Instagram and on my morning walks I was careful not to cut across Patrick Nelson's property. I understood now why he lived in that dump of a cabin. He wanted privacy because no one wants to serve beer or pump gas for the school shooter's dad. He was hiding. I didn't google his son and fought the urge to think about what had made him snap—a bully. Or maybe a teacher. Or video games like they always say.

I was eating healthy and reading myself to sleep every night, working my way through the books I'd ordered about scrapbooking, which were aiding in my attempt to stay objective. Derrida argued that archives are machines that operate with their own death drive, and that the process of archiving creates as much as it records. In turn, the process obstructs reality—sabotaging any hope of real preservation. I had laughed out loud, thinking that maybe my dad, shuffling around in his slippers, plunking my mother's possessions in the metal trash can had the same effect as Naomi slipping papers into Container Store boxes. It was all obliteration, one way or another.

Propped up on a pile of dirty clothes, I read about Marion Stokes, a woman who had recorded 840,000 hours of news footage over thirty-five years on 70,000 VHS tapes. She was, of course, a hoarder but also deeply concerned that the details of contemporary news would get lost, and with it, truth. Day and night, Marion and her husband changed out the tapes on the fourteen TVs in their home, and even rented out extra apartments to store the thousands of cassettes. What was Naomi's death drive in all of her hoarding? I reminded myself to take a breath; it didn't matter. It was just a job.

I texted Naomi dozens of examples of spreads to her burner. She responded via WhatsApp with her usual barrage of voice messages.

Darling, I love them! I am so excited. The pages look great. Her voice was poppy and overexcited.

Me again—I just did a second look through at the images, in the fourth spread you've mislabeled Gregor Salloway as Benjamin Molton, he's the one with gray hair. Could you fix that?

Oh, and another catch—in spread twelve, let's label the restaurant we were all at "City Oven on 23rd." Thanks again. I am so-so-so excited. I'm working on my calendar and I want to come see the books in person to add some of my own notations. I have some other "special business" to attend to in Asheville, so I'll call you later tonight to discuss my arrival.

Also, sweetheart, I just wanted to press the subject of secrecy. I know I've told you before, but under no circumstances should anyone see these books. Ok? This all has to go on my timeline. Ok? Sorry for being so over the top . . . You know. The birthday!

I was shocked she was planning on coming to see the books so soon. Would she really look through every page, hovering with a Sharpie, adding comments or correcting whatever I'd misspelled or just hadn't labeled? Naomi's sudden need for extreme precision scared me. I had spent months tranced out, letting the paper flow, what if she thought it was all wrong? What if she hated the most recent books? Would we eat dinner together? Would I cook? I forced myself to slow down. I wasn't going to fixate. I'd get my second payment, then be done.

Andra, the ceramicist who had let me join her class without formally registering, was in her eighties, and like most women in the craft world, wore loose jewel-toned layers over leggings with hiking boots. She had attended Black Mountain College and studied with all those brilliant minds just after the bombs dropped above Dresden and teenagers washed up on Omaha Beach. Sitting in Andra's class, listening to her talk about Josef and Anni Albers eating spaghetti with Merce Cunningham, made my heart sizzle. All those great minds releasing themselves from the grind of capitalism, dyeing yarns and dancing barefoot. I had spent the week in class focused on making cereal bowls. It felt therapeutic to work my way through the empty cabinets replacing all the essentials Jessica had taken with her. I even made a mug for Patrick Nelson, glazed in green, which I was planning on leaving for him at the post office along with a lengthy and honest note about my lapse into compulsive decision-making, and my sincere apologies for breaching his trust.

We were cleaning up our stations when Melis Khan, a retired bank teller, asked me if I wanted to join a craft show at a local co-op one town over.

"It's going to be about thirty artists, and we thought it could be nice to include a book or two."

"Sure," I said without thinking.

"Great. We're all chipping in for wine and cheese."

"Just let me know how much."

Melis smiled and walked off. I watched her sandals making a light squishing sound on the dusty floor, feeling grateful to be included. In little over a month, I would be done with Naomi and the scrapbooks and I would need to rejoin the world.

I placed my bowls away on the drying rack, hung up my apron, and walked out into the night. Before leaving campus, I paused in the parking lot to load my emails. I nearly laughed out loud. Brenda Millwater, the Dog-the-Bounty-Hunter private detective who I had written to ask the price for her to find the goth nanny Elena Tester, had written back. *Base rate is $1,500, not including incidentals. Cash or credit. Let me* *know if you'd like to proceed.* I snorted, embarrassed at myself for ever having written a PI and moved the email to junk.

The sky was purple with stars. I felt placid. A half mile down the road, my phone rang, splintering the silence. With Naomi's impending arrival, I had started carrying my burner and assumed it was her, but it was my normal phone. The caller ID flashed turquoise: JESSICA.

She was coming back. She missed me. I should go to the grocery store and get the hummus and stupid baby carrots she liked. I needed to change the sheets and take out the trash. I took a long meditative breath before answering. I had to seem cool.

"Hello?"

"Hi, Es."

"Jess," saying her name felt like Pop Rocks sizzling on my tongue. *Jess. Jess. Jess. Jess.*

"I hope I'm not interrupting."

"I'm just walking up the hill," I said casually.

I willed the steadiness of my voice to win her back. I needed her to miss me. I needed her to desire the blood in my veins and the ideas that bounded around my head like blind acrobats. I needed her to fantasize about the mole on my right hand and the smell of my mint shampoo. I wanted her to cry.

"Oh, I miss the hill," her voice faltered. I could tell she was thinking about it. The hundreds of times we'd walked home together from Hammersmith. The dark gravel. The bushes with blueberries and the sharp curve at the top.

"It's really nice to hear your voice," she said lightly.

My heart exploded. *SO WHY DID YOU LEAVE ME?* I wanted to scream.

"Yours too," I replied.

"Well, the thing is, I'm calling because we need to talk about the house."

"I can buy you out," I said matter-of-factly, annoyed at the bureaucratic turn of the conversation.

"Oh, that's great." Jessica sounded surprised. I knew she wanted to know more.

"And you, how are you doing?" I countered before she could follow up.

"I'm all right," she said too politely, "thank you for asking." Why was she talking like a robot?

"Lovely to hear," I replied just as mechanically.

Jessica cleared her throat, "I was worried you would be—"

"What?"

I felt my calm slipping.

"I had a feeling you would be angry," she said quietly.

She had broken up with me on pale blue stationery, and I had woken up every morning since, drowning in a sea of Greek tragedy. I wanted to scream at her. Instead, I thought back to the quote Andra had told us at the beginning of class and tried to find my center within the wobble—"I'm all right," I paused, "I'm taking a ceramic class. Making pots to replace the ones you so unceremoniously took," I said with easy liquid sarcasm.

Jessica laughed. My humor was an offering. She knew it.

The tension ebbed and suddenly, like a bend in a river, we picked up almost as if she had never left. I felt high. She was careful to not mention much about her new life. Or whatever girl she was or was not seeing. But she wanted to know about the neighbor in the Nelson house, and who was in the class at Hammersmith, and had they started building the new fiber arts studios. It was so relieving to be talking with the real Jessica, instead of the fake one that rattled around my head.

"I have to tell you about my job," I blabbed like an overcaffeinated teenager.

"Yeah, how the fuck are you paying off the house?" she asked with her chalky laugh.

"I got a job scrapbooking for this rich woman I met at Memphis's opening."

There was a pause, as if I'd shot an arrow over the phone. That was the weekend she had left. We both felt the sting. Then Jessica picked back up, "So, you're making her photo albums?"

"Yeah," I said blandly. Suddenly feeling guilty as if I were betraying Naomi. I knew I had to shut up or I'd end up telling her about driving to Nashville to see Tabitha or my theories on Marcella-Marie or my undulating obsession with the family. Jessica would have recognized the behavior. She would know I was spiraling.

There was silence.

"Well, I'm sorry for leaving those boxes of my stuff," Jessica filled in.

"I moved them all out to the barn."

"I just need some time to figure it out."

I allowed myself a Tic Tac–size nub of hope which nearly instantaneously transformed into a canyon of faith. Maybe she was planning on coming back. *Figuring it out.* Maybe my coolness had worked.

"So, you listening to any good Terry-Gross-out?" she asked. That was what Jessica always called true crime. She was not a fan. She thought the genre was catnip for understimulated white women, snuff porn for moms.

"A good Canadian one."

"The Canadian ones were always—oh, fuck, I have to go," Jessica said, I could faintly hear knocking in the background. Someone was coming over. My heart stiffened. "But let's do this again soon. It was so nice to catch up."

"It was," I said, warm as I could manage.

She hung up.

I cooked myself dinner in a cloud, frying up the tempeh how Jessica would have, spicy with extra yellow sauce, drinking wine out of one of my new lumpy mugs. The kitchen filled with the smell of curry powder and turmeric. I imagined Jessica driving down the highway, speeding to get here. I fought the urge to call her back. I wanted to tell her about Patrick Nelson shooting the snake and Derrida's archival death drive. I'd forgotten how good it felt to talk. Instead, I turned on the speakers and loaded a podcast about a seventeen-year-old girl who disappeared from Texas in 2010. I moved to the futon, resting the bottle of wine on the coffee table for ease of refill.

It was an amateurish podcast. I could tell the guy narrating had simply found the case online in one of those forums, Websleuths or maybe Reddit. High thread count, low substance. He was breathlessly narrating a dogpile of tidbits posted by strangers: search warrant affidavits, and links to Facebooks of ex-boyfriends and security footage from gas stations. Bizarre theories and recordings of phone calls. Most of it aggressive and speculative, but that was the point. It was simply motion—a cosmic throttle toward justice that soothed my soul. A commercial for a home-security system interrupted the podcast, I hated the ads which always preyed on various forms of female fear: hair loss, home burglary, bunions. I turned the volume down, refilling my mug. I was drunk and the quiet of the house was startling. I took my phone out and stared at Jessica's name in my contacts, I felt dizzy. Had I told her how much I missed her? I hadn't. I typed the words in:

Thanks for calling today.

I really miss you.

I sent, then waited. Nothing. No response. I turned the podcast up loud, letting the disappeared girl's sobbing mother fill the house. Leaving my phone in the kitchen, I drew a bath, and tried to separate myself from that fountain of anxiety that was Jessica. After my skin had turned apple red, I ran back to the kitchen buck naked to check. Still nothing. I remembered back to the faint knocking I'd heard in the background at the end of our call and the sound squirmed through my ear like a slug. Who had been there? It must be *her.* greenchristina1. Whoever she was. Still naked, I poured myself another mug of wine. I knew Jess missed me. I had heard it in her voice. Why else would she call? I wasn't making it up. Everything I wanted to tell her felt like unbounded confetti floating through the kitchen. I just wanted to see the words typed out, the ones we'd traded back and forth like a chain-smoker's lighter.

I love you.

A drunk girl's bionic force extended through my fingertip. I sent the text, then threw my phone into a pile of laundry and crawled into bed. Not even five minutes later, feral, I dug my phone out of the mound and called her. No answer. I tried again. And again. And again. Finally, it stopped ringing altogether. I was blocked.

Then, like lightning. My phone rang. I ran to pick it up. But it was my burner, it was Naomi.

"Hello," I answered trying to mask my tears.

"Oh Esther, what's wrong?" Naomi asked, surprised.

I coughed, it was no use, I sounded pathetic, "I'm sorry—my ex, I was expecting a call from my ex. I told her I loved her, and then she—she blocked my phone number."

"Oh darling, I'm so sorry."

I couldn't contain myself. I vomited the whole story about the house—*our life*—the note in the fruit bowl and what her sister Alisha had said about me being *too intense.* And Naomi, who usually took my calls on busy street corners, listened patiently, as if she were tucked away in some velvet room built for the express purpose of processing the meltdowns of loved ones.

She took a long breath, then began speaking, her tone stern.

"Never let anyone make you feel *crazy*. If they think you are too intense, it only means they aren't intense enough for you. And let me be frank, you probably don't love Jessica; you just love the idea of her. So, you have to take action. You can't mope around, all right? Plan the life you want. If you do that, everything else will fall into place."

It all sounded like Tumblr quotes, but I was grateful.

"And how about I come in a few days after Christmas, we'll go through the scrapbooks then go out for a nice dinner. I'll book a table."

I inhaled snot, "That sounds really nice."

"You take care of yourself. Make some plans, all right? No one gets to live your life but you."

"Ok," I managed before hanging up.

My conversation with Naomi had invigorated me to plow through the next few scrapbooks with bounce and speed. She had been kinder to me than anyone had in weeks. I felt mothered. I felt cared for. I now enjoyed walking to the barn and being surrounded by the photographs of the family, I felt oddly like one of them.

When I'd eat my burritos alone in my kitchen, I'd fantasize about Naomi and my upcoming dinner. I tried on clothes in the mirror to figure out what I would wear. I assumed she would book a restaurant in Asheville, maybe Cúrate or the Market Place. Everything I owned felt old and gross, so I drove to the secondhand place in Burnsville and bought a black button up. At home I paired it with my black pants. I was surprised, I looked clean and put together, like someone who might regularly change their windshield wipers and keep all their files neatly organized on a hard drive. I imagined after the appetizers I would broach the subject of Marcella-Marie and then Naomi would open up. I would console her, and maybe tell her about my own mother.

Over the next week I sent Naomi dozens of messages checking in about various details with the books, desperate for a response. For some flare of a reminder of her care from our previous call.

Thanks again Naomi for talking with me the other night. Attached are the final pages from the 2015 books. I had a question about who was next to Bryce on page 23.

Nothing. A few days later I texted again.

Hi Naomi, I just wanted to check in about the 2018 books. I am really looking forward to you coming, and if we want to stay on schedule, I need to finish them before you arrive—I'm sending some sample photos of the spreads—since the majority of the material seems to be financial statements, I was curious how you wanted it to be laid out. Let me know if this looks ok. Thanks! x E

And again.

Hi Naomi, it would be great to know if this all looks ok? The schedule is getting tight. Really looking forward to having you here!

Naomi was ghosting me too. It was nearly Christmas and I was well aware the Duncans and their fleet of monogrammed bags had already checked in at the Little Nell in Aspen. I had at this point read dozens of their yearly hotel bills, I knew the rosemary gin and tonics cost twenty-three dollars, and they always ordered the Alpine fondue and truffle fries. I also knew nine rooms were booked in their name, and the whole extended family went skiing every morning, tipping the lift attendants generously to secure the first ride up. It skewered my self-worth to imagine their family happy in Aspen. Now that I felt like one of them, Naomi's failure to respond felt like she was cutting me out.

The holiday crawled by like any other day on the mountain. I listened to a podcast about sex workers disappearing in

Arizona and continued gluing the Duncans' papers to the page. While eating Annie's mac and cheese on the couch, I got a text from my dad: *Merry X-mas.* I wrote back, *Same 2 you.* I exhaled, knowing that interaction would hold us till May 15, his birthday. I wondered how many pages of a scrapbook the detritus of my own youth could fill. Five pages? Maybe six? I wrote Naomi again.

Merry Christmas Naomi. When you have a chance, please let me know your thoughts on those spreads. I am just plowing through so as to stay on schedule :) Can't wait to have you on the mountain, there are some nice craft studios we could check out as well.

I left Patrick Nelson his chunky ceramic mug, wrapped in yellow tissue paper at the post office along with the note. And on New Year's I turned down an invitation from Chester the potter for a karaoke party, and kept gluing paper into books. Tabitha was now in high school. If I kept my pace up, I was on track to have the books ready for Bryce's sixtieth birthday. But not hearing from Naomi had started a brushfire in my stomach. It was like being dumped all over again. Had I done something wrong? Was Naomi mad at me? I called her burner again. No answer. I tried twenty-two more times, then I gave in. I called WAC.

"Hello?" a voice finally asked.

"Hello—I'm looking for Naomi."

There was a pause, a small intake of air, then a sigh.

"I'm really sorry to inform you that Naomi passed away a week ago."

"What?"

"Is there something I can help you with? Did she have an appointment with you? I'm still working through her calendar."

I hung up.

Everything felt off. I grabbed my bag and jumped in my truck. In the parking lot of Hammersmith, I pulled out my iPad and googled. The *New York Times* had published an obituary adorned with a smiling photograph of Naomi wearing a soft blue dress in her Hamptons garden. *Humanitarian Socialite Dies in Skiing Accident Christmas Morning.* Her work with WAC was outlined in detail. So was the story of her qualifying for the Olympic ski team. Followed by statistics on ski deaths. Her society life in New York. And a list of whom she'd left behind, Tabitha and her loving husband, Bryce Duncan. In lieu of flowers, donations were to be sent to WAC.

I kept refreshing. My head throbbed, maybe it was a joke? I read the article again. A skiing accident was such a thoroughbred way to go. Like a Kennedy. Or a movie star. It seemed bizarrely fitting and somehow completely abstracted the tragedy. I tried to remember the woman seated across from me at Memphis's gallery dinner, the gleam of her cheekbones, the warmth of her brown eyes, the perfectly placed red hairs on her skull, and how she had put her hand on mine and talked about fate and later reincarnation. Did she have a premonition she was going to die? I wondered if I should call back? Should I just explain the scrapbooking? I picked up my phone, let it ring once, then remembered the frost in Naomi's voice when she'd told me to not under any circumstances tell anyone.

I sat in the parking lot shivering. I didn't want to go home. I didn't want to be near the piles of paper printed with Naomi's name or see her face staring back at me. It was overwhelming. I couldn't believe she was gone. I needed to think. I pulled the truck out and headed toward Asheville, it was a little after five p.m. I wanted a drink but wasn't sure where to go. Despite being an advocate of craft, I despised craft beer and Asheville was soaked in expressive artisanal ales. I parked at a gay bar that I knew still sold Budweiser.

The interior was decorated with rainbow streamers and mostly empty. I drank quickly. Three successive pints later the bartender, who looked like a glitter-dusted Pillsbury Doughboy, asked if I was ok.

"My friend died," the word *friend* came out clunkily. Had Naomi been my friend? She had listened to me, she had been caring, and thanks to the scrapbooks, I knew everything about her and her family. Those things combined made it feel like we were in fact friends.

The bartender slumped his shoulders, turned, then reappeared with two shot glasses.

"I'm sorry," he said kindly while pouring whiskey, his forearm tattoo of a butcher's knife now facing me.

We clinked glasses. I sipped and tried to imagine Naomi's last moments, wearing her slick red Moncler puffer jacket on the ski slope. Had she been happy? Had they all watched it happen? Was it a tumble? A hardware malfunction? Or had someone pushed her? I'd seen dozens of photos of the family lined up, cheeks flushed, with matching blue helmets and Gore-Tex gloves, on those white snowy Christmas mornings. What had happened? I felt disgusted with myself for thinking it: how would I get my next payment?

The bar started to fill. I hadn't been around drunk people for what felt like years. It was loud. There was a birthday party unfolding near the pool table. Shots and bad dancing. Everyone had friends. Everyone seemed so happy and normal and dumb. I ordered another beer. I was beginning to feel woozy.

"Do you have Wi-Fi?" I asked the bartender.

"Yeah, the password is RuPaul."

I blearily dug around my bag until I found my iPad, then opened Tabitha's Instagram. The last post was a beautiful black-and-white photo of Naomi; young and smiling, her face freckled from the sun, holding Tabitha as a toddler on a beach. I had seen the picture in one of the piles, it was taken in St. Barts in 2002 or 2003. Underneath the post

Tabitha had written a note—*Heaven got one hell of a new angel; I'll love you forever Mommy.* Then a series of dove emojis and two hundred thousand comments beneath, most including hearts.

I sat dumbstruck. No matter my feelings about Tabitha, we now had this in common. Both our mothers had been consumed into the great void of gravity. Accidents. The combustible illusion of chance. An unexpected knife of heat ran through my body as the image of my own mother's car wrapped around the median flashed, her blonde hair matted with blood. The airbags blown out. Glass lodged into the right side of her face. She'd died in the hospital, a full two days after the accident, but I hadn't been allowed to see her. And I am still certain, if I had just been let into her room, to stand by her bed, she might have stayed on this earth. I wondered if Naomi died on impact or in a helicopter high above the mountain holding a well-trained EMT's hand. Had Tabitha cried on the powder below? Or maybe, I took a sip of beer to let the thought settle, maybe Tabitha pushed Naomi? I had convinced myself with little evidence she'd killed her sister. Why not her mom too?

In a bolt of drunkish urgency, I opened my junk folder and found the email written by the PI, Brenda Millwater, and wrote her back. *PRICE IS FINE. I am looking for Elena Tester, she was a nanny for Naomi and Bryce Duncan in New York City from 1998–2007. Please let me know ASAP. My credit card info is attached.* I needed answers again and Elena would have them. Just as I pressed send, I felt a tap on my shoulder. I looked up, a small girl, midtwenties, wearing a beanie over ratty blonde hair stared back at me. It took me a second to even remember where I was. A gay bar. On a Friday night.

"Are you Esther?" she asked, her voice surprisingly deep.

I nodded, giving enough of a smile to seem human.

"I'm Kenny," her eyes were a little glassy, her septum boasting a small silver arc.

"Hi," I said. I still had no idea who she was, but lesbians all know each other through some six-degrees-of-gay-Kevin-Bacon. Why had I come here? I could have ordered a pumpernickel grapefruit pale ale anywhere and been at peace.

"I was in Jessica's silver enameling workshop at Holyoke last spring." She paused, "You and I met at show-and-tell. I made the turquoise cheetah brooch."

Of course, she was a jewelry dyke. She had all the markers. Tattoos. Several interlooping artistic earrings, Doc Martens, and orangey-red lipstick.

"Jessica and I broke up," I snarled, enjoying the cruelty of my words. I was still angry she had never texted or called me back after our last conversation, my drunk confession: *I love you*. "She was cheating on me," I hurled with unnecessary intensity. I wasn't totally sure of that fact, or why I was telling this girl, but slander felt like the next step of grieving.

Kenny's face dropped, suddenly ashen, "Oh, so you know?" Her voice revealed its lisp from the birthday party's shots, "I'm so sorry. I thought you were OK with it."

"With what?" I asked.

Kenny flushed, "That we were—fucking. She told me you were open."

Flip a table? Punch her? Cry? I just sat there. We were not *open*. We were planning a family. We had bought a house. She had made me a ring. *Our life*. I said nothing, eyes hot, then I felt a flash of greed—I wanted every part of Jessica, why did I have to share her with this random vegan?

"I'm so sorry." There was a pause. "Do you want to come play pool with us?" Kenny eventually said hopefully, motioning toward the obnoxious group across the room.

"No."

"Please?"

"My friend died."

Kenny looked shocked then sad, "Do you want me to sit with you?"

I shrugged. She ordered a vodka soda, and pulled her chair close to mine, another pause, the gurgling brook of bar sounds filling in between us.

"Tell me about fucking Jessica."

She stared at me stunned, then looked away a few beats, "Will that make you feel better?"

I nodded. The greed returning. I wanted to consume their time together like a cold beer. I wanted whatever they had to slide through my body, fermented and mine.

She looked down at her chewed-up nails. I tilted my glass in her direction, prompting her to start.

"Well, it always happened at school—in my dorm. She would usually come over after slides, or whatever."

"The sex," I snapped.

I closed my eyes and listened to Kenny describe Jessica going down on her. How Jessica eventually fucked her from behind with the pink strap-on, the one we kept in our top dresser drawer, while holding her neck down into a pillow. She told me how it hurt. And how she had liked it, and how, for the last two days of classes Jessica completely ignored her existence.

I drunkenly leaned in to kiss her. Her tangerine lips were waxy, covered in mentholated lip balm, maybe Carmex or Burt's Bees. She glanced back at her friends then returned to my mouth, pushing her thin tongue across my gums. She dropped her hand to my crotch, and we made out in fast waves. Eventually, the sticky sludge of her lip gloss worked its way down my throat, and I felt like I was going to puke. I erupted in a coughing fit, then pushed her off, saying an ill-shaped goodbye, and stumbled outside. The air was cold, and the sounds of the bar were stretching into the parking lot, laughter mixing with tendrils of Dolly Parton. My mother loved Dolly. She'd sing "Jolene" while cleaning the house, a handkerchief dramatically tied over her hair. Then I heard Madeline's voice—*She's just more fun hammered.* I hiccupped with anger but was too exhausted to spiral. Would I drive drunk? I got into my truck and crawled to the back seat and passed out.

Five hours later I woke up freezing and certain the dangling seatbelt at my waist was a vindictive snake. The clock on my dash said it was five a.m., I caught my breath, then found my Nalgene. Gulping water, I blearily decided I was sober enough to drive home. Of course, Jessica had been cheating. I knew she kept a tally. Even when I'd think I'd gotten away with leaving the party early, not plonking my credit card down after dinner, hating her friends who came to visit, or forgetting to take the trash to the dump—it was always inscribed on my forehead, a line of strikes that I couldn't see; a line of strikes that allowed her to do as she pleased.

Charging across the highway, I floated out of my body, above the truck, like a camera on a crane in an action movie. I could see what I was—just a smear of light shooting down a dark road, so terrifyingly alone. I started to cry. After a few sobby minutes clutching the wheel, the idea arrived like a rock through my window. I could just burn all of it. The boxes of Jessica's shit. And all the Duncans' books. There were too many botched and wasted lives braided together in that refurbished barn.

I parked, then searched my truck for a lighter. I half expected the books to be gone, evaporating the second the news arrived that Naomi had left the earth—but there they were, in a haphazard line on the desk near the door and dozens of piles of loose material still laying on the concrete floor. I grabbed the flimsy, red-bristled broom and, sweeping up the remaining papers, imagined flames erasing all distinction between what was the Duncans' and Jessica's and mine in a certain blaze of finality. But then, something turned off inside of me, an invisible switch. I stood silently. In a near trance, I let the broom drop, then the lighter, and stumbled up the path.

7

I woke up to the sound of trees howling. The stormy weather felt appropriate for the cabaret of illness that my hangover had manifested: headaches, diarrhea, and an encore that brought me to my knees, face down in the toilet. All the while Naomi's death still churned like unformed butter in my brain. I kept returning to a looping image: Naomi in her Moncler puffer sailing through a Tiffany-blue sky like a duty-free perfume advertisement. How could she be dead? And what was I supposed to do with the books?

I wobbled to the kitchen to jam oatmeal down my throat then remembered the previous evening's near end in arson. I felt a slap of fear and pulled on my boots. Bracing myself against the wind, I held my coffee and ripped open the barn door, I needed to see it—to confirm I hadn't. There the lighter sat on top of the pile of papers.

"Thank fucking god," I said out loud.

I felt a flicker of pride that I hadn't succumbed to the striped needs of my rage. I had not transformed Jessica and the Duncans' ephemera into flames. Yet I still wasn't sure what to do, or even what Naomi would have wanted. I was too hungover to dwell on anything meaningful so I turned on a podcast about a boy who disappeared after a football game, his Durango mysteriously turning up parked outside a water treatment plant. Without thinking, I began reorganizing the mess of papers when a knock on the frame of the barn nearly made me barf with fear.

It was Patrick Nelson. I wondered if maybe he would shoot me this time, at least put me out of my hungover misery. I waved awkwardly then turned to pause the podcast just as the mother of the missing teen was blubbering about how reliable her son usually was at texting back.

"Can I charge my phone?" Patrick had a look of anguish on his face, his hands holding a black cable. "The power's out at mine."

I stupidly let my eyes wander up to the bright fluorescent tubes to check they were on. Before I could nod him in, Patrick was standing over a wall socket, pushing the button on the top right corner trying to revive the quiet plastic object.

A tree must have fallen on a line on the south side of the mountain, knocking his out but sparing mine. It happened often enough in the area. Hammersmith even had an elephantine generator that roared so loud I could hear it from my bed.

"Should I call Duke?" I asked.

Patrick nodded, without looking up.

I found Duke Energy in my contacts.

"Hi, it's Esther Ray, I'd like to report a power outage at 248 Mountain Ridge Road."

"Dammit," Patrick muttered toward his still dead phone which he was trying to turn on.

"They said they'd try and have it back up by tomorrow night, if not the following day."

Patrick huffed. I took the opportunity to stare at him—he was wearing jeans and a red T-shirt, his gray hair, scraggy in the back, needed cutting. A pack of cigarettes peeked out of his back pocket. I was so rarely around men. I avoided their lumbering forms in the aisles of the grocery store and dreaded taking my truck to the shop where I'd have to talk to *them*. The potato-shaped, wiry armed, stubbled middle-aged male was an absolute enigma to me, and I often wondered if they even had inner monologues.

Patrick was hunched over, his body aimed away from me. I could feel his annoyance at having to be here in the barn radiating in waves. Over the past weeks I'd always nodded to him in passing, hoping to catch some sort of reconciliatory eye flicker, but he was quick to turn away. He hated me. But I wanted to know if he'd liked the mug I'd made him—and if he'd read the note. After a few empty seconds, I knew the situation required an adult apology.

"I'm sorry about opening your mail."

Patrick continued to stare at his phone.

"I am. I have issues. I can be—impulsive. And I didn't mean to, well, open it."

"What do you mean, you didn't *mean* to?" he snapped, with a slug of anger.

I stuttered. It wasn't an adult apology I had given him. "No, you're right. I did. I opened it on purpose. And I read it. And I am sorry. There is no excuse."

Patrick pressed a button on his phone but nothing happened. I kept talking. "I just—I don't know—I get overwhelmed and then I do things," unexpected tears strolled down my eyes.

Patrick finally looked at me and something softened.

"I am sorry," I said again, firmly.

"Ok," he replied, and his shoulders fell.

There was a pause, our eyes held each other.

"Do you want coffee?" I asked without thinking. Wanting to escape the stinging silk of the moment.

Patrick looked silently down the hill toward his dark, powerless home, "Sure."

I turned to go, my hangover reappearing in a dolphin's leap as I made my way up the path.

When I returned, Patrick was looking over one of the books splayed out on the table.

"You gettin' a divorce?" he asked quietly as he took the mug.

"What?" I asked, wondering if he was talking about Jessica. Patrick pointed a tanned finger at one of the dense numerical spreads, "Asset assessments."

"Oh," I said, then added, "wait, what?"

"Asset assessments," he repeated. "What is all of this?" Patrick asked, looking around the books and the near-bonfire on the floor.

"It's, uh—a project for a friend."

Patrick simply nodded and returned to the books, engrossed in the numbers.

"Why does it look like a divorce?" I asked.

"Preliminary assessments, tracing tax returns from multiple years and different companies. Your friend's got a complicated one. Looks like she's planning a coup."

"My friend is—dead."

Patrick looked up, "I'm sorry."

"How do you know about these . . . assessments?"

"I'm an accountant."

"Can you see—anything—else?" I stuttered as if he were some sort of oracle.

"There isn't much else I can tell you from these without—"

A twist of mechanical Mozart ripped through the room, and Patrick answered the phone with gusto.

"Hiya, bud—how are you?"

It was his son. *Of course.*

Patrick nodded in my direction, then covered the mouthpiece with his hand, "And thanks for the mug."

He trotted off. I watched him disappear down the hill feeling grateful for the windy higher powers that knocked over the tree creating the opportunity for my mild atonement.

Instinctively, I turned the podcast back on, letting the annoying voice of the private detective hired by the missing boy's family fill the barn. My head was spinning. Naomi wanted a divorce? What sort of person serves divorce papers in a forty-book family album? Through the dullness of my hangover, I felt a strange lozenge of clarity dissolving in the back of my throat: the books weren't a gift, they were a Trojan horse, a delivery system for the end. It all made sense: Bryce's birthday, the dire need for secrecy and her urgency about the timeline. I tried to parse the columns of numbers which Patrick had been reading but understood nothing.

I sat on my stool chewing my nails, listening to the podcaster cautiously describe the missing boy's apparent diaper fetish, and the subsequent reaction of his high school ex-girlfriend. Zoning out in that moment, I felt a sense of loyalty to Naomi blooming inside my chest. I had to figure this out for her. She had trusted me. And my job was not done. *She deserved justice.*

I knew I needed to talk to someone who knew Naomi, who understood what her plans were with the books and her divorce. I dug out the dossier that Naomi had made of friends and family and wheedled my way through the list of names. Of course. Her neighbor and best friend, Chrissy Ash, *divorce lawyer to the stars.* Naomi had spent every summer with the Ash family and ritually attended benefit lunches and dinners with Chrissy, from all the information I had access to, Chrissy Ash was Naomi's closest friend and most likely her lawyer. I felt a shimmer of relief. I was visually rich with information about Chrissy; I knew she drove a silver G-Wagon and had salon-styled blonde hair, always brought yellow striped towels to the beach and on her days off cultivated a Gwyneth Paltrow-esque image with relaxed denim and light makeup. But I'd gathered from Google she was as well a tough-as-fuck Laura Wasser type. I needed to get ahold of her.

Back in the barn I searched for Chrissy's personal contact info, which I remembered had been printed on one of her son's birthday RSVP cards. The podcaster's nasal voice carried me on my quest as he extrapolated on the unseasoned sheriff who didn't think to check the Durango with UV light for blood spatter. While digging for the RSVP card, I kept stumbling over pictures of Bryce. He was the bright red button in the equation. He was a force I hadn't spent much time considering. In the books he'd come off like a blasé businessman with a thin smile and pronounced taste for khaki pants. He had been noticeably absent from the most recent years, which I assumed was because of work, but now the questions raged; did he know Naomi was planning a divorce? Did he push her down the mountain? *Divorce is a motive.* A silent chant pulsed through my head. *Divorce is a motive.* I found the birthday RSVP with Chrissy's number, I pulled out my phone and punched it in.

"We're sorry, the number you have dialed is no longer in service."

Fuck.

I could call her office. I reminded myself that good podcasters rarely call. They knock on the door during dinner. They catch their subjects off-guard. I knew Chrissy went to the Hamptons every weekend she could, even in winter. If I wanted to find her, I could go there. I had the welcome packet for Naomi's house, a disturbingly detailed ten pages typed up for Paul and Melanie Benton, who'd spent a few early fall weeks in the guesthouse, which included directions, internet passwords, and two pages with photos explaining how to set the alarms upon exiting and entering with the outdoor key-pad, all penned with automated Airbnb cheer: *Please enjoy the hot tub (extra towels are in the green hamper on the mezzanine) and if you need to turn up the heat, don't hesitate (thermostat mounted to west wall)! If you have any emergencies, you can always contact Chrissy Ash who lives next door and is usually around on weekends. We love that you're here!*

It took mere minutes to find the welcome packet. *Divorce is a motive. Divorce is a motive.* The chant returning like a drumbeat. I packed hastily, grabbing all my clean underwear, toiletries, black pants, and new button up. I threw in the scrapbook with the welcome packet from fall 2017, as well as the dossier on friends and family. As I was turning my truck down to the mountain, I remembered Patrick without power. I thrust my truck down his driveway and stomped to his porch. He opened before I could knock, wearing a headlamp.

"Patrick, hi. I have to help my friend—the one who died— so I'm going to New York. If the power doesn't turn back on at your place, you can charge up or whatever at mine. There's a key under the ceramic turtle on the porch."

Patrick looked grateful, and I hoped this final gesture would secure atonement for my mail fraud.

"Are you sure? Is, uhh, everything ok?" he asked, taking in my manic state.

"Yeah, I won't be back for a few days," I said, turning back toward the truck.

"Be safe," Patrick replied softly.

I parked in the Hammersmith School parking lot, opening the directions on my iPad. Thirteen hours. That was nothing. Two podcasts, maybe three.

8

My red truck crawling down the manicured street felt like an incoming herpes outbreak on Botoxed lips. Everything was too pristine. Too plump and perfect, except me. I had been to the Hamptons twice when I was Michael Valentine's studio assistant. Once to oversee the installation of two canvases in an oceanfront bedroom, and the second when I'd been chauffeured from Brooklyn in an UberX to touch up a painting that had been damaged by a belligerent dinner-party guest. I was still moved by wealth back then. I found the thickness of expensive drapery therapeutic, the hermetic seals of the front doors profound, and the precision of the hedges a sign of a superior intellect.

The Duncans' house at 271 Gin Lane was not oceanfront but still impressive, with round shrubs and grass that looked dementedly green even in winter. I eased the truck down the mouth of the drive, the house was far more extreme than it looked in pictures; it was not a rustic country estate, it was a muscular flex of wealth with an unexpected tang of Cruella de Vil. I tried to act casual as I punched the number from the welcome packet into the gate's polished silver pad. A mortifying pause. A black Porsche drove by and I was certain the driver was staring at me. Two excruciating seconds later, the gate rolled silently backward and the long-hedged driveway was revealed.

The Duncans never came out before June, so I confidently parked under the thatched carport and stepped out into the yard, admiring the pool cover's alarming shade of turquoise. I strode to the door of the guesthouse which resembled a near-shrunken photocopy of the blue-gray shingled main house and found another keypad. I checked the welcome packet. Again, a disturbing pause, then the alarm tutted, and the lock popped open. I was in. The air was neutral, the house suspended in the timeless clean of regular maintenance. I took a deep breath, letting the tension of the drive evaporate, and wandered around letting my fingers dance on the edges of the all-white furniture.

I wound my way up to the generous main bathroom and stripped. The glassed-in shower was nearly the size of my bedroom back home, and the torrential rainforest head had such magnificent pressure it felt like a baptism. I dried off and found a fluffy white robe in the closet and laid down on the bed. The sheets were exquisite. So comfortable I searched for the tag: *Frette*. I found my iPad and connected to the guest-house Wi-Fi, and I googled. The sheets were Italian, and cost two thousand dollars. I relaxed my body starfish style and promptly fell into a stone sleep. I woke cellularly rested: maybe it was the purified air, or showerhead, or maybe it was because I finally had decided on a plan. It was Thursday. Chrissy Ash would most likely arrive late tomorrow night. I needed to be ready.

I got in my truck and swung by the Citarella Gourmet Market and was horrified by the prices. A nine-dollar avocado? I bought the cheapest essentials and sprung for the twelve-dollar hummus and artisanal bread. Next, I drove to the Golden Eagle art supply store and proceeded to spend $1,986 on oil paints, gesso, plastic drop cloths, brushes, four canvasses, and an easel, which I rented for two weeks. When the heavy breathing, too-interested-in-my-artistic-pursuits cashier cut my debit card through the magnetic strip, I felt as if she were slitting my wrists. It was an absurd sum of money, but I had no choice. I loaded the materials into the back of my truck and tore off down the road and back to my gated compound.

I connected to the kitchen's Bluetooth and put on a podcast about an Australian housewife who went missing thirty years ago, then set about transforming the living room into my studio. First taping down the drop cloths on the bleached wooden floor, then situating the easel in a corner near the window. In a sad weepy tone, over the built-in speakers, an older woman described the missing Australian housewife as someone "who would have given you the shirt off her back." I released a snort. It is a phrase used in almost every podcast to describe the victim in question. Maybe this is the secret unifying similarity between all of these women who are disposed of by their rugby-playing husbands; they were all simply too kind or too generous, and too willing to peel off their shirts for others.

The podcast was gripping, but I knew the reason why I was hyperfocused on the lengthy descriptions of the "soft soil" where the police assumed the housewife was buried, was because I wanted to ignore the fluidity of my own movements. The ease of setting up a painting station, the thrill of laying out the brushes. This was the routine that had consumed the majority of my adult life. Craft had been my savior, my trapdoor from the pollution of the art world, but this still felt like coming home. After I was all set up, I wandered into the kitchen and found a hidden pantry which was stocked with various canned goods, noodles displayed in oblong glass jars, and a healthy rack of wine. I rippled with annoyance; I should have checked before buying my overpriced groceries. I took my time selecting a Chianti and poured a giant glass, feeling like a character in a Nora Ephron film. Now all I had to do was wait.

It was strange to inhabit their house. It was no longer a stage set, the world from the glossy photos of the scrapbooks was now my reality. The gleaming fridges filled with my food. The side table holding my half-drunk wineglass. The tub still wet from my bath. I hated how I liked the trappings of wealth. I felt my mother inside of me, the aspirational animal clawing up from my abdomen. And I had to remind myself I was here for a purpose.

Friday evening, I went on four walks, each time hoping to see the glowing lights of Chrissy Ash's next door, but the house remained dark. I took another decadent rainforest shower, then lathered my body in the La Prairie skin cream I'd found in the downstairs bathroom. I crawled in bed and started scrolling through Tabitha's Instagram, which was still a world of pinks and obscenely long eyelashes. She didn't seem to be mourning her mother's recent passing. She'd even posted a slew of photos of herself readying to go out, posing in a sequined dress in a hotel window, the New York skyline glittering behind her.

When I dove into the comments of the sequined dress post, I noticed people all talking hysterically about a viral video of her doing coke at Le Bain. I googled. Sure enough, there was a short, shitty quality video of Tabitha snorting something in the corner of the club. I watched it a dozen times, her head tilting forward then back, illuminated by a strobe. It had been only two weeks since Naomi had died and Tabitha was clubbing. I rippled with disgust. How could she not care? Maybe she was guilty? I wanted more. I found a link to her TikTok; as an elder millennial I had never ventured onto the app, which caused preteens to move like inebriated mimes at crosswalks, but my interest trumped my trepidation.

Seeing her in looping action was mesmerizing. I wasn't used to having internet at home and I lost hours in the large white bed chugging Chianti and scrolling. Somehow the algorithm immediately knew I was lesbian. It immediately knew I wanted to watch the hydraulic press exploding toothpaste tubes and that I would want to watch middle-aged women making oddly shaped candles and teenagers crocheting handbags from telephone cord. The performance of the small business-ification of the craft world consumed me and I was both horrified and enthralled, my feed was all women slapping labels onto plastic boxes while whining about customers, peppered with Tabitha's freakishly beautiful body in bathroom mirrors as she sponged on product and described her process.

"So, I like to start with a gentle toner to exfoliate. When I was younger I always overexfoliated because I loved the feeling on my skin. You know—like that aggressive feel." Tabitha was rhythmically massaging her face in a gray marble bathroom, the camera placed in front of the mirror, a halo of light falling at her shoulders and her eyes glaring in their greenness. "And repair oil is crucial, like never ever miss a day," she chirped. Then without warning, the video shifted tempos, speeding up to a Lizzo song as she finalized the makeup then made a kissy face at the lens. There was a mysticism to her relaxedness, like a dead fish that was somehow, miraculously cognizant of the fact that it was the most captivating thing on the planet.

In the morning I woke up with a hangover which I remedied by going on a long walk. The beach was nearly deserted. In the scrapbooks there were dozens of photos of Tabitha gathering shells and dragging pieces of driftwood, Naomi excitedly documenting as wind whipped her red hair into the camera's frame. Looking out at the ocean I was struck with the words Naomi uttered at Memphis's dinner; *it's fate*. The water was angry, lapping in violent waves. Naomi was dead, and I was here on her beach. If this was fate, fate was a motherfucker. On my way back to the Duncans' I craned my neck over the gate of Chrissy Ash's house but it was still dark. I spent the night in bed eating pasta and gorging on TikTok, trying to not let the high-thread counts and exquisite shower pressure corrupt me.

I assumed it would be another week before Chrissy appeared so I continued to focus on working my way through the wine rack. My last podcast about the missing Australian housewife ended in the rare and orgasmic clinch of justice. I savored the final episode in the bathtub with a bottle of Rioja, cheering as the brutish-pedophile-jock of a husband was arrested, and the podcaster was forced to stop reporting because the courts were *taking over*. The idea that this housewife, assumed to be buried under her own pool, was finally receiving due process electrified me. I wept with drunk joy and added more hot water to the bath, then started the podcast over from the beginning.

On Wednesday, early evening, I decided to go for another walk. Then I saw it, like a mirage: the lights of Chrissy Ash's petite Versailles on in full force. I sprinted home, brushed my hair, and changed. My nerves were trumpeting in my stomach but I reminded myself: I had a purpose. I was on a mission. I tamped down my fear and buzzed the brass rectangle.

"Hello? Who is it?" A quizzical female voice cut through the cold night air.

"Hi, is this Chrissy?"

"Yes?"

"My name is Jessica, and I'm a friend of Naomi Duncan. She asked me to come by and speak with you, before she passed."

There was a long pause, the gate buzzed. I walked the winding drive to her ominous entrance, all while second guessing having used a fake name. *Jessica, Jessica, Jessica.* I wanted to protect myself in case this ended up being a mistake. Naomi had been so careful with guarding the books. I owed this to her.

Twenty seconds later, the restaurant-grade refrigerator seal on the front door released, and Chrissy Ash stood in front of me in a beige cashmere sweatsuit.

"Thank you so much for seeing me, I wish it was under better circumstances."

"You were a friend of Naomi's?" Chrissy asked uneasily.

"Well—actually, it's a bit of a long story," I paused, trying to rouse an invitation into the foyer, but Chrissy stood firm with her arms crossed at the threshold.

"Well, the thing is, Naomi hired me to do a series of portraits of her closest friends and family. It was supposed to be a surprise Christmas gift, but of course—"

I let the image of Naomi hover between us. "She was really excited about the paintings, and she set me up in the guest-house as a studio, she had it all planned out, but—she was never able to tell you."

Chrissy moved stray blonde hair from her face, "This is really—unexpected."

"She told me she was thinking a lot about legacy, and that a portrait was a meaningful way to preserve presence."

"When did she ask you to do this?"

"She arranged the gift nearly a year ago," I added hastily, making it a longer plan seemed like it would add value to the gift.

Something relaxed in Chrissy's face, as if the timeline was paramount to her agreeing.

"Well, I guess this is very Naomi," she said releasing a sad laugh. "Over the top and always planning years in advance."

"So, you'd be willing to come sit for it?" I asked, near pleading.

She looked up at the ceiling, maybe fighting off tears.

"I have the easel all set up so you can come by whenever it's convenient."

Chrissy took a breath, "Of course, I have some work calls in the morning, but could be by around 12:15 during lunch."

"Great."

"It's nice to meet you, Jessica."

"It's lovely to meet you, Chrissy. Naomi spoke so fondly of you."

Chrissy stood there looking momentarily uncertain, maybe about to say something serious.

"See you tomorrow," Chrissy said finally, letting the door close.

I knew it would work. A portrait is a black hole of narcissism—a portal that opens between the sitter's own image and the rest of time, and all that trust lays entirely in my hands, their vanity on my eye. And it's always the same; at first the sitter brings their projections of who they are and they pose initially as if for a camera. Neck tilted, back straight, cheeks pursed in a soft smile, but after a few hours they relax, revealing the crook of their personality and the shape of fear in their body. I ask questions, and eventually their answers become liquid, truthful, tranced out. This had been what I did at Michael Valentine's studio for countless women of Chrissy's breed. This was my bread and butter, and this was how I would find out more about Naomi.

It was hard to sleep. For breakfast I forced down half a toasted bagel, then cleaned the house. I readied my palette, premixing gray tones on the overpriced slab of glass I'd bought at the Golden Eagle. I wondered what Chrissy would choose to wear. Maybe black in some form of mourning for her dead friend. Maybe soft neutrals as if she was about to be interviewed by Oprah in a backyard flanked by florals. I arranged one of the white chairs by the window and draped a beige blanket off the right arm and dragged a potted lemon tree to the background. It wasn't the world's most dynamic frame but the Duncans' minimalism didn't leave me many props. Chrissy arrived at 12:16 in khaki pants and a pale blue cashmere sweater. Her blonde hair was down, and it was clear she had applied a precise, yet subtle, dusting of makeup.

"Hi Jessica."

"Thanks so much for coming. How are you?"

Chrissy looked around at the living room. I realized the plastic tarp–covered floor might look more *kill room* than *art studio*, but Chrissy seemed unfazed.

"I'm fine, just deadlines. Should I sit there?"

I nodded. She walked over to the white chair.

"Would you like some tea?"

"Sure, anything herbal. Chamomile if you have it."

I let Chrissy settle in and slipped to the kitchen to turn on the kettle. I was nervous. When I returned with a steaming mug, I gave her a warm smile.

"Thanks."

"What I'm going to do first is the sketch, and then I'll begin on the underpainting. So, you don't need to focus on your facial expressions, but I would like to find your form on the canvas, so let's get you comfortable."

"Sure," Chrissy said, still sitting rigid in the chair.

"You can lean back, if you'd like."

Chrissy nodded and she shifted backward. I let ten silent minutes unfold while I sketched lightly with a pencil. Chrissy checked her phone again.

"Are you working on something in particular?" I asked, I hoped charmingly.

"The usual miseries, I'm a divorce lawyer."

"Ah, nice."

Chrissy took a sip of tea.

"I set up my weekend office here, it's a bit of a hassle but the change of scenery tricks me into feeling like I have more time off than I do."

I nodded, focusing on her shoulders which appeared spiky even under the plush cashmere. It was clear that Chrissy's brand of casual-chic applied only in style; I wondered what it would take to make her relax. Maybe a sedative. She looked back at her phone and flared her jaw. I began tracing the space around her body, gently mapping how her head cut against the muted greige of the wall.

"How long does this normally take?" Chrissy asked.

"It's a process, so it takes as long as it takes."

"Could you just take a photo maybe and work from that?"

I was surprised. Most rich people see themselves as modern day Medicis, they understood the value of presence.

"A painting from a photograph may as well be a photograph," I replied firmly.

Chrissy didn't respond. Silence filled in, I slipped from behind the easel, "What's your favorite type of music?"

Chrissy looked out the window, "I love The Weeknd right now, they play it in spin."

I put on "Blinding Lights" and watched as Chrissy started to ever so slightly bob her head: she was relaxing but something told me it was too soon to pry. She still seemed wary of the situation, and I didn't want to give her any reason to be suspicious. So silently, I continued sketching out the underpainting. An hour passed before she checked her phone.

"So, how do I look?" she asked.

"Like a stunning gray blob."

Chrissy laughed, "I have to take a call in fifteen, but I could come back over tomorrow, my lunch is always at 12:15? Does that work? It was honestly sort of relieving to do nothing."

"It can be quite meditative—12:15 is great."

Chrissy nodded, and got up to put on her jacket, stealing a look at the canvas. "I really am a gray blob."

"We'll get there, but wear the same thing tomorrow, ok?"

"Sure."

After Chrissy left, I looked at my sketch. It would be easy enough to paint her as she was, forensically scanning each part of her body, but I still had to capture the carbonation of her being. It was cringe, I knew, but the difference between my portraits and those made from a photograph was that I could reproduce that tinsel of truth that lived inside of a person. Michael Valentine had recognized this when I was a student, which was why he'd chosen me to work for him. I wasn't merely a copy machine, I was a thief, able to catch what others could not: the golden snitch. All day the bright smell of gesso and oil paint in the guesthouse brought me back to Michael Valentine's studio. It was like his cologne. It made my skin crawl. To be painting again was to be close to him, which was one of the main reasons I'd had to stop.

The next day Chrissy returned wearing the same outfit, with the same precise dusting of makeup, which informed me that she was taking the process seriously. She cared. I had The Weeknd already crooning from the speakers.

"Ok, one last thing," she said pecking at her phone, before dramatically pocketing it. "Now, I'm ready."

Chrissy was noticeably less guarded, and she seemed to be enjoying herself, she was even holding her chin with a new tilt, which I assumed she'd found the previous evening in the mirror.

"So, how's the case?" I asked lightly, hoping to ease open the subject of Naomi's divorce.

"Everyone wants everything. A lot of what I do is figuring out what they really need while making them feel like they are getting everything."

"How many cases do you work on at a time?"

"Five to six."

I let silence return. I was beginning to block out the details of her body, the way her sweater bunched at her waist, and the triangle of her crossed leg.

"And how did you first meet Naomi?" Chrissy asked, startling me.

"At an opening in Chelsea, we were seated next to each other," at least that was the truth.

"She liked supporting artists," Chrissy said wistfully.

I nodded, relieved she had brought her up.

"When was the last time you saw her?" I asked delicately.

Chrissy released a shot of air, "It had been months, maybe almost half a year. She was dealing with a lot. I mean, she was—she could be a little out-there with all her WAC projects. And I was busy. I have some guilt that there was a lapse in our communication."

My brain twisted.

"So, you weren't working on anything with her?"

"Like what?" Chrissy asked vaguely surprised.

"Oh, you know . . . plans whatever," I said, trying to abstract my interest.

Chrissy huffed, "I mean, usually we do Easter out here, but it would be too early . . ."

"Of course," I replied.

"And did you know about what she had planned for Bryce's birthday?"

Chrissy's entire body tensed, but she swiftly responded, "Well Bryce always screens a film and has a big dinner. Bryce knows the chef at Rodeio, and he always cooks."

"So, there was nothing special planned that you know of?"

"No, why?"

"Umm, it was his sixtieth birthday, right?" I asked trying to thread her along while seeming casual.

"I know for certain he wanted to do his usual thing, if Naomi had some other idea, well that's news to me—but probably would have annoyed Bryce. He likes to—be in control."

I sucked in a shot of air, she had no clue about me or the books.

Chrissy was staring out the window, "It's incredible Bryce really doesn't look sixty though. It's probably all the jogging. Have you been in touch with him for his portrait?"

I hadn't actually planned on doing anyone's portrait other than Chrissy's. It had simply been the tool to get her to sit down, and answer my questions about the impending divorce, but she knew nothing. She was staring at me, I had to say something.

"I want to be as considerate to Bryce and Tabitha as I can be. Grieving is such a complex process. I didn't want to shock them with the news of the portrait gift from Naomi."

Chrissy popped the joints in her wrist. "Bryce, I think, will be fine, but I doubt you can make him sit still for this long," she released a high string of laughter. The subject of Bryce was filling her with a new energy. She liked saying his name. I could see it in the firmness of her smile and the openness of her shoulders. I wanted to keep her talking.

"How is he handling things?" I asked.

"Bryce is sad of course, but strong for Tabitha."

"And is he still working? Or did he take time off to mourn?"

"I mean, he's always working. Red Rock Capital is really his baby."

I wanted to ask her directly: do you think Bryce wanted Naomi dead? Instead, I began mixing her skin color, oxide white and a dab of cadmium yellow. I'd begin with her neck then work my way to her clothes. I still wasn't sure about her face. I didn't understand Chrissy's soul.

"How is Tabitha?" I asked casually.

"Well Tabitha is Tabitha, she's pretending like she's all right, but it will hit her sooner or later."

121

Chrissy grew silent and I busied myself painting. Twenty minutes later, she left jabbering about being late for some conference call and in the emptiness of the guesthouse I felt even more confused. Who had Naomi been planning the divorce with if not Chrissy? I felt the sinking feeling I'd made a mistake in coming here. I opened a bottle of what looked like a very fancy Merlot and numbed my brain on TikTok, drinking myself into an early sleep.

The next afternoon, Chrissy informed me she had decided to work from the Hamptons for the whole week. She explained that she had no court appearances and all the other meetings could be done over the phone, but I knew she was staying because she liked being painted. Narcissism is a drug, and I was serving high doses. But Chrissy's lack of insight into Naomi's final months was frustrating, and I had been looking forward to my week alone in the guesthouse. I wasn't sure what I was doing and I needed time to figure out what was next.

Chrissy was punctual for our session.

"You know I have a big art collection?" she said without prompt.

"Oh, that's great, anything good?" I asked, despite my zero interest.

"I mean, tons. I have a Basquiat, and a really amazing Hockney. One of the pools."

There was no difference between those paintings or a piece of property in Switzerland. It was asset management, and those were the safest bets on the planet. I felt tempted to sabotage Chrissy's portrait, adding some bloat to her cheeks, or inflaming one of her nostrils. I was desperate to make our conversation constructive.

"Naomi was devastated after Marcella-Marie, right?" I blurted.

"I mean, SIDS is awful," she said, putting her phone down. "But if she told you about Marcella-Marie, I guess, then she must have been going through something. She was usually so tight-lipped about it all, like she never talked about her with me even after all these years. It always struck me as odd."

I returned to painting, agitated that she couldn't even provide insight into poor dead baby Marcella-Marie. This had all been for nothing.

After Chrissy left, I was feeling nauseated from the smell of oil paints and slipped outside, staring at the main house. I remembered Naomi had included the code in the welcome packet in case of emergencies. Moved by dull curiosity, I grabbed the paper from inside and tapped the numbers on the hooded metal box. The alarm tutted, then the wooden door swung open revealing the living room that I knew from photographs. The decor was similar to the guesthouse: white furniture, blond wood, blank walls, sand-colored throws. I wound my way up the staircase, the door was open to the main bedroom. Again, no seashells in glass bowls or nautical tchotchkes, just a stark room with thick taupe curtains, a big white bed, and two matching side tables. Then I noticed the rose quartz lined up on the windowsill, in descending size, largest to smallest from left to right, the type of pink rock that had hung from Naomi's neck at dinner. It was the only sign of her I'd seen in the house. I lay down on the firm mattress.

More than my frustration with Chrissy's lack of insight into Naomi's divorce plans, I had become annoyed with my own quiet joy at painting again. I'd spent all these years and money on craft classes and here I was, in the Hamptons, servicing another wealthy body, and for what? I inspected my paint-splattered hands, then mindlessly walked to the bathroom, turned on the taps, and got into the tub. When I first started working for Michael Valentine his whole thing had been portraits of blue-collar workers. He painted twelve of MoMA's janitors for his show at the museum, and elementary teachers for a show at the Albright-Knox, and sanitation workers in LA at LACMA, always working to invert the power of painting.

Despite coming from solid upper-middle-class comfort, Michael initially pitched himself as a man who championed for labor unseen, adding the workers to the pantheon of the masters. But Michael was also a man who adored German engineered cars, and had once told me that the most profound moment of his life, when he'd felt closest to God, was cruising down the Tioga Pass in his Audi A6, listening to Leonard Cohen's "Dance Me to the End of Love." But what he really meant is that was the closest he had ever felt to *being* a god. His vanity bloomed wildly and exotically as his career exploded. His clothes became designer. He got hair plugs and bought a condo in a spindly glass building near Hudson Yards. He pumped money into his brand-new studio he'd constructed upstate which he called *his church*, buying a ridiculous Italian espresso machine he couldn't use on his own, and installing a seven-person sauna. Success corrupted him, and the strangest thing was he didn't have a clue; by the end, all of his portraits were of rich society women, and his girlfriend, Rosa.

In the Duncans' bathtub I tried to wash Michael from my mind by focusing on the present but there was nothing positive there either. I had been sucked into someone else's demented world again. Naomi was not my mother. Chrissy knew nothing. This was not my house. These were not my fluffy towels. The full Talking Heads song applied. I knew I needed to make peace with the fact that whatever happened to Naomi on that cold mountain in Aspen wasn't my responsibility. I let my body slip underwater, my head disappearing into the suds, and promised myself I would go in the morning. I was nearly done with Chrissy's painting and if I spent the evening finishing the last two layers of glazing, I could leave it on her doorstep and be gone. I let out a belch of relief.

I toweled off and was about to put on my clothes when I heard it. The unmistakable tutting of the alarm. Then the thud of a bag. Someone was in the house.

9

Tabitha was holding a butcher's knife in the kitchen.
"Who the fuck are you?"

"Hi Tabitha," I said from the stairs, "I'm a friend of your mom's."

"What?" she asked dumbfounded.

"Just put the knife down, ok?"

Tabitha, even terrified, looked beautiful. She was wearing tight black pants that shot out into bell bottoms and a mustard-colored hoodie with the word *Drew* written in childish font, her hair tied up in two buns.

"How—did you know my mom?" she asked shakily.

"I'm an artist, and she hired me to do a series of portraits of your family and her friends. It was supposed to be a Christmas gift. Your mom set me up in the guesthouse as a studio, I've been painting Chrissy. And was waiting for the right moment to get in touch with you."

Tabitha looked incredulously at the backyard.

"Then why are you in her bedroom?" she asked, as if it was the only question she could think of.

"Because the guesthouse is filled with the smell of oil paints, and I needed a break."

Tabitha took a long pause, drinking in the black of the windows. "My mom really wanted a portrait of me made?"

"Yes," I lied. "She said she was thinking a lot about legacy."

Tabitha, still clutching the knife, sat down on one of the white stools and proceeded to burst into tears. I watched as she shook, and all of my dark feelings for Tabitha momentarily diffused. I gathered the courage to walk toward her sobbing form and placed my hand on her shoulder. I felt the same electricity I'd felt in Nashville, and it hit me in a hot static wave; she could recognize me. I thought about running to my truck and simply driving away. But then I remembered I had been masked by Desirée, rendered cubist with contour and was wearing my baseball hat. I was safe.

Tabitha turned her head nearly choking, "I'm sorry, I'm a mess. It's been a fucked-up week."

I nodded, I understood.

"Can I see Chrissy's painting?" she asked after she'd calmed.

"Umm, sure, it's not done yet . . ." I said, then led her across the foggy yard to the guesthouse.

I flipped the lights on, and there in the living room sat the portrait. I'd just finished the first layer of glazing and Chrissy's cheeks now had that old master's Flemish glow.

"Wow, it's beautiful. It looks so—real."

"Thanks."

"Wait, what's your name? I didn't mean to be psycho with the whole knife thing. I just didn't expect anyone to be out here."

"I'm Jessica Washington," I felt guilty for using Jessica's name again but I had no choice.

"Can we start now?" Tabitha asked. "The painting?"

"We should start in the morning when the light is better."

"No, I want to start now."

I nodded, giving in to the bizarre bratty urgency of Tabitha's voice. I pulled out the other canvas I had primed and eyed the room. "I think we should do it over there, so it's a different frame from Chrissy's," I said, feeling the old swell of pride in my work. Tabitha agreed and dragged one of the white chairs next to the large bay window, removed her hoodie, revealing a pastel green tank top, and assumed a perfect pose; her body relaxed but her posture straight. I began to sketch with pencil.

At one point Tabitha cocked her head to the side, "Have we met? At, like, one of my mom's events? You look weirdly familiar."

I felt a flush of fear travel through my body, "No, I don't think so. I only met your mom in person once."

She ingested this information with seemingly little thought, "Cool. Can I have a glass of wine while we do this?" Tabitha asked.

"Yeah, of course."

Tabitha got up to fish a bottle from the pantry and I waited for the sound of cork. That loud-wet-plop felt as if it were ushering us into a new universe; one in which all my old questions evaporated, and new ones were being formed, and maybe Tabitha would have the answers. Maybe she was why I had come. Maybe Tabitha wasn't evil, maybe she was also a victim. Tabitha returned from the kitchen with a glass for me, then settled back into her chair, and I continued sketching, enjoying the lines of her face.

"So, where did you meet my mom?" Tabitha croaked, interrupting my hand.

"At an art opening," I responded.

Tabitha gulped her wine down, then refilled her glass. Twenty minutes later, her spine slackened, her head drooped, and she passed out snoring. I stood awkwardly and debated my options. I wasn't strong enough to carry her into the main house. After a few minutes of watching her sleep, I brought one of the starched blankets from an empty room and turned off the lights.

When I came down, groggy, ready for coffee the next morning, Tabitha was standing at the kitchen's marble island in her workout gear, covered in a perfect brine of sweat.

"Jessica, I had an idea." I was too stunned by the unearthly iridescence of her exposed skin to know how to respond, and without caffeine I'd nearly forgotten my name was now Jessica.

"W-what's that?"

"I want to make a series of videos of you painting me."

I felt momentarily warm from the idea but knew I couldn't have my face on her feed, she was too famous and God forbid she google me and find out I wasn't Jessica Washington.

"That's—umm sorry, I hate having my photo taken," I said to her as I moved toward the fridge.

"Why?"

"I keep myself off the internet."

Tabitha's eyes bulged, "Weird, what? Why?"

"I had a stalker once, an ex—so I basically scrubbed my online presence completely. No social. No nothing."

Tabitha looked impressed, "That's crazy. What did they do? The stalker, I mean?"

"She just like, got obsessed. Followed me everywhere I went so now I just prefer to keep it low key."

Tabitha nodded, unaware that in our current arrangement, I was describing myself; I was the stalker. "Well, you could just be behind the canvas, and like then I can take videos alternating between your hands painting and me sitting or whatever. We can leave out your face."

I looked at her and huffed, "Ok."

"I won't post them for like a month anyway."

"So, where would you post them?" I asked as if I hadn't spent hours watching her mystical TikTok dead-eyed dancing on my iPad.

"I'm an influencer."

"What does that mean?"

"It means I run accounts and sell my soul and body to the devil by the second and I also hawk diet tea which gives you the shits."

I laughed. I hadn't expected her to be funny. Tabitha trotted off to the main house and changed into the outfit she'd worn the previous night, without me even asking. She was professional. She sat down and a gentle smile tugged across her face and her sheer desire to become an image fueled the morning.

After a few hours of posing, she took a break, and on her way back from the bathroom, held up a dark glass square. Then I realized it was my iPad. I rippled with fear knowing my search history would reveal all my digging into her and her family.

"Oh, I love true crime, shall we listen to one?" she said, now looking at my iTunes.

"Sure," I replied, nervously.

"I love these girls," Tabitha said, just as the speakers filled with the chipper voices of the two best friends obsessed with murder. The women were obnoxious in the giddiness toward shilling violence, selling coffee mugs, hoodies, and bumper stickers with their glib murder-centric phrases.

"I think they're hilarious," Tabitha added.

The hosts chatted inanely about air fryers until they finally got into discussing a guy who was dismembering women and storing their bodies behind the drywall of his house. Apparently, the smell of rotting flesh consumed the entire block, but the stench was blamed on the fish market next door, for which the owner had to install three different types of vent systems to try and eliminate the odor before the police figured it out.

"That's fucking rank," Tabitha said as she got up to shake her legs out.

"The police are idiots," I added.

Silence settled. And after a few empty minutes, I decided maybe it was time to do some light digging, "So, do you have any siblings?"

Tabitha responded sharply, "No."

There was no room for me to bring up Marcella-Marie without revealing what I knew so I returned to mixing paint.

"You know, we have some steaks in the freezer next door, should I grab them?"

I nodded.

While Tabitha was gone, I wondered what a podcaster would do in my situation. Should I be recording our conversations? Should I be pressing harder? Tabitha returned with two thick steaks sealed in plastic, I prepared a bowl of water to let them soak.

"I'm so hungry."

"Same."

I was stunned by the blossom of our friendship. I knew I had come here on a mission. I wanted to find out what had happened to Naomi, but there was something about Tabitha that oozed innocence. Maybe it was because she seemed somehow dumb, or sad. Or confused. Or maybe because she was so profoundly young. Despite trying to keep my investigative distance we had developed the tempo of an endless sleepover. I wanted to paint her nails while telling her my secrets.

The next morning, we continued with the portrait, and at lunch Tabitha suggested we order Thai, which she did silently from her phone without even asking me what I wanted; she got one of everything. When the hunched-over sweaty teen arrived with a dozen red plastic bags of food, I peeled with embarrassment. I refused to make eye contact with the kid, feeling caught in having become something I shouldn't have: comfortable in one of these beach houses and ordering one of everything.

Just as I'd decanted papaya salad and Pad Thai onto our plates, Chrissy burst through the door.

"Knock, knock. So, I heard through the grapevine there was a new model in town?"

Chrissy sauntered over to Tabitha, smothering her in a gust of perfume and cashmere.

"How are you doing, sweetheart?"

"I'm fine," Tabitha said coolly, returning to her plate.

"And how's it going in the studio?" Chrissy said looking at Tabitha's canvas, which was still just gray underpainting.

"Umm, it's going well," I replied mid-bite. I wanted Chrissy to leave, I felt like she was sucking out all the air in the room.

"I'd like to invite you girls over for dinner this weekend. I'll have a big case behind me and I'd love to celebrate. Does that sound good?"

I waited for Tabitha to respond first, "Sure, when?"

"How about Friday, seven thirty."

I smiled, Chrissy's phone rang and she answered, then waved to us and traipsed out and across the lawn.

We spent the afternoon in a cocoon of warmth. Tabitha took dozens of videos of my hands as they painted the canvas, along with selfies of herself posing in the chair. She spent an hour editing them together and adding automated voice-overs, which she workshopped with me.

"Does this sound good?" She held up her phone, which was broadcasting the captions in a droll voice, "Here I am getting my portrait painted like the mother-fucking-queen-I-am."

I nodded.

When Tabitha paused from filming, she asked, "So, when you just randomly met my mom at that opening, she was like, 'I want portraits made,' or like did you give her the idea?"

"It was her idea," I said, which felt like a generous lie.

"It's just surprising."

"Why?"

"Because she was a total bitch right before she died, family portraits didn't really seem on the agenda."

"Oh, I'm sorry."

"She was just different at the end, like colder. That's what I keep thinking about."

"How so?" I asked.

"I don't know, we didn't really get along."

I cocked my head as if to ask why, and she looked suddenly engulfed in sadness. She took a careful sip of Coke Zero, then seemed to let it go.

"Well for starters, I'm pro-Trump," Tabitha said with a laugh, stood, and began practicing one of her dances, crossing her hands across her waist then dropping her hips, ending with a disconcerting smile toward the fictional camera which was me.

"And Mom wanted me to come like help with this fucking WAC project in Kenya. And like, I don't know. It sucked. It was hot and gross. And like my friend Tamen was having a birthday party in Mallorca, and I didn't want to miss it. We got into a—fight."

Tabitha paused, there was something stony and unsettling about how she'd said the word *fight*. I remembered back to the description of the metal pencil case imprinting on her classmate's face. Tabitha looked up, then released a cherub's smile, as if she could see me doing the arithmetic on her cruelty.

"We barely talked since then, but Mallorca was really cute. I got a tattoo."

I was stuck on the fight in Kenya, how Naomi had been abandoned to her disappointment while Tabitha soared off to some glitzy birthday party on a stone cliff, with white linen tablecloths, champagne, and stick-and-pokes. A hush settled between us.

"Do you think your mom and dad were on good terms before she died?"

"What?"

"I was just curious."

"My mom and dad had a weird relationship. My dad always said mom was crazy, she had some, I don't know—issues. But

I also stopped paying attention to them like a bazillion years ago. Why are you asking me this? That's random as fuck."

"Sorry," I said sheepishly. "So, they weren't fighting?"

"I mean, my dad is ultracontrolling. Like with money, and well, everything. He can flip when things don't go his way, so they fought a lot."

"How does he *flip?*" I asked, trying to hide my searing interest.

"The man can rage," Tabitha said as she picked up her phone. "Like he doesn't take no for an answer. He always tells me, *business is war*, and I'm like, *Dad, it's TikTok.*"

"Would he kill someone?" I asked bluntly, then regretted it.

Tabitha burst out laughing, she thought I was joking. I flickered with relief.

"Honestly. There isn't anything he wouldn't do to protect Red Rock," Tabitha said as her chuckles faded, "he's ruthless."

Then she began scrolling. I was left to stare at the symmetry of her features and wonder how Bryce had pulled it off.

An hour later Tabitha opened a bottle of wine, it was only five p.m., but we drained two glasses.

"You know, the truth is, someone took a video of me doing coke at a nightclub and put in online. That's why I'm actually out here."

"I'm sorry."

"I mean, as if I'm the first person to do coke, but like it was either go to rehab or disappear for a month. My manager is barring me from posting which feels insane and is why I'm just editing these videos over and over and over."

"I'm sorry."

"I mean, after mom died, I partied for like a week straight. Which I know sounds fucked up, but it kept it from being real."

I nodded, "My mom also died."

"How?" Tabitha asked too quickly.

"In a car crash."

"Oh." She said, unsure of how to continue.

"What happened to your mom in Aspen?"

"You mean like on the slope?"

I nodded.

"I guess her ski boot malfunctioned, and broke out of the holder or whatever, and she was going really fast. I wasn't there. They said it was over in an instant. Freak accident. I stayed at the hotel restaurant because I was hungover but I keep thinking that like, if I'd just gone . . . then maybe it would have been different."

Staring at Tabitha, her green eyes and overly moisturized skin, my heart opened. Whatever slivers of journalistic-podcaster distance I had maintained melted away. She was just like me.

"Someone is to blame—but it's not you," I said, my voice filled with assurance.

"What do you mean?"

"I mean, there is no such thing as an accident."

"You mean like manifest destiny—or whatever?"

I was revealing too much. I needed to backpedal, "I'm just trying to say, I get it."

The next few days cruised by in the lazy calypso of two friends on vacation, but instead of long stints on a towel slathered in SPF, we sat on a tarp and I stared at Tabitha, translating her body with linseed oil and pigment. I understood exactly what Tabitha was going through, but I also knew she didn't understand how to help herself. Doing coke in clubs wasn't going to bring justice for her mother. I was no closer to figuring out what had happened, but at least I was determined.

Friday, the night of our dinner with Chrissy, arrived. "Honestly, I find her grating," Tabitha said while watching herself rhythmically roll her arms in the darkened reflection of the window. "Let's cancel and order Chinese."

I was relieved. Tabitha texted saying she felt sick and batted off Chrissy's insistence to drop off food. I put in a few hours filling out the texture of Tabitha's hair in the painting, then we spent the evening watching a reality TV show about airbrushed women in cartoon-villain power suits selling real estate.

When I woke up Tabitha was in the kitchen tapping her aquamarine gel-tipped nails on a fresh can of Coke Zero. "It's my dad's birthday, I have to go back to the city," she took a sip, "I told him about the portraits. He wants to meet you."

A chill descended on my shoulders. It was Bryce's birthday. All of Naomi's plans were supposed to unfold today. How could I have forgotten the date? I felt a strange surge of energy, then fear; I was not prepared to meet Bryce or return to the city.

"A car is coming to pick us up in like thirty. You should pack."

"What about your portrait?" I huffed desperately, motioning to the half-finished canvas, trying to create a reason for me to stay.

"We'll come back out in like a few days. I wanted to avoid going, but obviously with everything, I have to be there with my dad. And don't you have to paint him also?"

"I just hate New York City," I said without thinking.

"But you live in Bushwick?"

I nodded. I'd forgotten I was Jessica who lived off the Myrtle-Wyckoff stop. I hadn't even had coffee; I wasn't ready for this sort of disruption to our pattern. Then, without knocking, Chrissy's assistant appeared in the glass square of the door frame carrying a person-size black box with a gilded black ribbon.

"This is for Bryce," the assistant said neatly. Tabitha wordlessly nodded.

Forty-one short minutes later, unable to come up with an excuse, I found myself hurtling down the Long Island Expressway with all my paint supplies in the trunk, and Chrissy's huge black box cutting the circulation off of my legs.

10

"So, you met her at a dinner?"

I nodded.

"Where exactly?"

"Franco's, after an exhibition of Memphis Emerald."

Bryce was much more incisive than I had imagined. In photos his face seemed dull and lifeless, but I could see now he was alert with the air of a human calculator, doing the math on my story. I told him the lines I'd already fed Chrissy and Tabitha, including Naomi's comments on legacy.

"Dad, she's cool. And a really good painter," Tabitha said without looking up from her phone. Bryce took an awkward inhale, his hand firmly placed on the large mahogany bar in the kitchen.

"Well, who is supposed to have this portrait? I mean, where is it supposed to hang when it's done? What were her intentions?"

"She just hired me to paint them, I have no idea what her plans were."

Bryce released a spike of air that I couldn't quite read, maybe disbelief.

"Dad chill, she has her stuff with her," Tabitha said shifting her head in the direction of the empty canvas leaning in the entranceway, "you just have to sit there. Just indulge in the last of mom's nuttery."

Bryce looked at Tabitha and softened and I instantly saw the demented hall of mirrors that had been constructed for daddy's little angel; Bryce might be a control freak, but Tabitha controlled her father. Bryce turned toward the large stainless-steel fridge to remove a glass cylinder of what looked like carrot juice, then nodded to me, "I can give you one hour tomorrow."

The birthday's order of events had been explained to me by Tabitha: dinner then a movie, his tradition. The chef of Bryce's favorite Brazilian restaurant always came over in the afternoon and prepared a massive feast, and then they'd project a movie on the hulking empty wall in the living room. "This is what we do every year," Tabitha said quietly. I tried to act surprised, as if I hadn't seen dozens of photos of the family propped up on oversize white pillows. "We were supposed to have a bunch of people, and like performers, and speeches, and even some fancy videographer. Mom went all out 'cause it's his sixtieth, but dad's depressed so it's just going to be small. Total sausage fest, mostly work dudes."

I feigned fatigue as Tabitha pointed me up the stairs toward the guest room, but her eyes were glued to her phone and didn't even clock my faux yawn. Once alone in the hall I looked around, the house was completely void of detail. No art. No carpets or framed family pictures, just a stark modernist mansion in the sky with ebony floors. In the guest room I instantly recognized the white Frette bedding, the same as in the Hamptons, and released an audible chord of relief. After taking a shower I called Blick Art Materials and made a next-day order for linseed oil, rags, and paint tubes. I was nervous about painting Bryce, worried that in the process he would see through me.

The annoying digital doorbell began ringing at six sharp. I was on edge. Was I supposed to join the party? It felt surreal that the sixtieth birthday where the scrapbooks were supposed to be revealed was taking place beneath my feet. I wondered how Naomi had hoped to present the books; would she have wheeled them in on a cart? Or maybe she'd have had him laboriously unwrap all forty tomes as the bored guests watched on? I knew to unsuspecting eyes the books would have seemed like a sweet, albeit over the top, gesture of love and family. How quickly would Bryce have realized something was off? Would he even take the time to flip through the pages to recognize the asset assessments while his guests ate coxinhas? Would he have contained his reaction? Or blown up on the spot?

A little after seven I heard a tap on my door. It was Tabitha.

"Are you coming or what?" she asked, wearing a slinky satin yellow frock, her hair still tied up in a messy high ponytail. I felt underdressed as I shuffled behind Tabitha's clacking green heels. The large kitchen was buzzing. A chef in a comically crisp outfit was stirring a large pot on the stove. The buffet was covered in fried foods and salads with a proud plate of glistening meat perched on a metal rack in the center. Bryce was talking to a group of men all in near-matching pale blue button ups. There were a few I recognized from the scrapbooks. I had no idea how to behave.

"Do you have friends coming?" I asked Tabitha as I ate a fried fish ball.

"Well, I'm currently canceled. So, no."

I nodded; it reaffirmed why Tabitha was so open to our friendship: she had been tossed into the digital wastebasket. Tabitha shrugged then poured herself more champagne. The dinner dragged on with the guests all serving their strange linguistic sandwiches of condolences and birthday greetings. Naomi's death hung like grease in the air and no ventilation system, no matter how state-of-the-art, could remove it. I studied Bryce's face every time her name was mentioned, looking for signs of guilt: a slash of perverse pleasure, a twinkle of malice, but he never slipped.

A guy drinking a Rolling Rock and laughing near the fridge started telling a story about a robbery gone wrong in Queens;

the punch line was that the getaway driver had an epileptic seizure on the highway. All the pale blue shirts laughed in matching walrus tones.

"Who is that?" I asked Tabitha bitterly.

"That's Conor Copeland, he's like the city police commissioner or something."

I remembered him from the dossier. He went fly-fishing with Bryce every year. My stomach acid began to boil, I thought about spilling my drink on his khakis or spitting down the slick green barrel of his Rolling Rock when he wasn't looking. Yes, I hated everyday cops, the racist meat bags that pulled over drivers for being Black and failed to take domestic battery seriously—but what I really hated was police administrators. The men who sat at desks. The background warlords of corrupt ineptitude. I glared at him over the rim of my glass; he was tall with broad shoulders and had the rubbery face of someone who had long since abandoned his morals.

"Am I blocking your way?" he asked, noticing my stare, assuming I was trying to get to the buffet.

"I just don't find epilepsy funny," I said without thinking, then turned to walk away, reminding myself that I needed to keep my cool. I couldn't risk stirring trouble. Not now. Not here. Not as Jessica Washington. Not with Bryce *who figures everything out.*

We all filed into the living room where the fat white cushions already dotted the black floor. Tabitha never looked up from her phone for a single frame of *L.A. Confidential.* It was a predictable dad-movie choice, and I'd already seen it, so I let myself space out. I thought about Jessica, about our beautiful house and the baby we never had. I wondered if she was trying to get pregnant with her new girlfriend. Maybe she'd kept that fertility clinic appointment. And then I thought about Michael Valentine who was probably in his apartment only a few blocks away, watching Netflix and cupping his balls. Being in the city made him feel too close. When the lights came up, I noticed a few of the blue-shirts had already crept out, including police commissioner Conor Copeland. Everyone got up to say goodbye. That was it. An utterly boring birthday. I wished I could have wheeled out the forty scrapbooks just to liven things up.

The next morning Bryce was in the kitchen reading the *Financial Times*. I always loved the dusty pink of the paper and took a moment to enjoy the sharp white light from the windows cutting across the top of the bowed rectangle.

"Let's get this over with," he said, closing the paper.

"You mean the portrait?"

"Yes," he replied curtly.

"The light in here is nice," I said.

"I have until one thirty."

While I set up the easel and removed my palette from the hastily applied Hamptons cling wrap, Bryce settled into the slice of light that split through the room. He then closed his eyes. I waited for him to reopen. Five minutes passed. Nothing. Then another five passed. In all of my time painting portraits, no one had simply closed their eyes. Maybe it was something one did at the dentist or while getting their hair washed at a salon—but this felt positively serial killer-esque and affirmed my beliefs: Bryce had something to hide.

"So, how does sixty feel?" I asked a half hour in, hoping to get him to open his lids to make sure he wasn't just asleep.

"Fine," he responded.

"I'm so sorry about Naomi," I sputtered.

Silence. Eyes still closed. It felt impossible for me to pry with this set-up.

"You know, she was really excited about having me paint you," I lobbed.

"I'm only doing this because Tabitha requested. If it's ok, I'd really rather not talk."

I gulped and continued painting. Ten minutes later, Bryce grunted, indicating our session was over.

The next day, the ritual repeated, I walked down to the kitchen where he was reading the paper, and he assumed his position, eyes closed.

After a silent hour, he finally croaked, "Let me know when you get to the eyes."

I jumped at the sound of his voice.

"Soon, but not yet," I replied, now nervous for him to look at me.

In the middle of filling out the weight on his cheeks, a beeping sound chopped through the room from Bryce's phone, which was sitting behind me on the counter. I turned, startled. The ID read *Chrissy Ash*, her big blonde face filling the screen. Bryce sprang to life, removing the object from the buffet, then bounded out of the room to answer.

As I stood alone in the kitchen, I remembered the way Chrissy talked about Bryce, how her body surged whenever he came up, and her habit of overusing his name. When Bryce finally returned to his position near the window, I noticed his cheeks were slightly flushed, his shoulders oddly proud, and I felt a burning suspicion: he was fucking Chrissy Ash. It would explain the oversize gift she'd forced us to deliver. Had Naomi known? Was that why Chrissy hadn't been her divorce lawyer? I tried to keep my face blank as I painted Bryce.

"Could you open your eyes?" I finally asked, wanting to see what was there: maybe an answer. He did. And I jumped. His eyes were too bright. I felt like an animal who knew instinctively they needed to run; they were being hunted. I quickly filled in the whites, mixed ochre with a dark brown to fill out the pupils.

A few minutes later Bryce shifted his weight. "So, how did you and Naomi communicate?"

"What do you mean?" I replied, uneasily.

"I haven't been able to find any mention of the paintings in her emails."

He was staring directly at me. Why was he reading her emails? I inhaled, then added more yellow to my paintbrush.

"She wanted it to be a secret, since it was a Christmas present, she was very insistent about that. We only spoke on the phone. Why?" I asked.

"Just . . . wanted to make sure you had been paid for your work."

I could tell he was lying, but I had no choice but to play along, "Yes, she did. Cash."

"How much?"

"Two thousand per painting," I lied. I would have charged ten times that, but making it cheaper made cash seem reasonable.

"I'm still trying to sort out her accounts," he said tightly.

I was grateful his eyes were shut again. I finished up the painting as fast as possible without saying another word.

Even in the plush guest bed I could barely sleep; my mind was rotating like a fidget spinner on the axis of Naomi's paranoia and Bryce's questions; she had been right to be careful. In the morning I was groggy while painting and certain that Bryce's laser eyes were drilling directly into my brain. I tried to stay focused. Then again at 12:15 on the dime his phone rang, and he answered and exited toward the living room. It was Chrissy calling on her lunch hour. I sat in the kitchen feeling clammy and certain; an affair was motive, but I needed proof. When Bryce returned, he kept his cold eyes on me and I flew through the motions, finishing his painting that afternoon, in a tenth of the time I'd taken with Tabitha.

"It looks good," Tabitha said, filming the canvas then zooming into her dad's face seated in the window.

Bryce got up to look at it, "It looks like me."

"That's as big as a compliment you'll get," Tabitha said with a wry smile.

I nodded graciously.

"I have to get to work, I'm really not sure what to do with this?" he said, indicating the painting.

"I mean, you hang it on the wall," Tabitha said with Valley-girl twang, "Never mind, you're the minimalist Nazi." Bryce looked at his daughter like she'd just taken a shit on the floor.

"Don't speak to me like that."

"I'm just saying . . ." she let her gel tips flutter around the stark room, then released a sigh, "never mind, it was a joke."

Bryce checked his watch.

Tabitha pulled out her phone, "Well whatever, hopefully it's the last of mom's gifts from the grave."

Bryce looked uncomfortable but said nothing. I thought about my own desire to have a child. What if it turned out like this? What if we said terrible things to each other under track lighting in a travertine kitchen?

"Jessica and I are going back to the Hamptons," Tabitha clipped, "I want to finish this TikTok of my portrait."

"Tabitha you're not supposed to be posting," Bryce chided.

"I'm not. Just editing it together . . ."

"Well, I'll be out on Friday," Bryce added.

"Why?"

"To see you," he said, then turned to exit.

Tabitha postponed our return to the Hamptons by a day, something to do with meeting with her agent to plot her media comeback. So, I was left alone in the massive apartment with the fleet of housekeepers. While fishing leftovers out of the fridge, I could hear the faint sound of a vacuum bumping in another room and I took the opportunity to slip into Bryce's office, which was at the far end of the first floor. It was stark. All black wood, which matched the black floors and black desk. Six large windows looked out at Central Park. Three modernist leather chairs sat next to a glass table. Again, no art. No decorative lamps or even an ornate envelope opener or tape dispenser. I walked behind the large desk and sat in the swivel chair. I could understand Naomi's urge to hoard when in this house. Everything was too clean. My fingers were still greasy from the cold coxinhas I'd eaten, and I trailed my index finger along the center of the desk, leaving a perfect smudge.

Next, I looked through the cabinets on the right side of the desk, which were filled with binders. I leafed through the pages: floor plans of the apartment, a map of the electrical wiring, paperwork from contractors, and household bills. I assumed Bryce had his real office with the real paperwork at Red Rock Capital. In the top shelf of the desk sat a beveled silver cup with three pens: red, black, and blue; a pair of scissors; and a stack of perfectly aligned paper clips. A chill moved down my spine at the extreme order of the drawer as I realized then that Bryce would have lost his mind looking at the scrapbooks, not even because of their contents, but their glaring craftiness. I moved on to the next room, which was similarly furnished but more diminutive in scale. The only decorative embellishment was on the windowsill; five lumps of rose quartz which were arranged in descending order, largest to smallest. This was Naomi's office.

I sat behind the desk and opened the bottom drawer. Sure enough, sitting on the shelf was a white Container Store box with a tapered bottom, just like the hundreds I had in my barn. I held my breath and opened the lid, but it was empty. I closed my eyes and tried to imagine Naomi sitting at the desk, her well-moisturized hand dipping out of sight to deposit an envelope of Duane Reade photos into the box. When I opened, I looked down and realized I was bleeding through my jeans.

I'd left a small spot on Naomi's black rolling chair. Barely noticeable, just a slick black circle the size of a dime. It felt somehow fitting: the trail of grease on Bryce's desk, and my blood now on Naomi's chair. Proof I had been here. Proof I was getting closer. I wandered up to Tabitha's room hoping she had a tampon or pad. I knocked loudly on the door frame but there was no answer so I let myself in. The room was a teenage fantasy, like Cher Horowitz's closet in *Clueless* on ketamine; each corner of the room was a perfectly styled set, replete with its own tonality and ready-to-roll ring lighting, and each I recognized from various TikTok videos and Instagram posts.

I walked to the bathroom which boasted four more ring lights on moveable stands, the whole place felt like a spa for the camera. Everything marble. Everything clean. Everything organized. A cell phone holder attached with a suction device was mounted to the center of the mirror. I opened the top drawer of the vanity and found hundreds of lipstick tubes and eye makeup in every conceivable shade. The next shelf held dozens of brushes laid out on crushed pink velvet, and it dawned on me: this was the epicenter of Tabitha. Like being inside of her brain. And looking at her vast array of makeup brushes I realized how similar it was to my own painting practice. I understood why she had liked sitting for me so much; she was both a painter and a canvas, coaxing herself into reality with brushstrokes every morning.

After a few minutes, once the glamour of the bathroom had faded, I felt the operatic solitude of Tabitha. She spent all this time getting dressed up while her audience remained invisible; tucked away in their own bedrooms and cubicles. Tabitha was simply an image on a phone in a sweaty palm. She was fiction. Something to be devoured like a bag of potato chips. I opened the other shelves, two contained nail polish, one contained tiny samples that were neatly organized in bamboo trays, but there were no tampons. Maybe she was beyond bleeding. So fictional she didn't need to bother herself with the shedding of her uterine lining. I hastily grabbed a wad of toilet paper and made an impromptu pad. Unlike Tabitha, I bled in buckets.

Since the house was empty, I decided to keep looking. I wanted to find where they stored their skis. I imagined there might be a clue or some message from Naomi about the crash, evidence that Bryce had tampered with her bindings or pushed her down the hill. After wandering through the rooms of the gym on the first floor, I found a closet lined with sports equipment. Two pairs of skis were mounted to the wall but one rack was empty; Naomi's had never come home.

I sulked back to the guest room to get my coat, then shuffled along the sludgy bank of the sidewalk trying to avoid the piss-stained snow, and eventually found myself outside of Duane Reade. The store's wet gray carpet glistened with the glop of the street and the overhead lighting felt like a slap in the face. Without thinking I wandered to the photo printing area and touched the worn-down keyboard; Naomi had been here. All those photos of the family had been rendered by this machine: the whites of their smiling eyes and the flame red of Naomi's hair. The printer nozzles knew the Duncans intimately, just as I did. Eventually, I moved past an exasperated mother and her toddler to the sanitary napkin aisle. I wrinkled with disgust at the term "sanitary napkin," as if I were covered in ketchup and simply needed a wiping off.

"Yo bitch, are you fucking joking?" A voice cut across the store, just as I'd reached for a bundle of pads.

I looked up in horror; it was Memphis Emerald holding a thin paper bag, filled with what was probably Adderall. Unsure how to respond, I waved my wad of pads.

"Why didn't you call? Why the fuck are you in town?"

"I'm, uhhh," I mumbled, knowing I couldn't tell her the truth. "I'm uhh, just here for a class—bookmaking stuff."

"That's great. Well, you have no fucking choice, you have to come to dinner tonight. Kristian Weber is in town from the Kunsthalle Basel, and we're going to Franco's."

"I can't, I have . . . class."

"Well, get out of it. That's your punishment for not calling."

I could feel a small clot of blood sliding out, then absorb into the abyss of my underwear. I needed to plug my hole. I felt a wave of frustration at Memphis for having caught me here. I didn't want to have to deal with my old life, I was supposed to be figuring out what the fuck happened to Naomi. But I reminded myself that Franco's was the point of origin, and maybe returning to the restaurant where I'd sat across from Naomi would unlodge something.

"Bitch, you're coming," Memphis was texting, her chewed up nails stuttering across the glass.

"Fine but I have to run, I'm bleeding," I nodded to the pads.

"Always dramatic, see you at eight. Don't be late."

I had grown accustomed to the emptiness of the Duncans' and was surprised to find Tabitha splayed out on the white couch in the foyer. Her face fully done-up with glitter, wearing a tiny outfit with five twisted buns that crowned her head.

"Where were you?" she asked.

"Duane Reade."

"Gross."

"How was your meeting?"

Tabitha huffed, "Fine, actually, they liked the videos I made of you painting my portrait, they think it's—" she made bunny ears—"*wholesome*. And will, like, make a good follow up to my apology video or whatever."

"Oh cool," I said nonchalantly, "just don't put my face on the internet."

"Lol, I know," Tabitha shot back.

I felt nauseous as I backed down the hall to the guest bedroom. The air in the apartment was heavy. What had Bryce done? Whatever had happened to Naomi was radiating through the hallways, a poisonous gas I couldn't see or understand. Once I got to my room I curled up in bed, closed my eyes, then, immediately, received a text from Memphis confirming dinner. The last thing I wanted to do was go out. I just wanted to bleed to death in my Frette sheets.

I took the train downtown. The hostess, this one with geometric tattoos adorning her neck, waved me to the table and I was horrified to see that the Chilean Swiss curator was scrolling through his phone by himself. Where the fuck was Memphis? I tried to duck my head and turn, hoping to wait outside, but the curator made eye contact with me. I was stuck. I walked over.

"Hi, I'm Kristian—are you Memphis's friend?"

"Yes, I'm Esther."

He didn't remember me. I'd sat next to him at an after-dinner for a show of a Belgian artist at PS1 where he had talked endlessly of his love of Brazil, and how he was planning on buying a house in São Paulo. But he was one of those fags who couldn't remember women. I hated gay misogynists. They were worse than the plain-old straight misogynists because women weren't even worth fucking to them. I sat down, taking him in; he was short and muscly, wearing a low-cut T-shirt that was aggressively white and expensive.

I craned my neck to the left where I could see the table that Naomi and I had sat at. Four NYU girls who all looked like watered-down versions of Tabitha, with too-tanned skin and thin gold jewelry rattling on their collarbones, were competitively talking. I wanted to close my eyes, to roll backward in time and see Naomi; the way her face had lit up when she'd described her *special project* and how she'd leaned her head in to ask me if I'd be interested in working on the scrapbooks, but I couldn't do any time traveling with this man staring at me.

"Zo, how do you know Memphis?" Kristian asked lethargically.

"We went to art school together."

"Ah ja, great school."

"How do you know Memphis?" I replied dumbly.

"Ve are working on a show for next fall, at zee Kunsthalle Basel. Ve are very excited."

An unexpected sprig of jealousy crept up my throat. Ever since getting sucked into the gold-leafed world of the Duncans, my long-abandoned ambitions had returned in unsettling waves. Maybe I wanted a show at the Kunsthalle Basel?

"Let's order some wine, shall ve?"

I nodded as he selected a Grauburgunder, noting the *excellent soil* in Baden. We sat in silence as we sipped, Kristian engrossed in his phone, me watching the NYU girls, then finally, Memphis stumbled through the door in a startlingly trendy outfit replete with large sunglasses and cowboy hat.

"Darling, you look amazzzing," Kristian squealed with new energy.

"It's chic right? Gucci gave it to me, I'm in the next campaign. They shot in my studio, insane right?"

I smiled, remembering why I wanted nothing to do with the art world.

Dinner was a meeting. Kristian ignored me completely as they discussed the number of works and the hang of the show, Kristian going so far as to ask the waiter for a pen to draw a diagram on a piece of paper. I let my mind trail off, finishing off glass after glass of wine; every now and then I would throw in a "that sounds great" or "cool," and continue staring at that corner of NYU girls, willing the ghost of Naomi to enter and shoo them off so we could continue our conversation from all those months ago. Memphis kept glancing at me, and when Kristian went to the bathroom, she put her hand on my leg.

"Are you all right? I didn't realize this would be so work heavy."

I nodded to indicate I was fine.

"Why do you keep staring at those girls?"

The NYU foursome were now drinking glasses of prosecco. I didn't know what to say but Memphis's hand on my leg felt uniquely stabilizing, like a ballast. I released a sigh, and in the buttery glow of the restaurant, I was hit with a sense of relief; I could tell Memphis about Naomi. Memphis was already part of the story; it had been her gallery opening where I'd met Naomi. Maybe she knew something, maybe she could even help? The waiter returned and refilled our wine.

As I watched the liquid throttle into the glasses, it dawned on me how alone I had been in the past months. I hadn't even told Memphis about my breakup with Jessica. And I knew if I explained the scrapbooks, she would sigh, and tell me that I was obsessing over someone else's problems again. She'd tell me to get on a plane to North Carolina, get my shit together, get back to the studio and just pretend like none of this ever happened. Maybe that was what I wanted to hear. Before I could let it all fall out, Kristian returned to the table.

"Should we go to Boiler?" he asked.

Memphis, who was *very* dressed to go out, lit up. I shrank. The Boiler Room was a gay bar about two blocks away, a seedy packed shithole filled with gropey gays and their overexcited straight best girlfriends. I fantasized about strangling Kristian.

"How often do you get to go out-out. You live in a cabin in the woods," Memphis chided.

I needed to talk with Memphis. I would follow.

Kristian was now brimming with hot air, or maybe cocaine. His eyes were bulging and he was buzzing as he ordered a round of tequila Red Bulls while greedily taking in the crowd of boys. I leaned my head into Memphis, feeling as if I was about to bubble over.

"Do you remember that woman who I sat next to at your gallery dinner?"

"No," Memphis replied flatly.

"Naomi Duncan. Red hair, wearing like, a giant chunk of rose quartz around her neck."

"Not ringing any bells," Memphis said taking a swig. "Oh, wait, the bazillionaire."

"Yes, well she hired me to work for her and now she's dead . . ."

"She died?"

I nodded.

"How?"

"Skiing accident."

Memphis made an intrigued head bob, "She is, I mean *was*, a really good friend of my gallerist. I think she worked with her on some water thing."

"Exactly. WAC. Well, she hired me to work for her on this project . . ."

Kristian screamed something in Memphis's ear. I paused. All the curatorial diplomacy had evaporated; the gay bar had released some sort of demonic energy in him. He was smiling grotesquely as twinks walked by. In one seal-like gesture, he downed his cocktail and hoisted himself onto one of the pleather stools to order a round of shots.

"What sort of project?" Memphis asked, returning her head to mine.

The bartender couldn't understand Kristian. He screamed the order again holding up three fingers. I felt a rush of strange, spine-tingling air. A force felt like it was holding me

154

still. I paused, then shook it off, and just as I was about to open my mouth to tell Memphis about the scrapbooks, Kristian lost his footing and slammed to the ground, his nose catching the metal rim of the stool. He screamed. His snow-white shirt was covered in a fan of bright blood. Memphis called to the bartender for a first aid kit. Gauze appeared and was quickly applied. And I just stood there, watching it as if it were happening to complete strangers, the air still cold and tingly around me. And in the bloody-disco chaos, I felt certain it had been Naomi that had caused the accident; I hadn't been able to tell Memphis what she had hired me to do. Her secret was still safe. I decided to slip into the crowd, past the coat check and out into the dark. It felt fitting. The day was haloed in blood.

When I got back, no one appeared to be awake at the Duncans'. I was halfway to the guest room when I noticed the big black box Chrissy Ash had sent, propped up in Bryce's office. I walked over. The card had been opened and was resting on top. I looked around to make sure no one was watching, then lifted it to read.

To my darling B.
With all the love in the world.
C.

I made a triumphant huff; I knew it. Just as I was putting the card back, a voice cut through the stillness of the hall.

"What are you doing?"

It was Bryce. I turned, my stomach hard with alcohol and fear. I said nothing.

"What are you doing?" he asked again.

"I was just, curious what the—the—present was," I stuttered.

Bryce walked out of the hall's shadow. "Golf clubs."

"That's nice," I said uneasily.

"It is. I've been meaning to ask you, Jessica. Where did you go to school?"

I gulped. I didn't have much time.

11

It was late afternoon and the Hamptons were already dark and deathly silent. We had spent the morning after our arrival working on Tabitha's portrait but she had been called into another meeting with her agent. After a few hours alone, zoning out to TV, I was drawn into the yard by the shifting glow of the lights in the main kitchen. I watched as Tabitha sat on one of the tall blond chairs, crying while filming herself. She kept starting, then stopping to replay the video on her phone. Repositioning. Changing the lighting, then briefly turning the waterworks back on. When she finally settled into a frame, she began to talk, punctuated by controlled sobs. What was she doing? Eventually she paused recording and I pushed open the door.

"Everything ok?" I asked.

"Oh yeah, sorry, just my apology video."

"For what?"

"My followers, just like explaining my dark spiral and battle with depression after my mom died, hence the coke in the club video. Honestly, it's not my first, but this one is easy thanks to the dead-mom-card," she said with a low dry laugh.

I felt a heavy sadness curl its way down my spine. Tabitha checked her face in the screen, then applied a smear of lip gloss.

"I'm going to go for a walk," I muttered.

On the beach I took a gulp of salt air. The truth of the situation had surfaced, and it was a classic; Bryce was having an affair with Chrissy, so Naomi had wanted a divorce. I tried to

157

imagine Naomi in her scarves and beaded necklaces, on the beach having a Nicole Kidman moment, eyes glistening, looking out at the dark frothing waves. I felt a profound ache for her. I knew Red Rock Capital's fund was built off Naomi's father's fortune so it was easy enough to see that Bryce foresaw losing everything in the divorce. Naomi's death was too convenient to be an accident, and on top of all of that, it was obvious that Bryce was suspicious of me, but I was resolute, Naomi deserved justice.

It is always the husband. I had listened to almost every episode of *Dateline*. I could hear the host, Lester Holt, spitting some cheap line about how *it was a perfect Christmas day on the slopes of Aspen for the Duncan family, until it went sideways—right down the mountain.* But where was my proof? As I was turning back, I was struck with the sinking feeling that the proof, whatever it was, was in my barn— hidden somewhere in the scrapbooks. On the way back home, I called George at the post office.

"Hi George, it's me, Esther Ray, I wanted to ask if you could do me a favor. I'm out of town, and I've left my spare key with Patrick Nelson, but I can't seem to find his number, guess I've misplaced it . . . do you happen to have it?"

George loved his role as mountain switchboard, and rattled off Patrick's cell.

"Hello?" Patrick answered skeptically.

"Hi Patrick, it's me, Esther, your neighbor."

"Oh, hi. The power's been back on for a while, but I did charge my phone and computer there, hope that's all right."

I'd nearly forgotten about the blackout. "I'm calling because, well . . . I have a weird favor . . ."

I knew we weren't on even ground, but he was the only person I could ask.

"You know how you were able to figure out my friend," I added a dramatic pause, "who's dead," then continued, "was getting a divorce from looking at the numbers in those books I had in the barn. Could you look at them again, and see if you see anything else?"

There was a padded silence.

"I can take a look but I don't know what good it will do," Patrick said uncertainly.

"I'd really owe you."

"But what are you looking for?"

"Well, firstly I'd like to see if you can figure out who she was preparing her divorce with, if it was a lawyer or an attorney," I inhaled, "and maybe just like skim the numbers, let me know if anything seems off. I think the husband was having an affair."

"All right . . . I can't make any promises. You all right?"

"I'm fine," I responded, startled by his attentiveness, "I just really need to help my friend. The key to the barn is hanging next to the kitchen door, on a red lanyard. Thanks Patrick."

I hung up. As I entered the backyard, I saw Chrissy in the living room of the main house talking with Tabitha, I slipped past the window and retreated into the guesthouse, trying to avoid whatever conversation they were having. A few minutes later Tabitha appeared in the kitchen in one of her signature oversize hoodies.

"So, I guess Chrissy wants us to eat dinner with her tonight, I couldn't get out of it."

I nodded. At the very least it would give me an opportunity to try and find solid proof she was fucking Bryce.

"Sounds great," I said.

"Whatever," she lobbed.

Two hours later we walked the hedged drive and turned into Chrissy's, the gate rolling back before we could even ring. The housekeeper, dressed in a muted blue uniform, opened the door, exclaiming with bass-y vibrato, "Welcome. Chrissy will see you in the kitchen." Tabitha didn't take her shoes off, which felt deranged, as the whole house was dotted with cream carpets and we'd just traipsed through the soggy driveway, but I followed her lead.

"Hi dear," Chrissy gave Tabitha a deep hug while I sipped from the champagne flute I'd just been handed.

"What a gorgeous night," Chrissy said in high hostess mood. "So, how was the city?"

I smiled; Tabitha replied with a monosyllabic "Good."

"And did Bryce like his clubs?"

Tabitha stared blankly.

"My present," Naomi clucked, "the golf clubs."

I flinched remembering back to meeting Bryce in the hall.

"Yeah, he did," Tabitha replied.

"Well, you know, Jessica, I've been really enjoying my painting. I'm trying to figure out where to hang it. It just feels so beautiful that Naomi, bless her, brought us all together. I've been meditating on how meaningful it is."

I nodded.

"Here's to Naomi," Chrissy said holding up her glass.

"To Naomi," Tabitha and I added, but not nearly as brightly.

"You know, I am still so amazed that this happened, and that she opened up so much to you, Jessica."

I smiled cautiously. Chrissy began to refill our glasses.

"You know your mom talked with Jessica about Marcella-Marie? Isn't that incredible."

Tabitha shook her head, her face suddenly sullen.

"It just makes me think that maybe she was finding her peace. You know, I was chatting with Stella, our friend from California. And I told her it feels somehow like destiny, or fate, that we get to be here together."

My heart fluttered. *Fate.* The bizarre wind that had carried me to this overly pruned piece of earth.

"Well, I hope you like conchiglie ripiene, it's vegan, but I shouldn't have told you that because you would have never known."

Chrissy's striped pot-holdered hand pulled out a tray of bubbling green-and-red goo.

"It looks great."

"I've set us up in the formal dining room. I always eat in the kitchen, so it's nice to change it up with company."

We followed Chrissy and her steaming pan into a room with vaulted ceilings that overlooked their backyard. The mahogany table was set with bright yellow china, and a crooked bottle of white wine sat in a bucket next to a fluffed spinach salad. Tabitha sat down, but kept her nose glued to her phone; I sensed Chrissy wanted to swat the rectangle out of her hand.

"Are you having a nice break from TikTok?" Chrissy asked Tabitha glibly.

Tabitha nodded.

"I mean, I think digital detoxes are so important. Jessica, would you like some salad?"

"Sure," I replied.

Just as I was extending my plate, I noticed the wall to my right, which was hung densely with artwork. Three of them by Michael Valentine. I felt my stomach flip. My mind skidded. I forced a breath. Maybe it was just a coincidence. Lots of people owned Michael's work, but these were the last three of the portraits I had painted of his girlfriend, Rosa.

"Oh, those are great, aren't they?" Chrissy said, catching me staring at the triptych. "They're by an artist named Michael Valentine."

Tabitha was still engrossed in her phone, I tried to gather myself, but I felt like I was about to throw up.

"They're lovely," I gurgled.

"We had a great little dinner for him out here when he dropped the works off, he told us the craziest story. Actually Tab, you and your mom were here that night. Remember?"

Tabitha was still furiously swiping, not listening.

"Apparently, he had this studio assistant who worked for him, who was like totally obsessive and tried to sabotage him and, get this, literally burnt his studio down, but he couldn't prove it. These were the only works from the series that survived, isn't that a miracle?"

"Oh," I said, casually as possible, loading salad onto my fork. The truth was, the works had only survived because I'd put them in Michael's car before I'd left. It was a decision, not a miracle.

"He said his assistant was obsessed with murder podcasts and had a demented idea of justice, and disagreed with him on something, and then just snapped. I guess now they weave baskets in the woods or something." Chrissy paused, took a sip of wine, "I'm not doing the story *justice*." She said the word *justice* with an ironic twinge that made me want to bash her head in with the wine bottle.

"I'm sure," I shuddered.

Chrissy pointed to a large purple canvas on the far wall, "And that's a Nicolas Party, he makes the sweetest fruit paintings. We have one in the kitchen in the city."

I gulped, trying to steady myself.

"I need to use the bathroom," Tabitha announced, then abruptly got up. I was relieved she had been so distracted with her phone, assuming that maybe the sheer mention of murder podcasts would be enough for her to draw a connection.

If Naomi had met Michael Valentine, it meant she had known who I was at Memphis's gallery dinner. It was not *fate*. I remembered back to the folded rectangle with my name in try-hard cursive. She had probably arranged to have us seated next to each other. My brain felt like a washing machine with a rock in it, circuitously thudding.

"Are you all right?"

"Yeah sorry, long day painting," I said holding my forehead.

"I totally understand, I've been up since four arguing with assholes. More champagne?"

"No, I'm fine," I replied.

Chrissy continued babbling about work. Ten minutes had passed and Tabitha was still in the bathroom. I couldn't mindlessly chat with Chrissy about assets division and try and untangle what it meant that Naomi had sat at this same table with Michael Valentine.

"My son sent me that meme of a couple dividing Beanie Babies in front of a judge, and it's just like that. Every time."

I forced a laugh, then felt a buzz in my pocket. I pulled it out. Patrick Nelson had sent a text: *call me when you get a chance. I noticed something.*

A few seconds later the doorbell thundered through the house.

"Who could that be?" Chrissy said with pronounced zeal and rose to get the door.

When Chrissy disappeared, I found myself alone at the table and couldn't help myself, I pulled out my phone to call Patrick and listened to the rings while I stared at the triptych on the wall. The reds in the background still shimmered where I had underpainted with gold, and Rosa, seated on the green sofa, looked happy, which I knew was because she'd just found out she was pregnant. Then I heard footsteps, I turned: there were two policemen standing on one of the living room's immaculate taupe carpets, shoes on.

"Esther Ray?"

Tabitha trailed the officers holding up her phone to show me something. There we were. Pixelated on the small screen, posing in Nashville at our own private bachelorette party with the glittery backdrop.

163

"I knew I recognized you from somewhere. It clicked when Chrissy mentioned Marcella-Marie in the kitchen, because that was what you said your name was in Nashville," Tabitha was snarling. "You're a fucking stalker. My mom never talked to anyone about Marcella-Marie. *Ever.*"

"I can explain," I said calmly, but I could feel my body shaking and my throat closing.

"And I just found that creepy scrapbook in your truck, filled with pictures of our family."

The cops took their cue and approached me, grabbing my shoulders. Just as I was being led out the front door, without thinking, I called back, "Tabitha, Chrissy is fucking your dad."

12

Jessica, one of the only three numbers I knew by heart, did not answer my one allotted call, so I returned to the fecal-scented holding tank where a drunk woman was snoring. I had sat here before. Not in this cell, but one very similar to it upstate, where I waited until I was questioned for Michael Valentine's studio fire. Somehow sitting in this disgusting cube, so far from my idyllic home in the mountains, made it feel like time was just a looping rodeo, and no matter how hard I worked, I was bound to repeat myself.

In the morning I was moved to a small tiled room with three chairs by the young-ish Officer Wallace, who clearly cared too much about his facial hair, and the Officer Mendelson, who had a stoic's blank smirk. I basked in my hatred for them; their cow-like stances and bellies filled with processed food paid for by tax dollars.

"So, Ms. Ray, what were you doing on the Duncans' property?" Mendelson asked.

I looked down at the steaming coffee cup in front of me, overwhelmed by the urge to take a bite from the Styrofoam lip. I was faced with a decision. I could explain all the deranged charms on this bracelet of faux-fate that had brought me to this tiled room or be silent. And if I were to talk, I honestly wasn't even sure where I would begin; at the gallery opening? Demonstrating the way Naomi had firmly pulled my sleeve and steered me toward that corner table at Franco's?

"Look, your record isn't perfect, Ms. Ray. We can see here you were a suspect in an arson case three years ago."

I shook my head, "I had nothing to do with that."

"And now you're trespassing in the Hamptons using a fake name, and painting pictures of the owners under false pretenses."

"These aren't going to be light charges," the stoic said matter-of-factly.

I looked back at the Styrofoam cup. I wanted a sip of coffee, but I didn't want to fall for their placation tactic. I knew the other option was simply to cut to the chase and explain that Bryce killed Naomi. Tell them that I too was an investigator, a podcaster sans podcast, but the reality hovering above the three of us in this tiny room was Bryce's fly-fishing buddy, Conor Copeland. Men like Bryce had all the power. I couldn't tell these flesh sacks a thing.

"I'd like a lawyer."

"Do you have one you want to call?" Mendelson, the stoic asked.

"No."

"Well, we can supply you with a public defender, but I'd suggest we keep talking."

I shook my head and mouthed the word, *lawyer*.

Sleeping in a cell made me realize how accustomed I had become to the furnishings of the Duncans. I yearned for those sheets, the oversize support of the pillows, and the uncluttered expanse of the bathroom's marble vanity. I closed my eyes and willed myself to return to the Hamptons guesthouse, relaxing into the lobotomy of luxury, until the next morning when my public defender Rhonda showed up, sweaty and exhausted.

Rhonda informed me my bail had already been set at $15,000, and she had exactly eight minutes to hear my side of what had happened.

"All right, but why were you there?" she asked pushing her burgundy bangs back.

"I was working for Naomi Duncan, she had hired me to make artwork for her family before she died," I said, feeling that that was a close enough rendition of the truth. I was desperate to keep the existence of all the scrapbooks in my barn off the official records and away from Bryce.

"Do you have proof of her hiring you? A contract? Emails, anything? And why did you use a fake name with the family if she hired you?"

"I wanted to protect my identity," I replied coolly, "Naomi wanted me to keep the work I was doing for her quiet. She was extremely secretive, she even had me sign an NDA."

"You have a copy?" she prodded, checking her chunky off-brand Apple watch.

"It was on a tablet. I never got a copy. But I have a note she wrote me . . . and a packet of information about the family. I'm not a stalker, I swear I was hired by Naomi Duncan. I have voice notes from her on my phone."

"And we can get those?"

I nodded.

"Eventually the judge will be looking at your priors, so can you shed some light on this arson situation you were involved with upstate?"

"I wasn't involved," I said firmly.

Her watch beeped. My eight minutes were up.

"All right, well I'll do what I can to write something up for your hearing."

As the door banged shut, I felt an overwhelming sense of dread and in the din of the cell, my mind floated back to the Michael Valentine triptych hanging on Chrissy's wall.

Michael had had no choice but to treat me well; by the third year in his studio, I was making most of his work. He would decide on the compositions, but I was the one who actually painted the images. In the beginning he'd make a show about adding in some flourishes and details, performing his genius for me in the studio, but after a while he'd merely add his signature. The execution was irrelevant he'd always argue, he could have hundreds of paintings a day cranked out in China—"It's the ideas that are sacred." And thus, I, Esther Ray, his human paintbrush, flew with him everywhere: Shanghai, Sydney, London, Oslo. And for the most part I loved it, the carpeted hotel rooms in Austria, the fog of the cafes in Paris, and the sterilized scent of museum libraries where we discussed the hang of exhibitions.

And when Michael started showing with a gallery in Switzerland, he had decided to do a series of massive paintings of heiresses, à la Warhol. Michael had barfed his usual conceptual sonnet about the history of portraiture to the gallerist, but I knew he just preferred to be around these women, curled up in their electric envelope of wealth. Which was how I ended up spending my Christmas at the Boletto Haus in St. Moritz to paint Bunny Lilienthal, an heiress to an old logging fortune.

A car picked us up at the Zurich airport, and after three hours twisting through the Alps we were dropped off at a warm castle-cum-villa tucked in a snowy valley that looked like something off of a chocolate bar. Bunny met us at the revolving door. She was blonde and deliriously tall, which she later credited to her Dutch heritage. Michael loved women like this. He knew exactly how to flatter, erupting in a stream of banal jokes and references to bags, niche holiday destinations, artists, and delicacies of Tuscan regions. After I got the gold key to my room I headed up, leaving Michael and Bunny in the bar where he would describe his vision for the portrait I would soon paint.

To my relief, Michael's girlfriend Rosa, a Croatian poet with a Saharan-dry sense of humor, was flying in the next day.

Rosa could drink everyone under the table and loved to make fun of Michael, which I adored. She was the valve that brought oxygen to these trips, and she'd always pull me away from work to join her on long walks. The Boletto Haus, with its impossible hot-chocolate mountains, seemed like the ideal place for us to traipse, Rosa leaving a trail of Marlboro Reds like breadcrumbs.

The following morning, we set up a makeshift studio in Bunny Lilienthal's sitting room. The hotel had put down a thick layer of brown paper and a perfectly taped drop cloth to protect the burgundy brocade carpet beneath. We had coffee and exchanged pleasantries while Michael made a big show of sketching out the base of the canvas. Despite his general ineptitude, Michael was excellent at framing, always positioning his subjects sturdily in their backgrounds, but he was lazy when it came to detail. He simply couldn't be bothered with execution. After Michael finished, dramatically waving his wand like a conductor to an absent orchestra, I set about erasing his marks to begin in earnest.

Bunny Lilienthal had a horsey face, long and beautiful, with the overly pronounced features of aristocratic breeding. She expertly relaxed into the tweed chair by the window, where a slice of the startling snow-covered mountain rose above her right shoulder. While sipping her third espresso she asked questions. Where was I from? How long had I been working for Michael? And in turn I asked about her life, and she enthusiastically rattled on about her sons, Grover and Jack, and her daughter, Olympia, who was off horse riding with some famous trainer on some famous horse, who, *no*, was not named Seabiscuit. Then as the clouds thinned and the light in the room intensified, we settled into the frothy silence of portrait painting; me carving Bunny's features in ivory and pink on the canvas, and her chest quietly rising and falling.

A few hours later Michael returned in the annoying Euro scarf he always wore when he crossed the Atlantic and assumed his role as conductor, gripping the paintbrush fanatically yet barely touching the canvas. I hated his maestro act, so I moved to the window, watching the scene on the ice rink below, where old and young men were shouting as a gray orb moved across the slick ground.

Bunny caught my stare, "It's curling. The Brits are obsessed with it, but I tell you—it's utterly boring."

Just then, the door burst open, and in a haze of sweet sweat and blonde hair entered the young Olympia clutching her riding helmet. Michael Valentine's eyes dilated like a cartoon wolf about to release some terrible *awoooga* sound.

"Olympia, dear, meet the renowned Michael Valentine, and his assistant . . ."

She'd forgotten my name but it didn't matter, Olympia smiled warm as pie, then moved across the room to kiss her mother on the forehead. Michael could barely remove his tongue from the floor. I busied myself looking at Bunny, tracing her jawline, which, after Olympia's entrance, seemed now ancient and loose.

After a few minutes Michael cleared his throat, "You know, I have a thought—maybe I should paint your portrait as well, Olympia?"

Olympia blushed with obvious excitement. I was staring directly into Bunny Lilienthal's eyes when Michael posed this "thought" and I could see it—jealousy hanging like a neon twist of lemon in a cold martini glass. But Bunny simply smiled, not missing a beat, "What a wonderful idea, don't you think, O?"

Michael Valentine was famous. Everyone said yes to him. When he had been my professor, he had consumed me and I'd felt truly lucky. *Chosen.* But this was my sixth year following this man around, absorbing his paranoia of gallerists,

170

competitiveness, narrow vision of success, jealousy of younger artists, obsession with money, and fear of his impending irrelevance. It was exhausting. I knew he cheerfully sold work to the Sackler family and arms dealers, and that a diptych I'd painted hung above the dinner table of a man who had overthrown a fledgling democracy. Somehow, I was always able to make excuses, but that Christmas I began to crack.

The following morning after a mortifying performance of Michael pretending to sketch Olympia seated in the opposite window from where her mother had sat, I set to painting. Olympia glowed. She was wearing an outrageous purple Oscar de la Renta dress, and I enjoyed transferring the puff of youth that cupped her cheeks to canvas. We talked about her horse Jäger, and how she liked skating on the black ice of Silvaplanersee, which was only possible before it snowed. She told me that every New Year's the dinner has a different theme. This year was Carnival. Last year had been Casino Royale but her all-time favorite had been ABBA because of the costumes. After a few hours, Michael came by again, and pretended to paint.

"You know, Esther, I can take it from here for the night," he said holding the brush in the crook of his mouth, in what looked like a Salvador Dalí impression. I sighed, not enthused about whatever idiotic strokes he'd add in my absence, but relieved to have the evening off.

I wandered to the bar and downed a series of forty-two-euro glasses of Primitivo. My gothic wardrobe had improved since college, but my combat boots still didn't fit the mix of gluttonous Russian billionaires, old moneyed men in tuxedos, and genetic-lottery-winning teens drunkenly slurping their fifth gimlet. After a few hours of listening to a podcast about a gay woman living in a gated community who was murdered while walking her dog, I checked my phone. I had a text from Michael Valentine: *CANT FIND MY GIVENCHY BLAZER*

171

ITS IN YOUR SUITCASE RIGHT? I vaguely remembered some airport crisis which ended in spillover from his Rimowa being moved into mine. I needed to piss anyway, I left the bar half-drunk, swaying to my room to procure the blazer and relieve myself.

After I'd done my business, I walked up two flights of stairs holding the jacket on a hanger, then knocked, but there was no answer. Remembering Bunny's lengthy explanation on how none of the hotel guests locked their doors because of "Swiss tradition," I pushed on the oak door. The image instantly seared to my eyes; Olympia on all fours, her knees and hands pressed into the brocade carpet, her purple dress half off and Michael pounding her from behind with a sour bullish look on his face. Olympia twisted her young neck upward, saw me, then cried out, tears shooting down the perfect chub of her cheek as she tried to hide behind the bed. I closed the door.

I spent the evening roasting in hate. Should I have stopped it? I debated calling Rosa but she was already on her flight. I could call the cops or the concierge. I could tell Bunny. There were a million things I could have done, but I chose to drink another bottle of wine and take a sleeping pill.

He found me at the breakfast table hungover the next morning. "How dare you enter my room without permission."

"Fuck you. You texted me about your blazer."

"I texted about the blazer hours earlier."

I hadn't checked the time stamp, but that wasn't the point. He was trying to make this about me being a shitty employee. "Michael, she's sixteen. She's a fucking kid. You're a pedophile."

"Sixteen is the legal age of consent in Switzerland."

"Did you google that before or after you fucked a child?" I asked, loudly.

Michael turned white, hushing me.

"My private life is none of your business," he whispered, "and she pursued me, thank you very much."

I scoffed and took out my phone to google the Swiss legal age of consent. It was sixteen. A waiter in cream uniform pranced over, taking Michael's coffee order. I looked around the room, it was like a scene from *Titanic*, we were surrounded by old ladies wearing jewels sitting next to men scowling at newspapers. I willed the room to fill with freezing salt water.

"I'm telling Rosa."

"No, you won't."

"Yes. I will."

I didn't.

Instead, I let Michael buy me a Patek Philippe with a silver band. And when Rosa arrived, we went walking through the Alps, and I silently listened to her blather on and on about trying to get pregnant with Michael. This was before I'd wanted a baby of my own and I was still young enough to find her mooning over impending motherhood sad, like a woman grasping for her own noose at the tip of a curling branch. Wasn't our life fun enough? Didn't she like flying to these countries and dining at fancy restaurants and sitting on designer couches while ogling art collections? With each step on the snowy paths that crisscrossed the ski slopes, I knew I should tell her about Olympia on all fours. Rosa was well aware that Michael was an asshole but this was bad, even for him. I had heard whispers he'd fucked students, but I had no proof, his lechery toward me had been purely work related. I selfishly asked Rosa about the progress on her latest poetry collection. I didn't want her to leave.

Back in New York the incident with Olympia clawed at me. He was a teacher. And the rumors that had once been abstract now had an image; that purple dress and her tear-streaked cheek. I had to do something. After a string of near sleepless nights, I resolved to talk with the dean of the painting department, Chuck Blankolm. Chuck was not the ideal recipient for this type of information: he, a seventy-year-old man, whose own stagnated career rained over his every decision like an unhappy monsoon. But I had studied with Chuck and I had seen his flashes of empathy when it mattered. He would listen. It was winter and he was sitting at his desk, looking over a pile of papers with his usual chiseled scowl. I explained I was worried about Michael's behavior with underage girls, and he looked up at me in all his pre-Me-Too-security and responded, "He's the most high-profile staff member we have. What do you expect me to do?"

"I expect you to at least . . . look into it?"

"How? Do you have proof?"

"I saw him with a girl in Switzerland."

"A student?"

"No."

Chuck made a sigh, "If it's not a student it's not my problem, and to be frank no one enrolled here is under eighteen, he can do who he likes."

Chuck looked down at his paper, uttering one final statement in my direction, "You should really hope I don't mention your coming here to him."

I shuddered. On the train ride home, I half-heartedly took my resolve in having tried.

The ceiling of my cell was sharkskin gray and perpetually wet. I had resigned that this awful color was my future, I would go to prison. And maybe it's where I belonged with all the other scaly creatures. I knew my actions indeed belonged to the realm of gray area; I could see that I shouldn't have gone to the Hamptons. I had acted outside of the journalistic boundaries. Even as a podcaster, I had gone too far. And if Bryce wanted to prosecute me to the full extent of the law, he could and probably would. He had all the power in the world. I took a breath, and wondered if there were craft classes in prison. I had a friend in Asheville who did still-life drawings with inmates. Just then the door to the holding cell rolled open and a cop with slicked-back hair and long fingernails pulled out a beat-up clipboard: "Esther Ray, your bail's been posted."

13

I kept looking over at him while he was driving, his tanned arms lightly flexing as he shifted the steering wheel. Patrick Nelson had driven eight hours to pick me up, and we'd been on the road for an hour and a half, and he still hadn't made eye contact with me.

"How did you know I was there?" I asked finally, ripping through the iron silence of his Jeep Cherokee, and willing him to look at me.

"You were calling me when the police showed up. Remember?" he asked, his eyes glued ahead.

The past two days were a scrapyard of facts in my skull, but yes, now I remembered; he had texted me saying that he had found something in the books, and I'd dialed his number while sitting in Chrissy Ash's living room and staring at the triptych. Patrick had been on the line when the two officers entered the room. Revisiting that moment filled me with electricity. He had noticed something. I reanimated. "So, what did you find? I mean it must have been something big. I know Bryce was cheating on Naomi. Was he hiding money? Or something illegal?"

Patrick was unmoved by my burst of questions.

"What did you find?" I prodded.

Still nothing.

"Patrick. What did you find?" I asked again, "Please."

Patrick snorted angrily, "Don't you want to know why I came to get you?"

I felt myself shrink. I had thought he had wanted to play detective with me. I had thought maybe this was the beginning of our buddy-comedy, the one in which the old man and the lesbian solved the murder on a ski slope. I assumed that was why he had bailed me out.

"I came because I have a son in prison. And I've watched it change him, strip him of his soul. Esther, I don't understand what this mess is you're in, but I have spent my life thinking about what I didn't do for my son. And you had an option to leave, to get bailed out. I never had that option with him. And I never will."

There were tears in Patrick's eyes, I didn't know how to process this gruff man who reeked of cigarettes, spilling all of this emotion behind the wheel. I wondered if I should touch his arm but couldn't bring myself to do it.

"I'll pay you back the bail money," I said pathetically. "I have cash at home."

Patrick didn't reply. We were silent for a long stretch, trees hurtled by the window and a few minutes later the sky turned indigo.

"And thank you," I added, feeling a rush of gratefulness.

He nodded.

I knew twenty-two minutes had gone by before he spoke again because I was staring at the turquoise numbers on the dashboard's digital clock. His voice was stern, "Whatever got you in trouble. Let it go. Whatever this is, this crusade you're on for your dead friend, let it go."

I didn't say anything.

We were in West Virginia when my phone rang. I answered. It was a call from Rhonda, my public defender, who briskly explained that Bryce had formalized an agreement, all charges against me would be dropped by the Duncan family if I would sign an NDA and agree to a restraining order. I could never contact or speak of the

Duncans again. I had twenty-four hours to decide. The forms were in my inbox. She urged me to take the deal, then hung up before I could ask any of the millions of questions I couldn't yet form.

"They'll drop the charges if I sign an NDA and agree to a restraining order, she just emailed it to me," I said out loud, not necessarily to Patrick, more to the molecules of air that filled the car. It was a miracle I knew, a release from the metaphorical impound-lot of my life, but it was my third NDA. It was a pattern. When you get too close to power, to secrets, to money, this was the only outcome.

"The lawyer already sent it?" Patrick said.

I nodded, then added, "I won't sign it."

"You will," Patrick responded.

My mind began whirring. Patrick must have uncovered something big. Why else would Bryce be so desperate to keep me quiet?

"What did you find in the books?"

Patrick shook his head. "Just be thankful you get to go home."

He then swerved the car to an off-ramp and we rolled into a Taco Bell drive-through.

While eating our greasy burritos in the parking lot, I tried to explain the urgency, "Patrick. Naomi was murdered and I have to prove it."

"What good does proving it do?"

"Naomi needs justice," I scoffed, my mouth full of rice.

Patrick finally looked at me, his mustache vibrating. At first, I thought he was going to cry again, then I saw it, his anger like a vat of blistering oil. He erupted, "Esther, there is no such thing as justice. There is no balance. We're animals and we don't understand each other enough to ever truly settle a score. The whole story, the real story, well that's above our heads. Sometimes we just have to walk away," his voice was lashing at the empty parking lot. "Promise me you'll sign the fucking paper and walk away," he shouted.

Stunned, I nodded.

"Say it."

"I promise."

He was talking about Jupiter Nelson. His son, who'd shuffled into his high school one autumn morning with a semiautomatic rifle hidden in a gym bag, killing two classmates and a teacher. He was talking about his son's double life sentences as the court's attempt to serve justice. He was talking about whatever score Jupiter had tried to settle when pulling that trigger. But he was also talking about me. In the aftershock of his speech, I felt myself wince, it was almost as if he knew what had happened at Madeline Lancaster's, but that was impossible. I swallowed the rest of my burrito and sat silently. Patrick was right. I needed to let this go and I needed to stop feeding my gut-shaped justice-furnace with true crime podcasts, I had to get better.

After twenty minutes back on the highway, Patrick swerved off and into a Staples parking lot.

"What are we doing?"

"We're printing the forms and sending them back."

"Now?"

Patrick huffed, marching me into the disgustingly overlit store and making me log in to my email on one of the ancient tan computers. There they were, two attachments, seventeen pages, which would rupture my ability to contact or speak about the Duncan family for all eternity. I printed them out, and Patrick pressed a flimsy blue pen into my hand. I signed, and he slipped the pages into a FedEx sleeve. It was done. His fatherly action completed.

The sky was pitch black when the car finally took the turn around the grassy knoll of Hammersmith but I was elated: I would return to my house. I would find my center within the wobble. I had been given another chance, being cut off from the Duncans felt like a gift. The Jeep whined as it climbed the driveway. I took a breath and listened intently as my boots hit that familiar crunch of gravel. I was home.

"Thank you, Patrick," I said, looking back to his open window.

He dipped his head with a cowboy's nonchalance, then cruised back down the hill. My house was just as I had left it. Lonely but mine. I sucked in the stale air then flipped the heating on and filled the mildewy tub. I let the bathwater scald my skin. I wanted to burn the past weeks off my body.

While soaking, my brain wouldn't shut off. I had one searing question and I couldn't help it. It was late but he would be awake. Dripping wet, I grabbed my phone then lowered myself back in the tub and punched in his number, the second one I knew by heart: Michael Valentine. I had to know what happened at that dinner at Chrissy Ash's house, then I could stop. Then I would be done.

"Hello?" he asked in his usual pompous tone, as if him answering his own phone was some magnificent act of service.

"It's me."

There was a pause. He knew.

"I thought I paid you to disappear."

I ignored him, and asked, "How did you know Naomi Duncan?"

"Who the fuck is that?" he snapped.

"You met her at a dinner, at Chrissy Ash's house in the Hamptons. You were there because she bought the triptych of Rosa, with the gold underpainting."

He was silent, but I could tell from his breathing he remembered. He huffed. Maybe he was thinking about the fire in his studio or maybe he was thinking about the photos taped to the inside of my junk drawer.

181

"Why?" he asked, finally.

"Naomi Duncan was murdered. And for some reason she hired me to do some work for her before she died, and I'm trying to figure out why: why me."

"Why you? That is what you want to know. *Why me?*"

He was slipping into his cruel tone. I braced myself.

"You haven't changed. You're still so self-absorbed. You think the whole world revolves around you. *Why me?*"

He laughed.

"Let me guess, you're trying to play God again."

"Stop."

"Oh, so I'm right?"

"I still have the photos," I said, throwing my only dagger.

Michael was quiet.

"And my dear little Esther, I have the security footage of you burning down my fucking studio."

Now I was silent. This was the stalemate. This is why I had left. I had proof of his pedophilia but he had proof of my rage. And even Michael didn't know: this was not my first fire. If I was caught for one, I'd be caught for both. If I hadn't been so dumb. If I had just quietly put on my coat, turned off the lights, and gone to the police, he would be in jail.

"Just tell me how you knew Naomi Duncan," I finally gargled.

"Naomi Duncan was just another blasé woman at a dinner, who, if I remember correctly, had a cunty attitude. And her daughter wasn't even my fucking type. I wasn't hitting on her. Or whatever she said. If that's what you're insinuating. Does that help with your little *Why me?* fantasy? Jesus Christ, you know what, Esther, you're going to be sad and miserable for the rest of your little life. I feel sorry for you. And never ever fucking contact me again."

I felt the familiar throb of self-hatred and guilt as I slid back into the tub. Of course, Michael Valentine had probably slipped a hand onto Tabitha's thigh. Had Naomi seen it? Was that why she had chosen me, because she hated him the same as I did? It seemed plausible enough. I leaned my head against the cold curve of the ceramic tub. Someday I would fix this. He would be held accountable. After the bathwater turned cold, I padded to the kitchen and pulled out the top junk drawer and blindly traced my fingers over the bulge, taking solace that the square was still firmly taped into place.

Four Polaroids of Michael in a king-size bed at the Bowery Hotel with sixteen-year-old Rachel Mulligan. Rachel, with her bright auburn hair and too young smile, had interned at the upstate studio for a few weeks in the summer because she'd "loved art." I had been in Brazil finishing an install for the month that she'd "worked." I should have known. I should have never let it happen. I'd found the Polaroids of them in bed late one night after my return, not even hidden, just floating at the top of his desk. I gagged in rage and looked around the studio in panic. The whole place was stuffed with over-priced objects: the $20,000 Italian espresso machine, the plotter printer we never used, the Marcel Breuer chairs askew on the Persian rug, the German speakers, and the leather sofa which I was certain he must have fucked Rachel on. The truth was it didn't even look like a studio, it looked like a bachelor pad and I was his maid. I cleaned up his messes and tended to the altar of Michael Valentine. I hated myself for what I had enabled. I was done.

Standing in the track-lit studio, holding those Polaroids of Rachel's sixteen-year-old body draped over Michael's hairy torso, it came at me like a baseball to the jaw, fast and curved: *I'm just going to burn the whole place down*. I felt the insatiable need to obliterate the possessions that Michael Valentine held most dear: his artwork and the chapel he'd built in his own image. And this time I knew for sure, there was no one home. There was no one around for miles. I lit one of Michael's cigarettes, then threw it into the highly combustible bin of linseed oil rags.

In the kitchen of my cabin, the tentacles of Michael's cruelty were still lashing around in my brain as I cooked a box of Annie's mac and cheese, and finally, I let myself cry. All of my pain leaked out over that sparkling bowl of white cheddar and shells. The truth was, I didn't want any of this. I didn't want to obsess anymore. I just wanted to be home with Jessica. I wanted to put my hand on her fat pregnant belly and ask her what she wanted for dinner. I wanted a family. And I knew in part that that was why I had driven to the Hamptons. I had absorbed enough about the Duncans' lives to feel like I belonged. Naomi had just become another stand-in for my own mother. Just as Marcella-Marie was a stand-in for the baby with Jessica that vanished with that note in the fruit bowl. And I knew, standing under the warm glow of my kitchen lamp, I was a stand-in for Patrick's son. I needed a fresh start.

In the morning I drank coffee, and walked down the road to Chester's and asked if I could rent his extra car, a dusty mini-van he'd inherited when his grandma died. Chester wearing a tie-dye T-shirt and, agreeable as always, refused to accept payment. I drove immediately to Walmart to buy cleaning supplies and groceries. I started with the kitchen. In my time scrapbooking I'd ignored the basics, and the cracks between the sink and wall were ripe and the windows were so dirty they seemed fuzzy. I scrubbed the floor, I used baking soda and vinegar on the toilet, and brushed down the cobwebs from the ceiling with the broom. But I couldn't clean the barn. I knew seeing even one picture of Tabitha or Naomi would make me relapse. I was like an addict avoiding one of their old corners. I decided I would keep it locked up; I would deal with it when I was strong enough.

Vigorously scrubbing, I felt like a criminal in those precious moments right after a murder, cleaning for absolution. There were so many podcasts where justice was cinched by the receipt from the hardware store: bleach, gloves, heavy duty trash bags, a circular saw, Windex. But I was simply trying to strip away the past with each dramatic thrust of the sponge, and once the house shone with that incriminating luster, I tore off in my borrowed van toward Asheville. I was determined to meet someone new. I wanted to fall in love. Aching for affection, I returned to the gay bar where I'd made out with that jewelry dyke Kenny, but I didn't want her. I didn't want anyone who knew about Jessica, or any part of my past. On the bar's Wi-Fi, I downloaded Tinder and swiped through the slog of hikers, astrological tattoos, neurodivergent farmers, vegans, and self-described *dog mamas*.

While sliding through Tinder my phone rang. It was an unknown number. I was vaguely horny and answered hopeful that, maybe by some miracle, one of these Tinder witches had summoned my number. A stern voice replied to my boozy hello.

"Esther Ray?"

"Yes."

"This is Chrissy Ash."

My body tightened. Chrissy was using her lawyer voice: all steel, no bubbles. Her pose from our portrait session popped into my head and I could see every pore. I knew about the freckle near the inside of her nostril. I knew how her hair naturally parted when she turned her neck. I knew the ridges of her shoulders, but I had never heard this voice.

"Bryce didn't want me to call you, but someone had to."

"I signed his papers," I snapped.

"And he appreciates that, but I just want to make sure we're clear here. If you are to ever contact me, or him, or our family, or speak about us in any capacity publicly, we will come for you."

"Is this a threat?"

Chrissy let out a dismissive sigh, not even willing to reply.

"So, he'll kill me? Like he killed Naomi?" I prodded.

"You're insane, I can't believe you came to my house. I can't believe I sat for your painting. You're *so* lucky you're not locked away," Chrissy nearly screamed, then hung up.

Chrissy was already saying "our family." I was filled with rage and her hard voice rang like a bell in my skull, empty and cruel. I tried to imagine Naomi's brown eyes, watching Chrissy slink around her own stone kitchen with a glass of pinot. Did she know she was fucking her husband? Did she want to snap Chrissy in half? Or had she rolled her eyes, relieved she no longer had to drain Bryce's cock? It's always better to know. I wished I had known that Jessica was fucking other women. I wished I had been granted the opportunity to make her cry. To make her taste my pain. I took an inhale and looked around the room at the gay bar and tried to shake it off. I needed to return to me. To my body. To my desires. I looked back down at Tinder.

I spent the next month and a half fucking. I wanted to spawn. And in the midst of each date, I wished my strap-on was a real dick so I could fuck a child into Sarah with her dyed blue armpit hair, or Lisa who worked at a zero-waste brewery, or Franzi who loved gothic romance novels. I wished that pregnancy could be an accident. An operatic twist to an arbitrary Thursday. Not a didactic plan involving kitchen equipment, medical-grade freezers, and endless conversations. After a string of dates, none spectacular, I realized I was looking at these women as egg sacs: potential hosts to my future, and I hated myself for it, assuming this was what being a heterosexual man was like.

I decided I liked Sarah with the blue armpits. Not enough to ask her yet to host my progeny, but she taught a yoga class in the neighboring town on Thursdays, and she'd come over after with a roast chicken from the one good restaurant. She liked to eat on the porch. Always barefoot. She was constantly talking about food, planning our next meal before the one we were eating was over. I took solace in the inanity of her voice as it listed possible sides: fried plantains, Cobb salad, Cajun grits, coleslaw. I convinced myself that maybe this was how life should feel—numb, with a stretched stomach lining.

Patrick and I had returned to the quiet orbit of each other's lives. The intensity of our car trip lingered but not outwardly, we, as usual, merely nodded to each other when we passed on the road. A lump always formed in the back of my throat as the echo of his voice at Taco Bell, loud and fatherly, returned. I had kept my promise. I had walked away. I hadn't even opened Instagram or TikTok or googled the Duncans. I'd let the tangle of whatever Naomi's reasoning for hiring me lay dormant in the corner of my brain. I was even auditing a weaving class, keeping my mind occupied, threading bamboo cotton under and over, under and over, on a huge old loom that looked out at the Hammersmith knoll. Craft was again a salve, a place where I could give over to process.

On the nights Sarah slept over, she'd wake at dawn to make coffee and twist into a series of complicated positions in the living room. When I finally got up that Friday, coffee was on the stove and chicken bones danced in the sink, but she wasn't in her usual yoga spot. I wandered around, mug in hand, calling her name. Then through the window I saw the barn standing doors open. I jolted. My internal siren blaring. I tore down the path, spilling the hot liquid on my flannel legs.

"Babe it's such a beautiful space, I would love to hold a class here someday," Sarah said opening her eyes as she heard me clobber toward her.

Taking in the hollowness of her surroundings my face contorted. The barn was completely empty, her bright-orange yoga mat placed dead center.

"What?" she asked, confused by my mouth hanging agape, "It's perfect for yoga."

"There was . . . supposed to be . . ." I was stuttering. How could I explain what was supposed to be here? All of Naomi's plastic boxes were gone. All of the extra material and the organized piles of papers, including the line of finished books which had sat in their proud row on the table by the door. There was nothing. Not even the boxes of Jessica's shit or my own filing cabinet that held my passport and birth certificate. Sarah's mouth was moving, she was saying something but I couldn't hear her because I was busy doing the mental inventory of everything I had lost. After another stunned moment, I ran back up the path to the house, I needed to know the four photos were still taped to the top of the junk drawer. I thrust my hand in and felt for the edges. They were there.

"What's wrong?" Sarah asked, now standing in the doorway with a look of extreme bewilderment.

"I was robbed," I said hoarsely. I elbowed her out of the way and marched down the road.

Sarah followed, "Babe, what? You were robbed?"

"You need to go," I snapped over my shoulder, "I have to deal with this."

"What's wrong?"

"Just go, ok?"

Sarah was pissed, "Are you mad at me? I only went in the barn because I was bored 'cause you slept in so late. Jesus."

I was almost at the top of Patrick's drive, I paused to look back at her, "Sarah this isn't about you. Just go. Ok?"

"Explain what's going on," she demanded.

"No," I yelled, now marching forward.

"Esther, I can't deal with your inability to communicate. If you can't explain this to me, it's over."

From the corner of my eye, I saw Sarah storming up the hill, her svelte limbs swinging. I felt a small pellet of relief forming in my gut that it was, in fact, now over. I kept walking until I got to Patrick's.

"Who's there?" Patrick grumbled in response to my knocking.

"Me. What did you do with all of the books?"

Patrick opened the door in a ratty red robe.

"And the boxes. And the papers. And my filing cabinet, where are they?" I shouted.

Patrick looked confused, "What are you talking about, Esther?"

"The barn is empty. What the fuck did you do with all of it?"

"I didn't do anything. I don't even know—"

"Yes, you did. You knew where the key was."

Patrick rubbed his face, unbothered, which infuriated me.

"You're not my fucking father, you had no right."

The word father triggered something, a crest of anger spreading, "Esther, I didn't do anything with the barn. I put the key back after looking through that mess. I did you a favor."

"You got rid of everything," I sneered, "because you think you're some sort of savior."

Patrick took a deep, frustrated breath, "I have no idea what you're talking about."

I looked at him, his brows deeply furrowed like two supine worms, and realized he was telling the truth.

I waited on the porch while Patrick put on a pair of jeans and a sweater ringed with moth holes and followed me up the hill. We stood side by side staring at the barren barn.

"They would have needed a big truck," he said, removing a cigarette from its pack, "we would've seen it come up the hill."

I was silent, remembering the whale-like moan of the black vehicle revving up the drive, and the time it had taken to unload all of Naomi's boxes.

"They must've cleared it out when I went to go get you. That's the only time I've been off the mountain longer than the post office."

"But who is they?" I asked.

Patrick took a long drag of his cigarette, the wrinkles next to his mouth deepening as he inhaled, "I reckon whoever runs Red Rock Capital."

14

I'd watched a bizarrely addictive TV show with Jessica in which professional cleaners intervene with a usually disheveled, often near-senile hoarder. The hoarders always blubbered, releasing high-pitched whines because every Almond Joy wrapper had a deep and singular meaning; and how could they be asked to throw out that misshapen Reebok when it was an epic poem which only they could understand? On the show they explained it was a process; de-hoarding had to be done piece by piece, as each decision to throw something out was a trowel-scrape toward a brand new neural pathway. If the cleaners had just thrown everything away while the hoarder was in Bora Bora, there was a one hundred percent chance that the hoarder would return home and simply begin hoarding again. And I now understood. Each piece of the Duncans' papers had had meaning. Each scrap was a piece of a puzzle I had not yet solved, and I wanted desperately to fill the barn back up.

I forced Patrick to come with me to talk with the ever-cheerful Chester, who lived at the bottom of the mountain.

"I mean, yeah—it was about a month, maybe more, back in March."

I nodded. Patrick was silent. Chester offered us pert little clementines from a ceramic bowl he'd made himself. And I knew from his darting eyes he wanted me to compliment the vessel.

"Nice," I said, nodding my head toward the bowl.

"Oh, thank you, Esther!" Chester clucked.

"They came at night?" I asked.

"No, early evening, around six. I remember because their truck hit Bear Break Curve the same time as my clay delivery, and my guy had to back up about a half mile so they could pass each other up on Hemsley Hill."

Patrick nodded. He'd been right. And if it was Bryce, then it explained why he had dropped the charges as he knew I'd had the documents; the pieces of paper that traced two decades of Red Rock Capital's intricate tax fraud. Patrick explained the details as we walked back up the hill: that the scrapbooks contained documents that revealed a nearly impossible-to-trace pattern. Assets ritually disappearing and quietly resurfacing in the wrong place. Between puffs of cigarettes, he'd likened it to the sort of information which ends companies and puts Patagonia-vested men in cushy jail cells.

We walked back to my house and I made coffee. Patrick's masculine form in my kitchen still seemed out of place. I yearned for him to transform into Jessica, into any woman, then I could relax. Patrick kept a nervous eye on his phone while the coffee spittled on the stove.

"I think you should count yourself lucky," Patrick said solemnly. "But I can't believe you didn't look in the barn all month."

"Well, I was trying to move on and like, *let it go.*"

Patrick sighed, knowing from the tone of my voice I was blaming him.

"They took my stuff too. My fucking passport and birth certificate, social security card . . . everything. All I have left is the deed to this place which happened to be taped to the fucking fridge."

"You can get it all replaced," Patrick replied oddly light, "happens all the time."

"Yeah, but I can't let Bryce get away with this."

Patrick accepted his mug, "Esther, I was an accountant for small companies my whole life. Nothing major, but people when they cheat, they're desperate to keep it quiet. He did you a favor taking it all back. You signed the NDA and the restraining order, you don't have a choice. *Let it go*," he said, borrowing my annoyed tone.

"I have photos of three of the spreads."

"Delete them."

I released a pathetic, "No," then pushed back in my chair. "The question I keep asking myself is why she put that sort of financial shit in the scrapbooks? What had she wanted to happen?"

"None of those questions are relevant."

I rolled my shoulders back, annoyed at his return to that fatherish tone.

"He should go to jail."

"Bryce dropped the charges and he took his stuff back."

"He murdered her."

"She died in an accident skiing. Let it go," Patrick's voice was hard.

I was whining now, "But it was tax fraud, he should at least be held accountable . . ."

"Everyone fudges."

The truth was, I had no real proof. Of the three spreads I had photographed, only one had a spreadsheet and it probably wasn't enough. My stomach knotted. We sipped in silence as my feverish urge to refill the barn grew hotter.

Patrick downed his coffee then got up, slapping his knees with his hands.

"Just try and take it easy, ok? And promise me you won't contact him."

I nodded. The second Patrick was out the door I ran to my iPad and opened up my cache of true crime podcasts. I needed fuel for my rage. I relapsed, choosing one from my trove of tales about people who had vanished. Leaning back, my brain was instantly relieved by the podcaster's nasal voice. I listened as the low electronic music buzzed underneath the story of a near-blind, chain-smoking mother, who disappeared in the middle of the night without her keys, eyeglasses, or cigarettes.

I spent the next hours greedily consuming descriptions of individuals who seemed to simply have dissolved into the ether. I imagined there was a run-down nightclub, some limbo, with dark clanking music where all of these missing beings were forced to line dance until justice was served. Thinking about them all there, the birthday girl, the charismatic boyfriend, the nearly blind mom, and the college freshman in her short blue skirt, all sifting through the haze of smoke, sipping cheap drinks with thin red straws electrified me. Naomi wasn't missing, but somehow, I knew she was there too. She would be dressed in her Moncler jacket, moving in time to the music because she too needed justice.

It was barely noon, but I opened a bottle of wine and listened to another podcast, this one about a girl who disappeared walking home from a friend's house in southern Texas. On popped the voice of the missing girl's father, a shaky baritone, who explained that he has handed out flyers on the corner she was last seen for seven years, because, he said, "Someone knows something."

As I drank down my glass, I let my mind wander, and imagined Naomi's face on the flyers. It crept up on me like a yawn. I may be frozen out from speaking *to* or *about* the Duncans, but I could stand on a corner in Asheville and hand out her face. I knew she had been working on something in town, she'd kept talking about her "special project." *Someone had to know something.* I finished my wine and walked out of the house and into the van feeling euphorically buzzed. In the parking lot of Hammersmith I downloaded a photo of Naomi looking happy at a ribbon cutting for one of her WAC sites, zoomed in, cropped it, then traipsed up to the copy room in the school store. I printed one copy with her face centered on the page. In Sharpie above the image I scrawled, DO YOU KNOW THIS WOMAN?? writing below, SEEKING ANY INFORMATION, and then my phone number. I debated adding Naomi's name, but in light of her perverse commitment to secrecy and pseudonyms, decided against it.

Before I tore off in the direction of Asheville, I loaded Tabitha's Instagram to my iPad. I was surprised that there was nothing new, her grid was just as it was when I'd last seen it. Maybe she was still digitally detoxing. I guzzled the old images of her young body framed in square proportions, briefly stung that she'd never even posted the videos of me making her painting. All of our hours together in the Hamptons seemed like a hazy dream. I had to fight the urge to slide into her DMs, to tell her I was back on the trail and everything was going to be OK and I was going to figure out what had happened to her mother, but I held back.

Asheville was crawling with App State, Duke, and UNCA sweatshirt–wearing dudes sifting from brewery to brewery. These were the type of bros who owned multiple Yeti cups and wore their sunglasses on thick nylon cord. I couldn't imagine that any of them would have any information on Naomi but I tried to channel the energy of the desperate father of the missing girl from the podcast and pressed one of my black-and-white pages into the hands of one from each cluster.

"Who is she?" A big drunkish dude in cargo pants asked, pointing his whopper of a finger at Naomi's face.

"My friend, I'm looking for information," I said tightly.

"She missing?"

"Yes," I lied.

195

The brute looked at the paper, then showed it to his friends with surprising care. His comrades all shook their heads and lumbered off. I watched intently as a few feet away, he paused from the chorus of belches to neatly fold the page and tuck it into his bulging cargo pocket. Next up was a round of young mothers. I felt flush with jealousy at their exhausted forms, their wrists beeping with meticulously planned reminders on smartwatches. All they had had to do was trip on their husband's dick. How would I have my child? I wanted to scream at them, but instead I handed them one of my papers with a forlorn smile. The prettiest mom, pushing a beige Bugaboo, took the page and gave me a sad shake of her curl encrusted head.

I handed one to a man in a wheelchair and a woman in a tie-dyed dress who, after gazing at Naomi's face, told me she could sense my "missing friend was still with us," and "just be patient." I thanked her and watched them roll off. It had only been two hours, but I already felt the insane pathos of looking for the flint of recognition in the face of strangers. I handed out another fifteen or so then realized I could pop my headphones in and listen to podcasts.

I chose an episode about a guy who went on a walk to "cool down" after getting in a fight with his friends about Black Lives Matter and never returned. He had been barefoot and in shorts. It was the middle of winter; how far could he have gone? The next episode was about a guy who disappeared after booking a hotel room for his friend's bachelor party. There was another about a thirteen-year-old girl who went to a party and never returned. The cops, as always, assumed she'd run away and waited seven months before genuinely looking. She was never found.

I kept handing out flyers spinning in rage on the thread that connected each maudlin podcast: the families were failed by law enforcement and forced to search themselves. Fathers hiring cadaver dogs. Sisters going door to door. Moms selling their jewelry to pay private detectives. Twin brothers calling unknown numbers on their Verizon bill and begging Walmart to provide access to security footage. Standing on the street corner, I felt a sense of camaraderie. I was one of them. Naomi had been abandoned by law enforcement. It was easy to imagine Bryce and his fishing buddies, tossing evidence into a Jersey river. I listened to two more podcasts until my calves ached.

I walked into a fairly crowded bar that smelled like a blend of cedar and mold, and sat on a stool near the window. I knew there was probably a more precise method for finding out what Naomi had been doing in Asheville, but I felt an odd inking satisfaction knowing her face was safely tucked away in purses and cargo pockets around the city. I took out my iPad, logged in to the free Wi-Fi, and began googling water nonprofits in the area. There were around a dozen.

Naomi had said she wasn't working on WAC stuff, but I didn't know what I believed. She had said *hydroponics*. Was it a weed farm? I googled *Weed Farm Asheville Hydroponics* then ordered a beer from the too peppy bartender covered in flora tattoos and set about writing a boilerplate email with Naomi's photograph attached. HAVE YOU SEEN THIS WOMAN? I laughed when I stumbled on *Asheville Craft Cannabis*. That had to be it. I wrote to them while I chugged another beer and pressed send. Just as I was about to flag the marigold-spangled waitress to pay my tab, a big butch with cold blue eyes and dimples that made me want to die walked through the door. All the girls I'd fucked in the past few weeks had been an attempt at cleansing my palate: from Jessica, from the Hamptons, from Naomi. But this was different, I had no choice.

I waited for the butch's Highland IPA to arrive, then took one of the Xeroxes with Naomi's face and walked over.

"Hi, sorry to interrupt, but have you seen this woman?"

The butch turned her hard blue eyes to me and briefly drank me down, then she focused on the page in my hand and made a sweet little gulp of air as if she were sorting through all her terabytes of memory. Her eyes squinted, dimples flexing, her tongue pointing out in concentration. She was so focused, I thought for a moment that maybe she had every answer to every question in the history of time, but then she simply shook her head.

"I'm so sorry."

That flyer was the easiest pickup vehicle of my life. I ended up three blocks away in a hippie bachelor pad replete with tabletop charcoal water filters, getting fucked within an inch of my life. The butch out-butched me by miles, and I felt oddly femme for the first time in decades. I thumbed my uterus and imagined our life together. If I could, I would have punctured the condom or stealthily shoved its contents up my pussy in the privacy of my postcoital piss. Instead, the next morning the butch, whose name was Larson, cooked eggs and sautéed kale.

"So, this friend of yours, how long she been missing?" Larson asked while throwing the dish towel over her shoulder. I swooned.

"Uhh, a few months."

"So, when was the last time you saw her?"

It was the question everyone asked on podcasts. I answered with the practiced tone of the despondent, "When I was in New York, but she told me she was working on some things here in Asheville, and I'm just trying to get a better sense of what she was doing before she vanished . . ."

"Babe, I'm so sorry," Larson cooed as she dropped two East Fork ceramic plates onto the table.

"Thanks . . . it's really upsetting."

The eggs were perfect. Larson explained she loved to cook and had a "hookup" for the freshest year-round kale through

198

her work, which had something to do with the intersection of tech and green energy. It wasn't long until we were back in bed. After another rough session, Larson brought up Naomi again.

"But like, if your friend was working on something here, what was she into? Outdoor stuff?"

I scoffed at the idea of Naomi kayaking.

"She was," I corrected myself, "I mean, is, rich-rich, and into philanthropy and water management stuff."

"Well, if she's rich why were you handing out flyers downtown? Go to the Grove Park Inn."

The Grove Park Inn was the one fancy hotel, a regal old stone building that I had avoided like the plague because it had the same tenor of the Swiss chateaux I'd visited with Michael Valentine. It felt like a bootleg incantation of my past. I had no use for the picturesque terrace and fifteen-dollar martinis, but Larson was right. It was undoubtedly where Naomi would have stayed.

"Would you come with me?" I asked Larson pathetically, still half-nude and not wanting our morning to end.

"I have work, babe."

I hated being called *babe* or *angel* or *sweetie*, but I would have let Larson call me anything.

"Also, I realize we sort of jumped into things without discussing my situation."

I sat up, my insides curdling.

"I'm hierarchically poly. And married to my main partner who lives in Seattle, Sharon, and I have three regular intimate partners here in Asheville. If we want, or you want, to do this again, then I would have to ask you to meet my partners. It's our agreement. They're great, you'd love them. I'm sure."

I wanted Larson to cook me and my daughter eggs and bore us with facts about wind turbines. I had already planned our future and I needed her to myself. With the dream shattered, I got up and found my pants.

Standing outside the used bookstore on Lexington, I checked my Wi-Fi. I had two responses. One from WATERWORKS and another from American Hydro Engineers. Neither knew Naomi, but they both extolled syrupy tendrils of sympathy. *We are so incredibly sorry to hear of the situation with your friend.* The tang of fear was present in their kindness. *Wishing you all the luck on your search and let us know if there is anything we can do to help.* Oversympathy was one way to keep the problem foreign, because the fact that joining the dusky limbo of the disappeared was just a wrong turn or remark to a stranger at a gas pump was too much to process.

I drove up the hill to the Grove Park Inn, and let my old New York impulses take over, absentmindedly throwing my keys to the unhappy valet. Walking into the grand stone building I was immediately disappointed. There was nothing glamorous about the ancient men wearing North Face vests or their wives drowning in bright polar fleece. Ever since returning from the Hamptons the twitch for softer sheets, better water pressure, and designer objects had returned, but the Grove Park Inn would satiate nothing. I knew F. Scott Fitzgerald and Zelda had stayed here in their heyday, and I willed myself to imagine them knocking back whiskey and bickering in front of the massive stone hearth, but a middle-aged couple was clogging my sight line, digging dog-like through a nylon cooler rendering awe impossible. I ordered a glass of red from the corner bar and sucked down the overpriced Malbec before pulling out my flyer with Naomi's face.

The brunette bartender had a round southern accent and seemed oddly annoyed despite the fact that I was the only person she was serving at 1:15 in the afternoon.

"No, my dear, I'm sorry, I've never seen her," she said turning back to aggressively punching things into her POS system and flipping through receipts. Where was her sympathy? Why wasn't she dripping in sorrow for my plight? Maybe she was sociopathic. I picked up my second glass of wine and meandered out onto the terrace. It was a spectacular view that had the surreal pinch of a screen saver, but I had a view at my house too. I didn't need this. After a few minutes a sandy-haired busboy covered in freckles came by to clear my already empty glass. Again, I whipped out my flyer. He shook his head and frowned, at least meeting me with a proper amount of sympathy.

"I hope you find her soon," he said.

"Thank you," I clucked, and meant it.

A little tipsy, I wound down to the spa, and again was greeted by the sad shake of the receptionists' heads. They told me they were *so sorry*, and offered to pin the flyer up in the changing room. Next up was a barista in the disgusting airport-like mall in the new and poorly renovated wing of the hotel, making it clear F. Scott and Zelda would never be returning. The barista shook his head over the sound of hissing foam. In the granite bathroom I debated renting a suite just to avoid going home, the empty barn and my empty life felt like too much to bear. But if I drank the mini-bar down I'd have to pay for it myself. This was the problem. I had been a barnacle to wealth, and the truth was, in keeping up with the mortgage payments I'd already blown through most of Naomi's money. Before leaving the stall with a heaving sigh, I taped up a flyer on the mirror. Looking back one last time before the door closed, I caught Naomi's bright photocopied eyes as if we were seeing each other for the first time.

On the way home the podcast was blaring an age-old story: a girl accepts a ride from a guy, the girl is never seen again. I could barely listen, I was still wrapped too tightly in the blanket of pleasure I'd experienced handing out Naomi's flyers, collecting sympathy like a Salvation Army Santa. This must be some perverted brand of Munchausen syndrome, I wondered if it had a name or at least a WebMD entry. I had always been moved by the postdisaster images of people dazed and wandering around carrying photos of their missing loved ones. I thought back to the quintessential one from 9/11 that had been on the cover of the *New York Post*: that too-pretty blonde crying with a photo of her boyfriend just after the towers collapsed. When I got to Hammersmith I googled. I wanted to see the photo, I wanted to channel her pathos. And after plugging in the description, the image popped right up, but so did other articles. I was stunned, that innocent tank-topped sobbing woman had a decade later become the fake-tanned, botoxed Tiger Woods mistress. Maybe that's what happened when one is transformed into a piece of American iconography, the narrative inevitably goes off the rails, and now the Betsy Ross of grieving widows was wearing scarlet letter Louboutins.

15

It had been six days, and there were no responses to my flyers. I was spiraling. And Patrick could smell it on me, or maybe he could hear it; the tendrils of tragedy curling down the mountain as the speakers blared descriptions of violence. Patrick knocked on my door, which was standing partially open, and I jumped to silence the description of a double homicide.

"Esther, you busy?"

"What's up?" I asked uneasily.

"I was wondering, would you come with me?" he paused, "to see my son—Jupiter."

I didn't know how to respond.

"It would mean a lot to me," Patrick pleaded.

The true-crime fetishist inside of me wanted to meet Jupiter, but I was also wary of Patrick's fatherly impulses.

"Why?" I asked bluntly, pulling the blanket over my knees.

"Well, I think you'll like each other," he stuttered, "and I think, well, it would be good for him to talk to someone new."

I bit down on the inside of my cheek.

"Please," Patrick added.

"When?"

"Now."

"Don't I need approval or whatever?"

Patrick looked embarrassed, "I already submitted your name."

The last time I had been in Patrick's car he had been driving me home from prison, and here we were, on our way back. The odd symmetry hovered between us but neither said a word. After a few miles I let myself spin out into thoughts about Jupiter. *Did he know I was coming? Was he ripped? Getting beat up? Or in a gang?* The Jeep turned down another sunbaked highway and twenty minutes later the first green sign for the prison appeared with bright white lettering. MOUNTAIN VIEW CORRECTIONAL INSTITUTE.

We pulled into a hot dusty plain of asphalt filled with melancholic cars. I got out, my leg half asleep from the ride, and followed Patrick toward the sprawling complex. Just as we were about to enter the main building, Patrick looked back at me. "It's his birthday."

"Oh," I paused, feeling as if I had been tricked. "Should I have brought him something?"

"You're here," he paused, "that's enough."

A heaviness settled over me as I emptied my pockets into the circular tray. A dour guard pulled me aside and began frisking me. I cringed. It felt good to be touched. Her pasty hands running over the folds of my Metallica T-shirt reminded me of Larson's groping in the hippie bachelor pad. I closed my eyes as the guard grazed the undersides of my arms. I wanted to be loved. I wanted to be needed. When I returned to the fluorescent reality that was the visitation room, I was hit with the fact that there was no love here. Why had I said yes to coming? Because I'd wanted to squeeze this tragedy like an orange. A real-life podcast, but this was dark, this was a space filled with desperation spiked with institutional pain.

We waited in flimsy plastic chairs next to a young girl and her haggard mother. An older woman sat humming behind us, her jaw permanently extended in a state of ponder. Then the large metal door swung open, and in shuffled a dozen or so men in matching blue jumpsuits. I knew immediately which one was Jupiter because he looked just like Patrick, but I was startled by his age. Somehow, I had expected he would still be a teenager, his life's defining moment casting him in puka-shelled amber; but there he was, a fully formed adult with all of Patrick's rugged features. I took in the slight wrinkles in the corners of his eyes.

"Hi," I said dumbly as Jupiter took his seat in front of his father.

"Happy birthday, son," Patrick added brightly. "This is Esther, my neighbor I've told you about."

I smiled and nodded, feeling like a member of the world's saddest family.

"Happy birthday. How are you?" I asked.

"Good, I mean, yeah, pretty good," Jupiter let out a spurt of air, taking his hands and rubbing the top of his knees. He was nervous.

"Did you get to see the last episode?" Patrick asked.

Jupiter lit up, and the two of them began to gab about *Star Trek*. It was the banter of father and son, strange and unique. Jupiter listened to his dad's theories about a newly discovered space–time portal and when Jupiter responded his words felt too light, like they might lift off the table and fly out the partially cracked window. I could feel his sadness. He needed a hug. He needed a warmly cooked meal. Where was my softness coming from? I reminded myself he was a murderer. Forcing myself to imagine the lives he took, the weight of the gun in his duffel bag, the smell of the cafeteria, and the screams of his fellow students. From my googling I knew he had been seventeen. So close to being an adult. So close to getting a chance outside the clown car that was high school.

"Honey Buns all around?" Patrick asked, nodding toward the vending machine in the corner of the room. Jupiter said *yes* and I followed suit. Patrick ambled over to the machine and I was suddenly left alone with Jupiter.

"I'm happy he has a friend," Jupiter said softly, barely able to raise his eyes to mine.

Was I Patrick's friend? Jupiter missed my hesitation and kept talking, "It's just, he moved here to be close to me. And I just worry that he's all alone in that cabin. You know?"

I was hit with a slideshow of Patrick; he had killed the snake, he had driven me home from New York, he had posted my bail money. I realized he was, in many ways, my only friend.

"He's been really good to me," I said, my eyes welling up.

"What happened, why is she crying?" Patrick asked sounding angry as he returned to the table holding three cellophane wrapped circles of dough.

"I just told her I was grateful that you had a friend," Jupiter said defensively.

I wiped the tears from my face.

"It was sweet," I assured Patrick, who looked relieved.

"They were my favorite when I was a kid," Jupiter said, pointing to the confections Patrick was holding and trying to change the subject.

"The magnificent Honey Bun," Patrick said, placing one gently in front of each of us. There was a pause, Patrick's head was bowed. Was he praying? Then I realized he was singing under his breath.

". . . Happy birthday to you, happy birthday, dear Jupiter."

Jupiter gamely bowed his head blowing out imaginary candles.

There was silence, thick and strange as we ate our dementedly sweet Honey Buns.

"So, what do you do?" Jupiter asked finally, wiping sticky crumbs from his mouth.

"I was an artist, but now, I make books . . ."

"I always wanted to be an artist," Jupiter replied buoyantly.

"Anyone can be an artist," I said I hoped cheerfully.

"Not in here," Jupiter replied with a tilted smile.

"Sure, you can."

"What did you make?" Jupiter asked.

"Paintings."

Patrick looked up surprised, "You never told me you were a painter."

"I was good too," I said with a laugh.

"I mean if I didn't end up here, maybe I'd be like Picasso," Jupiter said with a self-effacing smirk. It was a tragic thing to say. He caught my eyes and something flickered between us, and for an instant I saw myself in his position. I was the one in a jumpsuit. After all, I had nearly murdered Madeline. Suddenly, the wall, which I'd so skillfully erected to keep my thoughts at bay, lifted, and I couldn't help thinking about it.

After my mom had died, I'd graduated high school a year early, desperate to get out of our sad house in Ohio. And by some miracle I'd been accepted with a full ride to a precollege summer art program in New York. I lived in a dorm in Harlem. I did my assignments. I went to get cheap drinks with people I didn't like after life drawing courses, but I still checked Madeline Lancaster's bizarre homemaking blog every few hours and I couldn't overcome my pulsing drive for vengeance.

Thanks to her blog, I was well informed that in the two years since my mother's death, Madeline had acquired three new Appaloosa horses and a Polaris ATV and begun building an extension off her kitchen. She was still throwing her weekly events, ritually uploading dozens of photos of *LADIES' NIGHTS* as if nothing had happened: images of Justine and Karen and Eleanor all dressed up, with their slurred smiles and fake-tanned digits clasping at glasses filled with brown liqueur. I could smell the mentholated cigarettes through the screen. And my mother's bitter words thumped like a drumbeat in the soft part of my skull: *Someday I swear, I'll just burn her house down.*

I was fixated. I knew Madeline had fed my mother piña coladas the night of her crash. I had watched the scenario play out in my mind over and over like a bad soap opera. I could see my mom, in her cheap purple Kohl's dress accepting another drink, then Madeline's squinched face saying something rude. Maybe about my dad. Or our rusting Chevy Silverado in the driveway. Or her impending all-inclusive vacation to Jamaica. Or maybe she just made a scene of showing off her new padded Chanel bag. Madeline knew how to twist the knife in my mom and I had witnessed a thousand idiotic fights and drunken outbursts, like erratic fireworks tossed between the two of them.

When I was a kid, I thought Madeline's house was the pinnacle of aspiration, with its wall-to-wall carpeting, backyard horse barn, and glassed-in pool. She was always giving tours, my mother rolling her eyes as Madeline pointed out the buttercream details. The curtains were redraped seasonally, the carpeting replaced every third year, and Madeline's beloved kitchen was in a near-constant state of renovation. I was hungover at Dunkin' Donuts on Second Avenue, scrolling through photos Madeline had posted of a new set of tangerine patio furniture, when I decided I had to do it.

I weighed the options. I knew I had harassed Madeline after my mother's death so I would be an obvious suspect. It would have to seem like an accident. Back in the stiff bunk of my dorm room, I filtered through the most recent images of the *LADIES' NIGHTS* then I saw it: the tiki torches glowing in the background. Prepackaged cans of accelerant dancing like showgirls around Madeline's kidney-shaped pool. And when Madeline posted about her upcoming trip to Atlantic City with her husband, Wayne, I decided it was time.

I stole my roommate's driver's license and rented a U-Haul, which was the easiest and cheapest way to get a car with a minimal paper trail. It was an eight-hour drive, but I'd bought two Subway sandwiches and was planning on making no stops. I parked near the summer program's studio in Long Island City and scanned my ID, taking care to make my face visible to the camera above the desk. A few minutes later, I let myself out through the emergency exit where there were no cameras. If I needed it, I would have a solid alibi. Around 8:15 p.m. I started my drive.

The drive was a blur of oldies on the radio and Subway sandwiches degrading on my lap. When I turned onto the familiar off-ramp, I felt oddly euphoric to be back in my hometown. I parked the U-Haul a few blocks from Madeline's house, then walked the empty street in the dark shadow of early morning. Madeline had made a post groaning about their 4:30 a.m. flights, so I knew there would be no one home. I waited behind a scratchy shrub and watched, checking to make sure there was indeed no movement. *Nothing.* Eventually, I gathered my courage and walked toward the back glass door of the pool. It was locked, but I knew where she kept the key—hanging beneath the ledge of the garden shed a few feet away. To my relief the key was there: I slipped it into the door and it swung open without a sound. I was hit with the smell of cold ash and chlorine. Wayne and Madeline had clearly had a party the night before. Bottles littered the glass patio tables and cigarettes dotted the floor. Their maid Rita would be coming soon, I had to move quickly.

I took the tiki torch that stood nearest the tangerine patio furniture and punctured the side of the can with a bottle opener, letting the gassy liquid ink onto the corner of the tangerine chaise. I lit the slick patch of oil with a lighter and greedily watched as the bright yellow flames scaled the cheery fabric. I took a deep inhale, molecularly calmed by the toxic smell, I looked around at what would soon become heather gray and felt finally that my mother could rest. This was for her. The KitchenAid appliances collapsing. The rows of MAC lipsticks liquefying and the drapes turning to dust. I left through the back glass door, remembering to lock it, and glided back down the street just as dawn cracked open on the cookie cutter houses that dotted Sable Road.

Nothing in my life has ever felt like that: me in that U-Haul. It was like bull riding out into the cosmos on a comet. I turned the radio up and found R. Kelly's *Remix to Ignition* playing and the song felt like a sign. *Ignition.* A confirmation that I had done the right thing. In a moment of ecstatic joy, I began to sing: *hot and fresh out the kitchen, mama rollin' that body* . . . I was ecstatic, my mind consumed with images of my mother, her iridescent beauty filled the cab as I bounced and sang. It was her funeral, her wake, her mass, and her birthday all at once. I didn't notice a car had pulled up next to me at the light and the driver, drawn by my gesticulating, looked over. In one gut flipping second, I felt my body seize. It was my dad, up early on his way to the office in his silver Toyota Camry. His brown eyes squinted in recognition at my face hovering a foot above him in the window of that U-Haul. Without looking back, I slammed on the gas, running the red light, and didn't take my eyes off the road until I was out of the state.

Madeline had been prolific on her blog, explaining from her hospital bed that she had been too hungover to get on that airplane to Atlantic City. Wayne had gone ahead without her, so she'd been sleeping and hadn't even smelled the smoke. But her savior, neighbor Carol Gotwin, had seen the blaze and called the fire department. Madeline was rushed to the hospital and put on a ventilator.

Madeline had posted dozens of selfies from her beige medical bed with long-winded captions, thanking God, and mourning the loss of her house and feeling blessed that her horses were unscathed. I learned from the local newspaper that because she had openly admitted to the fact that she couldn't remember blowing out the tiki torches, the fire was ruled an accident. My dad knew the truth, he had seen it in my eyes and I never went back home again.

Jupiter coughed, suddenly spiraling me back to the Monroe County Correctional Institute.

"So, do you have any plans this weekend?" Jupiter asked Patrick. I felt stunned, then wanted to laugh. Patrick and I were hermits. Two peas in the same pod of mountain misery, we never had plans.

"Yeah, we were going to catch a Tourists game," Patrick lied, as if we would ever go to Asheville to watch a baseball game together.

"Oh man, that sounds great," Jupiter said with longing.

Patrick shot me eyes, and I knew to play along, "Yeah, they're great."

A few seconds later a guard crankily announced that visitation was over, and we awkwardly said our goodbyes.

"I really liked meeting you," Jupiter said, "I hope you have a peaceful day."

"You too," I said, surprised by the loaded way he had said the word *peaceful*.

"Take care of my dad, ok?"

I nodded, the lump returning in my throat.

I followed Patrick out into the beating heat of the parking lot. We climbed in and let the din of the air conditioner fill our silence as we cruised out past the guard's station.

"It's my fault," Patrick said, "that's what I always think when I drive out of here."

There was no *Chicken Soup for the School Shooter's Dad* for me to borrow a passage from, I had no idea what to say.

"He was depressed. I wasn't paying attention. And now this is our life."

"But he made the choice to . . ." I didn't know how to finish. I knew Jupiter and I were in many ways the same, but I hadn't wanted to kill Madeline. I tried to remind myself that that's what separated us; he had wanted his classmates to die. He had wrapped a semiautomatic rifle in a hoodie and loaded it into that duffel and I had just wanted Madeline to lose what she loved most, her house. Her things. Her pointless objects.

"It's not your fault," I said limply.

"It is," he replied, "and all I can do now is buy him those fucking Honey Buns. And every time I do it, I thank God I can at least do this. How sad is that? A goddamn Honey Bun is the only thing that lets me feel like a fucking parent."

Patrick was nearly crying.

"You could have never known what was going through his head back then," I said with unexpected desperation because I was thinking about my own father's face when he'd seen me driving that U-Haul. I wanted Patrick to turn the car toward Ohio, I wanted to tell my father I was sorry. I wanted to explain that I hadn't wanted to hurt anyone. That I had been dumb and young. And if I could go back and change it I would.

Patrick took a big suck of air, "I should have known. Anyway. Sorry. Also, sorry about the baseball game thing. Jup's always worried I'm just holed up in that cabin."

I scoffed, "Well, you are."

He laughed, "So are you."

When the car was finally groaning up our steep drive, I released a sigh of relief. Whatever that was, was over. I never let myself think about my father's face on the day of the fire, because to remember it was to admit guilt. Patrick let me out at the top of my drive with his usual silent cowboy's grace, waiting to make sure I got in. I let my head drop when I saw the lights of his car turn back down the hill. I was deeply drained. I sat down on the couch and debated whether or not I was hungry. Then I smelled something. Musky and expensive. Before I had a second to process where I recognized it from, a hand was over my mouth.

"Esther, I am not going to hurt you. I'm just here to talk."

Standing in my kitchen was Bryce. And leering above me, with a gloved hand placed over my jaw, was a pink-faced man with ugly teeth. I tried to scream but my mouth was fully sealed. Bryce shook his head as if to shush me, then calmly said, "Tell me about the scrapbooks."

16

Bryce was uncomfortable in my house, his horror was obvious, like that meme of Hillary Clinton entering a cramped fluorescently lit kitchen. He stood firmly against the pantry as his eyes traced over the cluttered surfaces, as if making a mental tally of all the unwashed glasses.

"So, Esther, I learned a lot about my wife after she died. Turns out, not only did she want a divorce—which wasn't entirely shocking," he laughed, "but she also stole two hundred million dollars from Red Rock."

I couldn't help my eyes bugging.

"So, I'd like to ask firstly, do you know where it went?"

The pink-faced man removed his hand from my mouth to allow me to respond.

"No. Why would I know? And you stole my fucking passport, my birth certificate, everything."

Bryce continued, uninterested in my remarks. "You see. The books you made, they presented documents that make it look like *I* defrauded Red Rock. Which I absolutely did not. And I have poured over all of the documents with a forensic accountant, and I still cannot figure out where the funds went."

"Maybe you shouldn't have been fucking Chrissy."

Bryce's eyes sparked, but he didn't take the bait. "Do you know who was helping her?"

The pink-faced man again removed his hand from my mouth in anticipation of some sort of answer that might explain, but again I had nothing. Bryce looked annoyed.

"Maybe let's start from the beginning. How did you get the material for the books?"

The pink-faced man jabbed his elbow into my back forcing an answer.

"They just arrived, on a truck, in boxes mixed in with the photos and school stuff . . . I just glued in what she sent."

"And did you have any contact with the accountant? I mean, whomever produced the financial documents that you," he made bunny ears, "*glued in.*"

I shook my head and caught sight out of the window of a matte black Mercedes parked behind the house. I wondered if I would end up in the trunk.

Bryce looked at his companion.

"Well, why did you come to the Hamptons? Had she sent you?"

I shook my head, "I wanted proof."

"Of what?" Bryce asked disturbingly calm.

"That you killed Naomi."

Bryce released a trickle of laughter, "You think I killed her?"

The image of Naomi sailing through the sky came charging back. I nodded.

"I mean, maybe I should have. That much I now know."

The pink-faced man butted in, "Where's the money?"

What a dumb question. As if Naomi had buried two hundred million dollars in my own backyard.

"I don't have a fucking clue," I turned to Bryce. "Why did she take it?"

Bryce looked at the ceiling, "That is none of your business."

I felt offended. He had made it my business by showing up. And Naomi had made it my business by sending me all the documents in those boxes. I couldn't hold back.

"It is my business. I know everything. I know you always order the lamb on Christmas Eve. I know the names of your

216

aunts and uncles and companies where your best friends work. I know Tabitha was violent. I know she studied French. And I know about Marcella-Marie."

Bryce looked briefly stunned, then he gathered himself, "Esther. You know, you remind me of her. *Naomi.* You think you know everything. But in truth, you know nothing. I am going to ask you one last time. Do you know who helped Naomi with the accounting?"

I shook my head.

Bryce cleared his throat, "I haven't decided how to deal with you. Either I do it now," he made a shrug toward his crony, "or you find a way to disappear from my life. And if you so much as breathe in the direction of my family . . ." He paused, letting his eyes skim over the ceiling, "I don't think anyone would be surprised to find you hanging from that beam."

I felt a rattle of panic. This wasn't just Chrissy Ash on the phone yelling at me as she chugged Chardonnay. This was real. Bryce would kill me.

"So, can you disappear, Esther Ray?" he asked.

I nodded. Bryce cocked his head and smiled slightly. He then turned to the pink-face and motioned for him to cover my mouth, but this time he was holding a rag and everything turned woozy, my heartbeat thundering, my mind careening off into its own hallowed caverns as if snorting a gallon of poppers.

When I woke it was seven. My head stung and my lungs ached. I slowly regained my motor skills and sat up. The contents of my shelves had been removed, my mattress had been slashed, the broom closet emptied, and the mop, buckets, and refillable bottles of eco-cleaner were strewn across the floor. Instinctively, I ran to the junk drawer, tripping over a pile of silverware. The Polaroids were safe. I toured the rest of the wreckage. Bryce, or probably his pink-faced crony, had emptied my medical cabinet into the sink. My desk had been searched, loose papers and notebooks thrown to the floor. The entire house throbbed in violence. What was he looking for? Did he really think Naomi had stashed two hundred million dollars in my broom closet? And what had he drugged me with? I felt sick.

I tried to put the pieces together but kept circling back to his sad trickling laugh when he'd denied killing Naomi. I needed to clear my head. I needed to get the fuck out of my wrecked house. Without thinking I put my sweatshirt on, then hiking boots. Each step made me want to vomit. I tried to retch above the curling kudzu on the side of the road but nothing came out, and then I found myself on Patrick's porch and began banging on his door. No answer. His car wasn't in the drive. I felt angry that he would abandon our mountain in my time of need.

I aimlessly stomped off toward Hammersmith and wandered around the campus in a haze. I found myself in the library where there were soft overstuffed chairs and curled up. A few minutes later Ranger, a glass blower who worked dinner shifts in the kitchen, walked in carrying a stack of books.

"Sup, Esther?"

"Not much," I lied.

"You look a little overwhelmed, what you reading?" he asked motioning to the messy mound of books on the table in front of me.

I shrugged, unable to formulate a response. Ranger set his stack down, and picked up one of the stray rectangles.

"Clay pot firing."

"Complicated shit."

I nodded.

"You want to grab a coffee?"

I was still nodding from the earlier statement, and he took my general indifference as a yes. I blearily followed him out the door and soon found myself sitting on the front porch of the log building, blowing on a black cup of coffee listening to Ranger describe some new type of diamond sheers he'd ordered for cutting molten glass, but all I could do was replay the conversation with Bryce. Who had the accountant been? Then as if an answer to my question, Patrick's Jeep Cherokee blazed past the school.

I got up without saying goodbye to Ranger and queasily walked off back home. When I finally crested the hill and wound up his drive, I spotted bags of dirt from Ace Hardware piled in his open trunk, and I could see Patrick on his roof pulling moss out of his gutters. Patrick waved, and as I neared, I began gunfire explaining how Bryce had torn my house apart looking for millions of dollars and how he had drugged me.

"We should call the police," Patrick said throwing another green mossy blob onto the ground below.

"The police can't do anything," I said, remembering the idiots that had appeared on my doorstep after I'd torn down the *no trespassing* signs.

Patrick suddenly lost his balance, slid, then a crash, and his entire right leg was consumed into the rotten roof of the house. I hastily climbed the silver ladder and helped to pull him out.

"This fucking place is falling apart," Patrick mumbled, embarrassed to be needing my assistance, as he thrust his weight onto mine. When he got down, we both looked at his mangled, scraped-up leg.

"Should I drive you to the hospital?" I asked.

"I hate doctors," Patrick said breathily, his jaw gritted.

Once I'd hobbled him inside, Patrick sat on his maroon La-Z-Boy and stared at the new halo above the kitchen while talking, "I can't believe Bryce showed up here. You did everything he asked. You signed everything. You didn't bother him. And he trashed your place?"

I nodded.

"Why does he think you have the two hundred million?"

"I have no fucking clue. Wait, did you know that's how much was missing?" I snapped.

"I knew it was something around there," Patrick huffed. "We really should go to the police. He drugged you? That's too far. We have to deal with this properly."

It still surprised me that Patrick was such a firm believer in law enforcement, but I ignored him, "When you saw the tax fraud stuff in the books, could you tell where the money went?"

I handed Patrick a bag of frozen peas.

He shut his eyes as he pressed the cold square on his leg. "It was moved around through a string of opaque shell companies and then blockchain subsidiaries," Patrick let out a hacking chuckle.

"What's funny?"

"It makes sense now."

"What?"

"Why it was so obvious. The way the money had been removed was clunky, but the abstraction of where it went, well, that was clean. I tried to trace the numbers on my own, couldn't figure it out."

"So, she wanted someone to notice?"

Patrick nodded.

"Why?"

Patrick shrugged, "To frame him, who cares what she was thinking. Let it go. You clearly had nothing for Bryce. He left, and he left you alive. Amen."

I wanted to shake Patrick. I wanted to force him into a Sherlock Holmes hat and load him up with amphetamines so we could hit the road and get to the bottom of this Duncan family mystery. I wanted us to be Hercule Poirot and Veronica Mars. I wanted Miami Vice. I was trying to find just the right inspirational words to get him off his ass, but as I opened my mouth, I felt a wave of nausea. I looked down at the floor, heaving. Patrick didn't notice. His leathery grimace was fixed on his shin. It all felt suddenly clear; he was an old man with a busted leg, and I was a wreck. We would solve nothing. I needed to lay down.

"Let me know if you need anything, ok?" I said dutifully, as I got up to go. "I could bring you dinner?"

"That would be really nice," Patrick said pitifully and I instantly regretted my offer. I had nothing at home. I would have to go to the store.

"Sure thing," I tutted.

When I returned to my bludgeoned bungalow, I simply kicked the pile of broken ceramics out of the entranceway. I didn't have the energy to clean or even care. I grabbed my keys off their hook and sat on my porch for a dazed twenty minutes, then headed to Walmart to pick up some vegetables. I would make a soup.

Walmart always reminds me that humans are God's biggest mistake. What disgusting creatures. Pushing around carts full of food they will soon shit out, all wrapped in plastic that will never dissolve. It was fucking exhausting. Maybe I should buy a spool of sturdy rope and hang myself. Maybe Bryce was right. My head throbbed. I walked to the produce aisle and regretted entering the store. I regretted being born. I regretted whatever precocious fish took the first steps out of the primordial ooze. I bought two cans of beans and a head of cauliflower, one sweet potato, a pound of tomatoes, and four onions. I reminded myself I owed Patrick this, maybe that was something to live for—at least for today.

At home, I was too lazy to find the cutting board so I chopped the onions on the bare table, enjoying the flow of chemically coaxed tears. After everything was bubbling, I lay the wooden spoon on the counter and didn't wipe up the

221

tomato sludge. I decided I would never clean anything ever again. I would simply sleep on a sliced-up mattress in a torn-apart house until I died. Once the soup was done, I found a Tupperware and ladled in the hot liquid. When I opened the door to Patrick's he was sitting just as I'd left him.

"Is it broken?" I asked, nervous at seeing him so static.

"Just bruised," Patrick said with false machismo.

"It could be broken," I chided, "you really should go to the doctor."

"And you should call the police on Bryce."

"Touché."

I transferred the soup to a bowl and delivered it to him along with a fresh pack of frozen corn, returning the peas to the freezer. I began pacing. My anxiety obvious.

"Just ignore Bryce if you can," Patrick said, his eyes tracing my movements around the house. "He's a desperate man looking for answers where there are none. Take a breath."

"All right Yoda," I snipped, "but if you saw my house, you'd want revenge."

"If my leg wasn't fucked, I'd help you clean."

"Can I ask one question though: what kind of accountant would you have to be to hide money like that?"

"A very good one, and into fintech. Like I said, it involved blockchain. Which I don't really know that much about."

I nodded. Patrick looked exhausted and I helped him to bed, but before I turned to leave, he made a loud groaning *fuck* sound, "Esther, I'm supposed to go see Jup again tomorrow. He got extra visitation days for good behavior, but I can't drive with this leg . . ."

"I'll take you," I said, wishing I'd stayed a hermit and never made any friends on the mountain.

When I got home, I didn't even change out of my clothes. Without brushing my teeth, I crawled onto my gnarled mattress and drifted off into a hallucinatory sleep. I dreamt of

Naomi and my mother drinking espresso martinis. I dreamt of late-night parties and college friends I hadn't seen in years. I dreamt of bright blue acid rain. Hours later I was woken by a series of unexpected beeps. My heart raced. No one ever called. It was an unknown number. Maybe it was Bryce, back to finish me off? I sat up and looked out the darkened window. I saw nothing. No henchmen. No matte black car. The phone kept ringing. I rippled with fear but the truth was, I was too lonely not to answer.

"Hello?"

"Hi."

I knew that *Hi*. It was *Jessica*. *Jessica*. *Jessica*. My Jessica.

"Hi—" I finally remembered to respond.

She mistook my stunted excitement for confusion, "Sorry, I keep forgetting I have a new number. It's me, *Jess*. How are you?"

I looked around at our bedroom; the feathers from the pillows we'd bought together were scattered across the floor. The dresser was pushed over. Shards of ceramics trailed down the stairs.

"I'm great," I replied, which was true now. I could be in a sewer filled with human shit and if it was her on the phone, I would be happy.

"I'm delighted to hear you're doing well."

"Thanks."

"So . . ."

My chest cinched. I felt a strum of hope. She would tell me: *I'm coming home*. Then I would order one of the new fancy mattresses that came in a box and scrub the soup sludge off the stove. And soon we'd be saying those magic words, *we're over the moon*. We would be a family. I waited on her next breath; I could feel the words in her mouth. They had to be there. Why else would she be calling?

"I just wanted to let you know, I'm getting married."

223

"Oh," was all I could reply.

"I really wanted you to hear it from me, and not, like, Instagram, you know?"

"Thanks," I mumbled, then violently hung up, throwing myself back under the covers. I knew the dress she would wear: strapless ivory. I knew the type of flowers she would hold: hyacinth. The cake would be lemon with vegan cream-cheese frosting and soon she would have our child. She alone would have *our life*. I had nothing but a trashed bungalow.

I closed my eyes but there would be no sleep. When we had planned our lives together, I had imagined it all, not just the top-heavy wedding flowers bending in the afternoon heat, but the way she would look at me when we were in our seventies and she needed help carrying in the groceries. Or how her shoulders would relax after I double-checked there were no almonds in her salad at restaurants. Or the hyena laugh she would make chasing after our kid. Every time I tried to close my eyes, those imagined fictions, brutal in their detail and stored in the deep tissue of my brain, reappeared like IMAX projections behind my eyelids. I had to stay awake. So instead, I wrote a list of ways to commit suicide. Bryce was right, no one would miss me.

1. Shotgun to the head (don't have a gun)
2. Drink Drain-o (only have organic kind)
3. Jump off cliff on Sheldon Trail (fun?)
4. Drive car off highway (too much like mom)
5. Toaster in bathtub (classic)
6. Sleeping pills (have none)
7. Hang myself (as suggested)
8. Burn myself in kiln at Hammersmith (unfair to studio assistants)
9. Slitting my wrists (dramatic)
10. Leave car running in barn (fitting, but is barn too big?)

11. Eating to death (very Walmart)
12. Drinking to death (also fun)
13. Drowning (river?)

When I ran out of ideas, I decided to alleviate my sorrows with the trauma of others and picked out a podcast, which turned out to be a classic: insurance fraud. It always surprised me just how many true-crime tales involved life insurance. There had to be a statistic, if someone takes a plan out on you, you were x-times amount more likely to die. This one was particularly dark, about two old grandmas in California who found homeless men to groom, feeding and housing them for the two years it took for the claims to become incontestable, then running them over with their car. The women didn't even need the money, they were old and fairly well off. It was just greed. Greed motivated so much murder, it seemed like it should be love. Or jealousy. Or even hate. But it was always just payouts, inheritance squabbles, deeds to houses, jewelry, and stock shares.

The souring of so many families could be traced to the migration of wealth through fingertips and bank accounts. I thought about Bryce frantically looking for money in my broom closet. Had he taken out life insurance on Naomi? I wished briefly that I could have taken out an insurance plan on Jessica's love. It was pathetic and sad but I felt I deserved compensation. I too had been run over by a car, albeit mine was metaphorical. I watched the clock as it marched toward 8:30 a.m. I felt angry the birds still cheerfully chirped, unaware that I was heartbroken, unaware that Jessica was probably scrolling Pinterest for table setting ideas. I drank a glass of water, then dutifully readied myself to pick up Patrick.

"You look like shit," Patrick said, taking in my unwashed hair, sunken eyes, and yesterday's clothes.

"My ex is getting married."

"Good for her," Patrick said without an ounce of sarcasm.

"Good for her?" I snapped.

"Yes, it's good when people are happy."

"Fuck your Zen shit."

Patrick released a snort of laughter.

"I've got a fucked leg and a boy in prison for life, I think I deserve some Zen shit."

"I think I should take you to the doctor after this."

"I'll give it another day."

After a stretch of silence, Patrick grumbled, clearly lost in thought about the cabin, "Maybe I should just knock the place down," then turned on the radio. The car filled with Pharrell's delusional song "Happy." We both silently smirked. No one was happy. We weren't happy. At least we weren't happy together. I looked out at the cloudless sky, grateful to be away from my house, which had been consumed by the dueling tornados of the Duncans and Jessica.

The visitation room was skunked in its usual brine of sweat and low-grade antiseptic. We took a seat in the corner, Patrick's leg stuck out like he was trying to trip someone.

"Dad," Jupiter chirped, as he shuffled in the room, "Oh. Esther, hi, I didn't realize you were coming."

"Well, I fucked my leg on the roof," Patrick said quickly, trying to explain my presence and his bizarre position, "she had to drive."

Jupiter's eyes flashed, "Are you ok? Should you go to the doctor?"

"He refuses," I clucked.

"Dad, come on."

Patrick looked defensive, "I think it's just bruised. You should see the other guy, and by that, I mean the hole in my roof."

Jupiter took a breath, "You know that place was falling apart back when I was there and that was—twenty years ago."

"I'm fixing it up," Patrick said defensively.

It was nice to watch Jupiter care for his father, I sat back and relaxed into the ritual performance of the world's saddest family. "So, what's up with you?" Patrick asked Jupiter.

"The usual, trying not to get my ass kicked."

"Don't," Patrick said, prematurely exhausted by Jupiter's sarcasm.

"No, I mean—things are fine. I'm glad I get extra visitation days."

"That's great Jup, I'm real happy about that."

"How was the game?" Jupiter asked.

"What game?" Patrick replied.

"The Tourists game?"

"Great," I lied.

Jupiter looked at us quizzically as if he knew I was fibbing.

"Who won?"

"We did," I lied again.

"Honey Buns, on me?" Patrick said with the tone of a grandpa in an ice cream parlor, trying to thwart the conversation.

"I can get them," I offered, not wanting to watch Patrick limp.

"Nope, this is my favorite part," Patrick said as he hobbled off.

Jupiter looked at me, then around at the depressing room, "You didn't go to the game, did you?"

I shook my head. Jupiter smiled.

"Must be weird for you to come here, huh?"

"Your dad actually bailed me out, not so long ago."

Jupiter looked surprised, "What? Why?"

"I assumed he told you."

Jupiter shook his head, indicating for me to continue.

"Well, I got sort of—I don't know. I was hired by this family, and I may or may not have trespassed on their property, but I was just trying to solve—it sounds crazy—a murder."

"Really?"

"Well, I may have gotten a bit obsessed."

Jupiter cocked his head, "Obsession almost killed me."

I didn't know what to say.

"Most school shooters kill themselves. Did you know that?"

I nodded. It was as if Jupiter knew what I had done the night before. My list.

"Every day I think I should have. But I also read a lot on obsessive thinking. Which is why I ended up the way—I have. I was depressed and being bullied. But none of that matters. All I can have is acceptance. Like I just have to accept I fucking did it. And there is no version of control. Not here. Not back then. This is how it is. I meditate a lot. Do you meditate?"

Patrick hobbled to the table with three Honey Buns, "What are you kids talking about?"

I looked to Jupiter.

"We were talking about meditation," Jupiter said.

"Right, my hippie," Patrick said, "this is where I get the Zen shit from."

"Well, you named me Jupiter."

Patrick scoffed, "Your mom named you Jupiter, she was into astrology, or whatever."

I could see the hurt shuttle across Jupiter's eyes at the mention of his mother.

"Come now," Patrick said, pushing a Honey Bun toward his son.

"You should really try meditation," Jupiter pressed.

I nodded unenthused.

"He's even gotten me into it," Patrick said with a laugh.

"Shit works," Jupiter put his hands up.

"I mean, I have bamboo toilet paper and I compost, but like, I just can't get my mind to shut down," I said earnestly.

Jupiter laughed, "There are tricks, like if you have a thought—acknowledge it, label it, then come back to your breath. If that doesn't work, focus on your body. Focus on your feet. Think about how they feel."

Patrick rolled his eyes ever so slightly, and I shoved a wad of ecstatically sweet dough in my mouth to keep from having to respond. But when I got home, I tried it.

Every girlfriend had always said it in some form; *sweetheart, relax, take some breaths, close your eyes*. But I hated being told to "chill." I could almost calm down when I was weaving or binding books or throwing pots on the wheel, but I couldn't *just do it*. I cleared an area on the floor, put my hair up in a ponytail, closed my eyes, and immediately saw her: Jessica was standing in the doorway of our house in her sweats holding the baby. Then Jessica spitting toothpaste into the sink, smiling like in a Crest commercial. Followed by Jessica enameling in her daffodil dress. I was desperate to expel the images. So, I did what Jupiter said, and tried to label the thoughts.

On each beautiful image I tried to scrawl *j's junk,* just as I had done to the boxes of her shit in the barn. I took a breath and forced myself to slap the words on her glowing smile, obliterating the fictional envelopes of happiness that I'd been hoarding. I wrote it on the image of her, seventy-five with the grocery bags, and her in bed, and by the windowsill; over and over I scrawled *j's junk*. It was like a type of scrapbooking, the fantasies taped down, transformed into an alternate reality, one that now belonged exclusively to the world of sepia-toned sentimentality, the past.

Eventually my thoughts slowed. I focused on my breath. On my body. On the pressure of the floor underneath my ass. I felt my chest rise, then the coolness of air running up and down my throat, and I simply let myself exist. It was relieving, and I felt a small amount of pressure exit my skull, like a tire being softened. Maybe I could exist. Maybe this world wasn't built simply for me to hang from the ceiling.

Patrick came by the next morning and rapped on my screen door.

"Esther," he called.

"What?" I croaked, I was mid-meditation and groggy.

"You asleep?"

I didn't want to give him the satisfaction that I had been meditating so I simply grunted and shuffled to the door.

"I got us tickets."

"To what?" I asked as I ushered him to a chair on the porch, noticing his limp had greatly improved.

"To the Tourists game."

I knew instantly that Patrick had done it just to rectify his lie to Jupiter.

"When?" I asked.

"Today?"

"What if I have plans?" I said incredulously.

Patrick looked genuinely embarrassed and I felt a stroke of shame.

"I don't, when?"

Patrick sighed, "Two-thirty."

That was in an hour and a half.

I made him stop at a gas station so I could pick up sunscreen. I hadn't been to a baseball game since I was a kid, the Americana of it all was making me nervous. My dad had loved everything ball related. Football, basketball, baseball. The TV had been a constant hum, with the voices of men ebbing and flowing to the tide of games throughout the house. But I never watched, and despite being a dyke I had never played softball or volleyball or any of the other gay-adjacent sports. I was an artist. A dork. And I burnt easy. We parked down by the river and walked because Patrick didn't want to pay extra.

"You like these sorta things?" he asked as we took our place in line at the stadium.

"Little late to be asking."

Patrick snorted.

"I'm happy to be out of the house," I responded, taking in the buzzing crowd.

"Jup played shortstop," Patrick said proudly.

"Wow," I replied, despite not knowing what that meant.

We crept forward in the line with the other yokels, beer-buoyed men, and screaming kids in sporty sunglasses, as the sun beat down. Our seats were all the way at the top. We stood for the national anthem and the solemnity of the crowd as they held their caps to their hearts struck me as Rockwellian. I had no idea people were still doing this. Didn't everyone know about our war crimes? Didn't everyone hate America at least a little bit? Waterboarding? Guantanamo? I was relieved when Patrick ducked his head toward mine and asked if I wanted nachos and beer. I nodded, and he hobbled off just as the majority of the denim-clad butts were sitting back down.

"I got Budweiser," Patrick mumbled as he handed over a large plastic cup.

"Thank God," I replied.

I liked the slowness of the game. It was mostly just guys standing around on the iridescently green field watching for things: the white ball, the umpire, their coaches, the wind. The first major cracking of the bat against the ball felt ecstatic. The crowd whooped. The afternoon heat slanted upward and I felt a pulse of euphoria.

"Did Jupiter play in high school?" I asked Patrick as I dipped a corn chip into the chemically soft cheese.

Patrick shook his head, "He quit at the end of middle school, around the time his mom left."

I concentrated on chewing but was desperate to know more.

"What was she like?" I finally asked.

Patrick looked up at the cloudless sky, "Monica, well, she was very funny. And she was free-spirited, but at the same time, she could get real wrapped up in things, same as Jup."

"What does that mean?" I asked.

Patrick laughed, "For a while, she was really into selling makeup door to door."

"Oh, so like pyramid schemes?"

"Technically multilevel marketing," Patrick said with an accountant's disdain.

"Right."

"She was a good mom. But after the makeup thing went bust, she got into a frozen food sales thing, but it didn't work out, and then she got into this religious group."

"Ooof," I responded.

"Not quite scientology, but pretty much. She ran off to Utah and didn't even really stay in touch, which crushed Jup."

"You think that's why he . . . ?" I asked, and I instantly regretted the words escaping my mouth.

"I could blame her for what he did, it would be easier. But the truth is harder; I was the one who was there."

The other team scored a home run and a ripple of frustration ran through the crowd.

"How about your parents?" Patrick asked nonchalantly.

I took one of those heavy, for show, breaths. "My mother was beautiful but miserable, and a bit of a lush," I said, "and she died in a car crash when I was fifteen."

"I'm sorry, Esther."

My eyes unexpectedly filled with water. The lights of the stadium danced. I didn't want to be crying at a baseball game about my mother. It felt like something out of a bad TV show. Patrick awkwardly nudged his shoulder into mine, a silent, but salient gesture.

"And your dad, what's he like?" he asked, hoping I knew for a more cheerful response.

I blinked back the liquid, "My dad switched off after my mom died. I mean, he was never like the world's greatest dad, but he had held us together. Like he drove me to things, and tried to give my mom everything he could. He worked a lot, but then, like I don't know, he just sort of evaporated after she . . ."

"You keep in touch?"

"We text on Christmas and birthdays. His is in two days."

"You should call."

I thought back to the disappointment and confusion I'd seen in my dad's eyes the last time I had seen him while in the U-Haul. He knew what I had done. I only texted him because if we spoke, we would have to discuss it. If we spoke, we would inevitably have to talk about mom. We would have to feel all the things I knew neither of us wanted to feel. He and I were the same. We bottled things up till we burst.

The other team scored a run. The crowd audibly booed. I was startled by the collectivity. Everyone cheered when a brunette struck out. There was stupidity to the fervor that was relaxing, I liked being another idiot in the mass. I screamed when we hit a run. At the next inning I got up for our second round of beer, and when I returned Patrick was whistling with two fingers in his mouth, then became bashful at his exuberance as I handed him his cup. We were having fun. The game rolled forward with the bizarre elasticity of a dream, the afternoon turning thick with cheer.

We lost, but I felt high as Patrick's Jeep wove through the blue mountains, the energy still threading through my veins. I wondered where everyone was. The maddening crowd now dispersed to separate bedrooms and lonely kitchen tables.

"That was nice," I said, and meant it as I climbed out at the top of the drive.

"It was," Patrick said.

"Call your dad," he chided, as the wheels backed down the hill.

Call my dad. What did Patrick know? He didn't know how it had felt in my house after my mom died. He didn't know how my dad was practically mute, going weeks without talking, accepting longer and longer stretches of work away from home. And Patrick had no idea how I could see it; something awful in my father's eyes when he looked at me. *Pain.* For a while I wondered, half hopefully, that it was because I looked like my mom, but I knew that wasn't it. It was something else. And he never wanted to talk. Not about dinner, or where he was heading for work, or what we should do about the racoons that were breaking into our trash can. Eventually a bungee cord appeared on the silver container so I knew he at least listened, and there was always food in the fridge, and he came to graduation, but he wasn't present. Not really. Maybe it was depression. He could never ask for help.

I sat down on the futon feeling heavy from the sun and pulled out my phone. I dialed the house number instead of his cell. I knew the curved yellow rotary phone that sat in the kitchen would shake violently as it rung, and there would be no caller ID. He wouldn't know it was me. I wasn't sure I wanted to talk. Four rings. Then his heavy voice, "Hello?"

I put my hand over my mouth. After all these years it was too much.

"Hello?" he asked again, then started coughing.

I kept my hand firm.

"Hello?" he chided, now gruff.

I said nothing. He hung up. And I sat, tranced out in the echo of his voice. What could I have told him? Maybe about the baseball game. He would have liked that. I couldn't bring myself to call back.

I took a breath and crossed my legs. I would meditate. I focused on my breathing; labeling the stray thoughts as Jupiter had taught me. But just as I had lifted off, I was violently wrenched by my phone. My eyes tore open. I felt my universe exploding; it would be my dad. We would talk. The number was unknown, but maybe there was a reason; he was calling from a payphone, or he'd gotten a new cell. I tried to make a mental list of things we could talk about in case the line filled with dead air, then answered.

"Hello?"

"Hello?" An old lady's voice ricocheted through my ear.

"Who is this?" I snapped.

"Oh, maybe I have the wrong number. I'm so sorry."

I sat up, pushing the phone into position.

"Who is this?" I asked again.

"My name is Becky Archer. I saw the flyer with Amanda's photograph on it at the Grove Park spa. Is Amanda all right?"

"What?" I asked.

"This was the number on the flyer at the spa of the Grove Park Inn for Amanda Elliott. Perhaps I put it in wrong?"

My mind was ringing. The Grove Park Inn. My flyers. *Naomi.*

"No, no, it's the right number. I'm sorry, I was just taken by surprise."

"I understand. Well, Amanda rented my brother's old house on Walnut Hill. And I just wanted to make sure every-thing was all right."

"Really?" I blurted.

"Yes, it was very jarring to see her face taped up on the wall. Is she ok?" she asked again.

Was Amanda Naomi? Had my flyer actually worked? Or was this simply a dementia-riddled-bingo-player who thought all middle-aged women looked alike?

"We're just trying to piece some things together as a family. Would you be willing to meet?" I asked, feeling the only way to gauge this was in person.

"Of course, but wait, who are you?"

I stuttered, "I'm Amanda's daughter, my name is Tabitha."

"Oh, you poor thing, would you want to come by today?"

"You're in Asheville?"

"Yes, at 45 Summit."

I looked at my watch, it was only six p.m.

"I can be there in an hour."

"Great, but I have to get my dog from the groomer at seven thirty. Any dietary restrictions?"

"What?"

"Do you have any restrictions? I'll make us a nibble."

"Oh, no, I'm a—normal."

17

Becky Archer's Victorian home sparkled, it was clearly recently painted and boasted stained glass on a gleaming navy-shingled turret from the center of the roof. I got out of the van and noted that the lawn was pristine with a large cross-legged Buddha sitting in the East corner. It was one of the nicer houses I'd seen in the city. It reassured me; Naomi was close. Becky came to the door wearing all-black spandex in varying shades of cling. She was in her late seventies. Her collared workout shirt was snug on her shoulders and her gray hair was tucked back in an athletic headband.

"Oh darling, you must be so shaken up."

I nodded, enjoying the onslaught of sympathy, my Munchausen rushing back with a curtsy: yes, poor me.

"Come in, have a seat. I mean, just to be completely transparent with you dear, I did not know Amanda very well. I mean, we met maybe three times. I prepared us some nibbles. All healthy, hope you like hummus. It's not fresh-fresh. I mean, I just hate cleaning up the food processor. You know if you run it through the dishwasher, it degrades the plastic and then it enters whatever food you're making?"

I winced at Becky's blathering as I followed her lithe elder form into the large room, my eyes scanning tribal masks, indigo couch pillows, Peruvian carpets, and prayer flags flapping in the window frame.

"I'm on a fact-finding mission, so whatever you know is valuable."

Becky pointed to the tray of small hors d'oeuvres she had spread out. I sat and obliged, grabbing a carrot stick and dunking into the store-bought hummus.

"Delicious."

Becky looked pleased.

"Well let's see. How did we meet. Amanda actually wrote me directly. I had just listed my brother Robert's house on Sotheby's, he passed two years ago."

Becky paused, letting her dead brother dance between us.

"I'm so sorry," I said, finally remembering to be polite.

"It was a very bleak moment; my brother Robert was a lawyer. A real Renaissance man, and he loved bluegrass music. He was generous, and kind, well, he was also a little lonely, but he poured everything into that house, he called it *his sanctuary*. The thing about Robert was he was gay, but never really out-out, as they say."

Why was Becky telling me this? I took stock of my outfit, an oversize T-shirt, hiking boots, and baggy pants. I looked undeniably like a lesbian. Was I supposed to mourn Robert with her? My fellow fag? I made a sad, understanding face, bowing my head ever so slightly, which seemed to work. Becky paused to chew on a carrot stick.

"Naturally Robert had impeccable taste, but he had no one to pass anything on to. He was also very into auctions. He has a really wonderful collection of artworks. Anyway, your mom, after seeing the house online, wrote me saying she loved it but she wanted to rent it, two years. Cash up front."

"That sounds like her," I said wistfully, imagining the mountain of bills missing from Red Rock Capital's account.

"Amanda was picky about not involving paperwork, but she was paying. I mean, it wasn't cheap. It's a really beautiful house. A modernist jewel and Robert had such an eye for detail, he worked with that architect for years on the plans. Your mother was very pleased with it, and the cash was nice. I

238

mean, she seemed like someone Robert would like, you know, that's important to me. I can't just let anyone live there."

I nodded, silently, fearful Becky would continue her verbal diarrhea about gay dead Robert. Becky took a long sigh, "I mean, I haven't really heard from your mom since she moved in, but I thought that was a good thing. I've never been a landlord before." She snorted, "I despise the term *landlord*, it sounds so feudal."

I laughed lightly.

"Well, like I said. I just assumed she was away because she traveled so much. She told me she was a big jet-setter. You know, I'm sure that's it. She's probably just on some adventure. She was a funny one, very direct, and a little hard to read, but really beautiful too."

I nodded.

"You inherited her good looks," Becky said, with a celery string stuck between her teeth.

I nodded, it felt good to be Amanda's daughter.

"I'm happy to loan you a set of keys. Jerry, my gardener, said he hadn't seen Amanda on any of his visits, but her things are still there . . ."

I let out an audible gasp. The house was still around, and it was hers—she had things.

Becky picked up another celery stick, then looked at me solemnly, "I hate to ask this. Do you think something bad happened to her?"

There Becky was, dipping her toe into limbo: the line-dancing disco of the disappeared, the kaleidoscope of unconfirmed danger.

"We don't know, we just want to find her."

Becky stood to retrieve a silver set of keys from the kitchen.

"It's on 140 Walnut Hill. I really hope your family are holding up during this," she paused, "unsettling time. If you need someone to talk to, I am here and happy to chat."

I blindly nodded.

"I am sorry I have to get to the groomer before they close, otherwise I'd love to join you."

"It's no problem. I can bring the keys back to you this evening?" I said, trying to hide my relief that she wasn't accompanying me.

"Perfect, and there is an alarm, let me find the code. You'll need to put it in before you can open the door."

I could barely contain my excitement, nearly flying through a stop sign. I didn't even take the time to find a murder podcast to fill the emptiness of the hot van, instead gospel poured from the radio—it no longer felt like tragedy's angels carrying me forth, it was as if full-blown musical-techni-color-jacket-Jesus had taken the wheel. I had no idea what I expected to find, or what I wanted, but I was a devout hoarder on their way to replenish their cup. I wanted all of Naomi's things. I wanted every scrap.

The house on 140 Walnut Hill was just as Becky had described, a modernist jewel tucked up at the top of the Montford neighborhood. All steel, concrete, and glass, with a big oval gravel driveway. I had goosebumps as Chester's ugly van crunched to a stop. I paused before pulling the keys out of the ignition, letting the chorus of Christian gospel swell; I was on the cusp of Naomi's secrets. I got out, noticing the massive pile of newspapers on the stoop, then punched in the code. The house had the sheen of modernity but was bursting with eclectic taste, all *just right*, as if staged for photographs for *Southern Living* magazine. A collection of handwoven baskets dangled near the foyer. Three Rothko-sequel abstract prints hung framed on the entrance wall, and I spotted an ornate clay pitcher made by one of Asheville's most popular potters on an Eames credenza.

A hummingbird feeder drifted empty on the large wooden balcony. The marble counter was spotless, one white dish lay dry in the deep ceramic sink. I opened the fridge, finding a rotting container of yogurt. Expired orange juice and a withered husk of broccoli. I turned toward the office. There it was, a line of rose quartz sat along the window ledge near the fireplace, in descending order, largest to smallest, right to left, just as they had been in the Hamptons and in New York. She had been here. The old chill inched down my spine as I entertained the notion that maybe it had all been a big game of hide and seek, and I had just won.

"Naomi," I called her name out to the silent house.

No response.

I walked up the metal and glass steps to the second floor. The bedroom door was open, and the California king was wrapped snugly in my favorite Frette sheets. I checked the bed stand and was met with the usual pile of trash novels, a deck of tarot cards, a bundle of sage, and a file of papers on WAC. I poured over the papers: PR proposals and updates on a well in Nepal, nothing of real interest, but more concrete proof that Naomi had been here. Then, nearly hidden from sight on the wall, was a cheap OfficeMax-brand calendar, opened to December. I walked up to it, and flipped through the proceeding pages. The only marking was a pale blue Post-it, stuck on March 3, the day after Bryce's birthday. Written in Naomi's slanted handwriting was the word *EXIT.*

I moved through the house like an impatient detective, noticing the dust on the floor. Noticing the limp towel on a doorknob. I touched the white bowl of the bathroom's sink, it was dry. I moved to the closet, there on velvet-clad hangers hung three of the MoMA Design Store–style saris I'd seen her wear the night we'd met, along with a few choice pieces of cashmere. Deep purple underwear was neatly laid out on a top shelf. A stack of clothes lay folded near the door, and a row of twelve hulking Rimowa suitcases lined the wall. My brain twitched back to the pale blue Post-it: *EXIT.* I dropped to my knees and undid the main zipper on the first; it was packed tight, Marie Kondo style, everything folded into bizarrely efficient squares. I opened the next. Pants, shirts, large brimmed floppy hats, vacuum sealed bags of cosmetics and sunscreen, I kept digging. Each suitcase was bursting with items all neurotically organized as if she were going on a ten-thousand-year trip.

The last case in the line was a smaller carry-on, and upon inspection was completely empty, but the main flap, which had flopped over upon unzipping, felt extremely heavy. I undid the inner compartment. Out fell dozens of stacks of cash and a passport. I hastily flipped opened the first page of the passport and released a hiccupy laugh; it was Naomi but with blonde hair and bangs, like something out of a Carmen Sandiego cartoon. I looked at the name: Amanda Elliott.

I felt sure of it, Naomi was alive. She had staged her death and all of this meant that she was out there. The passport and suitcases were proof that she'd had a plan and multiple aliases. And why all the cash? Maybe to her it was petty. A mere fraction of what she'd stolen. Maybe she was wearing a sunhat sitting on some million-dollar boat rereading a trashy Dan Brown thriller. I liked imagining her red hair in the heat. Her natural sunscreen mixing with sweat. Her cooler filled with ice. Paranoia shuttled into my fantasy. For now, I was one step ahead of Bryce and I wanted to erase all trace of Naomi from the house. I packed the suitcases into the back of my mini-van, the twelve oversize rectangles barely fit, but I wasn't going to leave anything.

Back in the house, I shoved the rose quartz hunks into my pockets and cleared out the remaining clothes in the closet, then threw the tarot deck and stack of bedside books into the passenger side of the van. I did a final sweep, emptying the wastebaskets into a tote bag I'd found in the kitchen. And before dropping the keys off at Becky Archer's house, I made a copy at Ace Hardware, just in case I had missed something and would need to return.

I parked at Becky's and was startled when she, still in head-to-toe black athleisure, popped into the van's passenger window, a small white dog trailing her on a leash. My stomach dropped. She would see the suitcases. She would stop me.

"Oh darling, sorry to sneak up on you. Just out walking Winston. He's a very good boy."

I wanted to throw the keys and drive off, I didn't want to get sucked into another Becky talk-hole, I needed to bring home my new hoarder's trove. I needed to get out my microscope and inspect every inch of what Naomi had left behind.

"Winston, come here and meet Tabitha, come show off your fresh haircut."

I huffed audibly.

The animal reluctantly climbed into Becky's arms and was soon breathing its canned-food breath into my face. I fought off my grimace and petted the half-extended shaking creature.

"So, did you find anything?" Becky asked.

I sighed. "You know, Becky, it was just as you assumed. She's just on one of her big trips, off somewhere in Madagascar with limited communication."

Becky looked triumphant, but I wanted to make it airtight, so I added, "She left a note on the counter, which I assume she'd meant to bring to the post office, it had a stamp on it and everything."

Becky let out a swan moan, "Oh, well, I told you so!"

"You did, Becky. Thank you so much," I said releasing the keys into her palm.

"Do you know when she'll be back?" Becky asked. "Not to pester, I know she has several months left in her rental period, but a few interested parties are looking to tour."

I took a pause, "She'll be back soon."

"That's fabulous, will you tell her I say hello?"

I nodded. Winston whimpered, and Becky suddenly leaned in, her eyes scanning in the inside of the van. I froze. She was looking directly at the suitcases. She paused, her lips pursed, then her gaze landed on the passenger seat, and the stack of books I'd cleared from the bedside table.

"She loved a trashy read," I said mechanically, desperate to distract.

"It's a travesty how many trees have been cut down for Stephen King," Becky said, then pointed to the dog-eared copy of *Gone Girl*, "You know, your mom was reading that when I met her, she said it was a nearly perfect book—except the ending, she said it didn't make any sense. I never read that sort of stuff. You know? I prefer the classics, I studied literature at Vassar. Robert and I liked to read from . . ."

To my great relief, Winston began barking and I was saved from having to learn anything more about Vassar or classics or dead gay Robert and his good taste. I hastily said my good-byes as she turned her attention to the dog.

Just as I was pulling out into the street, I turned and saw Becky running after me. Arms waving. My heart sank. I debated stepping on the gas. Instead. I took a breath and rolled the window back down.

"Honey, one last thing, my niece Courtney, not Robert's, of course, from Angelica, my half-sister, well, she just opened a salt cave downtown, if you want to relax, salt can be very healing, it's a life force," she said as she pressed a business card into my palm. "Maybe you and your mom should take a visit when she gets back?"

I smiled and thanked her and tore off as fast as I could. A fucking salt cave? Asheville never failed to deliver. Once on the highway, I threw the card out the window.

Soon I was paranoid that every car was Bryce or one of his henchmen. I kept glancing over at the other drivers. How did everyone know when they were being looked at? Neck after neck snapped toward me. I felt surrounded. I swerved off at the next exit and took the backroads. Bouncing across the dark dirt curves, I was filled with a sense of relief that the van was packed. It felt sexual. I fantasized about laying out each piece of Naomi's clothing, my fingers running over the ridged slickness of the vacuum sealed bags before slicing them open. This time I would figure it all out, this time I wouldn't miss a thing.

18

I unloaded the van like a coked-up valet, desperate to spirit the contents of the cases to the vast floor of the barn. I selected a generic podcast, a young blonde girl gets into an unknown car at a Canadian mall, then shows up in a ditch a year later. The story was so rote, it could have been Enya. I decided to lay all of Naomi's things in neat rows. She had seventeen shirts all in varying shades of cream and lilac. She had six sleep sets made by Vera Wang, ten pairs of shoes. No heels. Just hiking boots, sneakers, and sandals. Four swim-suits, all black one-pieces in varying cuts. And what puzzled me most: one suitcase was filled with clothes for a small child.

In an effort to summon her, I laid out the rose quartz in ascending order on my table then opened the tarot deck. Jessica had taught me you can ask the cards a question, so I mumbled, "Where in the world is Naomi Duncan?" I pulled the Wheel of Fortune. The card was illustrated with an ornate green wagon wheel, and in cursive below claimed itself to be "the token of fate." Naomi's words flooded back to me and it was confirmation that Jesus really had taken the wheel. I dropped the slippery card back to the top of the deck knowing I was entering into the final episode of my podcast with Naomi. Instead of sleeping I pored over the objects in the barn.

I opened a ziplock bag filled with generic white pills, then dug through the contents I'd salvaged from her wastebaskets, but there was nothing of interest other than CVS receipts for seven bottles of melatonin and blonde hair dye. I tried to imagine Naomi and her perfect red scalp using a box of store-bought dye. It made no sense. I counted the money, which came out to a little under $90,000. All of this made it feel like Naomi was likely out there. I wanted to stay up, but my mind began glitching. I couldn't help it. I passed out on the sofa. Hours later, I jerked awake. My next step was to try and get in touch with the coroners in Aspen to get my hands on their report. If Naomi had faked her own death there had to be some trace, some obvious clue. I drove to Hammersmith and found the number online. A woman with a husky voice answered.

"Good morning, coroner's office."

"Hello, my name is Tabitha Duncan, I'm the daughter of Naomi Duncan, and I was hoping to get a copy of my mother's coroner's report. She passed away a few months ago."

"Oh darling, I'm so sorry. There is an intake form you can print off online, and you'll just have to fax a copy of your ID, and then we can send you the report on over. But it's going to cost twenty-five cents per page. Is that all right?"

I *mhmmmed*, and dutifully copied down the fax number, promising to send everything over later that day, but had no idea how to get ahold of Tabitha's driver's license.

Thinking about Tabitha made me pause. She should know Naomi was alive. If my mother had walked away from that car crash, I would have been desperate to know. Maybe I could have been different. I could have healed. I could have lived another life. I had an uncontrollable itch to see, or at least look at Tabitha, so I gulped down the new photos she'd posted online. She was out, celebrating a friend's birthday at Cipriani wearing a gold dress and holding a Perrier bottle with a pouty smile. She was flouting her sobriety. A day later she posted a photo of herself reclined on the leather bank of a private plane, her blue nails tapping at her chin as she looked out at the cotton candy clouds. The next photo was Tabitha in front of the Eiffel Tower in full-on *Emily in Paris* drag. I was not a teenage girl, but even I felt the thunderbolt of desire, not to fuck her, but be her. Tabitha was so skilled at producing the bite of jealousy: the image of an unattainable life. But I knew the truth, I could see it in the green pulp of her eyes, she was unhappy. She would want to know about her mother. She needed this.

I wrote her a message: *TABITHA IT'S ESTHER. I HAVE TO TELL YOU THIS: YOUR MOTHER IS ALIVE. I HAVE PROOF. I KNOW IF OUR SITUATIONS WERE REVERSED, I WOULD WANT TO KNOW. CALL ME. I WILL EXPLAIN EVERYTHING. HERE IS MY NUMBER.* I pressed send and released a sigh, feeling relief from having done the right thing.

Just as I was about to pull out, Ranger, the weekend cook, knocked on my window. I jumped.

"Es, you want some lunch? I roasted lamb."

My stomach growled. I hadn't eaten anything since Becky's pathetic hummus spread. After all my manic driving, the loading and unloading of Rimowas, and all my deranged detective work, I maybe deserved a meal.

I robotically followed Ranger up the stairs and into the silver kitchen of Hammersmith. The smell was all-consuming. The most perfect, delicious, round, caveman, life-affirming scent. *Lamb.*

"Oh, hi, Esther," Lily from the textile studio chirped.

I had been so focused on the lamb I hadn't seen her. She was wearing a yellow tank top, and the giant dragonfly that ensconced her chest was staring at me. I shivered. Why did everyone in the craft universe need a tattoo of nature to confirm their union with it?

"It's so nice you're going to join us!"

I flashed with panic. What was I joining?

Lily filled in, "I think you'll love my slides from my stone weaving trip to Sweden. I brought the lamb from my boyfriend's farm. It's smells great right?"

Now I understood. I had to sit through slides if I wanted lamb. My stomach decided I could afford an hour of stone weaving. I waited for my plate.

The lights were already off in the lounge, and there was a half-blurry image of Lily with a backpack standing outside of an ancient cottage. Lily had a caustically high voice, and went on to explain the intricacies of the Viking tradition, in which stones acted as weights at the bottoms of looms to create tension for weaving. I liked the pictures. There was something eternal about the photographs—they were all blurry, as if Lily had illegally traveled back in time to rob the past of its knowledge. The part of me that always calmed down around craft kicked in, and I watched blissfully as Lily blabbed. But when the lights slapped on, I slipped out—God forbid I have to chat.

Before finally turning the van home, I opened Instagram. A red circle appeared in the corner of my anonymous account. I had never received a message before. I opened it. BITCH UR FUCKED. I JUST TOLD MY DAD YOU CONTACTED ME. HOPE YOU ENJOY PRISON. The full weight of Tabitha's response fell like a *Looney Tunes* anvil falling on my head. Why hadn't Tabitha wanted to know about her mom? Why would she tell Bryce I'd messaged her? Wouldn't she at least want to know about the passport? Or the house in Asheville? Or the suitcases? Or the pale blue Post-it that said *EXIT* in her mother's handwriting? I started the van, then realized I was almost out of gas. I had no choice but to go down the mountain to the Texaco. My mind was reeling on the logistics; how close could Bryce's assholes really be? How much time had I wasted on Lily's stone weaving? I gunned it. As trees shot by, it struck me as funny that I had wanted to die. Now, when the time came—all I wanted was to live. And find Naomi.

The Texaco always reminded me of Ed Ruscha's paintings. It was a vintage postage stamp. A somehow functional image of the past, all red, white, and Lana Del Rey blue. My tank was nearly full when I noticed it, the matte black Mercedes with tinted windows parked near the vacuum station. I tensed. He, or his crony, was here. I wondered if he had followed me to Becky Archer's. I wondered if he knew Naomi was alive. I slowly turned my neck, trying not to draw attention, and saw the pink-faced man, the same one who'd put his hand over my mouth, paying for a Monster Energy drink, standing next to a small man in a matching suit. The pink-faced man's phone rang, he was instantly consumed in conversation. Maybe it was Bryce.

I needed to buy time. I sliced my credit card to pay for the gas, then ducked down to scramble through the contents of my back seat. What did I have? I found my toolbox. I grabbed the awl, the same object that had punctured all the holes in the pages of the scrapbooks, then I slipped across the busted, oil-pocked pavement, and in one, surprisingly seamless gesture, I slammed it into the tire of the Mercedes. I had maybe thirty minutes.

I wasn't sure where I would go. But I knew if I stayed, Bryce's Monster Energy–slurping henchmen would hang me from the ceiling like a chandelier. Back in the barn I began to frantically gather things up. Then, as if on cue, a figure appeared in the barn's door frame. I screamed.

"Esther?" Patrick asked, taking in the grid of objects on the floor and my manic state. "What's all this?"

"Oh hi. Sorry. I'm uhh, sorting through some old stuff, I want to give it to Goodwill."

Patrick looked at me suspiciously. He knew better.

"It was my ex's stuff," I lied. Given the recent and devastating wedding news, this made more sense, but Patrick wanted to ask more.

"What's up?" I blurted, trying to stop the next question.

"Contractor said I need a whole new roof. I got a tarp over it now."

I nodded. I needed him out of my barn. I knew the pink-faced man would be here any minute. How long did it take to change a blown tire?

"You want dinner later? I'm making my chili."

"I can't," I nearly screamed.

Patrick looked hurt. I didn't care. I had to get him out of the barn.

"I have . . . to call my dad, it's uh, his birthday and the only time he can talk is in a few minutes and I need to prepare myself."

Patrick was a sucker for the familial, and despite having no intention of doing so, calling my dad had been his idea, so he accepted the excuse. I needed him to leave. I didn't want to put him in danger. My fear of Bryce's crony trumped the guilt I felt watching Patrick limp back down the hill. In a tornado-esque haze I repacked the suitcases sans Marie-Kondo precision and threw each one back into the van. I would leave nothing for them. I went inside and surveyed my torn-up house; I only wanted the Polaroids. Using a butter knife, I removed the duct-taped square.

Just as I set my hand on the doorknob, I felt the old urge. I wanted to light the whole place on fire. To tip another life into flames. It would be so easy to simply erase it all. I walked to the stove and retrieved the long silver BIC lighter I used for the grill. The butane compartment at the bottom was full of slithery liquid, all I had to do was smash the plastic chamber and let the accelerant soak into the wooden dining table. I could use the meat cleaver. It would take only swing. I wanted to drive away with flames leaping in my rearview mirror. I wanted it to be done. This old life and all its material trappings. My hand clutched the cleaver, but my movement was slowed by the sound of dry brush clattering against the window screen. I remembered the brown forest, and the recent lack of rain. If I lit the house on fire, the whole mountain would go. It wasn't fair to Patrick. He had already lost so much; I took a breath, then solemnly walked toward the door.

Outside the air was crisp and I felt proud for not having slammed the cleaver to the table. Progress. I drove slowly down the driveway so as not to alarm Patrick, the less he knew the better. I stuck to the backroads feeling safe the goons were not yet on my tail. My first stop was the bank. Since I hadn't burnt the house down, I may as well pay it off. I assumed I would never have a suitcase of cash with me again. I parked in the back, then lugged the Rimowa with $90,000 through the door of First Citizen. The old lady with Reba McEntire hair looked shocked as I stacked the cash on the table.

"So, you wanna cover your mortgage in full?"

"Yes, ma'am."

"Ok, well give me a moment," she said as she pecked at her computer.

"All right honey, looks like you owe $42,285."

I nodded. If Naomi really was sitting on some yacht with $200 million of Red Rock Capital's cash, she could spare it. The Reba McEntire bank teller sucked in the side of her cheeks as she sent the cash through the counting machine. I looked at the clock.

Once the machine quieted, the Reba teller clucked, "Ok my dear, I just need you to sign here and here."

As I twirled the pen I felt an immense weight lift off of my shoulders. Debt was the violent aura of this country; everyone walking around weighed down by the shimmering cloaks of what they owed. As I strode out the door of the bank, I felt I had become a new person. My poisoned aura had been released from my shoulders. For now, I was free. Next, I had to ditch my phone, iPad, and van.

I turned the van on and headed down the highway, I didn't want to listen to a podcast. I wanted to be fully present. I wanted to remember the light. I wanted to remember the smell of rubber and heat that hung in the van's air. I reminded myself: I wasn't running from Bryce—I was on my way to find Naomi. I was headed toward the maternal fold. This was my second chance. I had never allowed myself to daydream about it—what would have happened if my own mother had simply slipped out into the night? Maybe found a rich man and a house of her own filled with KitchenAid appliances and thick carpet. I imagined her as she would look now, midfifties, barefoot and twirling in the empty silence of a housewife's afternoon. Beautiful. Bored. Probably Botoxed.

When I got to the overpass that hovered above the South Toe River I pulled onto the shoulder. I walked to the edge and, saying a small prayer of thanks to the inane objects that had tethered me to the world, I threw my iPad and phone into the gurgling current. I felt another slither of freedom. No one could get ahold of me. Next was Sally's Beauty Salon. I had driven past the run-down trailer a thousand times. As I grew closer it seemed to be bursting, the edges held together by expanding foam, like a tube of Pillsbury croissant dough. I had always wanted to know who Sally was. I imagined she was some sort of mountain Miss Piggy, living in a kaleidoscopic universe of powder and hairspray. There were no other cars in the lot—I parked behind a dumpster, out of sight from the road. A hazy bell tinked when I opened the door.

"Hi hun. How are you today?"

The woman who greeted me had an overdyed, several-haircuts-at-once look and seemed half bewildered that I'd walked through the door. She smacked her gum as she stood and pocketed her phone. She was not Miss Piggy, she was more likely to ask for the manager at Applebee's.

"I'm good," I said, "are you Sally?"

The woman got an amused look on her face. "I'm Melissa. Sally's been dead for, oh—nine years now, I took over after her but I thought it woulda been disrespectful to change the name. She was *real* nice."

"Oh," I said.

"What can I do for you?"

"Haircut, and color."

Melissa nodded, and I took my place in front of the mirror, where she had previously been scrolling her phone, the seat still warm from her ass.

"So, what are you thinking?"

"A blonde bob," I said, handing Naomi's passport to Melissa.

Melissa looked at Naomi's photo, then took a handful of my black hair in her Day-Glo manicured fingers.

"Oh honey," Melissa clucked, "this is going to be a *real* transformation, you sure you're ready?"

I nodded.

"Well, you know what they say," Melissa looked up, her pale blue eyes meeting mine, "transformation has no end."

I decided I liked Melissa.

There was no choice about the blonde bob. I needed to get out the country and there wasn't time for an emergency pass-port process; I had to use Naomi's, or rather Amanda's. Melissa worked quickly and soon I was haloed in tinfoil strips and she retreated to the back of the trailer to scroll on her phone while the dye waged its war on my follicles. I looked at myself in the speckled mirror. My eyes were sunken. I was exhausted and still unsure of where I would even go. I opened to the first page of the passport and tried to commit Amanda's birthday to memory, as if border control would quiz me like a bouncer. I looked back at the picture, it was undeniable, Amanda looked older than me. But I took comfort in our similar bone structure, and hoped the hair would obscure the difference.

Melissa slimed me with yet another layer of viscous dye. I checked the clock.

"How much longer?" I asked, as she buzzed around.

"Sweetheart your hair is *black-black,* it's gonna take a while."

After an hour of staring at the array of eighties-era head-shots taped to the trailer's wall, the best plan I could come up with was to simply buy a plane ticket to Madagascar where the most recent wells from WAC had been drilled. Maybe Naomi left some sort of trail of rose quartz and prayer beads I could follow. Melissa returned for another inspection.

"Honey, can you hand me that photo again?"

I handed the passport back to Melissa.

She began to manically flip through the pages, "Aren't there any more pictures in here?"

I cocked my head, "They usually just have the one," I replied trying to hide my surprise at her ignorance.

She huffed and did one more aggressive flip through the little book.

"Oops," Melissa said, bending over to pick up a Post-it which had just fallen out.

It was the same pale blue as the one that had said *EXIT.* Melissa slid the square back in and handed me the passport.

"Should be about another forty, then we can wash it out."

I waited till she'd walked toward the back of the trailer to remove the Post-it. How had Melissa plucked it so readily? And how had I missed it? Maybe because the light blue was the same as the pages of the passport. Maybe because I'd been too manic. Maybe because Melissa was my angel of tragedy. I held up the Post-it, which read *FLIGHT.* Then there was a phone number printed in Naomi's neat handwriting, followed by the numbers 4762.

"Melissa?" I called to the back of the trailer.

"Yes, hun?"

"Could I use your phone, I just realized I left mine at home."

Melissa paused, clearly unsure.

"Umm all right darling, you can use mine."

A few seconds later she appeared at my shoulder with her beat-up Samsung Galaxy caked in makeup dust and finger grease. She watched as I punched in the number. It began ringing. Then I started to panic. What if it was Bryce? What if this had all been some sort of trap? Maybe even Melissa was in on it? The rings continued. My mind was spinning, slow and hot, like a rotisserie chicken. I had so many questions. Then an automated too cheerful voice kicked on, "Hello and welcome to the VistaJet prebooked guest center. If you have the four-digit code for you booking please insert it now followed by the pound sign."

I greedily punched in *4762*. Light jazzy music filled in. Melissa seemed to grow bored of watching me and had shuffled to the back of the trailer and flipped on a small TV.

"Hello Ms. Elliott, apologies for the delay. Are you calling to set a time for your reservation?" a buttery voice asked.

I didn't know what to say so I just burped out a "Yes."

"Fantastic, and when would you like to depart?"

"Today?" I croaked.

"All right, if you'd like to stick to the original flight plan, departing from Asheville Regional Airport, I'm going to have to call down and confirm runway availability. Do you mind holding?"

"Not at all."

The jazz kicked back on. Fear sloshed in my stomach, but I decided I would flow.

"Hi Ms. Elliott, so we are all confirmed. There is a takeoff slot at five forty-five p.m. if that works for you?"

"Umm . . . I mean, yes."

"Great, as usual, you simply need to arrive at the private hangar, the entrance is off Lindbergh Lane, concourse N7. The concierge will take you from there."

"Perfect," I said, as I grabbed a pen from the Pizza Hut cup on the mirror's ledge. I was stunned. This was Naomi's *EXIT*. Or at least one of them. I was desperate to ask where the flight was heading, but I was too scared to tilt my hand and reveal everything I didn't know. And it almost didn't matter, anywhere was better than hanging from my rafters.

Melissa returned and inspected my foil-haloed head.

"Hun, thirty more minutes. Then we blow out."

I looked at the clock. I had two and a half hours to get to the airport, "Fine."

"While you wait, do you want makeup or nails?"

I looked down at the passport in my hand, flipped to the photo, and noticed the eyeliner on Naomi's lids.

"Can you do my makeup, how it is here?"

Melissa smiled, "Of course I can, but who is that?"

She wasn't stupid, she knew it wasn't me.

"It's my mom. She passed away a few years ago, and I woke up this morning and decided I just want to look like her. It's her birthday."

It was an impulsive statement. Maybe risky. Melissa could have checked the birthdate in the passport, but instead she just softened and gave me a smile. I felt a pang of guilt for all the lies, but after all, it was still my dad's birthday, lies could collide to make new truths; here I was.

"Oh honey, I will make you look just like her."

Melissa's hands smelled like cigarettes as she went about transforming my face. She was adept, better then Desirée at Tabitha's makeup launch. Melissa kept stepping back to match the photo to me, closing one eye like she was solving a magic eye puzzle. She carved my cheekbones with a smudge of something dark, then did my lids smoky just like Naomi's. When she was finished with my face, she whipped out an ancient yellow blow-dryer and set about blasting my hair. When it was done I really did look like the photo. I tipped

Melissa five hundred dollars of Naomi's money, and she looked like she was going to pass out.

"I mean, sweetheart, you don't—"

I did.

I got back into the van, knowing I had to ditch it. After twenty minutes on the highway, I pulled off at an overlook on the French Broad River and climbed into the back of the van to find an outfit. If I was going to show up to an airplane hangar pretending to be Naomi, I had to look the part. I pulled out one of her linen dresses and a flowy shawl with orange embroidery, then shoved my old clothes into the suitcase and slid on a pair of Naomi's Prada sunglasses. I caught my reflection in the van's window. I didn't look like myself, I wondered if this is what Jupiter felt like, picking out the striped blue polo shirt he would wear on the day that would define his life. I didn't have a gun, but there was something inside of me that felt like I was on a violent path.

I walked to the edge of the overlook; the current was strong and the water looked gray and amorphous, like elephant skin flexing in the sun. I inhaled, walked back to the van, and began my performance, standing dumbly in front of the popped hood; I was the blonde damsel in distress. It was an archetypal scene, it was Hollywood, maybe even biblical; blonde sends a flare into the universe, blonde needs an intervention from God. A trucker slowed down but didn't stop. A Southern Stepford-looking mom with two squawking children in the back of an Escalade pulled over to ask if I was all right. I told her I was fine. I didn't want her; I needed someone I could pay off. I needed moral swill—I was trying to disappear. I prayed the right person would come before the matte black Mercedes. A man in a gray Subaru Forester slowed; I smiled pathetically, but he kept driving. I was running out of time.

Finally, a twenty-something-year-old in a run-down sedan pulled off to the side of the road and asked with his sunburnt face and thick mountain drawl, "You havin' car trouble ma'am?"

Like everything biblical, it felt like a porno. I was myth. I was sin. And I needed salvation. I nodded, and pitched my voice higher, "And I have to get to the airport, is there any chance you can drive me? I'll pay you four hundred bucks."

"Four hundred?"

The sunburnt boy looked as if he had won the lottery.

"Five hundred if you promise to not tell a soul you picked me up."

His eyes pulsed. He may have liked the money but he was turned on by the telenovela. He puffed out his chest as he started loading my suitcases into his car. He was now playing his part. My bags barely fit, but he bungeed the trunk with a tired piece of cord, two of the suitcases still visible to anyone tailing us.

"What's your name?"

"I'm Amanda."

"I'm Buck," he replied shifting out onto the highway.

I felt Buck's eyes trace up my legs and when he noticed my calves were unshaven he quickly looked back to the road. I knew there was no such thing as a kind man. And it is not just the stranger in the busted sedan. It is the brother's friend. The dad's coworker. The neighbor's son. Safety for a woman in a dress even with unshaved legs was impossible. I leaned back in my seat. If Buck tried to rape me, maybe I would let him or maybe I would kill him. Buck looked nervous, he turned up a Kenny Chesney song about drinking beer in Mexico.

"Where you headed?" Buck finally asked, his chin nodding to the suitcases behind me.

"California," I lied. Women with blonde hair having car trouble were always headed to California. Buck just nodded. Six Kenny Chesney songs later we had arrived. I had never been to the private airstrip and obviously neither had Buck.

We pulled into the side entrance, and I told the guard my name, *Amanda Elliott*; he dutifully checked me off without even asking for my passport. Buck twisted on to the black pavement.

A concierge in a navy polo shirt and beige pants came bounding toward the car, he was good-looking in an overexfoliated way and eyed the sedan suspiciously. I nodded to the suitcases, deciding it was best to simply be quiet. I took five crisp hundreds from the small suitcase and handed them to Buck with an ingenue's smile. I fought the urge to go full camp and peck him on the cheek—men still repulsed me. This damsel had limits.

"Would you like to wait on the plane? We have another fifteen or so before we're clear to take off," the concierge said with a sheet-white smile as he ferried the last of the suitcases to his cart. I nodded with a rich woman's self-importance and slipped him a tip. Money was a distraction from truth; it vibrated in place of questions. As I walked toward the hangar, the concierge tried to remove the carry-on from my hands but I protested. I wanted to keep the money close. When I turned into the large metal hall, I was struck with fear; it was a small plane. There was no way it could make it across the ocean. Where were we going? Maybe this was just a vacation she'd planned and I'd find myself dropped off in Aspen or the Hamptons, directly into the lap of Bryce. I boarded silently, too afraid to say anything.

A bottle of sparkling water sat on the table next to a mound of fresh fruit, and I felt the strange urge to take a photo. I wanted to capture my decadence in pixels, to post it to Instagram, to make a TikTok. That was the thing about wealth, it was boring alone, it needed to be flaunted. Tabitha knew that. I took my place at the center of the plane and tried to imagine I belonged. I had studied enough rich women while painting portraits for Michael Valentine that I knew how they held their necks when they were bored, how they cocked their chins in disinterest, and how they subtly checked their phones mid-conversation. I tried to remember it all. To channel the conga line of unhappy wealthy women in designer clothes.

The concierge popped his head in to let me know that we were cleared to take off. He closed the door in a seamless gesture. I held my breath for what felt like the whole flight, tracing the land below with my eyes, trying to ascertain where we were going. Mountains undulated into flat ground, a patchwork landscape of brown, backyard pools, suburbs, then solid clouds. More clouds. Fluffy. Tubular. Then striated. Finally, as the plane dipped, the pilot made an announcement, "Syracuse is looking beautiful."

Syracuse looked like any American city. Why the fuck was Naomi headed here? I felt a rush of annoyance. The plane's wheels touched down and I craned my neck around the large black asphalt expanse. There were no ominous matte Mercedes or cops. I relaxed as we slowly taxied into a red metal hangar, and a man with a mustache and neon wind-breaker bounded forward to wave the plane in. The pilot exited his chamber and opened the plane door.

"Ma'am the next charter won't be ready for another thirty minutes or so, if you'd like to wait in the lounge," he said, extending his hands to the stairs.

There was another flight. I smiled; my overwhelming relief hidden by the shadow of the Prada sunglasses. Then I saun-tered behind the neon-clad man to the lounge, which didn't seem nearly luxurious enough. Six bottles of FIJI Water sat unrefrigerated on a wooden table, a gray couch stood near a window, and a corded phone was attached to the wall next to two plants in desperate need of water. I sat on the couch and watched through the glass door as the neon man removed Naomi's suitcases from the abdomen of the small plane I'd arrived on.

I was grateful to not be surrounded by other miserable travelers. My mother would have loved this, flying private. There were so many times when I was with Michael Valentine, at some Swiss chateau or collector's house, when I would try and beam my mother in. I wanted her to see that having wall-to-wall carpet and tangerine pool furniture in Ohio was not the pinnacle of living. There was so much more.

"I'm sorry to report, it's going to be another forty, do you need anything?" the neon man chirped, ducking his head into the glassed-in room.

"I'm fine," I replied, desperate to get back onto a plane.

I wanted to disappear into a white cloud and start over. I had so many lives to escape. I wondered where Jessica was? On the couch skimming wedding blogs? Patrick was probably puttering around the yard, Jupiter in the common room watching *Star Trek*. Where was my dad? Maybe eating steak by himself in the kitchen, football rattling away in the background. It was still his birthday. I hadn't texted him the usual perfunctory message, and my phone was now tumbling along the bed of the South Toe River. I felt a flash of guilt. The texts were all we had. I walked, zombie-like, to the thirsty plants that stood, contrapasso, next to the landline and punched his number in. While I waited for the rings, I poured out one of the Fiji bottles into the dry soil.

"Hello?"

Again, his voice snapped me, I wasn't prepared. The weight of my body jerked onto the wall, "Happy birthday, Dad."

He was quiet for a second.

"Thanks, Es. And thanks for calling me back."

"What?" I asked, still shaken by his familiar timbre. "When did you call me?"

"A few hours ago."

I could suddenly hear it; the fog of his breathing. Something was off.

"What's wrong?"

"Well kid, I got lung cancer. Figured I should tell you, promised myself I'd do it by my birthday. Here we are."

I slid down the wall, "Do you want me to come home?"

He scoffed, "Just wanted you to know."

"I'm so sorry, Dad. Are you sure you don't want me to come?"

"It's about fucking time for me to die. That's how I see it. All that smoking was finally good for something."

My dad's flashing darkness was a reminder of my own. We were the same. Unable to cope. Alone. Afraid. I tried to tamp down the quiet volcano inside of me wanting to blame someone else for his poisoned lungs: Philip Morris, capitalism, politicians, the Marlboro Man. Then, somehow, releasing myself from the twisted spaghetti of irrational blame, I was stunned by the fact that he had called. He never called. I never called. All of the things we had missed rushed in. Milestones. Dentist appointments. Breakfasts. Christmas presents. Photographs of sunsets, memes of otters, all the stupid things that a family shares with one another. We had given each other only space.

"But, Es. Here's the thing. There is something else. It's about your mom."

"Mmm?" I grunted, unable to find language, still tossing through the clutter of everything missed.

"You remember her crash?"

I forced out a "Yeah."

"I know you always blamed Madeline for getting her drunk."

I winced, my eyes pressing shut, remembering the U-Haul. The last time I'd seen his face.

"I didn't . . ."

"You did. I know you did. And here's the thing. Your mother, shit, Es . . ."

He sputtered off into a terrible round of coughing. I waited for him to clear his lungs.

"She didn't die that night."

I felt my soul crack open. A million sunsets collapsing onto my forehead. The room tilted. The universe bloomed in fast-forward like a mushroom in a David Attenborough film. My mother was still alive. Still out there, just like Naomi.

"She's alive?"

My dad was coughing again. "No, Es, she's not alive. She just . . . she chose to die. The car crash didn't kill her, it just severed her legs. The doctors gave her a choice. She could've lived, but they would have needed to amputate from her hip down."

"She chose—to—" I couldn't finish the sentence.

"I should have told you. But she made me promise not to—"

I tried to find composure, "She died on purpose?"

"Yes."

How selfish does a mother have to be to choose to die? How vain? How weak?

"Is that why I couldn't visit her in the hospital?"

My dad went silent, then coughed, "She thought if you came to see her, she'd change her mind."

Something hard had split open in my chest, and I was now bawling.

"What does this mean?" I finally choked out.

"It means you didn't need to burn Madeline's house down," he laughed, "but she deserved it." I released a gargled, mid-cry laugh, meeting his own sarcastic baritone.

"It also means. Well, that I'm sorry. I was so mad at your mom that I was mad at you," he said, his voice now solemn, "and I know that wasn't right."

I thought back to his anger after her death. To the sound of her possessions plunking into the metal trash can. To the frigid nights of silence that had passed between us.

"Do you think she regretted it?" I asked. "Deciding to die."

"I know she did," my dad said, "she told me, at the very end—but there was no going back at that point."

We were both quiet. My mother's beauty had been her gravity. That Betty Draper smile. Her perfect hair, her Coke-bottle silhouette. It had meant more to her than I did. Or Dad, or anything on this planet.

"I should have told you sooner."

I was quiet for a while. What would I have done with this information sooner? I flipped through the alternate versions of myself like a game of *Guess Who?*

"Thank you for telling me," I said, with kindness, wide and forceful. "I love you, Dad."

He was crying now, "I love you too."

We both let the foreign words hover between us. I looked around the airport lounge. "I might disappear for a while, just so you know."

"Me too," he said with a sad laugh. "Maybe we'll do better next time. Take care kid," then hung up the phone.

I sat on the floor for what felt like years, the Rubik's Cube of time unhinging and rearranging into a pile of jagged colored squares in my lap—my father was dying—my mother had chosen to die—but my father loved me—and my mother had chosen not to see me. What did any of it mean? I wasn't sure. But I felt somehow lighter, somehow filled with helium, as if I would no longer need a plane to cross the ocean.

"Ms. Elliott, the flight is ready," the concierge blipped, popping his head through the glass door.

I stood up, grateful again for the Prada glasses that masked my tear-stained face, and walked toward the slick winged machine. It was bigger than the last. I hoped this one could outrun the emptiness that now seethed inside of me. I was nearly halfway up the stairs when I turned back.

"Wait, I have to do something."

266

"No problem," the concierge said mechanically as I pushed past him.

Back in the waiting room I picked up the phone and dialed.

"Hello?"

"Dad, are you sure you don't want me to come? Maybe it could be good?"

"Es, no," he began coughing, then wheezing. "I'm in a lot of pain. And honestly, I'm ready to go."

"You sure?" I pleaded. I assumed I could get the plane rerouted. I could be there in a few hours. I could hold his grumpy gray hand as he tilted off this planet. I could be a saintly daughter for the last days. It could absolve both of us.

"I just, I wanted you to know. And I wanted to hear your voice."

"I have a plane, I could—"

"Es, this is what I wanted, all right?"

I gulped, "All right."

"Take care, kid."

He hung up.

I shakily climbed the stairs. Slumped in the back as we took off, I thought about all the hours of podcasts I had listened to. All of the thousands of stories of violence enacted from person to person like hard links of chain. I had listened because I had yearned for the velocity of justice. I had wanted each disappeared woman to be broken from the confines of her own circuitous victimhood. I had wanted vengeance, a hell raising; a return to the feeling of Madeline Lancaster's house turning to ash. But it had been my own mother—she had decided to die, there was no one to blame. All of that venom that raged in my blood was my own.

I lay my head against the champagne-colored seat and watched as the clouds scattered beneath me, my mind filtering through the meager images I could remember of my mother:

trying on dresses in a department store, laughing in her car, drunk at Madeline's. I felt sick. I ran to the toilet and dry heaved as the pilot made an announcement. I had missed it. He had said a city I had never heard of, then cracked a joke I didn't catch. I wanted to knock on the cabin door but I was too weak. I yearned for Naomi, for some sort of safety and a barrage of answers: Where was I going? Why had my mom chosen to die? What happened to Marcella-Marie? How had she faked her own death? I felt confused and feverish but tried to draw comfort from the fact that I was hurtling toward Naomi, and that we were bonded, both of us having escaped Bryce and our own families riddled with stripes of darkness. We were going to start over together. Fate: spikey and unyielding.

19

The flight was endless. I felt fidgety. After the sting of my mother's "decision" and the news of my father's impending death filtered through my body, I felt molecularly altered. I was worried if I checked myself in the mirror, I would look different. I inspected my hands and could barely recognize them. I desperately wanted to think about something else. The iPad mounted to the back of the headrest had a selection of movies, I lunged for it.

There were dozens of superhero flicks but gym rats in spandex did nothing for me. I didn't want anything sad either, so I settled on *Hustlers* with Jennifer Lopez. I wanted a lobotomy. Tits and ass. J.Lo plays Ramona, a stripper who starts ripping off Wall Street bros in the midst of the 2008 financial collapse. I could barely follow the plot, but I liked watching the girls' thighs flex around the pole, and there was something cathartic about the finance bros being drained of their wealth in bouncy montage: credit cards swiped while drinks tipped down throats. It was Robin Hood. Take what you can from the rich. When I was done, I dragged the cursor back to the beginning. There it was in white font, *Based on a True Story*. I felt my skin ripple. Like with all true crime, that iridescent cave of possibility opened up; this could happen to anyone.

I watched the movie again, this time imagining Jennifer Lopez as Naomi, writhing around the LED stage in a rhinestone G-string, surrounded by Red Rock Capital's bills. I felt slightly turned on. Then after a few more scenes, Jennifer drifted from Naomi to my own mother and I felt a flash of horror. I couldn't unsee it. My mother would have been a wonderful stripper; she loved money and her body, which seemed like it should be enough, but she hated sleaze. I tried to get the image out of my mind. My mother in a neon thong. My mother with highlights. My mother with her tits out. I closed my eyes. And willed her to leave my brain, to let me be. How could she have been alive after her accident?

I needed to find a new movie. I needed to distract myself so I wouldn't think about my mother's legs turning purple in the hospital bed, the doctors calmly explaining the options: to die or amputate. Did her life unspool in front of her eyes? Did she think of me? And what about my dad? Why had he waited till his deathbed to tell me? Couldn't we have hated her together? Bonded at baseball games? Talked shit while flipping burgers? I quickly flipped through the films and settled on *Ocean's Eleven*. Another movie about grifters, stealing from the rich, again heavy on montage, and Brad Pitt was always eating. Watching his mouth wrap around a burger in a hotel parking lot reminded me of my own stomach. I was fucking starving.

There was no stewardess to shuttle plates of overly salted food. I wanted care. I wanted a shoulder rub. I wanted someone to tuck me in to the cashmere blankets that lay folded at the sideboard. My loneliness fused with my hunger and I felt nauseous again. I took my shoes off and walked around the empty plane. In the back, below the slick tortoiseshell bar was a glassed refrigerator, I saw it: dozens of tall bottles of wine, two plates of antipasti, a steak tartare, and a chopped salad. Dinner. My mouth was foaming as I moved the trays to my seat. I watched *Ocean's Twelve* next, chugging Chardonnay and gorging on olives and crackers.

At some point I fell asleep. How long had I been out? I looked out the window and was faced again with only clouds. The monotony of the journey was clawing at me. I didn't want to watch any more movie stars in plastic scenarios. I wished I had an iPhone filled with photos. That was what everyone else did in the emptiness of flights, the ritual of shoveling through the emotional snowbank of pixels that constituted a life—but I knew my digital slush would have been filled with nothing but pain. I needed a distraction. I lunged toward Naomi's carry-on Rimowa, stowed horizontally next to me. I rummaged through the strange soup: rose quartz, bundles of sage, stacks of cash, Naomi's bedside thriller books, and my toiletries: a toothbrush, toothpaste tabs, and a bamboo hairbrush. I pulled out Naomi's favorite, *Gone Girl*, by Gillian Flynn.

I hadn't read fiction since college when I'd been forced to read Mary Shelley's *Frankenstein*. I found fiction manipulative and filled with hyperbole, but I needed something to fill my brain, so I cracked the well-worn spine. The first chapter was about the husband. Nick hated his wife. Or he was afraid of his wife, I wasn't sure. Either way he was selfish and sad, I didn't like being in his head. Maybe this was why I didn't like fiction, because it rendered men three dimensionally, forcing me to crawl into the bouncy castle of masculinity that I normally so easily ignored. I kept reading, then nearly dropped the book. The second chapter was from the wife's perspective, and her name was *Amy Elliott*. Stunned, I reached for the passport that lay perpendicularly in my pocket and opened to the first page. The spelling of the last name even matched. So did the description of the blonde bob. And *Amy* was a nickname for Amanda. What the fuck was Naomi doing? Naomi had Gone Girled herself.

The fictional Amy goes missing on the couple's fifth wedding anniversary and Nick is the main suspect. Nick is clearly a buffoon, fucking a younger girl, and filled with electric bile over the molting of his type-A wife, who is no longer the swirling laugh-easy-beauty he thought he'd married in

New York City. But Nick isn't totally wrong, Amy is vicious, manipulative, and vengeful. And Amy frames Nick for her murder, meticulously draining her own blood to spread on the floor and promptly cleaning it up, leaving a luminol-ready trail, quietly making friends with the pregnant village idiot to steal her urine, and writing a retroactive diary that plots abuses that never occurred, making it impossible for the cops to look anywhere else. Nick must have murdered his pregnant, terrified wife.

But it is the format that interests me, the gamification of the investigation as planned by Amy: the scavenger hunt. In her glittery life in New York City, before the move to miserable North Carthage, Missouri, Amy is a writer of personality quizzes. She likes riddles. She likes hints and clues, and every year for their anniversary Amy plans a scavenger hunt, and at the end lays his boring mannish gift: monogrammed stationery or a leather briefcase. But this time, the fifth anniversary, on which Amy disappears, the treasure hunt forces Nick to reveal a string of clues that implicate him: a storage shed of bullshit bought on maxed out credit cards, the bloodied murder weapon, and the diary filled with her fictive terror.

A bell was clanging church-like in my skull. The scrapbooks with their odd mixing of incriminating financial documents and family photos were the same type of corn-syrup classic-display-of-love laced with poison. I closed my eyes. I knew Naomi had been planning her *EXIT* the day after Bryce's birthday. If she had disappeared, the cops would have wanted to see the scrapbooks, and they would have certainly found the financial documents an odd addition. They would have called in a specialist. It wouldn't take long to see the pattern, the years of siphoned funds from Red Rock Capital. Naomi's anger. It was all there. All the proof they needed to put Bryce away, all within the innocent binding of a family album.

Two hours later, I'd gulped it down. Amy, despite engineering her own disappearance, decided she missed her husband. So, she returned to her Missouri McMansion covered in the blood of an ex-boyfriend who she'd blamed for her abduction. She was both hero and victim, and in the very end she knocked herself up with Nick's frozen sperm, trapping him in nuclear familial hell. I shut the book, closing my eyes, I remembered back to Becky Archer standing on the sidewalk in Asheville, extending her dog Winston into my van. What had she said to me when she'd seen the pile of books in the passenger side window? She said that Naomi had hated the ending of *Gone Girl*.

I felt frantic. I needed to get ahold of Becky. I got up and looked around the plane, the other flat screens on the edges of the seats only offered up a selection of movies, no internet. In a nook behind the bar, I finally found a white wall-mounted iPad that hung near a phone with an AT&T logo emblazoned on it. I retrieved the iPad, discovering I could control the lighting of the airplane and the music, speak with the captain, and log in to Wi-Fi. I furiously googled *Becky Archer*. Nothing but LinkedIn profiles of other Beckys. I checked her street and her name. Again nothing. Then I remembered her niece's fucking salt cave. I searched for it. There it was, in all its new-age Asheville glory. *Welcome to our caves! We like to call our unique salt "liquid love sunlight" or "liquid love-light energy" because it lives inside of all of us! We also call it "mother goddess soup" because salt is the physical representation of pure sun and light energy.* I scoffed. Then I found the number at the bottom, took the AT&T phone, and dialed. The receptionist on the other end was not in fact Becky's niece, but was nonetheless too agreeable, and released Becky's number without even asking my name.

I waited for the bleeps.

"Hello?"

"Hi, Becky—how are you, this is Tabitha, Amanda's daughter."

"Oh honey, how is your mother?"

"She's great," I lied.

"Lovely to hear. I've been trying to get in touch with her. I have a potential buyer in town next week, I think he is absolutely the type of person Robert would want to live in his house, a cellist from the LA Phil, very funny guy. But I haven't heard back from your mom. I called, and even texted a few times."

"Yes, she wanted me to tell you it was totally fine," I lied again, "just off traveling."

"Oh, wonderful."

"Becky, one last little thing."

"Of course."

"I'm trying to . . ." I paused; how could I ask this? "I'm doing some gift shopping for my mom, and trying to pick out a book. You mentioned her opinion on *Gone Girl*, that she didn't like the ending. What exactly did she say?"

Becky paused, "Oh gosh, well I only remember because she was so emphatic, she said she loved the book but the ending didn't make sense, because, why spend all that time framing your husband if you didn't have a plan for what to do after? Or something like that . . ."

Winston started barking in the background, and I took my exit.

"Thanks Becky," I mumbled before hanging up.

Gone Girl was the blueprint, but Naomi had wanted to plan the life after the miserable husband, not simply drive away to some dumpy hotel and watch the house of cards fall.

And then the clouds parted, and it hit me: Naomi had left this trail of crumbs on purpose. She'd wanted to see if I could find her. This was *my* scavenger hunt. That was why she had been so insistent on dangling the fishing lure of *fate*. I imagined Naomi waiting at the airport for me with fat white roses, the Monsanto kind, artificial and wrong. She would greet me with a hug, lead me to a waiting car, and we would twist off into the sunset with two hundred million dollars at our disposal.

In the quiet hum of the airplane, I no longer felt like an imposter. Naomi had planted clues. It had all been a game; she'd left me the Post-it and the passport and booked this flight. This was my *EXIT*. Feeling untouchable, I took the iPad and pressed the button that allowed me to speak with the captain, "What is the country code of our arrival airport?"

It was a simple question, unrevealing of what I didn't know.

"MLE," a happy voice chirped over the speakers, "should be smooth sailing, just another four hours."

I googled MLE. The first thing I saw was a photograph of a runway cutting across a thin island surrounded by topaz water. *Velana International Airport, Maldives.* I began to furiously read everything I could about the Maldives, starting with Wikipedia. *An archipelagic country in the Indian subcontinent of Asia, situated in the Indian Ocean.* Every photo online looked like tropical stained glass: undulating shards of blue, turquoise, and hot yellow light. There were photos of thatched luxury resorts and white linens draped on wooden tables. Great blooming plants. Small sun-white boats.

Next, I googled *passport control Maldives.* I was nervous that I would stumble at the last block and be sent back. A tourist to the Maldives was granted a single thirty-day visa, and all passports had to be valid for six months from the entrance date; I nervously checked mine. It was good for another nine-and-a-half years. There was no extradition treaty with the United States. There were five different types of sea turtles and the main export was frozen fish. To my relief there were no venomous snakes. Only a small portion of the 1,192 islands were inhabited.

The hours stretched like silly putty. I needed to be off the plane. I needed to run. I needed to scream. I kept googling the islands of the Maldives. Which was she on? I wanted to see a photo of Naomi seated at one of the fancy hotel's breakfast buffets. I wanted a picture of her laughing at the beach. I wanted the stock-photo version of Naomi to explain her obsession with *Gone Girl*. Instead, I googled old photos. Naomi at WAC events. On a green lawn in the Hamptons. But I eventually grew exhausted of ingesting her stiff old smiles. I wanted our future, I began pacing. Then I tried to sit cross-legged and meditate but it was no use. There was no calm, I resorted to another movie.

I couldn't follow the plot to save my life but it centered around another evil, maniacal financial warlord who could control time or at least reverse entropy. I liked the scenes in the free port where the time machine was located. A few years earlier, I'd spent an afternoon in the Geneva free port, doing touch-ups of Alizarin crimson to the background of one of Michael Valentine's paintings. The innocuous silver building had held over one hundred billion in art, all untaxed, and the air had had a specific tang, so clean it was unlike any museum, more like a spaceship. Absolute purity. I took a breath and looked out the airplane's window.

Fiction and fact were weaving in and out, I felt myself as every dark heroine, thundering toward a new life. Naomi had opened the gates. Then the plane lurched, dipping below the clouds, and I was greeted with an endless stretch of freakishly blue waters. We touched down, my heart now in my stomach. After a few minutes of taxiing, the captain exited the cockpit holding his white hat, "It's been an honor to have you on board, Ms. Elliott."

"Thank you for the—uh—smooth flight," I sputtered, grabbing my carry-on suitcase and heading for the open door. On the threshold I paused, overwhelmed as the recirculated airplane oxygen merged with the hot salt air. I scanned the tarmac for Naomi. A flash of red hair. A bouquet of roses, something. But there was no one.

"I believe your next flight is already at the port," the pilot said, in response to my eyes scrolling the asphalt.

My next flight? I wasn't done? I forced a smile, put my sunglasses on, and began my climb down the stairs. A minute passed, then a man in a cotton shirt and orange vest came to greet me, removing the carry-on from my hands. This time I didn't protest. Without saying a word, he loaded up a topless Jeep and we sped off across the tarmac.

The Jeep came to a stop in front of a small glassed-in booth where a man with Albert Einstein-esque eyebrows in a sweaty uniform checked my passport. I held my breath. My makeup from Sally's Beauty Salon had long smeared, but my hair looked the same as the photo. I tried to stand confidently. To exude the diamond certitude of Amy Elliott on her escape from North Carthage, Missouri. The man flipped through my passport, glanced at me, and then with no fanfare whatsoever, thwapped a rubber stamp onto one of the baby-blue pages. I heaved. The second I was back in the Jeep, the driver swerved to the right and a few jiggling minutes later we were at a sparkling port filled with parked seaplanes that looked like the overgrown toys of a wealthy toddler.

I didn't like watching the tiny planes bump with the tide and I stood uncomfortably as three men loaded my suitcases onto one with green wings. I wanted to stop them. It seemed like far too much weight. Instead, I took an uneasy inhale as the eighth suitcase was pushed through the white hatch. I closed my eyes and focused on my breath like Jupiter had taught me. The air in my lungs was delicious and alkaline. Clichéd scripted words about Dorothy and Kansas twirled in my head. Red slippers and tornados. *I was very far from home.*

When I opened my eyes, the last of the suitcases had disappeared into the tiny plane.

A tall man was walking toward me with a pilot's swagger, sunglasses suspended on his neck and clipboard in his hands.

"Good afternoon," he said cheerfully in rough English, then pulled out a set of keys, motioning for me to board the bobbing vessel. I hesitated, wondering what would happen if I decided not to, maybe I could just stay on land, but like all points of this journey, I succumbed to the flow, and climbed the rickety metal steps. Just as I was strapped in, the psychotically loud machine lurched forward, and we defied gravity and logic, dipping up and down, above the bright choppy water.

I puked four times. Hard, sour retches. The pilot with his broad smile kept looking back at me and raising his eyebrows as if that gesture might calm my stomach.

"I'm fine," I said, with a grimace, returning my face to the paper bag he'd handed me.

"We'll be at Naru in thirty," the pilot said.

Naru, I repeated in my head as I puked again. The pilot's eyebrows shot back up as he gave me another reassuring smile. I no longer cared where we were going. I would have preferred the plane to crash than withstand another second of vibration.

"There it is," the pilot pointed his thin finger to a dock jutting out of the green world, a swirl of foliage and pool-blue water.

Wet-eyed from vomiting, I again looked for Naomi, but there was no one standing on the long helix of sun-bleached planks.

As the island grew closer, I kept scanning, straining to follow the white-sand beach as it disappeared into dense tropical forest. Where was she? The plane landed with a queasy finale, ramming forward then back, bile cresting the hump of my throat. The pilot jumped out of the plane and, biceps flexing, unloaded the suitcases while I stumbled onto the dock. I dropped to my knees and released saliva into the Gatorade-blue water.

After thudding the last of the suitcases onto the hot dock, the pilot clapped his hands dramatically.

"Thank you," I managed to mumble, before turning back to the ocean for one last spit-soaked slob.

The pilot disappeared into the plane, only to return with a plastic bottle of water, which he left next to my throbbing form. Finally, I remembered to tip him.

"Good luck," he said with a laugh.

There was a rip of propeller. He was off. And I was completely alone on an island in the middle of nowhere. No phone. No computer. No way to contact anyone. Once even the drone of the plane faded, I looked up as if another plane would arrive and scoop me up like a fish in a pelican's throat. But there was nothing in the sky except a single gray cloud that slinked in front of the sun, and it dawned on me: maybe I had made a mistake.

I guzzled the bottle of water and stood. What was I supposed to do now? I had been shuttled from place to place by men in vests, khakis, and uniforms but now there was no one. Should I wait for some beacon of hospitality to arrive? A bellhop in board shorts? Was there some magical iPad with a call button or would I have to enter into the jungle like an episode of *Lost*? Without any other real choice, I set off, abandoning my bags on the dock, and was instantly washed in the sounds of the island; crickets, birds, buzzing bugs, and the electric symphony of shifting leaves. And after a few minutes, the path curved and popped out at another white beach, then I saw it, a massive house on stilts, and I felt an iron certainty: she must be inside. My feet moved quickly as I ran up the raised steps.

I pushed open the large carved wooden door.

"Hello?" I called into the tiled entrance hall.

It took a second for my eyes to dilate. The heavy linen curtains were drawn shut but light filtered in through the edges. The house was grand and decorated with care, the walls all shades of cream, the ceilings vaulted with dark shiny beams.

"Hello?" I called again.

Then I heard a baby's shrill unhappy cry.

"Hello—?" An adult voice spiraled back from the end of the hall. My heart lurched. *Naomi.* I gathered myself, smoothing down my travel-wrinkled clothes and took a relieved gulp of air, I had just won the scavenger hunt; I was here to gather my prize. I felt as if I deserved confetti or a balloon drop or at least a five-star dinner. A few seconds later a woman appeared with long black hair and soft unfocused eyes, as if she'd just been woken up from a nap. She was young. Twentysomething. It was not Naomi.

"I'm so sorry," my words stumbling, realizing I had trespassed into this house. Onto this island. And into this life.

"Amanda?" The woman asked, half desperate, rubbing her eyes.

"Yes?" I said without thinking.

"Oh. I'm so relieved you're finally here, we've all been worried," she said, in an accent that was vaguely Eastern European.

"Where is Naomi?"

The woman tensed, confused. "I don't know Naomi. I'm Sara. I've been taking care of Marcella-Marie for you. I was hired through the adoption agency, but since we couldn't get ahold of you, I stayed on . . ."

"Marcella-Marie?" I blurted. Was she here? Was she still alive? How old would she be now; eleven or twelve?

"She'll be so excited to meet you."

I followed Sara, who smelled faintly of lavender, down the cool hallway and into a big room with flowing white curtains. There sat a mahogany crib holding a six-monthish-old baby whose feet and hands were careening through the air. I gasped.

Sara gently cleared her throat, "Marcella-Marie, there's someone you should meet. This is your mom, Amanda."

I released an unexpected jet of air.

"I'll give you some time together," Sara said, putting her hand on the handle of the door.

20

I sat on the floor and stared at the baby's fat face, which was perfect, her brown eyes flaring with curiosity and distrust. I stuck my hand out for her to inspect. She promptly put my finger in her mouth, and I felt miraculously accepted. I looked around the room at the soft rugs and the bird mobile that dangled above the crib. This wasn't the same child I'd seen in the scrapbooks, and Sara had said *adoption agency*. Sara had called me *mom*. Staring at the baby I felt a cellular kick. I needed to hold her. I lifted Marcella-Marie out of the crib. She smelled like grass and dew and settled into my shoulder with heavy satisfaction.

Sara opened the door just a crack, "Just to let you know, if you're all right with her I'm going to run to the farm to pick up some groceries."

I nodded, grateful to get a moment alone to try to figure out what to do next. I counted to ten after hearing the front door bang shut and walked out into the hall with Marcella-Marie slumped over my shoulder. There were seven rooms on the second floor, and all of the doors stood open, all with identical furniture. Wooden headboards made from driftwood. Beds with no sheets. Oversize bathtubs that looked like ostrich eggs sliced in half. Towels in neatly folded rolls rested on shelves. Island-y paintings hung on the wall in gold frames. It dawned on me that this had been a fancy hotel or maybe a B&B, which explained the entrance that was a little too grand, and the hallways that were eerily identical.

Marcella-Marie started crying and I began the age-old bounce. Up, down. Up, down. Once she was calm and her pink smile had returned, I wound my way down the large spiral staircase and moved toward the back of the building where I found a kitchen that felt semi-industrial, or at least capable of cooking dozens of breakfasts at once. The walls were a cheery yellow and there was a large window that looked out at a sparkling pool.

"Where the fuck is Naomi?" I asked the baby.

Marcella-Marie responded with a spit bubble round as a marble.

On the stainless-steel fridge, I found a pamphlet with the name *NARU FARMS* in bright yellow cursive. I hungrily opened it. Glossy images of vegetables stared back at me. On the second page there was a map of the island with a gold star in the top right corner that read *Naru Farms*. In the *ABOUT US* section, I learned that Naru was home to around forty farmers and scientists from all over the world, who lived and worked on the island. Everything was organic, self-sustainable, and season-conscious. The farm specialized in *hydroponics, and is dedicated to developing new technology for our current climate crisis and rising sea levels.* The word *hydroponics* made the hairs on my arms turn to bumps—this was what Naomi had been referring to. I put the pamphlet in my pocket and continued my tour.

I slid a glass door on the first floor and found myself smacked with the smell of ocean on a massive veranda that looked at the ungodly blue water. The word *paradise* flashed in my head like a neon sign. The baby looked at me, then squinted into the sun. Marcella-Marie needed a hat. I slinked under the roof's shadow and sat down on a wooden deck chair. The baby closed her eyes. I was exhausted, I let myself relax, and felt myself fall down a dark tunnel. I wasn't sure how long I'd been asleep when I heard the front door bang, signaling Sara's return.

"Oh hi," Sara chirped, carrying a basket full of deep greens. "Everyone is *really* excited you're here at the farm, they wanted to have you over for dinner tomorrow if you're feeling up for it. They also want to give you a tour of the new hydro system. You're sort of a saint around there."

I nodded. Sara was staring at me cautiously. The sun was setting in a deep copper orange.

"I can put Marcella-Marie down, if you want to get some sleep. There is a lot of things to sort through in the morning."

"Maybe yeah, I should go to bed," then I remembered my suitcases on the dock. "Fuck, I need to get my stuff."

"Do you need help?" Sara asked, clearly surprised at my cursing, as she took the baby into her arms.

"I'll be fine on my own."

I walked back down the boardwalk while stripping off my clothes and jumped in the crystal clear water. I knew it in my gut, the lead bullet of truth: Naomi wasn't here. And I knew I had a decision to make. I weighed the options and the truth was cruel; I had nothing to go back to. No girlfriend. No parents. No job. No car. My debt was settled, and I was completely untethered. *I was free.* I dried off with my dress and gathered the last ounces of strength to drag the suitcases down the dock, one by one, through the sandy path and up the wooden stairs.

I slept hard and woke up terrified. It took a few minutes to remember the journey, the one in which I'd been dropped in like a pinball and bounced from place to place, plane to plane, car to car. I brushed my teeth in the gargantuan bathroom, sitting on the edge of the ridiculous bathtub. My blonde hair was matted from the swim in the ocean, my face redder than it had been in ages. I filled the tub, then looked at myself in the mirror and took a stabilizing breath. Floating in the ocean, I had made the decision; I was Amanda Elliott. I put on a pair of linen pants and one of Naomi's white camisoles and walked downstairs.

"Good morning," Sara said, "sixteen hours of sleep."

"I was really tired," I said defensively, unsure of what she knew, and how I should behave.

"You had a long journey," she tutted.

Marcella-Marie was banging her tiny hands on the flat expanse of her high chair, her eyes turning only briefly to meet mine. I kissed her on the head. That's what mothers did.

"Eggs?" Sara asked.

I nodded and she plated a yellow mound of fluff. I ate ravenously. Sara waited for me to finish, then opened her mouth hesitantly, "I'm sorry to do this on your first morning, but things have been a little—well, since we didn't hear from you for the last five months, I just sort of had to make some decisions. But there is a lot I couldn't do, and some of it is getting urgent."

Yesterday, while in the turquoise water, I knew I had to come with a reason for my, or rather, Amanda Elliott's absence. So, I lied.

"I was in the hospital, I had lupus."

"Oh goodness," Sara said, genuinely worried.

Lupus is what everyone had on that medical diagnosis TV show *House*. Jessica used to always complain that *it was always fucking lupus*.

"It's all fine now, but that's why I was unreachable."

"Well, if you need anything health-wise, there's a really good doctor on the next island. He checks up on Marcella-Marie biweekly."

"That's great," I said, concerned that I hadn't even thought about doctors. How could I be a mother? I wasn't prepared for any of this. I tried to keep myself from spiraling into all the things I didn't know. Sleep schedules. Feeding. What if she choked? What if she hated me.

Sara led me to the mountain of mail in the wood-paneled office. I tried to act natural as I took my place in the sturdy chair behind the desk and set about opening letters. As if this was my office. My life. My pencil sharpener. My silver pen.

"I know you'd discussed hiring someone to deal with the day-to-day but—they assumed you'd want to be a part of the process. John at Naru has been managing the practicalities at the farm, but the paperwork, I guess he just didn't want to get involved with."

"Yes, of course, well we can start working on that now," I mumbled half-terrified. I could barely open my own mail back home.

"Also, about the staff, well Ernie, he usually takes care of the house and the grounds, but he left to visit his daughter. And since no one knew you were coming . . . well. That's why he isn't here."

"It's fine, really."

Sara left me to sift through the pile. Most of the letters had to do with Naru Farms. It didn't take me long to understand that Naomi, under the alias of Amanda Elliott, had bought the fully functioning farm and the island for $22.6 million. There were all sorts of forms for me to sort through; letters from my Swiss bank, suppliers, credit cards, and invoices that needed my signature, and I enjoyed releasing my new name, over and over, like a gunshot across white paper.

Twenty minutes later, Sara returned to the office with an awkward look on her face, "And sorry to bring this up, but I've already considerably overstayed my contract. I was only meant to deliver Marcella-Marie from the orphanage in Warsaw and stay a week or so to make sure she'd adjusted."

"Was your overtime pay not arranged?" I asked with the hallowed tone of a disorganized boss.

Sara shook her head.

"How much do I owe you?" I asked, getting into the character of *Amanda Elliott*.

"Around five thousand."

"Dollars?"

Sara nodded. I got up and walked up to my bedroom and procured several stacks of cash from the carry-on suitcase. When I returned, Sara took a large gulp of relief.

"Thank you for staying on to help, it means a lot to me—and Marcella-Marie," I said, I hoped maternally, then returned to the pile of papers.

"Do you want me to take Marcella-Marie to the beach while you sort through this?"

"That's a great idea," I said warmly.

After Sara left, my eyes were drawn to a stack of unopened packages and padded envelopes that lay mounded on the floor by the door. I set about opening them with a kitchen knife; there were baby supplies, diapers, toys, new thriller novels, and a MacBook Pro laptop. Two new pairs of Prada sunglasses. An iPad. Kitchen appliances. Matcha powder. All things that felt intrinsically Naomi. And in one of the stiff white envelopes stamped with a government seal, I found two fresh passports, Maldivian: one for Amanda Elliott, one for Marcella-Marie Elliott. We were safe.

I opened the MacBook and set it up, using my own fingerprint. The Wi-Fi popped on automatically. I had listened to enough podcasts to know that one had to be extremely careful using the internet after engineering a disappearance, but I couldn't help it. I logged in to my old email. I had dozens. Mostly from Patrick. I knew if I opened them, they would be marked as read so all I could do was take in the subject lines. <WHERE ARE YOU? ESTHER?> <DID BRYCE DO SOMETHING TO YOU???> <ARE YOU ALIVE?> I had a sudden and

288

immediate flip in my stomach. *Patrick*. He was the only one I had left behind.

I thought back to my *EXIT*; the van parked at the overlook, the trashed mess in my house, my cell phone tumbling down the South Toe River. Patrick was right to be nervous. He was right to email in all caps. I itched to tell him I was ok, but I knew I couldn't. Bryce could be watching. I googled my name. *Esther Ray*. It had only been three and a half days since I'd driven away from our mountain, but there was already an article in the local paper on how I was missing and suicide was suspected. Two paragraphs long, the article included mention of police discovering a list I'd made of ways to kill myself, and quoted from my bereaved ex-girlfriend, Jessica. *I know she was going through a really hard time; I had just told her about my impending wedding, and I just feel awful. I feel like I pushed her over the edge.* I laughed out loud hoping I'd ruined her nuptials, and an odd sense of release washed over me now that Esther Ray was presumed dead. I could slip into this life. I could start over.

Sara returned, opening the door, "The guys at the farm want to know if you're going to join for dinner."

I looked up and nodded, "Sure."

It seemed like the only right answer, but I was nervous about the others. Would they know immediately I wasn't Amanda?

"Marcella-Marie is down for a nap."

"Great," I replied.

After another hour of sorting through mail, I headed to the beach. The air was hot and sticky. Rain was on the horizon. I stripped and walked into the resin-clear water, letting the buoyancy of the salt carry me out. I closed my eyes. Without willing them, images of Naomi in her Moncler jacket on the ski slope returned in telescoping intensity. The blue sky. The crack of her neck. She would have never abandoned Marcella-Marie; she was dead.

I returned to the house, showered, and dressed in one of Naomi's loose linen outfits. I even put on her makeup, trying to replicate the image of Amanda in the passport. When I was finally ready, Sara, Marcella-Marie, and I loaded into the yellow dune buggy, and we bumped across the dirt road that extended behind the house, Sara expertly navigating around the dense forest curves. Eventually we arrived at a series of large glass-clad buildings fogged with condensation and bursting with green. In the center of the area stood a wooden gazebo with a thatched roof that was decorated with twinkling lights. There were groups of people milling about, all casually dressed, all clutching canned beers and glasses of wine. Van Morrison crooned from a pair of speakers near a makeshift bar. There was an uncontestably jovial mood in the air, this was a party.

A man in a red shirt held his beer up, "Amanda is here."

The group made a bellowing cheer. I blushed. *Amanda is here.* The man in red came up to the car to introduce himself, he had a thick Australian accent, "I'm Luke, I'm so happy to finally meet you."

Luke said his name as if it meant something. As if we'd maybe spent hours on the phone talking. I released my widest warmest smile. Terrified he would know.

In a wash of hugs and handshakes, I met thirty-seven people. All of whom, in one way or another, expressed their gratitude to me, their benevolent benefactor, for saving the farm from the Hilton group who had wanted to develop the island and old B&B into some sort of ecologically genocidal resort.

"It's so amazing to me, that you would support the project so fully without having ever been here," Diwa, a scientist from Manila, said, as she refilled my wineglass. It felt good to be tipsy.

"I really believe in your work," I said in the most Naomi way I could manage.

"Well, I have to say, we were all a little nervous when you dropped off the grid," she said with a smile, "Saunders thought you must have had buyer's remorse."

I laughed it off, saying something about lupus. And Diwa gave me a tender squeeze on the arm, then poured me more wine. Sara went to check on Marcella-Marie who was sleeping in her car seat in the dune buggy. She returned to her place next to Luke, who appeared to have his arm around her. Sara caught my eye, and embarrassed, released herself to shuffle over and inform me that Marcella-Marie was fine.

A few minutes later, Luke walked over to me holding a beer, "So, how's it feel to finally be here, Amanda?"

"It's really great," I replied.

"You know, it's just the funniest thing—when we talked, you sounded really different."

I froze, turning my cheek away. I didn't want him to see my eyes calculating how to respond.

"Bad reception, I guess," I replied.

Luke cocked his head, "So, what did you decide to do about the old farm structures?"

This was a test. I smiled. I had to say something, I made an exasperated sigh, "Well Luke, I thought we should just burn them down."

Luke took a breath, then seemed to relax, "Good choice."

I had said the right thing. Or right enough. He sauntered off, but there was no denying it, he was suspicious. I would have to be careful. I would have to figure out what sort of contact Naomi had with everyone before her death.

At some point, gray-haired Saunders, the oldest of the bunch, stood up and made a toast.

"We are all very grateful for your support, Amanda. I am still not sure our deal is all that fair, but I promise you we will do what we can to hold up our end, and you will never run out of fresh vegetables."

I held up my cup, "It's a great deal. I am looking forward to our next chapter together."

Everyone clapped, and I was taken on a drunken tour of the hydroponic grow area, lit by a thin cable of LED lights. I *mhmmed* along but was genuinely moved by the level of excitement that beamed toward the heads of lettuce and frothing desalination tanks. It reminded me of Hammersmith show and tell, of the unbridled joy of craftspeople having made something with their hands. Something that mattered.

On the drive back, Sara, with a teenage glow, opened up about how she'd fallen in love with Luke.

"He's just so amazing, he's so funny. And smart, and like, he's just so invested in doing the right thing."

I smiled.

"But Amanda. I have to tell you."

I gulped.

"I have to go see my family. It's been months, and my cousin just had a baby. I have to go back, at least for a while."

Sara was near tears.

"It's fine," I said, nervously imagining being a full-time mother. I wasn't ready.

"But I want to come back," Sara said, wiping her eyes.

"For Luke?" I asked.

Sara looked over and nodded, "And for Marcella-Marie."

"Well, you'll always have a job here," I said with my new benevolent benefactor's smile.

We drove in silence for a while

"Can I ask you something?"

"Sure," Sara replied.

"Remind me again, what exactly happened to Marcella-Marie's birth parents?"

Sara looked back at the sleeping baby, and said only two words: *car accident*.

My own broken, exploded heart slingshotted out into the dark night and fell on top of sleeping Marcella-Marie like a heather-gray blanket of stars.

"She's lucky," Sara said quietly, "she survived, and she's here."

That was exactly how I felt.

21

I spent most of my time with Marcella-Marie but I loved googling myself. I devoured the dramatic fanfare over poor dead Esther Ray who'd committed suicide after finding out her ex-girlfriend was getting married. It was pulp lesbian tragedy. Everyone was posting about how much they loved me. How brilliant of a painter I was. How funny. How sarcastic. How beautiful. It was like watching a podcast be made in real time, and I was the glowing faultless victim. And then Memphis Emerald said it, she really said it, posting the line on Instagram: *Esther was one of those friends who would have given you the shirt off her back*. I laughed so loud I woke Marcella-Marie, who burst into a howling crawl.

In between a slew of selfies, Tabitha had posted the painting I had made of her, with the not-so-cryptic caption *RIP. Karma is a bitch*. But it was good. If she thought I was dead, Bryce thought I was dead. And her followers seemed to love the portrait, and I'd spent a good twenty minutes reading through their comments, plumping my ego on the inane clusters of emojis. Next, I googled Bryce Duncan and was greeted by the news that he was on house arrest for his pending financial fraud trial—trapped in his own minimalist prison.

I endlessly trolled online, discovering that even Madeline Lancaster had posted her condolences. *What a tragedy, I hope Esther can at long last find peace, and join her mother in heaven*. After everything my dad had told me, I was unsure my mother was in heaven. I was, however, certain I didn't want Madeline's sympathy. I liked that I had joined the dark clanging disco of the disappeared. I was line dancing into the abyss, because without a body there was never concrete proof. Whispers snarled across platforms. Maggie Billings, who'd lived in my dorm, posted that *Esther had run off before, after she left New York, she went on that craft odyssey and no one heard from her for months, maybe she's just done that again?*

So maybe I was rolling around at the bottom of the river with my iPad and phone or maybe I was learning to weld in the Adirondacks. But I knew that the real pain lay in not knowing. The families on *Dateline* faced with the most guilt were the ones who wished they had asked one extra question at the door: *Who is going to be there? Do you need money for a taxi?* At least I had left a note and I had reasons for ending it. Reasons created distance from the threat of the unexpected, it could all be filed away as the outcome of my unresolved issues.

I felt comforted that I had told my dad I would disappear. The online choir didn't even seem to know he had cancer. He didn't have a Facebook, he didn't even have an email, and he wasn't mentioned in anyone's poetic diatribes about their insightful and tragic friend *Esther Ray*. He would slip away, just as I had. Just as mom had. It struck me that I was in a way doing what my mom had: choosing to end my life. But being given the agency to do it this way was a power I had never imagined; it took money and planning and staging. Everything Naomi had. My mother was given a different set of choices. I still couldn't forgive her, but I could now faintly understand the allure of choosing to leave.

For the most part I enjoyed the posts, except from Michael Valentine. I found it early in the morning. He'd made a big slimy tribute on his Instagram, with a photo of us at an opening at the Centre Pompidou in Paris, his arm wrapped around mine, standing in front of a painting I'd made while he was on vacation in Saint-Tropez. *Esther Ray was an amazing talent who will be deeply missed. In the studio I witnessed firsthand her mental health struggles, so sadly, I am not so surprised by the news of her untimely passing—but in her honor I will be donating $500 to the suicide prevention hotline. I invite you to join me in supporting this great cause. And I hope we can all take a moment to cherish those around us. Tell your friends you love them. Send that text. Make that phone call. Lots of love. Michael Valentine.*

Five hundred dollars? Mental health struggles? I wanted to burn his studio down a thousand times over. And then I realized in a blinding flash that if I was dead, it didn't matter that he had footage of me setting the linseed oil rags on fire. I ran to my bedroom, carrying Marcella-Marie with me. She whined as I dug out the Polaroids, which were still in the front pocket of the carry-on. I walked calmly back to the office, careful not to look at Rachel's young body, and found a blank envelope and dropped the four squares in, then typed up a letter to the NYPD explaining Michael's penchant for pedophilia. I couldn't risk postmarking it from the Maldives, so I gave the envelope to Sara and she promised to send it when she was back in Poland.

Sara left by boat. Apparently, that's what nonmillionaires do. Seaplanes were for glitzy tourists with Swiss bank accounts. As the white-and-green ship revved, I gave Sara an extra thousand dollars. She looked deeply grateful, but she had held this world together. I owed her more. She promised to return soon. Marcella-Marie cried for two days straight and I thought I was going to lose my mind. I was still learning but I knew I loved her. There was some secret part of me that was still waiting for the buzz of propellers to mark the arrival of Naomi. And some days I wanted her to come, but mostly I was terrified she would rip Marcella-Marie from my arms. But with every sorbet-orange sunset over the water, I knew her arrival was less and less likely. This was my family now.

I decided I needed to fill my time. I couldn't just change diapers and watch YouTubes about blending vegetables into child-friendly pastes, and I didn't want to listen to murder podcasts. I didn't want to ice my own pain on that of others. I wanted to sort through the hurt. I needed to forgive my mom, I needed to forgive my dad. I needed to work on being present. On listening to my breath. On being there for Marcella-Marie who would someday have to work through her own pain and her own parents' car crash; another firework of fate.

I ordered a dozen canvases and oils which took two weeks to arrive. I had decided I wanted to paint the saltwater, the bright vinegar of existence. It was an endless assignment; light was a constant kaleidoscope. And I saw the humor, me the pyro, fixated by the ebb and flow of blue. Meanwhile Marcella-Marie and I were finding our rhythm, I would spend the mornings, before it got too hot, at the beach, and we napped after lunch, and early evening I brought her crib out to the terrace where I'd paint and she'd crawl around. We were fragile. Still tender, but I was happy. Patrick was the only thing that could crack through the warmth of these new days. I felt strangled when I thought of him. He had been my only friend. And he thought I was dead; worse than that, he thought I'd killed myself. He, the eternal failed father, would blame himself. I didn't know how to fix it.

On Naru, I was trying to seem normal. But I had no blueprint. I wasn't a mother and I knew nothing about environmental science or hydroponics or any of the things that Amanda Elliott was supposed to. I exuded a pensive silence whenever Luke or the others from the farm asked me a question, but my quiet was studded with fear. And they needed endless money. New generators. New docks. New equipment. I questioned nothing. Instead, I signed checks wearing Naomi's clothes, and prayed no one would put the pieces together. Money again silencing questions. My own name ricocheting through my head as Jessica's once had. *Esther, Esther, Esther.*

And I still checked my email. I never opened any of the messages but it was like a newspaper about a foreign planet, updating me on the schedule of craft schools and gallery openings. One evening, while drinking a glass of wine, I noticed an email from Brenda Millwater. I almost didn't remember who that was. Then it clobbered me; Brenda was the private detective I'd paid to find the hot goth-nanny that had worked for Naomi, Elena Tester. The subject line simply read: *Got Her.* I felt the old volcano of true crime erupt. I couldn't help it. I opened the message.

This was a hard one. Elena Tester: Lives in Toronto, may or may not want to be found, living under the name Ansley Worther. She works as a financial technology advisor for a company called Henrot. Her address is listed as 250 Yonge Street, Toronto, Ontario, Canada, and her phone number is +1416585393.

I copied the text, then quickly deleted the email from my inbox, then trash. If Bryce or the police were monitoring my online existence, I didn't want them to see Elena's details. But I knew if anyone had the answers to my questions, it was her. She had been there the day Marcella-Marie had died, and I knew now that Marcella-Marie lay at the center of everything; she was the strange pearl in this Maldivian shell. I thought back to the photos of the nanny and her tattooed torso and got vaguely turned on. I googled her new name. A corporate headshot popped up for her company in Toronto, she was smiling, her hair now auburn, the only flash of her former goth days was her eyeliner, which was still a tad dark for a boardroom. She looked good.

After some searching, I figured out how to make an untraceable phone call using a Nordic-themed VPN; after a few tries it seemed to work. The screen was bleating in aquatic tones.

"Ansley Worther," a clipped voice answered on the fourth ring.

I wasn't prepared. Who should I say I was? I couldn't say Amanda Elliott.

"Uh, ummm, hi."

"Who is this?"

"Hi, I'm a friend of Naomi Duncan."

"Who is this?" Ansley snapped, her voice now sharp.

"I, umm, I worked for Naomi. And I have some questions about Marcella-Marie."

Ansley said nothing, then growled, "Who the fuck is this?"

I caved. I told her the truth.

"I'm Esther Ray."

Ansley made a tongue-clicking sound, "Oh, the scrapbook girl?"

I sighed, deeply relieved to be temporarily returned to my old self.

"Shit, I'm sorry," all the hardness had drained from Ansley's voice. "I thought you worked for Bryce. Naomi told me all about the books."

"Oh," I said, surprised, "I have some questions."

"I'm sure you do."

Ansley was cagey, but once I'd convinced her I was trustworthy, she seemed relieved to have someone to talk to. Letting it all spill out: what happened on that rainy Sunday in Manhattan. Tabitha had been angry at Naomi. The tantrum had started in the park because Naomi had refused to stop at H&H Bagels, and the aggression had hung in the air like the day's humidity. It happened in a blink, back at their apartment, while Ansley had been checking on the laundry. Tabitha in her red rage had picked up Marcella-Marie from her high chair and dropped her head-first onto the marble floor. She'd died instantly.

"I mean, I walked in right after it happened—I could see it on Tabitha's face. I believed Naomi. It wasn't the first time she'd been violent with the baby," Ansley said, perfectly collected as if giving a deposition.

"Why did they say it was SIDS?" I asked.

"To protect Tabitha. But it all . . . it spun out of control—basically Naomi lost it. She was in a lot of pain and blamed herself, and Bryce convinced her to commit herself to a psychiatric hospital."

"That's why there was two years of material missing from the scrapbooks."

Ansley let out a small sigh, "Yes. And while she was there, she was really drugged up, and long story short, while she was fucked out of her mind, Bryce had her sign a bunch of documents which basically gave him full control of her money. He stole everything. And when she got out, he gave her an ultimatum, if she tried to fight him in any way, he would tell people Tabitha had killed Marcella-Marie."

"Oh," I said, then was quiet, drinking in the hard fact that Naomi had stayed silent to protect Tabitha. All the hours I had watched of Tabitha's body twist and slither on social media rushed in. She had been a violent specter. Malicious and brutally self-aware, able to bottle her cruelty and sell it as makeup, hiding her darkness in the spotlight. But despite it all, her mother had still loved her. She had stayed to protect her. I stung with jealousy.

"I mean, Bryce did give her the money to run WAC, I think that's the only reason she survived," Ansley said, her voice thick with sadness.

Ansley went on to explain that all those years ago, after the dust had settled around Marcella-Marie's death, Naomi was afraid of Bryce's ruthlessness. And in her paranoia, Naomi had convinced Elena to leave New York and change her name. "She was just worried he would come after me because I knew the truth," she sighed, "and like, she offered to pay my way through college, so I agreed. I moved to Toronto. And we stayed in touch. I think in some ways I was her only friend because I knew what had really happened."

I paused, trolling through all the new information before asking how Naomi had managed to steal the two hundred million. Ansley made another loud tongue click, "We came up with the idea about a decade ago, in one of our late-night phone calls. I work in fintech, I'm good with computers. She wanted what was rightfully hers, but she wanted to do it in a way that fucked Bryce. I suggested a blend of tax fraud and embezzlement. Then she read that book."

I made a knowing hiss, "*Gone Girl.*"

"Yeah, she was obsessed with the idea of like, framing him in a like fantastical way, and she wanted people to think he'd killed her. And that's when she came up with the idea of mixing in the spreadsheets with the scrapbooks. I tried to convince her to chill, but it just kept getting bigger. I mean, an anonymous tip to the FEC would have done it."

"Do you know what her plans were for after? Like once she had the money" I asked, desperately curious if she knew about Naru island. Or the baby in the other room. Or me.

Ansley's voice got sad, "No I have no idea, and that was the deal. All I knew was she wanted to disappear after Bryce's birthday. She kept telling me, *I have a second chance.* And then I'd always shut her up, I didn't want to know. It was safer that way." Ansley paused, then spoke softly, "She was so close, that's why it's so sad that she died."

The lead bullet in my stomach heaved. It was true. Ansley picked up speed and continued talking, "I mean, I didn't believe it. I thought maybe it was part of her plan. I even went down to Aspen with a private investigator, but it really was an accident. She just fucking died. I saw her body. Just one month before . . ."

A silence hovered between us, but I had another question, one that had nagged at me ever since I had become an inadvertent mother.

"Why was Naomi willing to leave Tabitha behind? Like it doesn't make sense to me, after she did all that to protect her . . ."

"Oh—well. God, Naomi did have reservations, even after everything Tabitha had done. But then there was the fight in Kenya. Tabitha pushed her down the stairs at their hotel. She didn't like *hurt her* hurt her, nothing was broken, but it snapped something inside Naomi—she finally realized there was nothing she could do. She needed to protect herself. It was time."

I remembered back to my conversation with Tabitha and the coldness in how she'd said the word *fight* when describing their trip to Kenya. It all clicked.

My final question was selfish and plagued me like a rash.

"Do you know why she picked me? To make the scrapbooks, I mean."

Ansley let out a little laugh, "Yeah, I guess she met this guy, some asshole at a dinner. Who kept talking about you, he said you were crazy and vindictive, and she thought you sounded great. She was always really sensitive whenever a man called a woman *crazy*. And then he said you were bookmaking in Asheville. She was so excited, because her astrologer had advised her to move her next project to Asheville, she felt like it was kismet."

The Post-it flashed in my brain. *EXIT.* I felt my chest heave. Then heard mumbling in the background.

"Shit, I have to get to a meeting, I'm at the office, but we can talk later if you want."

I took her up on the offer. We talked often. She was in fact a dyke, recently divorced. Her mother was Armenian and her father was Pakistani. She loved the TV show *CSI* and liked to complain endlessly about the idiots who worked at her firm. On our fourth or fifth call, I asked if she could do me a favor; transfer the deed of my old bungalow without a paper trail. Ansley had laughed, calling it *child's play*. And one week later, Patrick received an unmarked padded envelope at the post office that held the deed of the house and one Honey Bun.

No one gets to live your life but you. That was what Naomi had told me on the phone when I'd been heartbroken about Jessica not calling back. But lightning had struck, and here I was, living Naomi's. A ghost inside of a ghost. Two crazy women wrapped together. Maybe this was our strange brand of doom and rebirth; fate. As the months uncoiled on Naru, a rainy winter shifting into an electric summer, I fell into the ambivalent current of fortune, because maybe all of this is what I deserved. But it always glimmered, a pulsating unease, at the edge of my vision—the feeling that it could all fall apart.

So, I did what Naomi would have done. I opened an account with a new alias and steadily made deposits. I bought a secret boat and stocked it with gas and essentials. I had new passports made. If a solar flare of the past, my truth, ever arrived, we would be ready, we would have an exit.

304

Acknowledgments

Thank you to my father, who reads whatever I give him. And to my mother, who still insists on printing every version. To Max, my eternal editor. To Klara, for reading it in one sitting on that Berlin afternoon. To Rebecca, for her sharp notes. To Alexa, for her confidence. To Fred, for reading early. To Karen, for knowing where the stories hide. To my Penland family for giving me the mountains. To the diligent librarians at Villa Rossi. To Leidy, for the tidal editing porch. To my agent Eleanor, for everything. And to Jo, Ansa, Nico, Fede, and the brilliant team at Sceptre.